A Pact for Life

by
Grant Budge

Integrity

A Pact for Life

AUTHENTIC STORIES
© Copyright 2022

First edition: 2001
Second edition: 2022
Grant Budge has asserted the moral right to be identified as the author of this work in accordance with the Copyright, Designs and Patents Act 1988.

All rights reserved.

No reproduction, copy or transmission of this publication may be reproduced without written permission. No paragraph of this publication may be reproduced, copied or transmitted, except with the written permission of the publishers or in accordance with the provisions of the Copyright Act 1956 (as amended).

Any person who does any unauthorised act in relation to this publication may be liable to criminal prosecution and civil claims for damage.

ISBN 9781838236601

A copy of the CIP report for this book is available from the British Library.

Authentic Stories is an imprint of Integrity Media Ltd, a UK publishing company.
Visit us at www.integrity-media.co.uk

Printed and bound in Great Britain by Clays Ltd, Elcograf S.p.A

NOTES FROM THE PUBLISHER

Integrity Media is a publishing company focused on helping individuals who are or have suffered from poor mental health to tell their stories. In doing so, we enable our authors to move forward and our readers to better understand the challenges of poor mental health for their own education and support. Therefore, books published by Integrity Media, including this one, contain mature themes, frequently relayed in an open and honest manner. To enable our readers to decide if this work may be suitable and/or appropriate for them, we provide a list below of such themes contained in this publication.

We recommend that this book should not be read by readers of 15 years of age and below as the story presents topics of mature content, horror, violence and sex.

*This book is dedicated to my brother, and brotherhood.
A pact for life in its own right.*

1

Gloria's eyes sparkled as the candlelight twitched above the choir stall in front of her. To John, those eyes were more radiant than those of any other thirteen-year-old he knew in his class. He loved the clear blue irises and the plethora of deep emotions they expressed, washed together in the watery glaze. To John, she was flawless. From her unassuming character, which came from being the new girl in town, right through to her long, flowing blonde locks. She was pure gold. He even credited her with the pitch-perfect performances that the choir had been able to manage since her arrival, her voice soaring above those of her contemporaries. In truth, hearing her sing was one of the reasons that John enjoyed church so much these days. Not that he was a disbeliever. In fact, he was a strong and sincere harbinger of the faith. One of the few his age. This acceptance of Christianity had come from a firm but not overbearing upbringing by his adopted parents, who were regulars of the congregation. John had lived with them for the past ten years. He couldn't remember his own parents and had only vague recollections of the day he had been brought into Sean and Marlene Garret's home. They had been so delighted to see him, desperate to make him a part of their lives. However, they hadn't herded his real parents away, giving them time for a tearful farewell. Afterwards, he remembered the car pulling out of the drive and the feeling of loneliness that had come swift to his chest. However, the emptiness had been short-lived, being replaced by incredible warmth from his new guardians. They had given him time to adjust, holding back their tenders of affection. Showing him his bedroom, they had helped him unpack before bringing him into the lounge and leaving him to play with some second-hand toys they had bought in town a few days earlier. Soon, his childhood had become like everybody else's and by the time he was enlisted at the local school, thoughts of his real parents had been hidden deep in the recesses of his mind.

The church was heaving today, the space consumed by the thick jumpers and overcoats donned to keep the cold at bay. Electric heaters burned around the peripheries of today's Sunday disciples, but their heat was quickly absorbed by the first line of bodies. The few faces John could see from his prime position at the front, were chilled white as the air bit at their flesh. For the most part, the congregation sat in silence, watching and listening to the choir sing praise to the Lord. Some chatted amongst themselves, disclosing their true ambivalence to God. Others mouthed along to the words, remembering the old days when it had been them at the front, dressed in a cassock, surplice and a ruff. The rest sat in silence, taking the opportunity to pray for all those they held dear to their hearts and composing in their minds a personal verse for those less fortunate in the world. Sean and Marlene fell into this latter category. John pretended to but was really just utilising the time for adoration of his sweetheart. Daydreaming her to his side.

The architectural design of God's house was typical American mid nineteenth century. Fashioned in wood and with a single spire at one end, it stood proud on a mound elevated above the town. Every plank was coated in virgin white paint, symbolising the cleansing that took place within its walls. Plain windows lined its length and at the front, a stained-glass image depicting the Lord's resurrection shone down across the altar. In front of the Lord's table were the choir stalls, which sat perpendicular to the congregation. To the left of these stood the pulpit.

At that moment, the choir sat down, and the residual harmony quickly dampened against the wooden walls. As the last bottom hit the pew, Father Hill stood up and began his slow advance towards the pulpit, from where he would deliver his usual predictions of long-lasting damnation. His slow shuffle had become his trademark in the town since his arrival there thirty years earlier. His laborious walk wasn't due to any medical impediment but solely to emphasise his presence and authority. He wanted to grab everybody by the scruff of their necks and say, 'look at me and listen well, for it is the only thing that can save you'. Even the incessant gabbing of the Sunday gossipers ceased in trepidation at the sight of this seemingly fragile man. As Father Hill's feet hit each of the steps up to the pulpit, the hollow sound despatched a ripple of uncertainty around the congregation. They all feared that when this holy man was in full flow, those deep dark eyes would fall directly upon them and make it personal. John was amazed at how evil a man of the cloth could actually look, with his wrinkled skin and sunken eyes. His large ear lobes appeared to defy gravity, unlike the layered skin that hung from his chin. From the front row, John could also distinguish between the Father's real teeth and his dentures. This was the kind of detail he didn't need to witness, an image that haunted him every Sunday.

"Good morning, everybody," the Father said in an uncharacteristically soft tone.

"Good morning, Father," came the muffled response from the masses.

"Nice day, isn't it?"

People nodded reluctantly.

"I've spent the past week doing a lot of thinking, you know. A lot of time contemplating where I've been going wrong all these years." He took a short breath. "When I was given this parish to serve, I arrived excited and determined to make a difference. Do a little good in my short life. Become a figurehead for the community to follow. I think I started out alright. Didn't seem to get too many complaints. People always used to be cheerful after the service and stop around for a quick chat. Sometimes even a cup of coffee and a biscuit. Crime, under-age sex, drinking, taking drugs even, either didn't happen or the cases were few and far between. I discovered very quickly that I didn't have to fight as hard as I had prepared myself to, because I had landed in a community where people cared for each other, took pride in having mutual respect, for both young and old. No children played truant. Disciplinary action in the high school wasn't required. Circumstances have changed a lot since then."

He took a long pause and leaned forward dejectedly onto the lectern.

"For the last ten years, I've watched that utopia crumble away from around me. I've fought its demise at every turn but for nought. I still stand here every weekend, delivering the same message and each week viewing the same self-importance from all of you. Of course, I apologise to the few who are unaltered in purity. Don't worry, this is not condemnation of you. God knows who you are. But to the rest, I have to ask why? Hmm? Why?"

He stared around the faces that filled the nave, waiting for a response. But none was forthcoming.

"Please look at me when I'm talking to you and don't hang your heads in sorrow. Both you and I know that your guilt will be gone as soon as the Sunday roast hits the table."

The culprits looked up.

"Anyway, during my long bouts of self-investigation, I started to wonder about my methods, my beliefs and, most importantly, my ability to guide you. I tried to understand or even just remember the point at which I made a wrong turn, lost sight of the truth and led you all into hell."

He inhaled slowly and swallowed, relieving his mouth of the saliva that had accumulated.

"I think I found the problem! And part of the problem is

me! I've been banging on at a gradually increasing rate about the world's atrocities and the ills of our society. I've constantly relayed the effects of our problem, without showing the cause and without giving guidance to find the solution. I've served you poorly and for that I am forever sorry. But I know what to do now and I hope that you will bless me with the opportunity to make amends." He smiled. "Look at that. I've just asked you to bless me. You, who aren't ordained by a Cardinal to deliver and preach the Lord's gospels. But I ask you none the less, knowingly and reverently, please give me another chance. I ask you because you are the Church. Without you, there is no Christian voice. I need you and I hope that you need me. I've needed you for the past ten years, but I've failed to acknowledge it and I've failed to reach you. The only way forward from here is to work together. Guide each other. Parents, show your children what is right and wrong. Children, guide your parents when they argue over petty problems. If you see trouble, report it. If you have a problem, talk about it, don't keep it locked inside. Work with me!"

He stopped and turned to descend the steps but then looked towards the masses once more.

"I think that my lesson this week has been the most valuable of my career. I can only thank God for giving me the opportunity for further enlightenment and I hope that you seize the second chance that has been granted to you in the same manner I grasp hold of mine."

Then came a deathly silence, broken only by the hollow refrain of old feet smacking against the steps. Once at the bottom, he bowed his head towards the altar and began his steady shuffle back across to his seat. Then it happened. A clapping noise came from a few rows back. John turned to see who it was, but by the time he thought he had pinned down the source, the solitary applause had grown. People were standing up and clapping, young and old alike, in joint praise of the heartfelt speech. The event was unprecedented. In a few seconds, there wasn't a seated person in the church. Father Hill just stood there in disbelief, his jaw slightly ajar. He was the picture of a man dumbstruck. After a few seconds, he gestured for them to stop.

"Thank you for that very kind response. But please now make good on your word." With that he completed the journey back to his chair.

Following that historic moment of unity, the service continued as normal, though the atmosphere was altered. It was almost enthusiastic. No one remained seated during the hymns, every voice singing strong in praise to the Lord. However, by far the most noticeable difference was the replacement of the usual post-blessing lunchtime stampede by the whole congregation remaining still and praying. The church was silent for about three minutes before the loose chatter commenced. It sounded normal again, but John knew it wasn't. The conversations weren't idle but focussed on the Father's sermon. Some people displayed their true colours once more, taking exception to the criticism and finding cause enough to feel malicious intent towards their priest. These individuals were at the lowest echelon of congregational spirit and beliefs, who suffered church once each week to gain forgiveness for their sins. This classification characteristically housed the adulterers, the bigots, the racists and the deceitful.

Residing a couple of runs further up the ladder of spiritual guidance were the ninety-percent-of-the-time honest folk, who lived not in praise of the Lord but in partial fear of him. This fear wasn't a cerebral belief that God existed and if they didn't follow his desire, flames would engulf them in death. No, it was ever so slightly diluted from that. The dread was based on their own comprehension of his almost mystical power, so that they found themselves on the cusp of accepting faith but still requiring reassurance of His existence. That was their reason for coming every Sunday. It wasn't a particularly good one, but it was definitely a more deserving one than the aforementioned forgiveness freaks. In truth, John and his adopted parents were probably a single rung higher than the average of the category, but it was still the one that best suited them.

In the final section of classification were the soothsayers of righteousness. They were the individuals who praised the Lord with such ferocious devotion that they felt it placed them several paces ahead of the masses. There were few genuine people in this section. They were all hypocrites but refused to accept it, feeling obliged to sing and speak the loudest through every verse and prayer. They believed that they were delivering their own guidance to the less deserving. However, when the layers of deceit and self-convincing were stripped away, all that remained was the bare carcass of a human, flawed as much as the rest of them and in some extreme cases, worse.

The whole community was rife with insincerity and the Father was right in saying he had failed. They had all failed, because nobody cared anymore about their neighbours. With the exception of church on a Sunday, they hadn't united as a community for a single event in the past year and a half. Father Hill was right. It wasn't good and it was a far cry from Christian brotherhood.

John and his parents were one of the last groups to leave the church. As they exited, the scene was still one divorced from the normal. People had clustered in conversation, catching up on each other's lives. The Father was mingling with the worshippers, trying his hardest to refrain from smiling, but he couldn't help showing a couple of teeth. Despite John's young years, he knew exactly what the Father was feeling and discovered a similar sort of happiness from the occasion. The Father approached.

"Now then, Mr and Mrs Garret, how are we this fine morning?" He extended a hand towards Sean, which was met halfway.

"Just fine, thank you, Bill," Marlene responded.

"And how is young Johnny here?" With the words came a ruffle of John's hair.

"I'm okay, thank you, Father."

"Good, I'm pleased to hear it." He turned his head back up to John's parents. "I wanted to catch you before you left, because I want you to know that out of all my parishioners, that speech was meant for you the least."

Sean and Marlene remained silent, embarrassed and not knowing what to say.

"You two, I know, haven't forgotten what being a true Christian is all about."

"I don't know, Bill. I think we could all do with improving ourselves," Sean managed.

"Well, I think that is exceptionally charitable of you, but I will say no more. How's the shop doing?" Father Hill changed the subject.

"It's going very well. Mostly due to cheap staff," Sean said, giving his wife a hug and patting John on the head.

"I'm pleased to hear you're okay. What about your parents?" the Father continued, but John's head was wandering away. He could see some kids playing soccer in the adjacent field and wanted to go join them. He tugged at his father's sleeve, seeking approval. It was granted. Leaping into action, he wove through the throng and plunged into the long thick bladed grass. Struggling through it, he burst out into the field on the other side.

As John reached the other children, he recognised four immediately as Tim, Kevin, Ian and Nicola, all of whom were in his year at school and, in one way or another, he viewed as friends. Three others were from the year below and one from the year above. He knew them to look at but didn't know their names. John's arrival made their number odd.

"Join our side," Kevin said. "We're losing anyway." John didn't need asking twice. He threw himself straight into a successful sweeping tackle on the older kid. The ball flew out the far side and was picked up by Ian, who dribbled it a short distance before clipping a sideways pass to Nicola, leaving her completely unmarked and available to bash the ball through the makeshift goalposts. His friends went crazy with excitement.

The game continued for another five minutes, with the score staying more or less even now that the element of surprise had been removed. As the time between goals increased, John's interest decreased and he found his eyes drifting over to some activity on the verge of the woodland next to the field. He could make out three figures, one noticeably smaller than the others who appeared to be an unwilling participant in whatever they were doing. John strained his eyes to see if he could make out any more detail, at which point the football smacked his forehead. The impact caught him completely unaware, knocking him to the floor. Laughter erupted around him. For a moment he couldn't see anybody. Slowly the swirling in his head subdued, allowing his eyes to take in his surroundings once more. His team had closed ranks around him, their hysterics now slightly muffled with concern. As he stared back up to them for the first time, he could see straight away that Kevin had been the culprit. His face panic stricken, as if he was praying that John wouldn't burst into tears.

"Come on, mate." Ian reached out a hand to help him to his feet.

"Are you alright?" The voice was female. John turned round sharply to see Nicola looking at him all gooey-eyed. She reached out a hand to touch his arm, but he instinctively pulled away. He knew she had a crush on him and even though she was very pretty, his heart was still Gloria's. For now.

"I'm fine." The words were delivered harshly, and she cowered away. Brushing himself down, he looked back over towards the trees, but the three figures had disappeared. Doing a quick three-hundred-and-sixty-degree turn, he checked the horizon. Nothing.

"What is it?" Kevin asked.

"I saw some kids fighting over there a minute ago."

"Well, they're not there anymore, so come on. Let's play." With that, Kevin ran off and the game resumed.

However, John couldn't let it go. He had listened intently to every word that Father Hill had said, and the resounding message hadn't been, "keep yourself to yourself". No, it had been to acknowledge each other and in so doing, take care of each other. And if any one member of the community failed in that challenge, then they all failed. It was because of that, he had to investigate. He could see Nicola observing him closely as he ambled over to the woods, but he knew she wouldn't join him. She might have run along after him if he hadn't snubbed her so forcefully, but he had and now he knew she would be afraid of causing greater offence.

"Nicky, are you in this game or what?" Tim shouted at her and she snapped back into action.

As John reached the first wave of tress, he found a narrow drainage ditch running parallel down the side of the field. It was still partially filled with water from the previous night's rain, leaving the sides hazardously slick with soft mud. Taking a couple of steps back, he launched himself over, landing safely on the other side. The ground ahead was relatively even, but he had a steady clamber down into the thick. As he moved deeper into the woods, the deciduous forest canopy shrouded the daylight, leaving only sporadic laminated columns of light breaking through the gaps.

The dim environment made it difficult for John to pick out any signs of movement, but he continued to advance slowly, straining his ears. The more intently he listened, the louder the sound of his own footsteps squashing leaves and snapping twigs seemed to become. Glancing back to see how far he had advanced, he was disappointed to discover the extent of his progress was only about fifteen metres. He refused to retreat, though. As the forest expanded around him, his eyes adjusted to the environment and he gained comfort from his enhanced sight. The ground had begun to level out but was sodden, causing his feet to occasionally falter. With every dozen paces deeper into the woods, he passed a generation of trees, some of whose trunks were already a metre in diameter. The roots from the larger trees sprawled out in all directions, digging deep into the earth. Occasionally they would resurface, forming small archways, before plunging back down into the soil.

"Ahhhh!"

A faint cry of pain came from John's left. He turned towards it and approached steadily.

"Ahhhh!"

Another cry came, this one closer, its pitch accentuated with despair.

John adjusted his direction slightly and continued. After about ten metres, he arrived on the verge of a small basin, in the centre of which stood three boys, the group he had spied earlier. Hunkering down he remained out of sight. He recognised all three boys. The two older ones were Charles Manton and Lenny Fletcher. Manton was two years John's senior in school. His name was synonymous with bullying. He stood just short of six foot and had shoulder-length light brown hair. For the past year his hormones had been imbalanced, throwing his face into an array of teenage blemishes. Ironically, it was only as these spots had begun to sprout that he had turned into the lunch money lifter of Shifton High School. By his side was Fletcher, one of his regular accomplices. The boy was a year Manton's junior but had been sucked into his world due to what appeared to be a strong admiration of his work. In truth, Fletcher had mainly been prompted into the role of the bully's accomplice by the racism that festered within the community. It didn't reach the weighty heights of persecution that the Klu Klux Klan displayed, but for an impressionable teenager was sufficient to instil resentment. Then map that background resentment with the day-to-day indignity of public pranks and verbal abuse, and there could be no real surprise about his partnership with violence. It gave him the opportunity for some payback. Although to John's knowledge, he rarely took it. Physically Fletcher was a couple of inches taller than Manton and carried at least another ten kilograms in weight. His face was clean and smooth, his hair shaved close to his scalp.

The focus of their attentions was a young boy in John's year who held the bizarre name of Brighton Smythe. Whatever had inspired his parents to call him that, it had to be one hell of a story. Though for Brighton, there would never be any humour in it. It was as a result of his name that he became a prime candidate for Manton's attention. It didn't take a genius to think of suitable taunts for a boy called Brighton. The scope was incredible. Smythe was one of the smallest boys in the year, both in stature and mass. He was every pound the school weakling. But once John had got to know him, he had discovered a very determined character, and since then he had always been a loyal friend. Though the shoe was on the other foot, and it was time for John to display some allegiance.

Studying the situation, John knew there was no way that he could take on the two aggressors. Distraction was the only option. At that moment, Manton flung Smythe to the floor, kicking him lightly in the stomach as he landed. John's friend was evidently already too in pain to feel the sting from this latest attack, remaining silent in acceptance of the inevitable. John couldn't wait any longer if his actions were to have any significance. As he stood up to make his presence known, he thought of the Father's words during his sermon and found strength in them.

"Hey, stop that!" John's cry rose out through the woods, firm in its meaning. It was so loud that Manton actually jumped a little. As soon as he saw John, though, the momentary fear turned to glee.

"Well, look what we have here! If it isn't little mister goody two shoes." Manton started walking towards him now. "Stop, you say? And who's going to make me?"

"Look, I'm not stupid. Of course, I'm not going to take you on. But I can sure as hell run to get someone who can." He tried to retain the firmness of tone, but with every stride of Manton's advance, his voice wavered increasingly.

"Somehow I don't think you're going anywhere!"

With those words, Manton broke into a run, reducing the gap considerably. John turned as quick as he could, dropping his head and eyes to the floor, preparing himself for a sprint start. He was positive he could beat Manton in a race. He'd done it before. Driving his toes into the floor, he accelerated away from danger, but the forward momentum was short lived. He'd hit something. A person. Dazed from the collision, he staggered back to view a fifth person at their woodland congregation. It was the older boy from the football game. Suddenly everything came flooding back to him. That was where he knew the guy from. He was Chris Young, a part-time Manton groupie.

"What were you saying?" Manton reached them, standing so close that John could see the nicotine stains on his teeth as he grinned. Then they were gone again, as John bowed in agony from a punch to the stomach.

"Would you care to come down and join your friend?" He waited for a response, but John was incapable of providing one. "Bring him down, Chris."

As the frog march back to the hollow began, John managed to regain his breath and senses. He quickly realised there was nothing to be gained from allowing the course of events to be orchestrated by Manton, and if he allowed himself to be drawn back into his lair, that was exactly what would happen. However, the only alternative was to put up a fight and chances were that it would involve severe pain. But then as John looked at it with an open mind, both eventualities were inevitably going to involve pain and at least if he made a pre-emptive strike, there was a possibility he would come out relatively unscathed. Bearing that in mind, he lashed back blindly with his foot, hitting his captor squarely on the shin. For a brief second the grasp around his arms weakened, Chris recoiling in anguish. That brief moment was all John required to launch himself on a one-way course out of there. Breaking free, he retraced his steps up out of the hollow. As he did, an arm reached out to prevent him escaping, but John swept it aside. He was free and all he had to do now was stay in front. Climbing the shallow gradient out of Manton's pit, his feet seemed to brush the floor so lightly that he felt almost as if he was flying.

"Don't just stand there, you fucking idiot. Get after him!" Manton's voice screamed out from behind.

Breaking onto the flat, John's pace immediately increased, and he started to sense victory. There was absolutely no way the other kid was going to catch up with him. He'd seen him on the football pitch and there was most definitely nothing to write home about. As that thought drifted through his head, John's previous fleetness of footing subsided, his feet plodding heavier on impact. He refused to look behind to see whether his pursuer was gaining on him. He couldn't hear anything that indicated imminent danger. No breathing or twigs breaking. He began smiling nervously to himself, but then suddenly his grin was eating dirt. Crucifying pain ripped up from his ankle into his brain's frontal lobe. He winced in agony. Looking towards his feet, he saw one of the tree roots twisted above the ground supporting his foot. He must have hit it dead centre, for it to have felled him that hard.

All this contemplation was losing him vital seconds of advantage on his aggressor. Refocussing his attention, he could see that the foot soldier despatched to retrieve him was closing in, albeit at a breathless rate. As he stood back up, John's ankle exerted its reservations about moving. He could already feel the tendons stiffening. However, their disapproval was overwhelmed by the suffering he would receive if recaptured. Placing his full weight on it, John embraced the pain and continued his escape. His pace was severely impeded, his injured right foot consistently managing just a half step before buckling. John could now hear the gasps of his pursuer. They gained clarity with every step. He tried to increase his speed, forcing his weakened ankle to accept a greater load, but it only accommodated him for a couple of strides. Looking up ahead, he saw the sunlight breaking through the outer tree line. There was only ten metres to go before he would be out in the open. Chris's breathing was getting louder, and he could now hear firm footsteps. John continued as fast as he could, his injury forcing him to grimace. With every stride, the pain intensified.

Suddenly, a hand brushed against his shoulder, catching a piece of his shirt, restraining him. He leaned forward to break free, but the hand followed. Five metres to go. John knew there wasn't a chance that he was going to make it. Instinctively he ducked to one side, trailing his poor leg out behind as an obstacle. His move caught the older boy off guard. Launching him into the air only to plummet back down to the earth in a disadvantaged bundle. Unfortunately, this manoeuvre also left John in a heightened state of agony, as eleven stone of weight collided with his already handicapped foot. Plus, the initiative had also knocked him to the floor, though in a moderately more controlled manner than his pursuer. As John stood up again, he looked down at Young's body on the ground. He was silent, clutching at his stomach in an attempt to gain breath. Rolling over onto one side, he exposed the true cause of his agony – an elevated root that had hit him straight in the chest, winding him. John smirked at his aggressor's suffering and then continued to hobble toward the open ground. After crawling up the embankment, he screamed out for help. Two of his friends came running over. As they advanced, John peered back down into the woods to view how Young was doing, but the space was empty.

"What's up?" Ian crouched bedside him, quickly followed by Kevin.

"Manton's in the woods." John took a sharp breath. "He's beating up Smythe. Get some help."

Kevin instantly raced back towards the church. John watched in silence as he vanished through the deep shrubbery. By now, the remainder of his footballing associates had come over, headed by Nicola. She knelt down by his side and immediately took hold of his hand. John flinched, shaking her off as he had earlier. After this, he half expected her to run away crying, but she didn't. Instead, she retracted her hands with perfect composure, placing them on her lap. Her face remained for the most part concerned, but she couldn't help displaying the telltale signs of the sadness his action had brought. John stared at her intently, now desperately wanting to apologise, but his pride wouldn't allow it in front of the others. He felt so ashamed. Nicola had done absolutely nothing wrong except fancy him and he had treated her like a leper. She deserved so much better than that. Her gentle features weren't as distinct as Gloria's, but they were still beautiful. Her auburn hair, hanging straight down to her shoulders, lacked lustre but was tidy in a homely manner. Her eyes didn't sparkle like his heart's desire, but they did glisten with an unspoilt and unselfish sheen that he couldn't help finding captivating. Her skin was pale and smooth and ever so lightly smattered with freckles across the bridge of her nose and cheek bones. Like most teenage girls in the States, she wore a brace in her mouth, but fortunately for Nicola it was of the removable type. She was wearing a floral-patterned dress with a cardigan over the top. Her legs were dirty from the football and mottled purple from the biting cold, adding to her frail appearance.

Suddenly an exhausted voice disturbed John's concentration. "What's up?" He recognised his father's tone. Looking up John found a group of male adults including the Father and Nicola's dad. "What is it, son?" His father asked once more.

"In the woods...." John was a little nervous now that the focus of attention was on him.

"What's in the woods, son?" This time it was the Father speaking.

"Brighton Smythe. They're picking on Smythe."

"Where?" asked his dad.

John didn't respond immediately, because it took him a couple of seconds to transform his memories into directions.

"If you go straight in for about eighty metres, then go a bit more to the right. They were there."

His description was sketchy to say the least, but the adults obviously hadn't expected any better. They set off down the embankment without further questioning. By now the maternal contingent had caught up, headed by Marlene. As soon as she saw John's flushed face down on the ground, she rushed towards him. John was embarrassed by the attention, looking away from her. He could see the Father struggling with his frock on the uneven ground, but the rest of the eight-strong posse were already out of sight. This had to be community spirit in action. The Father had spoken of a state of being where the community cared for each other, a place where nothing but goodness stemmed from each of their hearts. This had to be that place, there was no other explanation. Maybe God really did watch over him and had given him this opportunity as a sign, to show him the way forward. He smiled contentedly.

Five minutes passed before activity returned to the nearby woodland. He saw his father guiding Smythe away from danger, closely followed by the Father. The boy looked in a much worse state than when John had left. His face was badly bruised around the left eye and his posture highlighted further hidden suffering.

"Father, could you take Brighton home?" John's father said, turning to offer the priest a helping hand up the embankment.

"Certainly, Sean." With that he took hold of Brighton's hand and led him off back towards the church.

"Who did that?" Marlene asked. John flicked his head around sharply, ready to answer but realised she was addressing his father.

"It was a couple of boys called Manton and Fletcher."

John was puzzled why they only had the two names but choose not to question it any further. If Smythe hadn't felt the need to divulge the late arrival, then neither did he. Getting up on his feet, he watched the townsfolk disperse, feeling a warmth seep into his spirit from the accomplishment of doing good.

2

It was a brilliant morning, a thin veneer of mist delicately drifting along the streets, above which the crystal blue sky was readily visible. As John looked out his window, he could see the paper boy coming down the street on his rollerblades. His name was Freddy. He was in John's year but assigned to another class. Freddy was one of the kids in school who fitted in and didn't fit in at the same time. He knew kids from both sides of the fence, bad and good, though he never favoured either and that was probably why both sides still talked to him. He had this ability to make everyone feel he was a close friend who always had time to talk and wouldn't belittle any aspect of life.

Freddy's physical attributes went a long way to explaining his casual demeanour. He was tall, with an athletic build and had an eye for dropping a basket from the court halfway line. This latter ability was one of the reasons he was at Shifton High to begin with, because at the time of his enrolment, his parents weren't actually living in the town. They weren't even living in the state, for that matter, but they had still managed to send him to the high school by virtue of a sports scholarship. This wasn't something that frequently happened. But in Freddy's case, the school wanted him as much as his parents wanted to send him. The school's desire was to find a cornerstone around which an average basketball team could be league contenders; and with Freddy, they were. His parent's motivation also arose from selfish grounds. They wanted their son to have the best possible opportunity to gain a good sports scholarship to college. And even though Shifton High wasn't historically one of the key focal points for college recruiters, it had supplied the talent for five of the ten key sports scholarships in the past three years. As such, it was currently guaranteed to have a watchful eye kept on it. Meanwhile, Freddy was tossed around in the middle. There was no disputing he enjoyed playing basketball, but he didn't need the academic pressure of having to retain a certain grade point average that went hand in hand with securing a scholarship. It wasn't that Freddy was a loaf of bread short of a picnic. But it could be said that he had a bite or two taken out of his sandwiches. Consequentially, he found the study of everything other than the aerodynamics of a basketball very difficult. And this led him to feeling obliged to study hard for the benefit of all the other parties concerned, at the expense of any social life. Yet despite this lack of time for friendship, he managed to know a little bit about everybody, including the assholes like Manton. Though John believed the roughnecks only endured his friendliness because he would prove too much of an opposition.

At that moment Freddy looked up and spied John. Then, raising one hand in a greeting, he flung the Garrets' daily paper towards the door with the other. He did this so effortlessly, never losing balance for a second. John automatically lifted a hand in acknowledgement, but his face was blank, transfixed by the way Freddy's feet glided across the pavement. Soon he was out of sight and the street was empty once more, which for six thirty on a Monday morning wasn't surprising. He looked up and down for any other signs of activity, but all he could see was the same old row of eighties mass-fabricated houses, with standard driveways, no perimeter fences and a customary patch of grass that separated the pavement from the kerb.

John watched until the sun had risen above the horizon and then slid back into his bed. Pulling the covers up around his neck, he soaked in the warmth. Contentment filtered through his pores, allowing his mind to wander. For some reason, his thoughts focussed on the exploits of the previous day and the expression on Manton's face when they had finally brought him out of the woods. The refined hatred that had dwelled in those eyes and the way it had been bestowed solely on John. His eyebrows had furrowed towards the centre of his forehead, adding greater depth to the expression as he had passed by John mouthing the words 'watch out' threateningly.

The remainder of the day had been occupied by deliberation over choosing a punishment fit for the crime. It had been a difficult balancing act. Manton's crime, after all, had effectively been grievous bodily harm to which Fletcher had aided and abetted. However, they were young and as such required a degree of action that didn't necessarily follow the line of the law. After two hours' debate, a decision had been reached. A compromise between legal justice and school punishment. The sentence began with a month's worth of Saturday morning detentions, during which Manton and Fletcher had to write an essay on the law pertaining to their crime. The writing element was proposed by the school English teacher, who happened to be an ex-lawyer. After this, they would be given release for lunch, which had to be eaten at home, followed by an afternoon of community service up until six o'clock. This latter punishment over-spilled into Sunday, continuing for a further five hours after they had attended Sunday morning worship. The best part of the punishment's design was the fact that Manton and Fletcher had to endure public humiliation as they carried out their physical labour. To all intents and purposes, they had become slave labour for the town. Sweeping streets, emptying rubbish bins and cleaning public toilets. Despite the humour John found in the sentence, he would have to be very careful to stay out of their way while they carried out their duties.

Rolling his head to the left, he checked the clock. It was

quarter to seven. Time to get up. Sliding his feet over the edge of the bed, he forced himself into an upright position. His head swooned from the sudden downward rush of blood. Gradually he came around enough to be able to walk, and so began his school day ritual. By the time he had got downstairs, Marlene was already washing up after Sean, who had just departed for work.

"Morning, darling. Cereal or toast this morning?"

"Nothing, thanks." He headed towards the fridge and poured himself a glass of orange juice. Gulping it down, he dropped the glass in the sink and headed for the door.

"What, no kiss goodbye?" Marlene called after him. He walked back towards her and she squeezed him tight. "Have a good day." She kissed him on the forehead. John smiled at her, then left.

Outside he found Kevin and Nicola waiting for him at the end of his drive. The three of them normally walked together, a habit prompted initially by a parental association that promoted safety in numbers. Now they did it because they were friends. As John approached them, he was struck by the sharp contrast of their styles. Kevin was positioned somewhere between retro seventies and grunge. His shirt was bright blue, with an excessively long collar, the buttons left undone, allowing it to hang freely around his ripped jeans. On his head he sported a New York Knicks baseball cap, and his feet were housed in a pair of sturdy caterpillar boots. Next to him was Nicola, in a flashback outfit from *The Little House on the Prairie* consisting of a flowery dress and hair plaited down her back. The only thing she lacked was a bright pink bow on the crown of her head. Nicola couldn't be blamed for her style. It was her mother's influence. At the weekends she was allowed to select her own wardrobe, and when she did, it was like any other teenager's.

"Yo, bro, how's it hanging?" Kevin raised his hand to give a high five.

"What you talking like that for?" John pulled a funny face,

leaving Kevin hanging.

"What? Can't I talk to the coolest guy in town this morning?" Kevin maintained his accent.

"What are you on about?" John started walking.

"You don't know? You are the man of the weekend! The talk of the town! The inspiration of the teenage masses! The man who broke Manton!"

"Piss off." He dismissed it, believing Kevin was just pulling his leg.

"No, honestly. Everybody's talking about how you rescued Smythe and slam-dunked Manton and his sidekick into the biggest heap of shit they have ever seen."

"Give it a rest." John was having none of it.

"Tell him, Nikki." Kevin gave her a poke in the arm.

"It's true. I've already had Gemma and Evelyn on the phone this morning."

"See – you're a hero. And at such a young age." Kevin nudged him on the back, but John didn't respond. "What's up, man?"

"Nothing, alright!" He walked on ahead. The town making him out to be some kind of crusader was all he needed. Manton's anger would be bad enough, but his retribution was bound to be greater, increasing proportionally to the degree of his humiliation.

"Hey, don't worry about it." Kevin caught up again. "There's no way he'll even touch you. I mean, just think what would happen to him if he did. They'd probably have a public flogging in the town square." He paused for a minute and made an exaggerated thoughtful expression. "Now, actually, that would be pretty cool. Maybe we should let him kick the crap out of you after all. I'll see if I can set it up."

"Shut up, you prat." John couldn't help but laugh at Kevin's final rhetoric, because he made it sound so ridiculous.

"There you go, that's better. Now start acting like a hero." He turned and grabbed Nicola by the arm, latching the two of them together. "Start with this. Heroes should always have a pretty young girl in tow." They both laughed briefly, before John dove at Kevin. He missed and ended up chasing Kevin down the street, leaving Nicola walking sadly behind. It was one of those instances where the young male bravado inadvertently hurt her, an event that recently happened a lot between John and Nicola. Kevin, however, was more sensitive to her feelings and called out for her to catch up. She accepted instantly, the corners of her mouth lifting. The bus pulled up just as they arrived at the stop. The three of them boarded and managed to squeeze themselves on to a two-seater, with Kevin sat in the middle.

The journey lasted about ten minutes and was for the most part silent between the three of them. However, John kept getting pestered by the other children over his Sunday heroics. What Kevin had professed appeared to be true. He had become an icon amongst the kids overnight. It was a title he didn't particularly relish, mainly because of his previous reservations about Manton being incited into a more severe revenge. On the other hand, though, it was nice to have street cred. It made him feel good about his deeds, establishing ever greater empathy for Father Hill's sermon. Finally, the bus pulled up outside the school and the three of them disembarked. Standing poised on the pavement was Ian. As soon as he thought they were in earshot, he began.

"Jesus, man, you're famous." His lips curled in a huge grin.

"Don't worry, he already knows." Kevin responded on behalf of his friend. "We've had continuous adulation for the past ten minutes. In fact, if you look up his butt, you'll see the sun is shining."

"What's up with you? You thought it was fantastic earlier." John questioned.

"Yes, I know. But that was before Garret mania back on the bus." He paused and turned to face his three compadres. "Now, I'm sorry to say this, but if this intense reverence continues, then

I'll have no choice but to terminate our friendship." He stopped for a second to view their response, which was a vision of disbelief. "That is unless you tell everybody that I was a heroic soldier of righteousness as well, coming to your aid when you feared capture and thought all was lost." Kevin started laughing, quickly followed by the rest of them.

"Shut up, you ding-dong." John thumped him on the arm.

"Oh, is that how you intervened yesterday? Jumped up in front of Manton and said, 'Stop right there, you ding-dong.' He must have been quaking in his boots."

"Shut up." John punched him once more, but he was laughing so hard it barely made an impact.

"Please don't tell me you hit him like that. I mean, that was as light as a feather. In fact, I'd wager that Nicola here could pack a bigger punch than that." Kevin grabbed her by the wrist and raised her arm in the air. "Yeah, feel that muscle." He squeezed her bicep.

"Hey, leave me alone." She pulled back, appearing slightly intimidated.

"You just keep going mate and I'll show you what I did do." John said, helping Nicola to break away.

"Ah-ha! I think we have discovered his weakness. He only helps those in distress. Okay, so, I'll kidnap Nicola and you'll have to come and save her. Come on, Ian, give me a hand." With that he made like he was going to carry her off. John stood still. "What, no action?"

"No. Because I know you'd enjoy having Nicola as your prisoner. It'd be a dream come true for you." John's comment was very close to the bone, because Kevin had recently disclosed to him that Nicola was the current object of his desire.

"You bastard."

Kevin dropped Nicola and leaped toward John, but he was already on the move. Leaving the others behind, John ran in the direction of their classroom. Kevin refused to give up the chase and John knew he could never outrun him. Weaving through the crowds, he managed to gain a few more feet breathing space before he had to turn left into the main building. On entering, he flung the door shut behind him, stalling some of the kids directly in his wake. He knew this would in turn force Kevin into defeat, but just in case he maintained a steady jog. It was only after he saw Kevin's head on the far side of the door, that he slowed to a walk. Turning forward to face his direction of travel, he collided with a T-shirt-clad wall of flesh.

"What a pleasant surprise. Nice to see you again, Garret. Is it nice to still be breathing?" The voice was unmistakably Manton's and it was definitely pissed off. John was still looking down at the floor, almost too afraid to raise his head. There were three pairs of shoes lined up next to each other, which meant the full team was present. "I'm talking to you, Garret, so lift your fucking head!" Manton's voice was slow, soft and sharp, somewhere just above a whisper. John was absolutely terrified. "I said look at me!"

"Look at him, you prick!" Another voice entered the conversation, followed by a dark-skinned hand that clasped around his chin and raised his head.

"That's much better," Manton started again. "How are you doing this fine morning, Garret?" John began to open his mouth in defence, but Manton didn't wait for a response. "I'm not doing so well, as you can probably see." He gestured toward his face and the bruising that extended up his left cheek, engulfing his eye in a half-swollen mass. "Don't worry too much, though. I've had worse. This is my father's handy work. He's been doing it to me all my life. Hell, it's no wonder I'm all fucked up and into beating up people smaller than me. It's bred into me. It's in my genes." He paused for a minute. John glanced either side of him at Fletcher and Young, who flanked their leader with head-dissecting smiles. "Hey, I don't recall telling you to look away!" John felt the clamminess of Manton's hand now against his cheek, pulling his head back around. "Where was I, anyway? Yes, it's in my genes to beat up small kids. So where do you get off trying to stop me and landing me in the shit for something I can't stop myself doing?"

"I'm sorr—"

"Shut up. Don't you think you're in enough trouble as it is?" He paused for thought one more time, taking a quick look up and down the corridor. "I think we had better find somewhere a little bit more private to continue this conversation. Don't you?" He grabbed John by the arm.

John tried to struggle, but his efforts were quickly suppressed by Fletcher and Young, one of them behind him and the other on his open side. He was marched quickly into the boys' locker room, which was only three doors up the corridor. Everybody had stared as they walked past, but nobody did anything. They were too afraid. The routine was clearly formatted between his three assailants, with Fletcher remaining outside the door on lookout duty. Once inside, Young did a quick recognisance mission down each aisle and into the showers. Then with a nod of the head, he signalled the all-clear.

"Do you realise how much trouble you have got me and my friends into?" Manton began.

"I'm—"

"Shut up when I'm talking." Manton twisted John's arm up around his back and pushed him against one of the lockers. "We've got next to no free time for a month and it's all because of you. I mean, when you decided to grass us up, did you ever consider the fact that Smythe wasn't complaining? Okay, yes, he was screaming a little, but did you ever hear him say 'stop, please don't hurt me'?" For once it seemed a response was required. "Well, did you?"

John shook his head.

"Exactly! No, you didn't! So, what gave you the right to stick your nose in where it wasn't required?"

"I'm sorry." John managed to get the full words out of his mouth this time.

"Sorry doesn't cut the draft I'm afraid. I mean, does sorry make it alright with you, Chris?" He turned towards Young, who shook his head in response. "You see it's not good enough for either of us. Chris, do you think sorry would be good enough for Fletch?" This time Manton didn't even bother turning his head to see the customary shake. "You see, Chris here doesn't think a simple apology would be good enough for our good buddy Fletch either." He paused, looking thoughtfully up at the ceiling. "Now, unfortunately, the only thing that's going to make us feel better is to take all our aggression out on you. And try not to take it personally, just remember it's in my blood." He started to cock his fist back.

"Please don't." John began pleading.

"You're not quite with the program here, are you? Smythe may have had a choice, but you don't."

Just at that point, the swing door out into the corridor opened and closed.

"Oh, I think you'll find he does!" Standing behind Manton was Freddy the paper boy. "Let him go."

"Get lost, man. This doesn't concern you." Manton looked over towards Young. "Get rid of him, will you." Like a puppet, Young advanced on the intruder, looking anything but confident about his impending fight. Freddy placed a handout in front of him and waved him down as he would a car.

"Why don't you just put your fists down for a minute and re-evaluate your situation?" Freddy spoke calmly.

Young stopped in his tracks but retained his predatory stance.

"You are about to pick a fight with a guy who is four inches taller, four kilos heavier and whose daily exercise routine is slightly more than getting out of bed. Now if you want to proceed, go ahead, but I would advise against it." Young glanced over at his boss again and received the customary flick of his head, ordering him to continue. "Wow, just wait one second." Young stopped once more, confused at what else Freddy could have to say. "If those weren't good enough reasons for you, have you even wondered where Fletcher is right now? I mean, I walked through the door he was allegedly guarding. Why hasn't he come in here to help? Could it be a) because he has a brain in his head and can figure out when he is outmatched or b) he's as much of an idiot as you are considering being." He took a breath. "Now, if you want to give it a whirl, fine. I'll not try to dissuade you any further."

Freddy relaxed his legs and dropped down into a defensive karate stance. Young's uncertainty grew. His face had turned a paler shade of white since the initial order was given. He stared over at Manton in panic, seeking a retraction of instruction. But Manton was in no mood to yield. He wasn't going to let some varsity basketball player get the better of him.

"Just kick the shit out of the asshole, will ya, so I can get back to business!"

With Manton's final verbal command, Young attacked quickly and directly. Arms raised out in front, he lashed out at Freddy's head but only made brief contact with one of his arms as it swept the attempt off course. The next thing he felt was a solid blow to the stomach, which left him crippled in pain. Freddy wasn't going to leave it at that, though. Grabbing Young by his shirt collar, he dragged him through to the showers and left him in a heap over the drain hole. As he returned to the locker room, he switched the ring main on and left his attacker to soak up the water. The entire event lasted seconds and John enjoyed watching every piece of it. He would have appreciated it more, though, if he had been just a spectator and not a participant who was still pinned up against a locker.

"Now, where were we? I think I was suggesting that you leave him alone." Freddy waited for a response and Manton obliged.

"Don't you fucking go anywhere." The words were meant for John, but Manton didn't take his eyes off the new player, he just threw John aside into the corner of the room. "So, come on then, hero. Show me what you got."

With that, he dove straight for Freddy's midriff, before Freddy had the opportunity to prepare himself. Manton's first effort, unlike his assistant's, had both conviction and power. As his shoulder hit home, Freddy was raised off his feet and driven straight back into the row of lockers behind him. They wavered slightly, as the hundred and thirty kilo mass hit them at full speed. John's saviour slumped to the floor, clutching his stomach, but his face remained staunch with determination. Manton, however, didn't allow him time for his true grit to be released, burying a hefty boot into his testicles. This second blow left Freddy bent over and unable to respond, but Manton hadn't had enough yet and aimed his steel toe cap once more at Freddy's curled body. At that point, Young returned from the shower, flush in the face and drenched to the bone, his face brimming with anger once he saw who was lying on the floor.

"Care to get some revenge?" Manton gestured at his dripping partner to join in the fun. John couldn't watch any longer. He had to do something. Standing up he took a dive at Manton, trying his hardest to emulate what he had seen him do to Freddy. Hitting his target square in the side of the ribs, he drove him in a straight line away from Freddy. The assault caught Manton completely by surprise. They smashed through the locker room door and out into the corridor. John kept driving his legs, until Manton hit the wall on the far side of the corridor. And as the brick made contact with Manton's right shoulder, John heard something give.

Manton fell to floor screaming in pain. John recoiled in shock, watching in amazement as for the first time he saw a tear appear in the bully's eye. For that brief second, his enemy became mortal. He wasn't indestructible. He could feel pain just like the rest of them. As John moved further away from the agonised wreckage of his attacker, his tunnel vision receded. Kids stood stationary along the full length of the corridor. Silence filled the air, spoiled only by the occasional whimper from Manton. Then it happened.

A single person started clapping far over to John's left. They were rapidly joined by others, until it seemed as if the entire corridor was applauding him.

"What the hell is going on out here?"

The rapture ceased.

"Well? Somebody answer me!" It was the school principal, Mr Stevenson. His question wasn't answered with any words, but by fingers pointed at John by several of the onlookers. Advancing quickly, Mr Stevenson's attention gradually rested on John. "Can you give an explanation for this, Garret?"

He tried to answer the principal, but the words just weren't ready to come out. So, he did as others had done before him and extended a finger towards Manton.

"Jesus! What the hell have you done to him?" Stevenson knelt down by the injured boy's side. "Go get the nurse, Garret!"

John didn't hang about for a second longer. He felt a massive release of anxiety in being ordered away from the scene. As he ran along the corridor, several hands respectfully patted his back, and he couldn't help but let a smirk appear.

The infirmary always sounded too grand a name for the large room with three examination tables and rail-mounted curtains for privacy. The nurse didn't even have her own office, just a desk in the corner, enclosed on each side by two filing cabinets. Her name was Mrs Vedder, and as far back as anyone could care to recollect, she had always been the nurse. That didn't mean she was particularly old. In fact, no one knew her real age, because she still looked like a firm-figured twenty-five-year-old.

As John entered through the opaque glass-fronted door, he found her sitting at her desk reviewing some notes. She had her legs crossed, forcing her skirt to ride up above her knees, exposing her stocking tops. In his cocky mood, John couldn't help but look down and as soon as he did, he was stunned into silence. This was one of those treasured moments that would get discussed in the locker rooms in years to come and wasn't to be taken lightly. Unfortunately, it was cut short when the sight of his gaping mouth and glazed eyes caused her to adjust her hem line.

"Can I help you, Mr Garret? Beyond your spectatorship, that is!"

His face burned with embarrassment, but he tried to act natural.

"Yes, Mrs Vedder. Manton's hurt himself up the corridor." He tried to look her in the face, but his hormones only allowed him to manage a shoulder-height glance, causing him further discomfort as he realised, she might think he was staring at her breasts. He looked away altogether, but she was already standing up and moving into his new horizon. His eyes diverted again, down to the floor this time.

"Come on then, show me!" She ordered him to lead on.

Back at the crime scene, none of the spectators had moved on since his departure, making it steady work to navigate through to the accident. As the principal came into sight, John could see that the rest of the story had unfolded in his absence. The changing room door was propped open and he could see Freddy resting battered up against a row of lockers. As soon as he saw John, he smiled and raised a thumbs-up towards him. By now nurse Vedder was tending to Manton, with the principal looking intently on. John took the opportunity to go and see his saviour.

"Hi," he said softly on approach.

"Hi." Freddy found it difficult to speak. "Thanks for your help."

"What do you mean? It should be me thanking you!"

"Maybe a little, but if you hadn't stepped in at the end there, I'd be in a lot worse shape than this. Hell of a charge, that. Did you ever think of playing tight end for the school football team?" He gave a small laugh and John joined him. "Despite that weak shit still beating on me, I heard you both smack into the far wall. Did you leave it standing?"

"Yeah, well, I surprise myself sometimes." He pretended to be cool.

"Well, you can surprise him like that anytime you like." He flicked his head towards Manton. "What's up with him, anyway? He's been moaning since you took him out."

"He's got two fractured ribs, that's what!" Nurse Vedder was standing in the doorway. "And I believe he's also got a sprained wrist from trying to push somebody off him." She stared at John as she knelt down next to Freddy. "Other than that, he's fine, but what about you? Where does it hurt most?"

"I don't know, Miss. Pick any spot and I'll feel something."

"Okay, if you insist." Raising his shirt up, she prodded him in his left ribs.

Freddy emitted a small complaint of pain, but she ignored it, running her hand forcefully down across his bones.

"I think we can definitely say you've broken nothing on that side." She traced her hands around to his other side. Freddy pulled a pleasured face as she did so, and John struggled to stifle a laugh. "And that side's intact as well. Can you move your arms?"

"Yes."

"Legs?"

"Yes." Freddy seemed confused by her apparent dismissiveness.

"Well, get on your feet and walk down to the infirmary. I'll give you some painkillers and then the best thing would be to go home and lay up for the rest of the day. John, you help him down there, will you?" She stood up and returned to Manton.

"Come on then, take the cripple away." Freddy stretched his arms up towards John, seeking assistance to get up on his feet.

By the time they shuffled out the door, Mr Stevenson had successfully dispersed fifty percent of the onlookers with the threat of detention and was now increasing his punishment to include non-admittance to the school dance, which took place at the weekend. They attempted to slide past unnoticed but failed.

"You two wait there a minute." He finished addressing a small group of about ten girls and three boys, who subsequently disappeared rapidly up the corridor. "Now, what have you two been up to? Hmmm? Why do I have two boys who look like they've just done ten rounds with Prince Naseem?"

John and Freddy looked at each other, puzzled, not knowing who the hell the principal was talking about.

"He's a boxer. Now answer my question!"

There was a moment's silence before John had formulated in his head the most diplomatic way of explaining the situation.

"Well, you see, Sir, Manton was about to start beating me up when Freddy stepped in and stopped him."

"So, you broke his ribs for that, did you?" Stevenson stared accusingly at Freddy.

"No!" Freddy asserted.

"No, I did that, sir, by accident," John cut in before Freddy could lodge a bigger protest.

"But I thought you said big man here saved the day?"

"He did, Sir, but after Freddy had managed to sort out Young, Manton had a go at him and knocked him to the floor, and that was when I intervened and broke his ribs." John could see Manton was listening in while he was being tended to, although he looked in too much pain to be bothered about it.

"Who threw the first punch?" The principal's patience was fraying.

"Young did, Sir." Freddy answered.

"But I thought you said Manton was trying to bully you?"

"He was about to, Sir." John paused to swallow, his mouth getting more parched by the second. "But that was when Freddy turned up and Manton ordered Young to get rid of him."

"This is all getting a little confusing." Stevenson looked back at Manton, who was now being aided to his feet by a newly reappeared Fletcher. "Take Freddy to the infirmary and then I expect to see you outside my office in five minutes and we'll run through this one more time from the top. Now go!" He ushered them away down the corridor before returning to Manton.

3

The rain cascaded down from the corrugated veranda roof and on to the lip of the porch, generating a continuous hollow drone. John stood there for a couple of minutes to see if the stream would subside for just a few moments, so that he could escape into the world without too much of a drenching. It had been raining since Tuesday morning, pouring non-stop out of the sky. Today was Friday. John continued to wait for a break. It wasn't that he was particularly bothered about getting wet, although he did hate it when the cascading torrent found its way past his collar. Maybe one day his adopted parents would stick a gutter up. Until then, he'd live with it.

John had now been standing there for about ten minutes, waiting for a suitable break in the weather, but it hadn't come. Nor, judging by the advancing clouds, did it look like it was going to any time soon. He couldn't wait any longer. If he did, then he wouldn't be able to drop in on Freddy before school, which had become a new routine for him this week since their joint collision with the Manton gang. Thinking the situation through in his head, he put on a determined face and dove through into the wet air. His baseball cap held back the majority of the streaming water, but a couple of drops still made their way past.

The street this morning was pedestrian free, a lot of parents having made the effort to drive their children to school. The few still making their way by foot and bus were wrapped up to the eyeballs in scarfs, raincoats and hats. Some poor boys were also forced to wear earmuffs, the ultimate in 'mama's boy' aesthetic. Walking down the drive to the sidewalk, he turned left up towards Boston Drive. Ahead, he could see Nicola being bundled into her father's car. One of her parents always dropped her off during bad weather. The only downside for her was that she arrived at school a good fifteen minutes before the rest of the kids, so that her mum and dad could still get to work on time. She caught a glimpse of him out of the corner of her eye and smiled. John waved back. Her grin expanded. He felt warm inside from the small bit of happiness he had imparted. It was a feeling he'd been getting a lot during this past week. Every kid in school was talking about him. This left him feeling good about himself when he was alone, sometimes it verged dangerously close to egoism, but he remained very benevolent in public. Recent events had led him to realise that he wasn't really one for mass adoration. He would have favoured quiet reverence, but that wasn't for him to decide. At least once he had got through today, he could hide from the town for the duration of the weekend. Give himself a break. As he arrived at the end of Nicola's drive, they were just reversing out. Her face still glowed from his wave and she gave him another direct beamer as she glided past. He stopped and smiled back, waiting for the car to pull off in the direction of school before continuing.

Gloria lived four houses up and in an unprecedented turn of fate she was leaving for school at the same time. She looked over towards him and stared before turning away again. But then, as if in sudden recognition of who he was, she flicked her head back up towards him, smiled and waved. John was caught off guard. He didn't know what to do. Raise a hand or scream out hello? Flustered, he awkwardly raised both hands in greeting. He watched her face crack into a small laugh, and he felt his own go red with embarrassment. It wasn't over yet though. The torture was about to be compounded, as he watched her deposit her bag in the back of the car before walking down to the pavement's edge. John's eyes followed her every step of the way. His heart began beating treble time. They had never conversed beyond the usual pleasantries and this event had all the indications of breaking that barrier.

Gloria was wearing a red raincoat with a wrap-around belt tied up at the front. Underneath she was obviously wearing a skirt, her bare ankles protruding from the bottom of her coat. Over her head she loosely wore a transparent plastic drape, which revealed a big black bow clipped to the back of her long locks.

"Hi," she called out from a few metres away.

"Hi, Gloria." John used her name, finding it peculiar to say it out loud.

"What are you up to this weekend?"

"Nothing much, really. Thought I might do some reading." He tried to be natural.

"You're not going to the game?" She sounded slightly distressed.

"I wasn't planning to, but you never know?"

"I'm going." Her smile drooped.

"Well, I may suddenly become inspired to attend." He played up to her, his confidence increasing as the conversation proceeded.

"I'll see you there, then." Her presumptuous response left no leverage for him to shy away from attending. And before he could reiterate his uncertainty, she was away.

He watched her run to her car, his heart tripping in time with her feet, thinking about what had just taken place. He couldn't wait to tell Freddy. Taking one final glance up the drive, he caught her reflection staring back at him in the wing mirror. Raising a coordinated and confident hand this time, he waved goodbye and continued on his way.

John's heart didn't stop pounding until a long five minutes after the encounter. His body and soul were on cloud nine. So far this morning's events had been comprised solely of the stuff his dreams were made of. In fact, having his ideal girl come up and talk to him was mind-blowing beyond anything his sleeping brain had conjured. Her approach had been blatant in the extreme. She had come to him. It hadn't been an accidental meeting. There had been clear intent. Likewise, she appeared to have firm intentions about seeing him again on Saturday at the football game. He was amazed. The wonderment carrying him the remaining hundred metres to Freddy's front door. With a smile so prolific that it almost looked as if it wrapped right around his head, he rang the doorbell. It was literally seconds before Freddy's friendly face filled the gap.

"What you doing out of bed?" The sudden appearance of his mate, who was supposed to be bedridden, startled John.

"I'm not an invalid, you know! I can leave my bed under my own steam! I don't need your permission!" Freddy was standing there in a T-shirt and boxer shorts, a dressing gown hanging loosely around his frame. "Well, say something, then!" he said in a disapproving tone.

"Piss off." John smirked back, checking either side of his friend for any nearby adults. They both began laughing.

"Well, are you coming in or what?"

"That depends. Are you going to invite me in?"

"Sorry. Forgot you required an invitation. You've been here so much recently, I just thought you were part of the furniture."

John couldn't top that, so he resorted to a punch on the arm.

"Hey, don't you think I've taken enough punches for you this decade?" Freddy said with a smile.

"I'm sorry. I was under the impression you were a man and could take it!"

"You're cruising for a bruising." Freddy raised his fists in mock preparation.

"I can't. It would be fair, with you in your weakened condition. Wait until you're better, then I'll take you on." John grinned.

"You're on." Freddy started bouncing on the spot. "When I'm back to peak fitness, I'll give you a real session of humiliation. You think Manton's intimidating? Wait until you get a load of me!" He managed a couple of air punches before they both started laughing again. "What's happened to you this morning, anyway? Did you get out of the wrong side of bed?"

"No and you'll never guess either." He raised his voice in a challenge, but Freddy didn't bite. "Gloria just walked up to speak to me."

"Why? Was she lost or something? Did she need the time?"

"Why don't you just shut up and give me a break." He took a breath and allowed the corners of his mouth to rise. "She asked me to the football game on Saturday."

"Bullshit!"

"Afraid so." John allowed a smug expression to form.

"What did she say exactly?" Freddy asked, an expression of disbelief on his face.

"She asked me if I was going to watch the game and I said I might do."

"That's not asking you out!" Freddy turned to enter the lounge.

"I'm not finished yet." John followed him. "Then she said that she was going and that it would be nice to see me there." He tweaked the truth to make it sound better. "Then I said I might suddenly get a hard-on to watch some football." Freddy was listening with greater interest now. "And then she said she hoped so and looked forward to seeing my hard-on." He couldn't keep a straight face any longer, breaking into hysterics at Freddy's gullibility.

"You prat." Freddy punched him. "I knew you were lying."

"No, seriously, she did come over to speak to me. And she did say she looked forward to seeing me at the weekend."

"I don't believe you."

"I'm telling the truth now." He needed Freddy to believe it.

"Well, if she did, that's great, but it's no big thing, you know." John's face dropped. "She does that to all the guys. She even invited me out last week, to go bowling of all things."

"You're shitting me?"

Freddy delayed his response, savouring watching John slowly deflate. "Yes."

"Bastard."

"That makes us even." He pointed a warning finger at John. "Okay?"

"Alright, I suppose so. What you doing?"

"A bit of reading."

"Why?" His mouth gaped open in amazement. "I'd be watching videos full time."

"Yeah. Well, I've already had three days of that and now I'm reading." John followed Freddy through into his father's study. The walls were layered with shelves, hundreds of books stacked in disarray on top of them. "Come over here and have a look at this." Freddy pointed at a large leather-bound book he had opened up on his father's desk. As John closed in, he could see one page was covered in illustrations and the other with verses of what appeared to be a poem. The writing was bizarre, shapes he had never seen before.

"What is it?"

"Well, I was watching a video." He paused and smiled at John. "Called *The Crucible*. You know, the one with Winona Ryder?" John's face remained expressionless. "You know, the one where she gets her kit off at the beginning and all she wants to do is hump Daniel Day Lewis into the next millennium."

"Yes, I know the one. Thank you for your graphic reminder."

"Hey, just didn't want you to miss out on anything." Freddy raised his hands submissively. "I was intrigued by the story. It's true you know?" He looked at John for some kind of a response. John obliged by shrugging his shoulders. "So, I came in here to sift through my father's collection, see if he had anything about it. He's always liked that stuff. Anyway, I found this! It's a book of magic that has been pieced together from the tales and documents that were around at the time."

"So?" John wasn't particularly impressed yet.

"For the first half it covers the same story as the movie, although it's a little more detailed than that. It traces back further. It gives accounts of two of the girls' activities a year before they arrived in Salem. Stories of practising witchcraft, long before the incident that brought about all the deaths." He took a sharp breath. "I mean, you watch the film, and you think it's all a big misunderstanding based around a lie that would expose them for what they really were. Well, that may have been the case in Salem, but for a couple of the girls it certainly wasn't true. They weren't just playing a game. They really could conjure up demons. They'd done it before."

"If they were known for being witches, why didn't anyone pick up on it? Why didn't they just kill the kids?" John still didn't believe.

"Because the only people who knew were the parents. And the parents knew that they would be persecuted, along with their offspring. Naturally, they were terrified. So they kept hiding the evidence from the successive communities they lived in, each time quietly packing up their possessions and leaving. They kept willing themselves to believe the places to be evil. So that they could leave the darkness possessing their children behind." Freddy had begun to talk with an air of mysticism.

"So, what's that meant to be?" John stretched a finger towards the picture on the left-hand page. It depicted two girls in a wood, standing with their arms stretched either side of a small fire. Each girl held a dagger in their right hand and what appeared to be a rabbit in their left.

"That's the girls trying to invoke the spirit."

"What's the spirit?" He spurted the words condescendingly out his mouth, desperate to prove that it was all a load of rubbish.

"The spirit of Shalek, as he is sometimes called, is the force of nature that exists all around us. Witches believed they could harness this power to their advantage."

"What, so they brought the evil to life and it did all that damage?"

"No. Shalek isn't an entity, it's a power. Whether it is good or bad is solely dependent upon the intent of the one who summons it. In this case the two girls."

"Is that supposed to be Salem?" He acknowledged the picture once more.

"No, that's the most unnerving thing about it. That's here in Shifton!"

"Bullshit!"

"Honest. It's supposed to be the woodland up near the church."

John's expression displayed his stubbornness to accept what he was being told.

"Have you never wondered why we have a newer church than all the surrounding towns? Says here that the original church was burned down and that the same day, farmers' crops withered overnight, and young girls were seen throwing themselves off rooftops."

"Did you ever think that the town may have just decided to tidy its appearance up a little and built a new one?" He played devil's advocate.

"Actually, I did! But I don't have any way of checking it here. For that I need to get to the library and go through the old records. It says in here that the church wasn't rebuilt until fifteen years after the incident. Which means it should be recorded somewhere in the library's archives, either in the newspaper periodicals or registered on a town plan or something?" Freddy looked at John pleadingly.

"What?"

"My mum won't let me out of the house until next week. You could go and have a look for me?"

"Come on. You want me to spend my Saturday searching through library books to see if a couple of kids burned their church down in a fit of pyromania?"

"Look, I'm not saying that it's all true, but if the church wasn't rebuilt for so long, it at least gives us cause to move on to factual proof number two."

"And what's that?"

Freddy didn't answer, just pointed back to the book and flicked his head for John to move in closer.

"You see that tree there? You see where the wood is stripped back and there are two names carved into the stump? Well, those names are the two young girls."

"Give me a break. That could just be artistic licence?" John wasn't going to concede to the possibility just yet.

"It could be. Although it does say in the book that after the families in question had left the village, a young boy found the tree and saw the names scribbled inside a five-pointed star. A pentagram. However, when the boy went to show his parents, they couldn't find the tree again, but that doesn't mean it's not there."

"So, you want me to go and have a look for that as well?"

"No, I want you to wait for that bit, until I can come with you." He broke for a moment's thought. "Besides, if this is really there, then that star represents the sacred location of their coven. Who knows what forces may still be present?" Freddy stopped talking and listened patiently for his friend's answer. Which was slow to emerge as John pondered the facts.

"Okay, I'll go to the library on Saturday morning, but I'm leaving to go to the football game at twelve o'clock. So, if nothing materialises by then, you're on your own."

"Fine. Besides, going to the game might be a good thing?" Freddy's face relaxed, shedding its intensity.

"Why?"

"I don't know. I was just thinking, that with all the time you spend dreaming about Gloria, maybe she's a witch as well and has cast a spell on you." He darted back out into the hall, just as John lashed out to punch his arm again. "Hey. It might be more fruitful on Saturday just to tail her. She could lead you straight to her own coven." John managed to catch hold of Freddy's arm and was about to punch it, when his mother appeared out of the lounge.

"Don't you think it's time you went to catch your bus, John?" she questioned.

John froze on the spot.

"Well, go on, then. You can visit Freddy again tomorrow." She moved towards the door to let him out.

"See you." John let go of Freddy's arm, then whispered. "Get you next time."

"Yeah, right. Just don't forget the library."

"I won't." He raised a dismissive hand and departed.

Outside the clouds had lightened, the rain turning into a fine spit. Checking his watch, he discovered Mrs Wayne had done him a favour by kicking him out. There were only five minutes before the school bus would arrive and depart. Tightening the straps on his bag, he started to jog. The jog quickly built up into a run, which had to rapidly increase into a sprint as his transport passed him on the final straight. Seeing it pull up forty metres down the road, he pumped his legs harder. A sweat broke out across his forehead. As the rear of the bus loomed, he could hear cheering and raised his head to see Kevin and Ian shouting from the back seat. He blushed a little as he passed beneath the reverberating windows, his bloom increasing when he mounted the stairs. Trying to salvage a bit of dignity, he took a quick bow, which was met with a ripple of applause from the whole bus. Then walking up the aisle, he took a seat next to his mates.

"So, what's the deal? You think you can catch the bus whenever you want, just because you levelled Manton?" Kevin started off with his gags as usual. "You do realise that this service existed for others before you decided to become a hero?"

"Yes, and you know that at the beginning of the week the jokes were funny, but you're really scraping the bottom of the barrel now," John quipped in an attempt to silence him.

"I'm so sorry. Don't beat me up!" Kevin pretended to cower down into his seat.

"Shut up." John laughed.

"How's Freddy?" Ian asked.

"Fine. He's up and about having the time of his life from what I can see. Videos, dressing gowns, chips and soda. The things that heaven is made of." He grinned and patted his stomach at the thought. "He reckons he'll be back to school next week."

"Great." Kevin butted in. "We can have a ticker tape parade for the both of you." He opened his eyes and mouth wide, pretending to wait for the rapturous response. Instead, he got a volley of punches from both Ian and John. "Okay! I get the point." He lifted his arms in surrender. "I'll say no more. My lips are zipped."

The remainder of the journey fell into silence. Due to the rain, there were fewer children on the bus today. The still was only broken twice by a casual murmur of voices up at the front and once by the noise of a discman somewhere in the middle. Since Monday the tranquillity of the present environment had been replicated at school, making it a very relaxing place to squander time. There was no school bully to contend with, because the motley crew had been suspended for the remainder of the week. Consequentially there was no continuous trepidation about being dragged into a dark corner and having your nuts wrenched for the sake of a dollar's lunch money.

"Are you coming?" The bus had stopped, and Kevin was standing halfway down the aisle, signalling for John to get off.

Outside everything was the usual early-morning, self-interested hustle and bustle routine, with every teenager in the town trying to make their own particular statement, whether it be musical, political, fashion or just plain old self-righteousness. The haircut was the key to categorisation. If the hair was dyed, spiky or clean shaven, it generally signified the individual had anarchistic tendencies. That didn't mean they were active protesters or rally organisers, just that they liked the standard appearance of the true faction member. The vast majority of these kids wouldn't be able to hold a ten-second conversation on the environment or the injustice of vivisection. That included talking to themselves about it. However, it would have been wrong to tar everybody in this group at the same level of intellectual mediocrity, because at least fifty percent of them were just idle. The other half were just too afraid of failure. They hid behind an image, hoping that the teachers would dismiss them as a waste of time. The regrettable fact was that both subsets, in a frenzy of coolness, were diminishing their life prospects.

The next cranium-covering genre was the styled, the gelled, the moussed, the perfectly combed, and for the girls, the eloquently French-plaited. These were the students who had sufficient intellect to seek their own identity, albeit usually based on the latest film or music stars' own inimitable style. They moved around in their cliques, each of them endeavouring to appear the centre of attention. Their capacity for academia was varied, ranging from the spoilt king who was void of any parental guidance and usually brought up the class rear in any test, right through to the spoilt and left alone, on the basis that their grades reached a pre-agreed level of acceptability. Sandwiched between these financially lucky were the middle-class kids who knew the true value of money, understood what was required to get it and worked hard, when out of harm's sight, to achieve good results. These, in truth, were the cleverest of the lot, holding the skills to mingle with an establishment that outwardly shunned schoolwork in preference for partying. They studied behind closed doors, so that in public they could meet up to the apathetic expectations of their socialite cohort.

Following swiftly behind the socialites were what could be referred to as the normal kids. They had no distinctive hair styling, just cut tidily, but presented on the verge of unkept. They were a little bit like Freddy, available to get on with anybody, never setting their stool out in any particular corner. They studied hard and without hassle. They joined in whenever they were around, and nobody made them unwelcome. In the teenage circles, they were accommodating middle-ground outcasts, and that was their strength, because it gave them the facility to infiltrate any sect. They were the most balanced of kids, with the strongest characters. The unseen future entrepreneurs and captains of industry. The untouchables of the student body. The inoffensive mass, with a friend in every camp.

Finally, at the top of the academic ladder, there were the bright sparks. Despite simple uninspiring functional haircuts, these were the ones perceived by all to be the pinnacles of future society. Yet, despite their undeniable intellect, the students in this category would nine times out of ten fall short. The persistent adulation from teachers and peers alike building their self-belief to an untouchable level, in the end breeding complacent attitudes that would only lead to average careers. It was fine and dandy that they had a wealth of ability, but history had defined the subconscious 'will' as the only prerequisite for success. All of this analysis wasn't to say they would be complete failures, because that would be a misperception of equal magnitude. All of them would probably end up being in the top fifteen percent of the nation's best paid. The snobbish tier of the middle class. The fact that they could have made a bigger difference to the world away from financial incentives would never occur to them or interest them. They were brainwashed into believing that the precious dollar was synonymous with their level of achievement. That was their problem, anyway, not John's. He didn't care if they missed a rung or two on life's ladder. It left more for him to play on.

The building that was Shifton High held no great historical significance, being relatively new. However, this failed to detract from the grandeur of its front elevation. Large dolomitic slabs had been used to frame the main double-doored entrance, their pale colour forming a sharp contrast to the predominant fired red-brick construction. Windows lined all three storeys, uniformly spaced apart, both horizontally and vertically. All portal frames were wooden and newly painted white, giving a warm, inviting feeling to the place as a whole. Unless you were a pupil, that was. This conglomeration of individual elements was all fused together by a rather distastefully coloured yellow mortar, the sight of which always made John's hair stand on end.

Passing under the arched entrance, he brushed the excess rain off his coat. Out of the corner of his eye, he saw Young being dropped off at the kerb side by his father. Initially a sensation of dread fell over John, but it soon dissipated as he realised Young was still on suspension. The only reason for him being here now was his community service punishment. This was the first time John had spied Young in public since their brawl earlier in the week and his mannerisms gave the strong appearance of a newly formed subservient nature. Mr Young was known throughout the town as a walking contradiction of character, achieving an unpredictable balance of tolerance and a short fuse, a sample of which he had obviously bestowed on his offspring. In a peculiar way, it was actually the father's fault his son had hooked up with Manton. It was after all Young's pocket money that had caught Manton's attention. Initially, Manton's only interest had been in periodically beating Young up, until the change fell in one lump out of his pocket. Young then took the initiative one day and bypassed the bruises, handing over a suitable sum of money first. To everybody else this appeared to be a strange thing to do, but then they weren't looking deep enough into the psychology of the action. Yes, it did reduce the periodic physical discomfort, but that wasn't the driving force. Young did it in an attempt to befriend Manton. Despite the savagery of their relationship up until that point, Manton was the only person showing the slightest bit of personal interest in him and that was lure enough. In a short space of time, the subsequent advantages of having Young on his team sunk into Manton's head and the notorious group was formed. Since then, they had collectively terrorised the junior years, the drain on Young's personal pocket money reducing concurrently. He had found his place in society.

"I'll see you later." No response. Kevin tapped John's shoulder. "What, are you deaf?"

"Sorry. I was somewhere else."

"Tell me about it! I'll see you in Phys Ed."

"Why, where you going now?" John was puzzled. They were supposed to have all their classes together this morning.

"I've got my medical and IQ test, remember?"

"Sorry, I forgot."

"So, in Phys Ed then!" Kevin started walking away, pointing his finger back, in a 'see you later' flick of the wrist.

"No, I'm not going to..." John started to say, but the words got lost in the crowd. Turning back to Ian, he continued, "I'm not going to Phys Ed."

"Fine, I'll tell him. We'll meet up with you at the arcade in town afterwards. Let's go." Ian grabbed his sleeve and started to pull him down the corridor. Just at that moment, Young walked through the door, brushing past them both. John froze slightly, but

Young's humbled eyes never strayed from the floor.

"Come on, will ya, or we'll be late."

John followed his friend on autopilot, his mind reminiscing about Monday's events. The terror he had felt, followed by the relief of Freddy's appearance. Then the subsequent anger, as he watched his saviour start to lose the fight, which led to John's assault on a guy one and a half times his size. All in all, it had been an incredible start to what was rapidly establishing itself as a week to end all weeks. But even with the admiration that streamed down on him for his now notorious take-out lunge, he wouldn't want to live it again. It wasn't him. He did something that he had perceived to have been right and it was, but he had no desire to exist as he did now, a target of revenge. His body quivered just at the thought of it. There was no way that Manton would let this slide. Christ, he'd broken the guy's ribs. That wasn't something you forgot about overnight.

Deep in thought, John almost overshot the entrance to his class, but Ian caught his arm and dragged him in, smacking himself on the side of his head and pulling a dunce's face at him. It was an act that John generally would have dismissed, but Nicola had been watching and found it humorous. So, John shoved his friend away in displeasure. The force with which he did this sent Ian careering backwards into the teacher's desk, leaving him slightly dazed. His friend's expression said it all. The whole response was alien to John. He had never cared before when someone had found humour in his stupidity, but this time an unconscious reaction had occurred.

"I'm sorry." John extended an apologetic hand.

"Don't worry about it." The forgiving words didn't match the face and John knew he would have to do a little more than the usual to make amends.

The morning dragged on and Ian's silence at each class break made John's embarrassment harder to suffer. Even Nicola seemed to find the atmosphere uncomfortable, such that she resorted to befriending a girly posse. By lunchtime, a form of polite conversation had resumed and with stunted smiles, they affirmed their gathering at the arcade later. After finishing his sandwiches, John decided not to pursue a resolution any further, sensing that it would come a little easier if they were separated for a while. So instead of hanging around after lunch, he made his excuses and departed for the town. Leaving Ian's presence lifted a huge burden of guilt from his shoulders. He felt so relieved that even his breathing felt smoother and less restricted.

Outside the rain had dispersed and the wind had picked up, allowing the school flag to fly proud. The grey backdrop complimented the purple flag, with its shield emblem, underwritten by a Latin insignia. The insignia lacked any inspirational merit, like carpe diem. Instead, it was long, unpronounceable and meant 'For life, we give thanks'. Hardly the epitaph for a success story. Nor did it provide suitable material for an uplifting football chant. Unlike Nashem High School twenty miles away, whose motto was 'In the face of challenge, accept no prisoners'. This of course led to the great roar of "No prisoners!" every time a Nashem sports team took to the field or court. Truth be told, Shifton's motto was probably greater suited to a convent.

It was only four blocks from the high school to the main street, and then to get to anything worthy of interest John would have to walk five blocks west. It was a journey he had done many times before and to make it interesting he varied his route, choosing a different way to zigzag through the streets each time. Today, though, he chose the simple route, taking each directional requirement in block.

As he hit Main Street, the first shop he encountered was Mr Satherswaite's butcher shop. As usual, he was in the midst of chatting up one of his clientele, a lady at least ten years his senior. There was obviously no level to which he wouldn't stoop in pursuit of a conquest. That wasn't to say that the lady was unattractive. She was actually quite pretty for her age. It was just the thought of the two of them together that made his blood curdle. Large meat on old meat! The thought was repulsive. Shaking his head to disperse the image, John moved swiftly on. On the opposite side, there was his father's video shop, a Texaco gas station and a large hardware store called Owen's, which was run by its namesake. It was the oldest shop in the town, currently managed by John Owen and his wife Sarah. They were third-generation town residents, their grandparents having moved here from Nashem to open up the store.

After this small local business area, there was a break in traditional trading posts, where the international giants took hold. On the nearside, the buildings had been levelled and the ground tarmacked, transforming the area into car lot paradise, occupied by a string of new and second-hand dealerships. Offices were set back from the road, allowing at least two rows of pristine polished cars to be displayed under 'Mr Pedestrian's' nose. Flag lines littered the sky, with small dazzling blue, red, orange, purple and silver fabrics that were almost as big as an attraction as the glistening car bonnets.

The following series of shops displayed clothing merchandise, from the specialised and garish through to the mundane and practical. Residing in the middle of these lower-cost shops was 'Bloomers and Bouncers', a rather more select underwear shop. Which, although it sold very choice brand names, still managed to give the appearance of a saucy sex fest through its window display. Despite this, it had the second highest average sales price per article in the town.

Scattered in between the fashion houses were record stores, bookstores, toys and comic shops, all suitably positioned to give the kids something to do while their mothers entertained their fashion fantasies. John usually hung out in the record store, flicking through the sale section, hunting for that ultimate bargain CD, or searching the more affordable racks of Batman comics. He had accumulated quite a formidable collection since his arrival in Shifton. It was a hobby that Sean and Marlene had started him on when they bought him the very first issue of the *Dark Knight* series for Christmas one year. He had been addicted ever since. Batman's portrayal in the comics was, in general, a far cry from the spoof nature of the seventies-television series. He was a bastard! And not just any bastard! He was a psychotic, reality-challenged, don't give a flying fuck you low-life piece of rat-eaten scum bastard! And when he kicked ass, the blood flew. This was always brilliantly illustrated in full-page graphics, detailing every droplet as it fell through the air. The perfect role model for an impressionable mind.

The town centre was relatively busy today. The activity had an end of week hustle to it. Bodies crowding the sidewalk such that John had to weave a path through the oncoming traffic to make any advance. It was as a result of this concentration that he was distracted enough to miss who was coming towards him. The first warning sign John had was when Manton's scarred hand grabbed him around his bicep and dragged him to the side of the footpath.

"It must be my lucky day!" he said. "Do you like my new features?" Manton gestured up to a fresh swelling on the left-hand side of his face. "That's nothing in comparison to the bruising I've got over the rest of my body. Some of which you gave me, you little shit."

"I'm sorry." John's voice quivered slightly, even though he knew Manton would do nothing in such a public place.

"Is that all you ever say? I'm sorry! Give me a break. It's going to take a shit load more begging to get out of what you got coming to you." He relaxed his grasp. "It may not be today. It might not be tomorrow. But it's coming!" With that he turned and walked away.

It was only then that John realised Manton was on public service duty, holding a litter picker in one hand and a dustbin liner in the other. Still paralysed, John stared blankly at the back of Manton's head. The suffering that had been referred to became clearer now – Manton had a heavy limp in his right leg. John caught a glimpse of the piercing pain in Manton's face as his leg buckled underneath him. He couldn't imagine what his father had done to inflict such damage. And it had to have been his father that did it. A man who was so blitzed out of his head every night with remorse over the way his life had panned out, that he took to making his existence even less tolerable by day, when he realised what his hands had done the night before. It was a sad repetitive life, but he had no apparent wish to change it.

Manton senior and junior lived alone in a trailer park off Fredrickson Avenue. Mrs Manton had died several years earlier. For her it had been relief a long time coming. Not only had she endured the pain of internal disease, but also the hand of her husband's poor alcoholic temperament. Charles had been four at the time of her passing and deep down he had never forgiven her for what he perceived as abandonment. Since then, Manton junior had become 'the bitch' of the house, taking the beatings, doing the shopping, cleaning and cooking. As he had got older, though, he spent less time at home doing anything for his father. It just wasn't worth it. In fact, sometimes at the weekends he slept in one of the car wrecks down by the railway tracks, knowing that if he returned home, the savagery would be more severe than the week-night attacks. All of this went some way to explaining the boy's violent nature, but ultimately nothing could justify it. John walked on.

4

John had risen from bed early on Saturday. There was a lot he had promised to do and limited time to do it in. His workload began with Freddy's weekend paper round, something he had agreed to do on Wednesday during a moment of weakness and indebtedness towards his new-found friend. Later in the week he had come to his senses, but it had been too late to back out then because Freddy had already notified his boss of the substitution. This meant John had risen at six-thirty, thrown his clothes on and departed with his breakfast in hand, consisting of a can of Coke, a Snickers bar and a left-over slice of chocolate cake from the night before. He pushed the cake into his mouth with two swift thrusts, interspaced by a single chew and swallow, then dropped the rest of the supplies into his backpack and mounted his bike. The convenience store was five blocks away and it took him a good four minutes to get there. He arrived to find Freddy's deliveries neatly piled, ready for collection. And after a quick word of explanation as to who he was, they were released to his care.

He had seen kids riding down the street in perfect balance a hundred times with the papers folded in their handlebar baskets and had witnessed Freddy do it on rollerblades. As a result, John had assumed it was an easy task. So, he took off at pace, mounting his bike when he was already in motion. But as he raised his right leg over the saddle, he failed to compensate for the weight of the papers. The centre of gravity of bike and boy shifting heavily in the same direction and dispatching both to the floor. The papers slid out of the basket, lining up like fallen dominos along the road. John's leg smashed down onto the tarmac, trapped beneath the bike. A rift of pain buckled up his spine. He winced in agony. Water swelled in his eyes. But without even a small cry, he quickly gathered up the papers, remounted and got on his way, not looking back once. The blood had already begun to trickle down his leg, but he was too embarrassed and afraid to stop. He peddled harder and harder, until he had reached the start of his round, then he let himself go. Coming to a halt, he dropped the bike down on the kerbside and nursed his injury. Bits of loose tarmac had embedded themselves into his soft skin around the gash and he brushed them away. The cut wasn't particularly deep, but it had opened up in an awkward place, allowing what appeared to be prolific amounts of blood to be released. Opening up his bag, John searched for anything that would substitute as a bandage. After checking all the zip pockets, he found a neck-tie. Wrapping it tight around his knee, he tied a double-knot with the ends securely to the front. The pressure of the makeshift dressing seemed to moderate the pain and he found he could support himself comfortably again. This small incident had delayed him by a good ten minutes. It was time he would have to make up at some point during the morning. More than likely, it would eat into his research period, but he was doing that for Freddy as well, so it wouldn't matter greatly. Pushing off steadily, he mounted the bike for a second time, this time with perfect stability.

The round passed by incredibly quickly and without anything of note occurring. John felt good from the rush of the cool morning air around his face, but other than that, he viewed the activity as pretty dull. Neither was the money attractive enough to take his thoughts off the repetitiveness of the job. This realisation compelled him to hold Freddy in even higher esteem. To endure such a tedious chore on a daily basis, was a feat worthy of much respect, particularly since it involved getting out of bed at such an unchristian hour.

Having completed this first task by eight thirty, it left him half an hour to take his bike home and hitch a ride into town with his mum before the library opened. He knew she was going in early that morning to help at the video store. When John reached home, she was already pulling the station wagon out of the garage. As he walked up the drive past the car, she raised three fingers towards him, indicating how many minutes he had to get in the passenger seat. John acknowledged her with a smile and pushed his bike through the garage doors, leaning it up against his father's workbench. After shutting the doors, he climbed straight inside the family car.

"What you done to your knee?"

"Fell off my bike." He was too embarrassed to say anymore.

"Is it alright? Do you want me to bandage it up properly? We've got time." She looked straight at him.

"It's alright," he responded abruptly.

"What? You going to walk around all day looking like Rambo?"

"I wouldn't know. You've never let me watch the movie." John relaxed and attempted to retain a straight face.

"Oh, that hurt." She smiled back and reversed out of the drive. "Maybe I'll just bring it home tonight, then."

There followed a moment's silence before she started asking what he was doing after the library. His mother's talk filled the air all the way to the library steps, at which point John turned, gave her a son-to-mother kiss and jumped out on to the kerb. Then wasting no time, he mounted the stairs towards the main entrance.

The library building itself was probably the oldest one in Shifton in full-time use. It had stood here since the early twentieth century, beginning life as the town hall. Then in the mid-fifties, it went under a part change of use, becoming half library. It suffered under this duality for three decades, before complete conversion arrived in the eighties. Ironically, it was after losing the statutory occupants that the council began spending money on its upkeep. The years of neglect, though, hadn't been excessively detrimental. In fact, it had added character to the shallow-cambered roof by allowing time to discolour the slate tiles. The same aging process had eaten away at the four limestone pillars at the front of the building, leaving them seemingly riddled with holes and weak in appearance. The stone steps that ascended up to the large dark wooden entrance doors were also worn. Smoothed at the edges and bowed towards the middle, they had been eroded by hundreds of feet using almost exactly the same spot to gain leverage for their climb.

As John entered, the magnificence of the hallway impacted on him with the first strike of his heel against the marble floor. He had only ever been in here on a couple of occasions in the past, both times with his mother and when he was less than five years old. Experiencing it older and on his own was a completely different ball game. The hall reached the full height of the building, up to a circular, lead-framed domed skylight was at least three metres in diameter. The two-storey void was dissected away from the slated column of light by a circular balcony that provided access to the rows of periodicals hidden in categorised rooms upstairs. As he stood there somewhat in awe of his surroundings, the massiveness of the enclosed space left him feeling very vulnerable. Very insignificant. Sat centrally in the light from the dome was the main book check-in and out desk. It was round, made up of two semi-circular, mahogany-stained wooden counters. Their fronts rose just over a metre, which meant that the leading edge measured up and into the average person's ribcage. Rather quaintly, to accommodate for the customer of lesser stature, there was a small-stepped ledge around a quarter of the circumference, which took a good thirty centimetres off the service height. From where he was standing, the desk appeared to be manned by three uniformed librarians, two of which were female and in their late thirties. The third, a man, was a recent high-school graduate, whose face John recognised but couldn't put a name to.

The library was separated into five key areas of history, science, world, fictional and biographical literature. However, the books in these sections were not necessarily categorised in the most logical manner. An example of this would be if someone was doing a search against the events of World War 1, their immediate reaction would be to look under history, but here that would lead them up a blind alley. Instead, to find the relevant material, they would have to sift through the directory in the 'World' area. In a similar sort of fashion, Einstein's theories of relativity were listed under history, not science. And books on the seven wonders of the world could be found under non-fictional, instead of world. It was for the most part a confusing categorisation of periodicals and novels, designed by an artistic mind, for a non-artistic town. No one knew who the real culprit behind the disorder was, but there was no desire among the current staff to begin a reshuffle. It would be too great a job.

The entire library inventory was logged on a computer, with two terminals available in each section. These allowed access for quick searches against author, title or even 'buzz words', for those with no clue what they were looking for. Taking a seat, he positioned the mouse on the 'buzz' search icon and clicked twice. This transferred him to a new display, giving the option to key in five fields. Each field allowed a single word to be inputted and ranked in order of interrogation priority. He began with what he knew, typing 'witchcraft' in the top space, followed by 'Shifton' in the second, and then pressed enter. The system was fairly advanced, in that when it undertook the 'buzz' word search, it analysed the abstracts of each paper and book filed. Unfortunately, this meant the processing time could be quite excessive, particularly as the software was being run on an old 386k desktop PC. John sat back and waited.

His initial search could have been a lot quicker if he had chosen to accept Freddy's direction and look for a record of the church being rebuilt. But he hadn't! Instead, John had started on the subject matter that provided him with the greatest interest. The computer groaned to a halt, presenting seven matched records on the monitor. Clicking over the print icon, he waited for his hard copy of the information before initiating a new search, keying in the words 'Shifton', 'church' and 'built'. This second interrogation of the system appeared much shorter, with two references to the town paper being churned out in a matter of seconds. One article was from an edition at the turn of the century and the other preceded it by fifteen years. At the bottom of the page, a flashing message informed him that these records weren't available in hard copy format to the public. But they could be viewed via another computer terminal upstairs, which contained a database for all town broadsheets issued prior to the paper's name change in nineteen seventy. Printing off a copy of the issue dates, he headed straight for the staircase.

The upstairs computer was slightly more powerful, a 486k unit with 64 megabytes worth of memory capacity. It required this level of capability to facilitate the storage of all the back-issue information in a readable format. The data had been scanned in by a professional firm down in Boston. This firm had subsequently employed a graduate 'systems analyst' student from the local faculty to read through the entire electronic database and enhance any areas of poor resolution. This student had then employed two undergraduates he knew, paying them five dollars an hour, and got them to do half the work. With the three of them doing the checking, the entire system was set up, checked and completed within two years. Which, considering the task covered the editing and upgrading of four thousand and twenty weekly newspapers that detailed town life for the eighty-five years preceding its transition to a daily paper, was one hell of an achievement. Statistically this level of work equated effectively to proofreading and modifying two editions per day, per person, and that was if they worked three hundred and sixty-five days a year. Now that was a tall order in anyone's eyes. So, to believe they managed the same task on a five-day working week, taking into consideration holidays, illness and the study time of the two undergraduates, was verging on the divine. In fact, it had to be impossible. Consequentially, the librarians had asked for a five-year warranty on the work, so that sufficient enquiries could be made on the system to establish its completeness. To date there had been no evident glitches and the warranty only had a year left to run. So, it looked as if the job had been done in full.

Sitting down at the console, John keyed in the publication dates and waited for the records to appear before him. In comparison to his last computer encounter, they were retrieved fairly quickly. This was probably due to their brief nature and low graphical content, which was a function of the era they were written in. As he scrolled down over the first paper, it took a few seconds to find the article he wanted. 'Church Torched' read the title in inch-high capital letters. Reading down the text, he discovered the fire had taken place on the evening of the twelfth of November in eighteen eighty-six. The source had never been discovered, but onlookers had commented how it appeared to burn from the inside outwards, with the spire plummeting vertically down before the outer paintwork had even began to score. The village folk had tried in vain for about half an hour to quell the flames, but the dousing only seemed to heighten the fire's ferocity. Eventually they had given up, standing back to watch their place of worship burn. There were several comments in the text about how the fire had lasted such a long time. Everything in the church was an ideal fuel for any fire and yet it burned fierce and slow, as if it held a will of its own. And in that will rested the fortitude to savour the moment and burn every last piece of wood right through to the final grain. Nothing was to remain but smouldering embers. At best count the fire had taken two and a half hours to complete its cycle, with an hour of that being on full burn. At times the flames had lashed out into the night sky for thirty metres, sucking the oxygen out of the atmosphere and leaving the villagers short of breath. In the eye of these flames, people had claimed to have seen unnatural images. Faces of demons. In truth, their eyesight had probably just momentarily blurred, leaving them to reconstruct their vision. And in this moment of vulnerability, the distortion had allowed them to project their fear for an explanation right into the heart of the blaze. Whether the faces had been fact or fiction then became irrelevant. They were an answer. A solution to the mystery.

John read on to discover how there had subsequently been an inquest into the fire. They had interrogated all the townsfolk, evidently some more rigorously than others. This was where

Freddy's story fell from accuracy. The process of elimination had left several people unaccounted for, but out of all of them, two girls had fallen under the eye of suspicion. The trail of guilt was thin to say the least, with three facts being used to convict them. Firstly, their alibi was that they were asleep in bed, which was corroborated by their parents. However, neither the mother nor the father could confirm that they had seen their children after nine o'clock. Secondly, they were both known for playing strange games out in the woods near the church. The fact that all the other children in the village played out there had become irrelevant. And finally, they had been seen fully dressed at the site of the fire by some townsfolk when they were supposed to have been in bed. Again, the inquisition's perspective on relevancy had dismissed the presence of ten other child spectators, all of whom were also in their daily clothes. The direction of the article impinged on the brink of slander and demonstrated nothing but guilt by speculation. It said nothing specifically about the witchcraft Freddy had spoken of, except a mention from the other children of how the girls could be seen dancing and chanting in the woods. In the end, the final nail in their coffin had been through the act of their parents, who had decided to move home under the shroud of night. In the eyes of the villagers, this had confirmed the children's guilt and they were erroneously sentenced by their absence.

John was even more intrigued now, because nothing had been satisfactorily confirmed. If the story Freddy told him had been the one he discovered, then he would have still found it easy to dismiss. Instead, the story was there in part and he could easily see how it might have been spun to tell a tale of witchcraft. But it hadn't worked out that way in the newspaper. He would have to do more digging! For the next three hours he searched both sets of archives for more obscure references like 'cults', 'devil worshipping', 'Satanism' and 'Angstan Forest', the latter, he had just discovered, being the name of the woodland by the church. He even did a search against missing children between eighteen eighty and nineteen forty. And even though the initial part of this period wasn't particularly well recorded, he still managed to find fourteen missing children in the run up to the fire and about one per year through until nineteen twenty-five. No explanation was given for any of the missing person cases. No bodies were found, with the exception of one who was discovered dead in the marsh, on the north side of town. For its population at the time, Shifton must have been a national statistic for lost children. It was a miracle that anybody at all had chosen to settle here and have a family.

He discovered several references to worshipping of all kinds, from Christian through to various rituals for blackened souls. It appeared that the hollow where he had found Manton and his cronies on Sunday was a focal point for all this religion. Initially, Christians had used the ground for special night-time services during the summer. Then, when the church was levelled, it fell out of use, the villagers choosing to believe that evil forces plagued the ground where the children use to play. This labelling had stuck to the woods for a long time, with travellers passing through on a frequent basis just to visit the ground. If the descriptions were to be trusted, these people were walking temptation to the locals – whores peddling their wares to married men and throwing scorn on the women who looked down on them. Then there were the women who didn't flaunt themselves in such an open fashion but did it quietly and seductively, requiring no remuneration for their service. Over the decade before the turn of the century, twenty-three bastards were born into the village by these casual ladies. Each baby's cry had brought mental suffering to the villagers in bucket loads and it was during this period that honest faith died out, through a naive belief that God would not have allowed it to come to that, if he really existed.

The male travellers were worse than the women. They brought death with them. They murdered husbands in cold blood for looking incorrectly at the whores. Which led to hangings of the men who did the murdering. A black nature had fallen across the town that refused to be shaken off. Then, around the turn of the century, a light began to grow once more. The travellers no longer arrived in their droves. Male vagrants were evidently drawn to different pastures for murder and corruption. However, while some of the women folk departed overnight, leaving no trace of their existence, others chose to settle in Shifton and suffer being humbled by the locals. Either way, the ill-conceived children remained as a legacy to the times.

It was then that the townsfolk rode on the spirit of resurrection and decided to rebuild the holy home. Grand schemes were detailed in subsequent papers, displaying ornate cloisters running the length of the church and allowing more room for a standing congregation than the last church. The published drawings were dressed in seemingly intricate ornaments, including a four-foot crucifix and array of candelabra that could only be perceived to be cast in gold. Enthusiasm for religion surged and the foundations had begun to be laid, but then the new Father had arrived. He had been shamed by the lavish nature with which the town were attempting to dress Christianity and had brought an end to the church's erection, calling a town meeting. The modest sanctuary that could now be seen was the result of this holy intervention. The Father, who remained nameless in the text, continued ruling the villagers in a similar vein. At times his actions read as verging on the narcissistic, but there was no disputing the good effect he had on the community. He had ceased to preside as the holy leader of Shifton in nineteen twenty-five, which unfortunately coincided with a steep drop in the number of missing children. On his departure, very few people knew anything more about him, beyond his ability for mesmerising speeches.

On the side of the occult, John had managed to drag up two more unearthly bouts, which had brought him through to present day. One of these had taken place in the forties and had involved a sect of four parents taking their sons and daughters up into the woods by the church. Once enveloped in the hollow they had stripped naked. The parents then paired up with whichever offspring they desired to indulge in carnal pleasure. This ritual had taken place around a campfire, with all the seething bodily embraces being in full view of each other. The sometimes-incestuous depravity had been brought to an end when one of the daughters had fallen pregnant. She had become ill at school and through subsequent medical attention had been correctly diagnosed. Her young age had prompted an investigation, through which the true father had been identified. Eventually all the detail spewed out into the public domain, including the fact that two of the mothers had given birth to their neighbours' sons' children. Needless to say, the four sets of parents had been imprisoned and the children had been taken across country and placed with new families.

The second dark incident had been nowhere near as foul, involving a misconceived night-time venture for a group of hippies in the sixties. They had decided to light a fire, smoke dope and attempt to summon the devil. The little shindig had lasted no more than three hours before the police had raided the gathering and dragged all the participants back to the cells for the night. No charges had been brought against the peace preachers because all evidence had been destroyed in the fire. Beyond this final recorded legal infraction, there was nothing else worthy of note. The town had been seemingly engulfed into sleepy middle America.

John looked at his watch and discovered the hands had nearly stretched to eleven thirty. The game would be starting at one o'clock. It was a good half-an-hour walk up to the school football grounds, leaving him at most fifty minutes more research time, to be on the safe side. By now he had perused the majority of references from his query searches, with the exception of those related to devil worshipping. With this in mind, he returned back downstairs to walk the aisles once more, tracing his finger across the book spines as he moved. Not surprisingly, the objects of his desire rested on the top shelf, far from a child's grasp. Fetching the ladder, he ascended to discover the gospels of evil. There were three chronicles where he had expected to find one. Each volume was two inches thick, bound with leather covers. Two of them still had a single metal clasp that kept the book closed and the pages protected. All three were labelled with the head title 'Keeper of Fallen Angels'. Then below this, each book had a different subtitle: 'The History', 'To Summon' and 'The Promise'. Pulling the first volume down, he took it back to one of the viewing tables, undid the clasp and opened it up. The pages were weathered yellow, with well-worn edges where generations had flicked through in intrigue. The opening page greeted him with a quotation by a Mr. C. Mather. It read:

"For any to deny the being of a devil must be from an ignorance or profaneness worse than the diabolical."

The words precipitated a temporary paralysis through John's body, but it was swiftly overcome by his anticipation. Turning the page, he started to read the preface, which endeavoured to establish the facts behind the myth. According to the author, the original concept of the dark lord came from the Jews. They believed that God had created the Devil. After all, it was their God who had allowed the serpent to tempt Eve in the garden. Which, when considered alongside his omnipotent image, left only the conclusion that he knew Eve would succumb. Further on in history, it was also God who despatched the evil spirit to possess Saul. He bet against the 'Evil One' on the loyalty of Job, and it was God who created the animosity between Abimelech and the Shechemites. From all of this ill-doing, the concept was spawned. John found it ironic that, for a religion based on faith, it read as though fact had needed to be sought to justify the existence of evil. Though this almost scientific approach wasn't allowed to extend to anything that could readily be written off as 'an act of God', such as the ten plagues of Egypt. But here, where dark forces potentially conspired, there was a religious requirement to explain their presence. This desire for explanation led to the following initial hypothesis. God had sent 'Watchers' down to earth to keep us on track and presumably notify him of any misdemeanours worthy of punishment. These keepers of biblical law were, in fact angels, some of whose hearts darkened in the presence of worldly freedom. These bad angels ended up mating with mortal men and women, creating less than innocent children. Thus, the evil multiplied. It was through this story that they justified the presence of mortal evil. This further supported their belief of God creating evil, because no matter how the facts were studied, God ultimately knew everything and had to have permitted everything. This postulation was again backed up by the two books of Samuel, in which it was made perfectly clear that evil is under the control of God and that the 'Evil One' reports to him. In short, the Devil is the earth-bound tempter and accuser, but God is the controller.

It was only after exile that the Jews picked up the Zoroastrian dualism and built Satan up to be an opponent rather than a servant to God. This was the creation portrayed as the adversary to God in the New Testament and was potentially the root of Judas's betrayal. But without Judas, there would have been no crucifixion or redemption and consequentially, no Christianity. So again, God had allowed the temptation, tricking the Devil into initiating his greatest scheme.

It is at this juncture that the Devil decided to forego his adversarial role, diversifying to solely earth-bound dealings of corruption that achieved his own amusement and financial gain. His work became localised, focussing only on increasing his stake in the world's population. The solitary catch to his plan was that mortals must come of their own free volition and in doing that, he evades the further undertaking of God's work.

Through the first chapter, the author of the book had gone on to explain the further evolution of the evil lord in connection with the Christian faith, through to the late nineteenth century. John was riveted. But by the time he had reached chapter two, the clock had already slipped around to twelve fifty and he was going to be late for the biggest potential date-like event of his life so far. Flicking back to the index, he saw the remainder of the first volume went on to explain the formulation of a Prince of Darkness in nearly every religion. And though he would have found that fascinating, it didn't really bear fruit to his quest. So, he returned it to its rightful place and extracted the second volume. Taking it to the counter, he booked it out for a couple of weeks. Then, placing it in his backpack, he set off out the door and up the street.

The air outside had started to take on its daily polluted aroma, the morning freshness that had been sucked up through his nasal passages earlier now diluted by diesel engine exhaust fumes. The street was jammed solid for six blocks, all the way back up to Mackenzie Street.

In the sky, the morning's clouds were in the process of dispersing to reveal a hazy light blue. Sunny days weren't a great favourite of his, but it was good weather for the game. Spectators and players alike would appreciate the beaming rays rather than a torrential downpour.

It took him as long as expected to meander his way over to the playing fields. As soon as he arrived, he only had to take one glance up into the stand before Gloria was standing up waving down at him. For a few moments he forgot himself, turning behind to see whose attention she sought. Then, with a rush of blood to his cheeks, he remembered. Head bowed down, he ascended the stairs towards her. She was perched on the very top row with a couple of her female cronies, Shauna and Simone, the same sycophantic followers who stood by her side day in, day out, watching the sun rise and set out of her anal tract. At least that was John's perception.

As he got closer, he could see Gloria was wearing a tight orange check half-cut shirt with extended frontal tails tied in a knot above her belly button. Jeans covered her legs, finished by a pair of high-heeled pixie boots. Her eyes sparkled as bright as ever, but for the first time, they were shining for him. Even though he didn't look up for the majority of his ascent, John sensed her beaming face was staring down on him. He could feel it.

"Thought you were never going to turn up!" She didn't wait for an answer. "Game started five minutes ago!" She failed to wait again. "What kept you?"

"I got caught up in town."

"I don't know. Playing arcade games instead of being here with me. That won't do!" She smiled, cocking her head to one side. John chose not to correct her assumption. "Well, come sit down here." She patted the bench next to her.

"So, what's the score?"

"I believe we're ahead by a touchdown. Though I haven't been paying much attention. I've been waiting for you."

John's skin began to prickle. It was like the twilight zone. Gloria had been ignoring a team made up of fifty percent of her ex-boyfriends and fifty percent of her future boyfriends as they ran around the field in preference for watching for him. Small, frail-bodied him. One of the insignificant masses, until he had a major mental block and had taken on the school meathead. Her hand dropped onto his thigh. John nearly left his seat in shock. Gloria just grinned. She knew what she was doing. He felt himself getting firm. Then it got worse. She turned and hugged him. And as she tucked beneath his cheek, he caught the sweet fragrance of her perfume. By now the entire stand's female population was watching, endeavouring to fathom what was happening between one of the school's beauty queens and a non-jock.

For a while they watched in silence. That was to say, John sat speechless, Gloria's hand firmly clasped around his thigh, tweaking it every now and then. The girls, however, jabbered away continuously. As far as he could hear above the general applause and chanting from spectators, they were discussing what to do after the game. Options like going to the mall or Chucks, which was an ice-cream parlour come video arcade megastore, were debated. John always went to Chucks. It was one of those fifties meets eighties flashback attempts. Waitresses on roller skates, drive-through windows and original period memorabilia scattered all around, like a jukebox and a soda fountain. All in all, it was a great place to hang out. At least, it was until seven o'clock at night, when the older kids turned up with their dates. Intent on impressing, they would throw junior high school kids off video games and generally poke fun indiscriminately.

"What do you think?" Gloria said in his ear.

"Huh?!"

"Have you been listening?" Her tone was semi-patronising.

"No, not really. Sorry."

"Well, you're going to have to do better than that, you know." She pulled closer to whisper. "If you want to stick around with me." John was stunned into silence. "So where do you want to go?"

"When?"

"After the game, silly."

"I don't mind. Chucks, I suppose."

"Chucks it is, then!" She squeezed his thigh and resumed talking to the girls.

John settled back in his seat and endeavoured to calm his heart, which had been pumping like crazy ever since she had stood up to wave him in. Breath by breath he managed to bring it under control. He stretched his fingers out across his thigh, accidentally touching Gloria's hand in the process. She turned, smiled and moved her hand on top of his. The pounding increased again. Five minutes passed before he managed to regain control. By then the first quarter was over and the home team was ahead by two touchdowns and a field goal. John continued to watch the game in blissful, if only internal, silence. He'd gotten used to the touch of his dream girl's hand and he'd even grown accustomed to the incessant inquisitiveness of spectators. In fact, all attributes of his present situation began to appeal to him.

Shifton Junior High were playing in plain royal blue, with white pants and a single red lightning bolt on either side of the helmet. Nobody had a clue what this graphic represented. The team's name was the Shifton Charlatans, which in no way led you to that particular piece of imagery. It did, however, provoke thought over which idiot thought of the name.

Matt Thompson was playing quarterback. He was a former boyfriend of Gloria's. He took charge of the position and the game as if he was born in a football jersey. His field presence was remarkable. He would duck and turn himself out of the opposition's grasp just long enough to get a clear line of sight to one of his wide receivers. Then, with a seemingly effortless flick of the wrist, the ball was unleashed over a fifty-yard stretch of grass, till it landed in the secure hands of Tod Stevenson or Joshua Minkins.

Thompson's erratic style of movement behind what could only be described as a weak offensive line pushed him to comparisons with Fran Tarkenton, former Minnesota Viking. Tarkenton had been credited with 47,000 yards' passing and 342 touchdowns in an eighteen-year career. And although Thompson's statistics at the tender age of fourteen couldn't match Tarkenton's, his evasive agility, right down to the final twist away from danger, was enough for comparison.

As could be expected, the quarterback was also at the pinnacle of school society, a position Matt had endeavoured to transform into godlike status. Kids adored him and he lapped it up. Gloria had been the goddess for a short period of time, drawing equal attention to herself. But in many ways, she was better than Matt at manipulation, because she managed to make the adoration stick even when they parted ways.

The game continued into the fourth quarter and John failed to notice the arrival of Manton and his crew at the bottom of the stairs. However, their eyes found him within seconds. Manton's patience rarely lasted beyond the ten-second mark, but in this instance, he found a new restraint. Maybe it was through fear of additional public humiliation. Or possibly, he was actually learning from the recent failure of his heavy-handed tactics. Either way, he stood still, his piercing gaze never faltering, his eyebrows centrally furrowed, emphasising his passionate resentment. Eventually, when his prey's eyes fell on him, Manton slowly raised an arm pointed straight into John's brain, marking him out of the masses. Then, with a single slit-throat gesture, he gave warning of John's impending fate.

The game ended in anti-climax, with the home side destroying the visitors thirty-three points to seven. Cheerleaders hugged their boyfriends, spectators walked off and Gloria turned to kiss John on the cheek, startling him once more. He turned towards her, his face having become pallid, then looked back to the foot of the stand. Manton had vanished.

"Come on." Gloria grasped his hand and pulled him down the stairs.

Initially he showed reluctance, feeling a strong sense of dread over what might be hiding around the corner, but Gloria's hold strengthened, and she led him on. As it was, Manton had disappeared altogether. Which in a sense made it worse, because if John could have seen which direction the hulk had been travelling, he could have taken an alternative route. Before they left the playing fields, Gloria had agreed to split up from the girls for a while and meet up at Chucks in an hour's time. From this point, her attention became firmly fixed on John.

"So, what do you want to do?" Gloria stared at him, a smile lashing across her face.

"I don't know."

"Not exactly one for pushing a girl, are you?"

"Guess not." She said nothing, so he fumbled his way out of the pregnant pause. "I've not exactly had much experience of this."

"Experience of what?"

She was toying with him, as if she wanted him to surmise that they were becoming an item.

"You know. I've never been particularly high on the girls' 'want to be with' list."

"Oh, I don't know. You're kinda cute."

"Cute has never been high on the key credentials list before." He smirked, feeling a touch more relaxed.

"I love the way you talk."

"That's never been high on the list either."

She laughed and he joined her.

This was the first time he had ever been alone with the girl of his dreams and he was emotionally static in a wilderness of disbelief.

"You still haven't told me what you want to do?" she said, disturbing the moment.

"We've just established that I've not had many girlfriends bef—"

"So, I'm your girlfriend now, am I?"

"Well, I thought..."

"Just kidding." She smiled again and reached out to tickle his ribs. "I kinda like the sound of girlfriend."

John was still in shock. He let go of Gloria's hands.

"Hey. I was only joking with you!"

No response.

"You're supposed to be happy now. At least, all my other boyfriends were." She pulled a peculiar face and John couldn't help but grin. "That's better."

He took hold of her hand once more and they drifted in silence towards the edge of the playing field. It was magical, but John still couldn't get over the difference between choirgirl and school goddess. Before he had established the difference to be purely a change to her physical appearance, which gave rise to her popularity. But now he was discovering a new dimension. A personality that wasn't reflected in the chapel anthems. They reached the grass verge.

"So, what now?" Gloria piped up again.

"Whatever you want."

"God, you're going to be a pushover," she joked. "If you really don't mind, then we'll nip back home to my house and I can freshen up."

John just shrugged his shoulders in acceptance, and they walked on.

5

Since Manton's mother had died, the seemingly endless barrage of drunken beatings to which he was ritualistically subjected each weekend became as normal to him as watching MTV all night in his room. His father, Mick, worked at the paper mill on the outskirts of town. He operated one of the sawing mills, cutting the bulk timber down into hand-sized pieces for further processing. In truth, it wasn't much of a job. The equipment did all the work, he just stood over it. A silent supervisor. Not that he would know what to do if anything went wrong, except go and get his own supervisor. When facts were faced, he was lucky to have a job at all. He did nothing but stand in a virtual daydream for the length of his shift. He didn't socialise with his colleagues anymore. And he always smelt of booze. Half of the time he was actually drunk. The sole reason he hadn't been fired was because Mr. Chanter, the factory owner, was his best friend since before his wife's death. He figured Mick had suffered enough.

Apart from Chanter, Mick, like his son, had few friends. His abusive nature had forced him into a world of seclusion that added to his pain. Manton junior bore the brunt of this solitude through his father's fists. He resented his father for that. Resented the lack of control he had through eternally blurred eyes. Resented the way he had shut his son out of his life, like he was severed from the family. An unwanted adoption that he no longer wanted to support. For such a young boy, Manton accepted his father's guilt over missed opportunity with greater maturity than he had ever seen displayed by his father. However, this burden had at least in part been the catalyst for his bullying tactics in school. But despite the grand bravado he exhibited in the corridors of education, going home in the evening still left him filled with dread.

The events that led to Manton's alienated domestic life were all immaterial now. His existence had been fashioned into a personal hell. His future was mapped for the worse, in slowly changing detail, commensurate with the end of each beating. None of this Manton acknowledged yet, even though he played the role perfectly. He no longer harboured thoughts of good grades, let alone future business success. Instead, plans for deception and theft already plagued his mind. In that way, suffering was like the worst of contagions, far more dire than the common cold. It didn't just temporarily affect a person's physical being, it was driven into the root of neural activity through every abusive act, pushed deeper and squeezed tighter into the very core of human thought. It couldn't be shaken off readily through medication or a few days in bed. Instead, it would take a willingness to accept his dysfunctional behaviour, followed by years trying to understand how the twistedness had been triggered from out of his genetic make-up. In Manton's case, the incendiary device was his father's fist and it had already sparked the darkness within his own genes.

In some respects, assessment of Manton, and in fact anybody, solely based on hereditary instincts, is an unfair psychological classification. Every human on the planet has a less than pure streak locked within their psyche. The only difference is how much duress it requires to be released. Manton could at one time have turned out to be one hell of a nice bloke, because it took him more than a year's worth of parental disregard for the disease to be released. This purer streak still lurked around inside him, surfacing in vulnerability with each step he took towards his home.

Manton opened the trailer door, as usual without having to insert his key. Another one of his father's less than admirable habits. Moving directly to the fridge, he pulled out a beer. It had just turned five thirty, which left a couple of hours before he had agreed to hook up with Fletcher and Young again. Tonight was going to be the night of retribution. An occasion where his authority through the school corridors would be firmly reinstated. Humility resided in someone else's camp this evening, and if that someone could be John Garret, it would be. Sliding into his dad's favourite seat, he brushed the TV remote ever so lightly, bringing the unit to life. Flicking through the channels, he paused on MTV and dropped the control to the floor.

The living room wasn't much to look at. The sofa was dark with dirt, the worn fabric displaying its age. A single mismatched chair sat at the far end, which on the surface looked newer, but it wasn't. It had been his mother's chair and he had only ever sat down in it once since her death. That beating took so long to forget he hadn't tried his luck ever again. Even when his dad was out. The last event had nearly been a hospital job. Behind the sofa stood a solitary tall glass-fronted dresser housing the best crockery, which had never seen beyond those glass panes since his father's metamorphosis. The cabinet stood as a living timeless classic of its day. Nothing altered. And no replacement parts available. Its existence served as a visual reckoning of his father's mental state. A blatant refusal to allow the memory of his wife to leave his mind. As if in doing so, it served as an epitaph of the injustice in her life.

The accommodation was simple and small, sitting in a trailer park on the outskirts of town. It had two bedrooms, one bathroom, a kitchen with dining area and living area. Its size exacerbated Manton's difficulties, leaving him space to hide from harm's way. He spent the bulk of his time in the bedroom, but even that wasn't a safe haven. The poster-clad walls were ripped from repetitive assault. A door from the wardrobe stood propped up against the wall and a sales tag on the bedside lamp gave evidence of its recent acquisition.

Manton spent an hour in front of the television, then had a shower and got changed, leaving him half an hour to walk across to Chucks. Outside the temperature had cooled considerably, leaving the night air crisp. After exiting the trailer once, he returned back inside to change his jacket from a denim to a red chequered lumber jacket with a thick wool lining. Then resumed his journey.

Like obedient dogs, Fletcher and Young were waiting as instructed on the corner of Jeffery and Diamond, next to Joe's Used Car Emporium. Fletcher wore a pair of jeans, faded denim shirt and a worn leather flying jacket.

Young stood to one side, his head lowered to the ground, studying his foot as it traced the cracks in the pavement. His left eye socket stood proud of his face, evidence of paternal discipline, though at least for him it wasn't a nightly occurrence. His attire was not dissimilar to Fletcher's, save for the substitution of a denim jacket. Their dress sense gave the immediate impression of togetherness, but their body language spoke another verse. Neither were speaking. Standing four feet apart, each acted out a scene of blissful ignorance to the other's presence. Fletcher was leaning up against a streetlamp, fag in hand, ever the young pretender to Manton's throne. His pose was relaxed, confident, strong. He brought the cigarette up to his mouth in one long, slow ark and grasped it firmly in his almost grimacing lips. He took a confident drag before returning his hand to his side. The staggered discharge of fumes filtered out through his nose and mouth; their trail tinged yellow by the lamp's light. Young, on the other hand, looked uncomfortable with his surroundings. Agitated and fidgety. Feet never at rest. His body was tense, his shoulders hunched forward in the posture of a weak man. Between the two of them tonight, Manton would have chosen Fletcher to be the greater in a fight, even though his experience told him otherwise. Fletcher spied him and raised a hand. Straight away his charismatic pose faltered, and he dropped his cigarette to the floor.

"So, what's happening?"

Young raised his head to see who Fletcher was speaking to.

"Payback time." Manton's words flew towards them, tainted with aggression.

"Alright!" Fletcher enthused. "Who's gonna get it?"

"Garret!" he announced as he reached them. "That's if the

little shit decides to show his face."

"Oh, I don't think you've got any problems there. He seemed pretty friendly with that Gloria bitch earlier, and she's always up at Chucks."

"Who you calling a bitch?" He grabbed Fletcher by the collar and watched as panic filled his eyes. Young stood back, preparing himself for a scuffle. "She's about to become my girlfriend." Manton started laughing and let go. Young joined in.

"You asshole," said Fletcher, clearly failing to see the funny side.

"Come on. I don't want to run the risk of missing the little shit head." Manton walked off without bothering to check he was being followed. They would, like trusting dogs.

As they closed in on their destination, the two 'puppies' began to jostle with each other. Manton was relieved to see some life come out of Young at last, though it was still a feeble reflection of his true capability. A smile temporarily broke out on Young's bruised face but quickly receded as fresh pain flared in his eye. He distanced himself from the other two once more.

"Hey, what the fuck's wrong, man?" Fletcher asked.

"Leave him alone." Manton dropped a calming hand on Fletcher's shoulder. "He needs some time."

"Time for what?"

"Just some time."

Manton had no intention of adding to Young's embarrassment. He understood how it felt. Besides, he needed three men tonight. Two wasn't an option. For once he was thinking rationally. He had been forced into playing a mind game as much as a game of brawn, which was exactly the reverse of what he usually strived to do.

The problem with Garret was his newly acquired iconic status, gave him an extensive, albeit invisible contingent of close friends. Manton knew he would never be able to exact revenge against the backdrop of such a mass, though the temptation for such humiliation of his foe was nearly irresistible. But it was vanity that had humbled Manton to begin with and he refused to falter down that avenue again.

Up in the distance, Chucks' streetlights were now visible. They didn't actually belong to the restaurant, they belonged to the town, but Charlie the owner had come out early one morning and changed the bulbs from white to purple. This effectively had given the perception they were part of the restaurant. Truth was, no one had gotten around to changing them back. The subdued light produced by the bulbs gave a greater sense of privacy to the clientele and with it, a higher level of intimacy. A dozen kids congregated around the street poles, wallowing in the purple haze that steeped the air. Talking, kissing and smoking, they stood tall, seemingly protected by the lack of incandescence, their facial features blurred by the monochromatic light. Purple noses blended into purple cheeks, into purple mouths, mopped by purple hair. Individualism was stripped away, beauty distorted, and style camouflaged.

Tonight was one of the busier nights of the week. Few vacant slots were left in the car park for newcomers. The overspill was further evident, with a group of twenty teenagers hanging outside under a veranda section to the left. This was a relatively new addition to the premises, designed to provide protection from the weather for any stragglers. The layout was simple, with fast food style tables and chairs fixed in a block pattern. Speakers wired up to the jukebox inside compensated for the otherwise plain appearance, making it still pretty cool to hang there.

Manton increased his pace over the last fifty metres, finally coming to a stop in the middle of the car park, where it was relatively dark. He didn't want to lose the element of surprise. Straining his eyes, he stared in vain at the external crowd, searching for just a glimpse of Garret. Nothing. This made him a little uncomfortable, because despite his external bravado, after recent events he didn't relish the thought of confrontation in front of a big gathering. Finding him outside would have been ideal. He could have yanked Garret out of his seat, dragged him into the car park and beat the shit out of him. But that wasn't to be.

"What now, man?" Young had just caught up.

"We go in!" Manton tapped him on the cheek.

As they entered, the jukebox started to play 'Bad to the Bone' by George Thorogood and the Destroyers. Manton grinned from ear to ear. For him that was fate. Not to mention the ultimate in cool entrances. Unfortunately, only four other people noticed the synchronisation.

Pushing a couple of juniors to the side, Manton and his boys moved to the bar. He ordered three large cokes and instructed Fletcher to pay. Then, turning around, he surveyed the tables one by one. This task was impossible from a single location, because the room was split into six different areas, through elevated floor sections and careful screening by plants, statues and waist-high walls. Four of the six splinter areas protruded from the main floor, with the final two being elevated off the back of these. The outer areas appeared uncomfortably packed to the brim, leaving space only around the main floor. The video games and pinball machines sat in a small open annex from the side of the bar. It was also bunged with kids.

Manton stood hawklike for about five minutes, scanning side to side, before he caught a glimpse of his quarry. Over on the far side, to the back of the second offshoot from the right, he had spied the peak of a baseball cap. Its owner's face wasn't visible, but he recognised the colour scheme of the Denver Broncos and there weren't too many of their supporters in these parts. In fact, there was only one that Manton could think of.

Without turning to aim, he smacked Young on the upper arm and signalled him to follow. Finding some gusto now, Young replicated the action on Fletcher and like a parade of elephants they swaggered across the floor. Manton was inevitably the first to mount the stairs and John saw him immediately, his eyes fixed in fright. Manton still had no desire to make a public scene, so raising a finger, he bid Garret to come out from hiding.

Manton could tell John was trying to ignore him, but then Gloria turned inquisitively to see what had captured her boyfriend's attention. As soon as that happened, the whole table became aware of his beckoning. Stares then turning sharply back towards John, the spectators waiting for a response to the challenge. Manton knew he had John physically and psychologically cornered. There was nothing John could do, but accept his bidding.

Standing up, John pushed his way around the table, all the while his head lowered towards the floor, deep in thought. When he got to the other side, he was surprised to find he was alone. Manton had disappeared. But then he spotted him again, on his way outside, leaving Fletcher to ensure his victim followed.

"Are you alright?" Gloria stood up and whispered in his ear.

"Yeah, I'm fine. Don't worry." He endeavoured to look fearless.

"Do you want us to sort him out?" Matt Thompson spoke up, pointing at himself and Tod Stevenson.

"No. I think I'm better dealing with this one."

Matt shrugged his shoulders and sat back down.

"Are you sure?" Gloria spoke again.

"Yeah, positive. Just stay here. I'll be back soon. I think."

With that he felt Fletcher's hand land on his arm and tug him toward the stairs. John gave no immediate resistance, but he pulled his arm free as soon as he had turned fully, glaring at Fletcher intensely as he did so. Fortunately, nobody from his table followed, although the challenge had brought interest from two or three other kids that John could see, who with initial uncertainty joined the procession. One of them was Kevin, who John hadn't even noticed was in Chucks tonight.

Once outside, he found Manton removing his jacket, in preparation for a brawl. John looked at him with a degree of awe. His T-shirt stretched tight around his upper body, displaying his firm torso. It was a sight very few people had ever seen before and added a new dimension of fear to his notoriety. The absence of a jacket had also exposed a number of scars up and down his forearms, which were too abundant to count. John felt extremely vulnerable. He may have taken Manton on twice already this week and won, but those encounters were nothing compared to the head-on collision that faced him now. Leaving his own jacket on to hide his muscular inferiority, he raised his hands up in an attempt to pacify his aggressor.

"Could we just talk for a second?" John began.

"That's all you ever want to do, Garret. And I've told you before it won't save you. Besides, I didn't see you talking too much the other day when you broke my ribs. By the way, they hurt like fuck, but you'll know all about that soon."

"Look, I'm not expecting my talking to save me, just to put an air of rationality into this situation. If that's possible? And—"

"Don't get smart with me."

"I'm not trying to be smart, but would you let me finish. I was about to say that I appreciate that I've resorted to fighting recently, but can you blame me? You were trying to rip me limb from limb at the time."

"I know. And I'm going to finish that off now." He grinned almost manically from ear to ear.

"Can't I finish—"

Manton threw a punch square across John's left cheek, the follow through clipping his jaw, sending him spiralling to the floor.

"No, you can't."

Lying on the floor, John felt the side of his head exploding in agony. Blood started to drip from the corner of his mouth.

"Get up, you pussy!" Manton taunted him. In the background he could hear the onlookers begin to add their weight, egging the fight on, not that Manton needed encouragement. The crowd had swelled to ten now, a few additional spectators having arrived to view the carnage. John tried to order his thoughts, ignoring his battered nerves. He knew it was not the time to pick a fight with Manton. There was no way he could win. He didn't have the strength. It would only result in his own humiliation, and that wasn't an appealing thought. Talking had failed him. Which as far as he could make out, left him with a single choice: run.

"Get up, you shit. Take your beating like a man."

John had no choice in the matter. Manton was pulling him to his feet, whether he liked it or not. Lapping up the moment, Manton playing the crowd for all they were worth. One arm raised his victim back to the slaughter and the other stretched wide, encouraging applause. He looked around at the watching faces, his grin fixed, paying no heed to John. That was when John's inspiration struck. In a single, swift burst of energy, he rotated around, lifting his knee up hard into Manton's groin. It landed home, eliciting a shriek of pain. Manton's hold gave way. Fletcher and Young paused in shock for a split second before diving at John, arms outstretched. Stepping to one side, he evaded Fletcher's clumsy attack. Then, with a duck of his head and a carefully positioned leg, he felled Young to the floor. The crowd had silenced in amazement. John took a brief glance down at his foe, then sprinted straight out of the car park. By the time he had hit the main street, Manton was already back on his feet and in pursuit.

John headed towards the school playing fields. There he would cut into the woods, which would bring him up past the church, down by the stream and into his estate. This route kept him away from the town, which wasn't good, but it was the most direct option. He glanced around to assess his head start, feeling momentary déjà vu.

As he jumped the gate to the playing fields, his lead had dwindled slightly, with an inspired Young now heading the chase. The football field slid softly under his feet, dampened by some rain earlier. Leaving the playing field, he dropped down the embankment on the far side and entered the woods. What little there had been of night light was shielded further now by the dense foliage canopy over his head. His eyes struggled initially, and he lost his footing, stifling his advance. Gradually they adjusted and he picked up speed once more. Behind him now there was nothing, at least nothing he could see. He wasn't sure whether his best course of action was to slow down and use the poor visibility to maximum advantage or keep running and increase the risk of them hearing him. He kept running and prayed for silence. Nobody was listening, though. Twigs continued to snap beneath him. He stopped abruptly and listened. His heart pounded from exhaustion, thumping in his brain. Trees rustled in the breeze, a short heavy gust bringing a shower of leaves, but still, he could see or hear no one.

He began running again. A couple of squirrels ascended a tree to his left, invading his peripheral vision and startling him. Through a break in the woodland up ahead, he could now see the glow of the spotlights surrounding the church. Their brilliance offered comfort and his nerves settled. Behind there was still nothing audible or visible and for the first time, he permitted himself to think of success.

The last few trees brushed his arms and then he broke free into open ground again. He was approaching the church from the west side, which meant he would be exposed for a good distance. Initially, the long grass impeded his progress, the twines catching across the bridges of his feet, holding them down. He raised his knees higher to gain greater ground clearance. Still, there was no sign of Manton and his boys. In the sky, the moon slid out from behind the clouds, illuminating the woodland verge.

The church stood tall and brilliantly white in front of him. It was about a hundred metres away now, its neatly trimmed lawns just a few strides ahead. If he could just get to the other side of the building before anyone saw him, then he would be able to get back into the woods on the east side before they could catch up sufficiently to notice his point of entry. Life sprang back into his feet, bouncing his body higher above the long blades of grass. But then it happened.

As he plunged his left foot down solidly to the floor, it landed straight in a rabbit hole. John realised the lack of support too late to make any difference. All his body weight continued down and forward, pivoting around his trapped ankle as he began to fall. Stretching his hands out to meet the ground, he cushioned the impact, dissipating some of the energy through his arms. It wasn't enough. His ankle's flexibility was pushed to the limit, the muscles stretched in agony. He screamed. There was nothing he could do to prevent it. The pain was so intense. He lay there for a moment, biting his lip, waiting for the torment to subside enough for him to carry on. Instinctively, he began to pray, the words of the Lord's Prayer floating unbidden from his lips.

The fall had left him shrouded in the thick grass, hidden from general view, but it wouldn't take the boys long to figure out where he was. Raising his head up into open space, he saw nothing. Both the woodland and the field appeared clear. Had they given up? He stood up and started off again immediately but failed on the first stride. His weakened ankle gave way beneath him, causing him to collapse back down to the earth. There was no way he was going to get home now. His only options were to remain where he was, covered by the grass and pray more that he wasn't discovered, or he could seek refuge in the church, if he could make it that far. At least there it would be dry and warmer for him. He got back up on his feet and, taking another quick glance around, began to stumble his way towards the entrance. Each step left him in agony, but he knew he must keep moving. He continued to pray, distracting himself from the pain. Eventually, he arrived at the main doors, which opened readily, allowing him access. Then, taking one final glance around, he closed them behind him.

Inside the church, John searched for a place to hide and rest his ankle. He eventually settled underneath the altar, because it was the only place he could be completely obscured from sight. The altar cloth draped down around all but the backside. Candles burned above him and to either side, spewing thick scented smoke. The central heating had been turned off and his breath hung heavy in the chilled air. If he was lucky, though, any escaping traces of breath would be enveloped by the candle smoke. Straining his ears, he listened for the sound of the door opening, with each second increasingly fearful of the future. Plans of how he was going to get out of his predicament flashed through his mind. All ignored the harsh reality of his immobility. Then, in desperation, he began to pray once more. First the Lord's Prayer, then grace and then he started again. The words spilled from his mouth so fast that they lost all definition, merging into a meaningless string of syllables. In the background, the wood boards of the floor and walls contracted and creaked as the temperature continued to drop outside.

Suddenly a cool breeze wafted underneath the altar cloth, chilling his spine. Someone had entered. He ceased prayer and strained his ears to hear footsteps. There were none. Minutes passed by and still nothing. He started to shake. Then another disturbance of air suggested a departure. Had he escaped? He lay still for a while, fighting off thoughts of success. Had he really beaten Manton again?

"Are you ever going to come out of there?" The voice came from directly in front of the altar. John's stomach dropped. "Come on out. We know you're there."

John trembled, sliding himself out from underneath the cloth at the back of the altar, wishing to keep at least something tangible between him and Manton. His efforts were in vain; emerging to discover Young and Fletcher flanking him. As soon as his arms became visible, they reached down and grabbed him under the armpits, pulling him to his feet.

"It seems to me that we have a shit load to sort out?" Manton was sat in the front left pew, his legs stretched wide open in a relaxed pose. "I mean, we never came near you in the past. As far as we were concerned, you weren't worth bothering about. But then you open up this one-man onslaught on us, which is impossible to ignore."

"Look, I just turned up in the wrong place at the wrong time." By now he had been brought around the front of the altar and stood directly facing the enemy.

"Haven't I told you about interrupting me before? I'm sure I have."

Manton pointed initially towards Fletcher and then at John's ankle. John saw a gleeful smile sweep across all his aggressors' faces and then his vision was instantaneously glazed by pain. Fletcher had kicked the side of his foot square on, inflaming the damaged muscle once more. As he tried to reach down and cradle his injured limb, Fletcher and Young let go, leaving him to crash to the floor in an unbalanced heap. Water streamed into his eyes, distorting his vision.

"How you feeling? I bet that really hurts." Manton faked sympathy. "I'd get used to that level of pain if I was you, because it's nowhere near over yet." Manton pointed at Young this time and then towards the church entrance. "Lock it! We're going to be a while."

Silence fell for a few minutes while Manton waited for his orders to be carried out. Even when Young had returned, he remained silent in observation of John's suffering, waiting for the moment when the pain had subsided sufficiently for a new dose to be dished out. John could tell Manton never wanted him to forget this experience. As far as Manton was concerned, when he eventually left this church tonight, he was going to be both mentally and physically scarred with reminders of what crossing Manton would mean in the future. The moment arrived.

"Are you feeling better yet?"

John remained silent.

"Okay. Well, we'll carry on anyway! Strip him down!"

"What?" Fletcher questioned.

"I said strip him down!"

"Why?"

"Look, do you care about how this shit just embarrassed us in front of fifty kids? Made us look like fucking idiots. Do you care about that?" Manton stood up and approached Fletcher.

"Yes."

"Then don't ask fucking questions. Do as you're told, and he will pay for that insult ten times over. Alright?" Manton shouted the words into Fletcher's face.

Fletcher said nothing more. Turning away, he did as he was instructed.

Meanwhile, John was uncertain as to the part he should play. He was unable to effectively fight them and if he tried, they knew exactly where to hit him. But at the same time, he felt an idiot just lying there, allowing a couple of weirdo kids to strip him naked.

"Hey! What you doing?" John spoke up, but Manton ignored him. "I said what do you think you're doing?" He was ignored again, but Young clearly knew what his boss wanted him to do. Another boot landed squarely against his ankle.

John remained silent in agony as they removed his clothes, putting up only a moderate struggle as he writhed around, trying to find relief from the pain. As each layer was peeled off, he felt the chill of the room with increasing intensity, his skin colour paling, hairs standing proud. This same cooling gradually quenching his courage, leaving him shaking from a lack of warmth and fear, as he watched his clothes scattered across the length and breadth of the church like rags. Until he was left undignified, wearing only his underpants.

"What have you left those on for?" Manton quizzed Young. "Get them off!"

Young executed the instruction immediately. John failed to offer any resistance. Silence fell around the chapel. Manton had sat back down, his head lolling toward the ceiling in self pontification. His two cronies stood to one side, afraid to disturb their keeper but lost without his direction. And in the middle of this confusion, John sat huddled in front of the altar, rocking backwards and forwards. Naked and frozen. He had begun to pray again, the same style of incoherently strung syllables mumbled through condensing breath. Thoughts of escape had completely evaporated.

"Give me your belt."

Manton was back on his feet, pointing at Young's trousers. Hesitantly he did what was asked. Manton yanked it from his hands as soon as it was free. Walking over to John, he lashed his hands together behind his back.

"Give me yours as well," he commanded Fletcher.

He looped the second belt underneath his victim's bound wrists and pulled John's back down to the floor, fastening the two free ends around one of the altar legs. This left his upper body splayed across the alter platform, while his legs laid lifeless on the steps. He continued to pray, distracting himself from the indignity. The world was moving around him, but he saw nothing, heard nothing. He still felt, though. It would take more than casual distraction to stop the cold eating away at his fragile frame. Closing his eyes, he started the Lord's Prayer once more. When the verse was complete, he called for help. Intervention of any kind, divine or mortal, it didn't matter. He felt hands clasp his ankles. A pair restraining either side. His prayers were left unanswered. Maybe he had done something to displease God. An act that had breached the pureness of his faith, dirtied his religion. He thought hard. To his knowledge he had undertaken nothing that was selfish, disrespectful or deceitful. Maybe it was just that his request was too much. Maybe God would provide through another vessel. John altered his tack, praying for strength from suffering. Power to endure the pain.

"You still with us?" A slap landed flat across his cheek. "Hey, shit head. You in there?"

John opened his eyes to view Manton's face inches from his. He was so close that John could smell the stale phlegm clogged at the back of his throat. John ceased praying.

"You ready now? Ready for your penance?"

Manton stood up, revealing a candle in his left hand, the flame stretching out to burn the air above it. Solidified wax streaks covered the shaft and even though John couldn't see it, he knew there was a pool of molten wax welling around the base of the wick. Placing the candle over his prisoner, Manton tilted it to one side. John watched in silence, bracing himself for the pain, as a stream of liquefied wax slugged over the solid rim. Time seemed eternal. Then it struck, hitting just to the right of his left nipple. The initial contact was painless, but then the wax began to transfer its heat into the skin, drying it out. John wriggled in agony.

"How was that? Was it memorable?" Manton's face grinned above him. "You want some more?"

John didn't answer. There was no point.

Placing the candle over John's chest once more, Manton lowered it closer to ensure greater accuracy. Then, tipping it, he released a larger quantity of wax, which enveloped John's nipple.

This time it burned his skin immediately, leaving it raw.

A fearful sweat started to swell from his pores. He could see in Manton's eyes that the event was still far from complete. He would carry on until the candle had burned down the entire stem and then he might just grab another and begin again. John's shackles bit harder into his hands as he tried to wriggle free, and at his feet Young and Fletcher continued to compensate for his every action. Manton aimed the candle again, releasing more wax down on to his other nipple. The pain felt less tortuous. His nerves were in disarray. There was nothing he could do except lie back and wait for it to be over. Focussing on the roof he started to pray again, though not for a saviour to arrive. This time he would settle solely for the strength to get through it. Above him Manton laughed insanely.

"Are you fucking stupid or something? He ain't going to help you. He can't! To show himself would destroy part of the faith. It's too easy to believe in something if you've seen physical proof of its existence."

Those words were the most intelligent thing John had ever heard Manton utter and for a moment they broke his concentration. If God couldn't help him, then what was the point in believing in him? What did he gain? Was it all just about 'sitting in God's kingdom' when he died? If it was, was that enough? Shouldn't there be more? It wasn't like he was asking for wealth or success. All he wanted now was protection. Surely that could be granted to him? He resumed prayer, which infuriated Manton, prompting him to ponder his next strike. Inspiration struck. Lowering the candle above John's penis, he poured a slug on top of his scrotum. Here the pain managed to manifest itself above that streaming in from John's upper body. It didn't just burn at his soft flesh, it felt like it reached inside and grabbed his balls, twisting them in a needle-ridden palm. He lay spasming on the floor, reeling in torture at the foulest pain derived by man, his prayers silenced.

Manton and his boys laughed, but the humour quickly dissipated. John knew Manton wanted to hear him scream. He wanted the suffering to cover every level of sense to ensure recollection. It couldn't be just any scream, either, it had to be the ultimate piercing shriek to know that there was nothing else he could do to enhance his retribution. Slowly, through a continuous assault, Manton achieved his goal. And with paralysed eyes, John saw the pleasure it brought to Manton's face. Revenge had suited him well. Eventually the three of them departed, leaving John limp and semi-conscious at the foot of the altar.

The pain from the burning sores was close to unbearable. Everything he did only seemed to inflame them more. His chest and legs were littered with clumps of solidified wax, with a mass the size of a tennis ball moulded to his dick. Lifting a hand towards his left nipple, he stripped back a clump, ripping hairs from his body and tugging at the skin. His head felt light. Lying back, he allowed the moment to wash over him before continuing. Steadily he removed the foreign masses from his upper torso and legs, then painstakingly uncovered his genitals.

Once the gruesome task was complete, he lay back on the floor again and rested, allowing the freezing night air to soothe the newly exposed flesh. As the minutes passed by, his nerves became anaesthetised, but he knew it was only temporary relief. His thoughts plummeted mindlessly through everything and anything, lacking rationality. He failed to grasp the scale of indignity and torment he had been subjected to. It wasn't supposed to happen like that in this day and age. Kids weren't meant to assault other kids. The law was supposed to protect all. And what of God? Where had he been? Why hadn't he helped? Why had God allowed him to be mottled by red sores? Hadn't John always been good? Hadn't he always gone to church? Was it really like Manton said, that "he couldn't display his power through fear of deconstructing the faith"? Was faith really that fragile? Was it truly strongest without evidence? Did any of this really matter? Should he care for a being that displayed no compassion for him?

Slowly the chill of the night air passed beyond a comforting temperature and John began to retrieve his clothes. As he put them on, warmth permeated back into his wounds, leaving them to deliver fresh suffering. The anguish now amplified by the aggravation of fabric rubbing the surface of each and every blemish. He tried to acclimatise to the pain, forcing himself on, seeking to break through the initial mental barrier. As he reached the back of the church, his head became light. The relatively modest additional pain from his ankle momentarily overcoming him. Resting up against one of the pews, he took a break. What was he going to do? How was he going to explain this to his parents? Should he justly serve blame or remain silent and hide the truth? The answer to that was really simple. He would lie. Nobody would hear about the end to tonight's proceedings from his lips. If he refused to speak, then the rumours would never hold substance.

Leaving the church, he continued towards his home, crossing into the woods where he had encountered Manton a week previous. It was ironic that the location for the beginning of his stand against the school bully was also the place where it had almost certainly come to an end. His walk was twisted and uncomfortable due to the scarred flesh, the pain from his ankle taking quaternary status compared to all other injuries.

His feet scraped the ground, sifting between the mass of fallen leaves. He clipped a tree root and for a moment his ankle twinged, before finally giving way. On his descent, he put his arms out in front to protect himself from impact. As his bum finally sealed against the earth, he started to cry. Not one patch of scarred tissue had remained undisturbed, his burned scrotum providing the highest level of suffering possible. He clutched at his genitals in an endeavour to find some comfort, but the contact only made things worse. Laying back against the tree trunk, he felt a wave of darkness begin to cloud his mind. Relaxing as best he could, he peeled the bark off the tree for distraction. It came away surprisingly easily, releasing in long chunks that ran lengthways towards the stars. It was only after the third slab had detached that John noticed the markings. Words scratched into a patch of pre-exposed wood. Girls' names. Dolores and Elizabeth.

6

"Have you heard about John," Kevin said, tugging at Ian's shirt.

"What?"

"Manton came and grabbed him out of Chucks on Saturday night."

"And?"

"They started to fight in the car park." Kevin took a moment's pause. "Well, Manton and his crew began beating him up. John took a hit and went down to the floor, everybody thought he was out for the count, but then he came back up, left Manton squirming on the floor from a kick to the jewels. And then dropped Young and Fletcher to the floor as he made an escape."

"Cool! Where's the king now?"

"Nobody knows. He never turned up for church yesterday. He wasn't on the bus this morning either and our queen here hasn't made any contact over the weekend." Kevin pointed towards Nicola, who was walking down the corridor.

"So, what's the deal, then?" Ian probed.

"I don't know. I've not seen Manton or his boys yet either. Maybe John took them all out of commission?"

Just then Nicola caught up with them.

"You heard anything yet?" Kevin asked her.

"No. I've not seen him since the library on Saturday."

"Oh, don't look so worried, my little princess." Ian started to play the fool as usual. "I'm sure your king is fine."

Nicola did her best to ignore him. "Have either of you checked with anyone else?"

"Just the entire school bus." It was Kevin's turn for sarcasm.

"What about Freddy? Anybody checked in with him? He is, after all, John's new bosom buddy," Ian said in a flippant tone.

"He's been off sick since last Tuesday, idiot," Kevin responded.

"Yup, but he's back today." Before either of them could say any more, Ian was off down the corridor, walking towards Freddy.

Kevin shrugged his shoulders at Nicola and they both followed. Freddy still looked as if he was seriously ill, with a pained grimace across his face and a single crutch tucked into his armpit. A chequered lumber shirt covered the bandages wrapped around his midriff, supporting his battered abdomen and ribs. One of his eyes still displayed the residual markings of a bruise, which he was trying to cover up by keeping the peak of his baseball cap tucked down tight to his eyebrow.

"So, how's the prince of cool today?" Ian said.

"What?" Freddy looked condescendingly back at him.

"Just ignore him, he's an idiot," Kevin cut in. "You alright?"

"Yeah, fine. Where's John?"

"We were kinda hoping you could answer that question, prince," Ian chirped up once more, only to receive scowls from the rest of the gathering. "Okay, okay. I was just trying to be funny. I'll shut up. Tell me if you want me to say anything."

"I've not seen him, but I heard he took a beating on Saturday," Freddy announced.

"No, you got that muddled up a bit. Manton started on him, but John definitely finished it off. I know, I was there." Kevin spoke authoritatively.

"This was after that," Freddy said.

Nicola stopped hiding behind Kevin and closed in to listen.

"Apparently John made it as far as the church before they caught up with him. That's when they set into him, stripping him naked and burning him all over with candle wax. If you can believe it, they even burned his dick."

Kevin and Ian cringed at the thought.

"How do you know all this?" Ian asked.

"Manton's outside bragging about it," Freddy said, shrugging.

"I'm not going to believe something that dickwad is spreading around," Ian said, defiant.

"Where's John? Hmm? I don't see him anywhere," Freddy quipped.

"That doesn't mean he had all that done to him." Nicola stepped in.

"No, it doesn't. But look at it. The story certainly fits better than the heroic one you're spouting." Freddy looked around at each of them in turn. "He's as much a friend of mine as he is of yours. I don't want to believe it either, but it isn't looking good."

At that moment, Manton entered the corridor, beaming from ear to ear. He had regained his throne. Spying them almost immediately, he approached, slamming a few kids into lockers on route. His hair was greasy, and his clothes crumpled as if they had been slept in. Young flanked him on one side, but Fletcher was nowhere to be seen.

"So, I guess you've heard of my triumph by now." He addressed them all.

"We've heard your side of the story," Ian said in a dismissive tone.

"I think that's the only tale you are going to hear for a while. Your little friend's not feeling too good." Manton's grin never faltered. "You'll see."

"Yeah, I'm sure we will." Kevin took over. "Where's Fletcher?"

"Unfortunate thing. Came down with a bug, so he's going to miss our homecoming parade."

"Ill? More probable John kicked him in the nuts and downed him just like he did you." Kevin had pushed it too far. Manton grabbed him by the collar and shoved him back against the wall.

"Look, you little shit. Your friend lost, accept it. And that particular incident you're talking about really hurt. You probably don't realise how much! Let me show you!" Manton took a step back to gain clearance, but Freddy thrust his crutch in between them.

"Hey, come on. You don't want your glorious mood destroyed just yet. As you say, you won, so why be bothered about anybody who says any different? Hmmm? Waste of energy, if you ask me."

"Nobody did ask you, but you have a small point." He relinquished his hold on Kevin's neck. "I'll be back for you some other day." He thrust a finger in Kevin's face and retreated. "In fact, I may come back and sort all of you out for just associating with Garret."

"Can't refute your logic, but today's not the right day." Freddy spoke placidly and Manton looked at him confused but didn't react. Turning away, he gave Nicola a light push, forcing her to stumble backwards as he continued his narcissistic swagger down the corridor.

"Oh, that's big," Ian said softly under his breath.

The group of them stood there in silence for a while, each waiting for the other to begin talking. None of them were sure what to say. There was no reason for Manton to be so triumphantly brash unless what he said had actually happened. But in their hearts, they still didn't want to believe it until it had come from John. They couldn't believe it. It was then that the outside doors at the end of the corridor opened wide once more, silhouetting a single figure in the middle. It was John. They all stared in amazement as he walked the length of the corridor towards them, and they weren't the only ones. Twenty other kids had also seen and witnessed Manton's boasting and had no reason to think it untrue.

John walked as if on air, a smile on his face identical to Manton's. Unlike his nemesis, though, who'd had to force his way through the gathered onlookers, for John the crowd parted, like in a biblical scene. The contrast between the two entrances could only be likened to that of good versus evil. John's eyes never once lost contact with his friends, as if he knew everything else around would move. His appearance was as usual, T-shirt, jeans and shirt undone, hanging loose like a jacket. There were no indications in the way he walked that he was suffering in any way. If he had been subjected to such a brutal assault as Manton had suggested, it wouldn't have been possible. A genital affliction of such magnitude couldn't be hidden. They were all speechless.

"Is there a problem?" John asked.

"Not if miracles are accepted as part of everyday life by the church," Ian responded. "What's going on?"

"You're going to have to narrow the scope of that question a touch there." John displayed a brash confidence that none of them had seen in him before.

"Okay. How come you are walking, talking and happy? When, by all accounts, you should be a crumpled mess, lying in your bed, sobbing you heart out," Ian expanded.

"Well, you must have heard an exaggerated story." John responded.

"Only if Manton is suffering from a sudden bout of delusional grandeur. I mean, okay, he's not at the top of my list for articulation and accuracy, but he'd have to be close to a loon to misrepresent what he did to you as badly as evidence dictates," Freddy said, having regained his vocal capacity.

"I don't know what to tell you."

"You could start with your side of the story," Ian suggested. Nicola and Kevin remained silent in awe.

"Okay, well, Kevin here saw the first bit, when they started to beat on me and I ended up kicking the twat in the nuts, before doing a runner. After that I made it as far as the church, where I tripped and twisted my ankle. They caught up with me there and decided to do a spot of sacrificial offering, with me as the lamb." He went silent, hunching his shoulders up as if to say, 'that's it'.

"And?" Ian wasn't satisfied.

"They burned me a bit with candle wax, but it hurt more then than it does now." He tried to conceal the extent of the horrors inflicted on him.

"You got to be kidding me?" Ian said, sceptical. "Let me see the burns!"

"Actually, they've already started to settle down." John was reluctant to expose anything. But then, realising they weren't going to back down, he lifted his T-shirt, displaying a vague red mottled tinge that smattered his stomach.

"If that's all he did, why the hell is he walking around like Ben-Hur?" Ian was confused. None of the facts matched.

"How the hell should I know? He's an asshole! As long as he thinks this is quits, that's fair enough." John attempted to de-escalate the situation once more. Finally, Kevin and Nicola's aghast faces broke into expressions of disbelief. "Is that it? No more distrust?" John questioned, but a silence fell.

"I've got to get to my class." Ian retreated, shadowed by Nicola.

"Yeah, me too." Kevin followed.

"Guess that leaves you and me then." John turned to look at Freddy.

"Yup, but we've got to get to our classes as well."

"Not just yet." He placed a restraining hand around Freddy's bicep. "We need to talk. I found your tree and I found your stories. I tell you, some freaky shit has gone down in this town. You wouldn't believe how many children have gone missing right through to the second half of this century. And those girls, Dolores and Elizabeth. I found their names on the tree. They were mental as anything."

"How do you know you were looking at the right tree?"

"Come on. How often do you find two girls' names graffitied on to a tree trunk? Besides, it was well off any beaten path and the carving certainly wasn't fresh; it had moss growing out of some of the lettering."

"None of that guarantees that it's the right tree." Freddy dismissed him.

"Hey. Where's your enthusiasm gone? It was you who sent me off to research all of this, remember?" John was a little annoyed at the overall lack of acceptance he had received this morning. "I'll take you to have a look at it after school. You can make your own decisions then."

"Can't do it today. Not while I'm on this thing." Freddy nudged at the crutch.

"Fair enough, but I'm going up there. Want to make sure I can find it again." John took a moment's pause to regain his breath. "You'll never guess all the other stuff I've learned from the library. I mean, did you know that if you spread bat's blood across your eyelids before you go to sleep and place laurel leaves under your pillow, you'll dream of demons?"

"No, of course I didn't know. And I'm not sure I believe it either."

"Me neither. But I can vouch that if you spread cat's blood across them and put any foliage under your pillow, the demons will talk to you." John raised his eyebrows to provoke a reaction from his friend.

"You haven't tried it?" Freddy questioned.

"Couldn't resist. Besides, the next-door neighbour's cat will recover." Freddy was visibly shocked. "Oh, don't worry about it. I only nicked him to squeeze a few drops out. He's not going to die or anything. Least not unless I have to sacrifice him."

John taunted. Falling into fits of laughter as Freddy's face froze in horror. John could tell Freddy found his humour inappropriate. There was something very different in his character and he knew Freddy had noticed. A confidence that Freddy had never witnessed before.

"Was Fletcher with Manton today?" John turned serious.

"No. Why?"

"No particular reason."

"Did you expect him to be a no show?" Freddy asked.

"Maybe. Wasn't sure."

"What made you think it at all?" Freddy began to sound concerned.

"Oh, nothing. I just got in a good couple of punches myself on Saturday. Wondered if they'd done much damage." He lied. "We should be getting to our classes. I'll see you later." Before Freddy could say anything else, John bolted off down the corridor.

Slowly making his own way, Freddy found himself greatly perturbed by John's behaviour. It wasn't normal. And to say he had stabbed the cat next door so he could rub the blood across his eyelids was deeply disturbing.

The day passed slowly, and he never caught up with John again as promised. However, he did manage to find Kevin and Nicola at lunch, sitting in the dingiest corner of the canteen hall. They spoke at length about the morning's events, but only Freddy harboured grave reservations about their friend's stability.

Freddy spied Manton enter the hall at one point, his mood several pegs below the egocentric heralding of earlier. Manton had obviously heard of John's return, his face drooping ignominiously as he watched his empire disintegrate around him. Freddy looked around the hall. It was clearly evident from the general student body attitude that Manton's presence no longer struck the same chord of fear. Despite that, Young still followed Manton as the devoted sidekick, but Fletcher remained notable in his absence.

"Either of you heard anything about Fletcher?" Freddy changed the topic of conversation away from John.

"No, not really. Just that he's gone down with some kind of bug," Kevin answered.

"One kid told me he'd lost five kilos in a day," Nicola contributed.

"Don't be so gullible. He'd have to shit bricks to lose that kind of weight." Kevin put her down.

"I'm just telling you what I heard."

"John asked me about him this morning," Freddy divulged. "Says he landed a good couple of blows on him last Saturday."

"Now that seems a more realistic explanation." Kevin gestured towards Freddy, while looking condescendingly at Nicola.

"Well, not entirely. I can't see how he could have injured one of them so much and have received so much in return. Besides, the other two appear almost completely unscathed. Doesn't add up!" Freddy said.

"Works for me better than flesh-eating viruses," Kevin said

before getting up. "I'm out of here."

"What do you think?" Freddy looked at Nicola. "Didn't you find John the least bit peculiar today?"

"No, not really." She cowered in her seat, still feeling shy towards the new clique member.

"Must be just me then."

Sitting upright, Freddy surveyed the room. Gloria was sitting over in the far-left corner, cavorting with her football friends and their cheerleader partners. Not really the sort of behaviour that was expected of a girlfriend. Maybe she no longer classified herself as that. Maybe she had heard the rumours and in the absence of the walking, talking wounded, now classed herself a free agent. If the miracle boy walked in now, though, Freddy was positive her stripes would change back to spots within seconds. Her fickle sense of honour was laid bare for all to witness by the way she sidled up to Matt Thompson, much to the annoyance of his current girl.

Freddy returned his gaze to Nicola, who was getting up to leave. She was smiling sheepishly, half waving her hand as she started to depart.

"Hey, let me walk you." He got up to follow. "So how long have you lot been friends?"

"Two years." She looked uncomfortable.

"That's pretty cool. It must be nice to have such close friends."

"It's alright, I guess."

"Only alright. I'd kill to be part of a group like yours. I've spent so long living on the fringes of everybody, that I don't really know anybody. That's until now. Now I've met John and you guys. Bit of a fluke, really. Makes me wonder whether it was fate." He kept babbling on, trying to make her feel comfortable. "So, you live near John?"

"Yes."

"Do you guys get together much at the weekend."

"Not really. I work Saturdays anyway."

"Yeah? What do you do?" He was surprised that anybody as young as her actually worked. He had his paper round, but that didn't really count.

"I work in the library."

"I've never seen you!" Freddy had spent a lot of time there over the past year, reading for pleasure and studying.

"Well, I've seen you." She started to mellow. "You read a lot of science fiction."

He laughed, amazed at the fact she had taken that much notice.

"How'd you get that gig?"

"My dad's the manager. He makes me work there so he can keep an eye on me."

"Less than noble means, but at least you must get paid well?"

"Only pocket money. And that only when it suits. My father says it's good experience."

"That's what my dad said about my paper route."

They entered into an uncomfortable silence. Freddy desperately tried to think of something to say to keep the conversation going. He failed, but Nicola picked up the ball.

"John was in the library on Saturday. Did you know that?"

"Yes. I asked him to look up some stuff for me."

"Well, that's some pretty weird stuff!"

"What do you mean?" Freddy was puzzled. He had only asked John to look up some history.

"He checked out a book called 'Keeper of Fallen Angels: Volume 2'. It's one of three books that according to my father shouldn't even be allowed into a library."

"What are they about?"

"Devil worshipping, mostly, some witchcraft and a little black magic somewhere in between. The one John's got apparently takes you through the summoning of the Devil. Didn't he tell you he had it?" Her conversation flowed freer now that John was the subject matter.

"No. Must have slipped his mind." He paused for thought. "Look, I better get off. Got an errand to run for my parents before dinner. See you tomorrow." He hobbled off down the corridor.

Nicola stood still, watching him until he was out of sight, before carrying on her own way.

John had watched his friends from the wings all day, not wanting to be drawn into conversation, but now he'd had enough. They had all gone their separate ways anyway and he wasn't in the mood for an afternoon of school. Besides, he'd lost all concentration since discovering Fletcher's absence. So, he left, retreating back into the forest to the etched tree. There he sat and read from the library book. He learned that to invoke Shalek, the spirit of the earth that Freddy had spoken about, he had to establish a link with the four elements of nature: wind, fire, sea and earth. From these forces combined, a power could be unleashed into the caller, granting wisdom and magic to defeat any foe. He discovered Freddy's understanding of Shalek was misguided, learning of Shalek's split nature. Some religions believing him to be a single entity, while to the others he was an unseen controller, a conglomeration of several spirit entities, that offered different treasures depending on the ritual used to open the gateway through to Shalek's earthbound ethereal plane. These varied ceremonies, tied together with the lunar cycle, presented five unique opportunities between adjacent full moons to invoke a spirit. However, for it to work, the caller had to be pure of thought. He or she had to have decided what their beliefs truly were, otherwise, a good caller could invoke an evil spirit, leading to corruption of their soul. In this situation, the evil force would reign supreme, possessing the body. There was no uncontrollable violence associated, no foreign tongue spoken and no physical exhibition of magic, unless absolutely necessary. The spirits obeyed this latter rule, so that they could walk alongside humans unnoticed. In this way their work could span decades, their mayhem and influence reaching thousands. Conversely, if a good spirit was invoked by an evil human, then its goodness would be rejected and lost forever.

The way the book read, it gave John the impression that the spirits were regenerative. Where one was lost or in cohabitation with a human, another would stand in to be called whenever required. In many ways, this tied together with the religious tale of fallen angels walking the earth. The only difference here was that they walked within people. They weren't lost souls. They were something else. The text failed to describe fully their semblance, save to say that their existence was derived by the earth and Shalek combined. In this way they represented the power of the elements, decanted and harnessed in small packages, fashioned in their maker's image. And Shalek was characterised as a Devil-like creature, with God-like powers. He could create life and inject it into God's design, allowing him gradually to taint the seven-day creation. But while this made him strong, his creations were based around a simple procedure that couldn't be broken and, unwittingly by the hand of God, generated as much good as evil. John failed to grasp the hypothesis being laid before him and had to re-read the passage.

What it broke down into was that God created the world in balance. Where he generated good, wealth and prosperity, he created equal proportions of evil, poverty and misfortune. The reason for this was that for God, one couldn't exist without the other. If people were incapable of differentiating between good and evil, principally because the two states didn't exist to start with, then how could they desire more from life? How could they know what was right and wrong? How would they evolve into a species that sought to help each other? And if they were emotionally and mentally incapable of doing all of this, then how could they pray? What would they pray for? Where would their faith be? The answer was nowhere. If he had created perfection, then it wouldn't have required his continued presence. He would have been redundant. So, in the early days he allowed misfortune to strike at his people. He allowed Saint Paul to suffer via a thorn in his flesh, which Paul requested be removed three times before God acted mercifully. However, bestowing pain and ignoring suffering wasn't a long-term solution to enhancing faith. To remain omnipotent, he had to distance himself from the hand of evil. The solution to his dilemma was of course to create an entity of evil and give this same form the opportunity to perpetuate itself without his involvement. This evil creation could only strengthen the faith of his subjects.

Again, the story bore resemblance to the religious text. So, God had created Shalek and granted him the powers described. But because everything earthbound was fashioned in perfect balance of good and evil, when Shalek used a specific element to create his 'called' souls, birth was given to an evil one and a good one. It was in this way that God allowed the situation to be kept in checkmate. But unbeknownst to him, things had changed slowly. Shalek had devised a way of swinging the balance, despatching good spirits to populate the evil and vice versa. In this way, his foot soldiers multiplied, populating the earth, while God's good intent was lost in the wind. And while Shalek wasn't allowed directly to incite humans to invoke a spirit, his henchmen could.

God hadn't been stupid, though. He knew Shalek would evolve and defeat his safety features. So as a supplementary guard, he set about nine keepers to watch over Shalek. Unfortunately, their deficiencies had also been exposed and exploited over time by Shalek, distracting them to other tasks away from his core desire, eventually causing them to fall from grace and sit within his own ranks. This hadn't been a particularly arduous task for Shalek, because to call them guardians had been to stretch the definition to the limit.

First, there was Amaros, whose objective was to resolve unnatural enchantments. He acted as a reverse cupid, flitting from continent to continent, testing people's love and breaking spells where he found them. He had been the easiest to foil. Shalek had trapped him into a lust of his own, forcing him to use his powers for selfish gain. Secondly, there was Arakiel; signs of the earth were her game. She would repair the earth where it fell afoul of evil, restoring damaged woodland, allowing earthquakes to heal and impeding man's instinctive expansion across the globe, where they consumed God's creation for personal wealth. Next was Azazel; war equipment, cosmetics, ornaments were his thing. His remit was to prevent war, remove vanity and assist Arakiel in quelling man's desire to hoard possessions. Then there was Baraquel; he was into astrology. For him all records were pretty sketchy; the author made no guess as to his purpose, nor to his demise. Kokabel was the fifth; he was supposed to cover the constellations. In truth, his was the greatest task. He was required to protect the skies from disruption by Shalek's hand. After all, the power to call the master forth was within the stars. Kokabel was the last to succumb and contributed the most to Shalek's plan, restructuring the stars and allowing the calling to take place five times during each lunar cycle rather than the previous two. Penemue was to cover writing of all forms, particularly words written by the vulnerable young. Sariel was to join with Kokabel in protecting the opportunities for 'calling'; her responsibility was the course of the moon. Of all the jobs, this had been the most worthless, because the moon's route already mapped out the maximum number of slots; it was only the stars that required realignment to open further potential. Semjaza, the eighth protector, was effectively the upfront force on Amaros's turf. Where Amaros was to rectify enchantments, Semjaza was to prevent them. To do this she would routinely sweep the globe, removing all magical power from root cuttings, eyes of toads and other emblems of the dark side. Finally, there was Shamshiel. She was to protect the sun, ensuring that its glow perpetuated and reached earth for as long as possible. God's theory was that maximisation of daylight would keep the demons at bay. Like Sariel's, this task was redundant because the same God had granted Shalek the ability to call demons from the elements, which he could then use to populate humans, who could walk at any time of day or night anyway. This oversight had been put down to the 'Almighty' being unaware that his nemesis could do this.

While the names confused John, the underlying facts were clear. But what of their lord? What of Shalek? Was he never released? Did he ever surface? Could he ever be brought within? John had already demonstrated that he didn't have to call a spirit to be able to use magic. He had used a spell that allowed him to bestow a curse on Fletcher: the Rakshasa, a disease that would gradually eat away at his body, reducing him to a skeletal frame, at which point the magic would fail, because evil couldn't directly take life. It could only aid it. Nudge it in the right direction. John wanted to progress beyond these primitive curses, though. His own God had allowed him to suffer, failing to present a shred of relief, despite John's continuous prayer. As such, any faith that provided action from request was the one for him. And if it existed, he wanted it all. He wanted the full power of darkness. Let his body be consumed if necessary. He would happily become a temple for Shalek but only him.

He read on. The book started to detail the method by which the ultimate spirit could be called, providing all information leading to the sealing of a pact. An agreement between parties, which in return brought powers to the initiator. If the book's words were true, he must combine his calling with a rejection of his existing faith. To say he no longer believed wasn't enough. He had to denounce his faith to God in person. Only then would Shalek reveal himself. Only then would he accept a subject into his fold, without spiritual possession.

The ceremony had to follow a set path, beginning with the open retraction of his faith within hallowed walls at dawn on the seventh day. The dismissal had to follow a set verse, which had to culminate in the partaking of an innocent's blood. For this, a child's blood was recommended. These words started to present a clearer picture of Shifton's history. However, John knew he couldn't bring himself to expend human life, even though it was the ultimate sacrifice, the ultimate proof that no goodness resided within the caller. But it wasn't the only way. Lesser offerings were available.

No later than twenty-four hours after this denouncement of faith, the subject had to carry out a second ceremony. This one could be taken anywhere and involved the caller standing inside a ceremonial circle. A virgin piece of parchment from a freshly born calf was required for the contract, along with a knife and quill, to draw the blood and scribe the deal. Blood had to be drawn from the left arm; should it fail to flow freely, heat was to be applied direct from a flame to induce it. Once the details had been firmly outlined, another verse had to be read out loud, the final section of which had to be repeated until Shalek appeared. At this point the parchment should be flung towards the apparition. Immediately on contact, the deal would be struck. A warning then followed. At no point should the caller step outside the confines of the circle. It was only the circle that prevented him from forfeiting his life on the spot, through having audacity enough to summon and demand from the higher being. The book then went on to explain how Shalek would not speak, but that he would honour the contract for as long as the subject lived.

There was little said of breaking the deal once it had been struck. Suggestions were made that it couldn't be undone. Yet religious sectors professed that denouncing Shalek and seeking forgiveness for all they had done while under contract, along with complete destruction of all evidence and symbolism of the pact, would suffice to break the link. However, there had been no records of this being attempted.

No matter what the authors said, John's conviction did not falter. He had smeared the sacrificial blood across his brow and been exposed to demons. He had held conversation with the spirit minions of Shalek – conversations he couldn't remember, but he knew them to have taken place. He had already felt the power of the elements, casting spells to fell his enemies. There could only be one logical next step and that was to embrace Shalek in all his glory, to contract him into a deal for success. He would break faith with God and accept a new lord into his heart, follow a belief that offered protection through self-inducing powers. A hands-on approach. A vengeful approach. A way of living that required no more rights and wrongs. Just reason to act against others.

7

Manton woke up in the middle of the night, his forehead dripping sweat, his T-shirt and boxer shorts saturated. But he was cold, ever so cold. Needles of pain tore through his head, his muscles cramping in sympathy. Inside his chest he felt a bubbling sensation, almost as if his blood was boiling. It had begun about an hour ago as a localised pain near his stomach but had rapidly spread to cover the majority of his frontal torso. It felt like his stomach acid had drained through into the rest of his body, leaving it to slowly digest his internal organs. Even his penis was in pain. Limply shrivelled and sensitive to touch, it blazed on fire. He had never been this sick in his life before. Maybe it was due comeuppance for living in such unhealthy surroundings for so long. Fair recompense for living like a bum. Never cleaning the bathroom or hoovering the carpets. Which given the size of trailer he and his father shared, was inexcusable if they had an ounce of respect between them. Maybe this was divine demonstration of the error of their ways.

His bedroom was a living example of this hygienic disregard. It sat at one end of the trailer and his father's, though it was rarely frequented, spanned the other end. Between the two, his father's was the biggest, which was probably a blessing in disguise, because Manton could have generated a greater mess if he'd occupied it. As it was, the floor of his room was invisible, covered with magazines, clothes and old dinner plates. In some ways the strewn clothes were better than the naked floor, because it was only linoleum tiling, which generally felt cold and harsh under foot. He'd had a carpet once, but then a little accident had occurred in his father's room. A stray dog had climbed through the open window and shed a generous portion of diarrhoea, from one side of the trailer to the other. It was vile. The little dog had left paw prints in his own discharge as he had staggered uncontrollably around the room, eventually collapsing in the middle of it all. He was barely moving when they had discovered him. However, the dog's weakened state had elicited no compassion from his father. He had simply picked it up and dropped it outside in a puddle, then returned inside to rinse his hands underneath the tap before ripping the carpet up and throwing it on the trailer park tip. The entire episode had enraged his dad to a point that someone had to pay. Consequently, Manton had suffered one of the worst beatings he had ever taken. He knew it wasn't really the dog that had riled his father so much. That was just an excuse. The true primer was the pain and loneliness he still lived, since the death of his wife. For that reason, Manton had remained silent in his suffering. It had, however, been one of the last times he had done so. He had been twelve at the time and his body had been assaulted so badly that he struggled to walk the next day. Yet while the beating had close to immobilised him, his father had displayed some intelligence, making sure that his lashes missed his son's face. He had also shown sober intellect the next morning, by calling his son in sick and leaving him at home to heal. The healing had taken almost a full two weeks, but only one had been spent away from school. None of the teachers had ever suspected a thing. All they had seen was a kid playing truant to physical education classes. It had been a classic scenario where playing truant shaped many a child's life, including Manton's. He had skipped the classes because he was too embarrassed for people to know what had happened. In doing this he had protected his father from true exposure and in return received detention and other punishments from the principal. This ultimately created his resentment for the establishment, and while he silently suffered through each day, he required no additional justification for resenting his father.

Three weeks elapsed in total before his father considered assaulting his son again, but this time the event wasn't so one-sided.

Manton had initially feared confrontation, but when the first punch landed home, those inhibitions had dissipated. For all his anxiety about retaliation, it had been surprisingly easy. His father's movements were drunkenly slow and cumbersome, giving Manton the chance to sidestep him and knock him off balance into the breakfast bar. His shoulder had hit the counter about halfway down. His head followed through with a hollow crack against the wooden boards. This action had startled and aggravated his aggressor in the extreme, and Manton had watched the change of expression with dread. Hauling himself back up on to his feet, his dad had lunged at him once more, with equal imbalance as the first time. Manton had shifted out of the way again and aided his father's plunge with a shove to the middle of his back, sending him head-first into the corner cabinet. The top edge of the cabinet had caught the side of his father's left cheek, stripping the skin and drawing blood. The warm liquid had swelled rapidly out of the cut and his father had passed out. Manton had watched for a couple of minutes, uncertain as to whether his father was bluffing. Eventually he leaned forward and prodded him. When no response came, he knew it was over. Strangely, he had then felt sympathy for his dad. So, tended to the wound before locking himself up in his bedroom and going to sleep. When he woke the next day, his father had already departed for work. They never spoke of that night again, but his father rarely abused him as violently afterwards.

Another wave of pain drifted up through his appendix and into his chest. He clenched his teeth, enduring the buckling agony, sweat breaking out across his face and body once more. The intensity of the attack this time was close to intolerable. His father still hadn't returned home, and Manton knew with great certainty that when he did, the smell of alcohol from his breath would be enough to bring pain relief. He had first noticed the symptoms a couple of days ago but hadn't told his dad. He wouldn't have been interested anyway. And even if his dad had listened, having paternal supervision at home more frequently than normal wasn't a thought to be relished. However, on reflection, Manton wished he had said something, anything. Just a few words. Maybe his dad's interest would have been genuine. Instead, he lay there alone and afraid.

As if inspired by fate, his eyes fell down to the chair that stood in the corner of his room. His mother had made it before she had died. She had loved carpentry. It was something she had learned to do from books, because she couldn't afford the night classes. Progress over the years may have been slow, but her attention to detail when fully submerged in a project was unquestionable. He had loved that chair up until her death. Now, he buried it under anything he could. She had died a year after finishing it. Cancer had eaten her up. Fortunately for her, the final deterioration had been rapid and remission free, but that shortness of suffering on her behalf had been shallow comfort for Manton. At the time, he had held a naive comprehension of the disease, which had been brought sharply toward the stark reality as he watched his mother's body fade away. The disease had never been explained to him. His father had been too grief-stricken to talk and there were no grandparents in his life. This lack of explanation scared him now. What if the disease was hereditary? What if the sensation he could feel eating away at his insides was the same affliction his mother had felt?

He rolled over, groaning. The pain was only just endurable. From what he knew, the sensations weren't that dissimilar to those complained of by Fletcher, and he was now on the road to recovery, though he'd lost several kilos. Apparently Young had also fallen under the same sickness a couple of days earlier. His deterioration had been much the same as Fletcher's according to the doctor, so they had put him on an identical regime of medication. All thoughts of treatment freaked Manton out now. Not because he disliked them, but because he wasn't on them. What if delaying the treatment had an effect on his recovery? He already believed his symptoms to be much worse than Fletcher's had ever been. His eyes began to cause aggravation, as if they were smouldering in their sockets. He closed them tight.

His mouth started to feel dry and claggy. His gums throbbed

under bacterial assault. He needed a drink. Sliding his legs over the side of the bed, his feet made contact with the cold floor. Then, pushing his torso up on his hands, he stabilised for a couple of seconds, letting the motion sickness in his head subside. Steadily, he acclimatised and moved on to the next phase, standing. His footing remained unsettled initially but then gave every indication that it had found firm foundation. Manton waited until the weak tremble at his kneecaps had elapsed before stretching out with his left leg. His foot trailed limply behind but remained strong as he flicked it into position to transfer his weight. Pausing to recompose himself, he shifted his right leg through a similar ark, nearing him to within a foot of the closed bedroom door. The knee quiver returned, and he could feel his consciousness evaporating, bringing with it a glazed world. There was no doubt as to what would follow. He had no strength to escape it.

He fell and the side of his head smashed into the bare floor. For a brief moment he remained conscious but then darkness swallowed him up.

Twenty minutes passed. His body rapidly harvested energy from his ever-thinning layers of fat, replenishing his weakened muscles, granting consciousness once more. The swirling in his eyes slowed, fixing on an image of yesterday's boxer shorts. His legs remained dead, but his upper body strength was sufficient for him to reach out and grab hold of the bed leg. He pulled himself back towards it. Once he had managed to get close enough, he grappled with the mattress, raising his upper body and bottom up on to it. Then, again using his arms, he retrieved his legs, placing them under the duvet. It was only when he had stopped to regain his breath that he realised how much time had elapsed since embarking on the fateful journey.

Lying there, shaking uncontrollably, he feared the future. Unable to walk, he couldn't reach the phone and call for help even if he wanted to. There were no other trailers near theirs, so shouting would have been a futile exercise. Besides, with his dry throat and mouth, he wasn't sure he would be able to shout loud enough. His brain blistered with transmitted signals of suffering and there was nothing he could do. He could lie there for the next three days and die before someone came looking for him. It was a Friday night, so school was out for the weekend. He had made no plans to meet up with his gang because they had been off ill during the week. And as for his dad – well, if he could see straight when he returned, it just meant he would have a soft landing on his bed, rather than the couch. Though despite that potential outcome, his father was the only person who presented hope. And whilst Manton felt reluctant to pursue the avenue, he had few other options. Unfortunately, the bedroom door was still closed, presenting a major hurdle even before having to put faith and trust in his only parent. The door opened inwards and operated via a handle. And he was positive the latch had dropped accurately into its hole, adding another obstacle. One thing was certain: whatever the solution, he would be remaining within the confines of his bed, which was at least two metres away from the door handle. He puzzled over the problem, allowing thought to force pain into taking a back seat. Skimming his eyes across the plethora of objects that littered his bedroom floor. He initially sought something long and rigid that could be used to bridge the gap in an instant. Nothing obvious presented itself. Innovation was to be the key. Unfortunately, that was one of his weaker attributes.

All the surrounding area had to offer were piles of clothes, an alarm clock and a dirty dinner plate. He muddled his mind over these same items again and again, all the while endeavouring to find a way to create this long rigid pole that he had set his heart and soul upon. Inspiration failed him and his head dropped back down on the pillow, his eyes shutting momentarily in despair. Then it came. The most ingenious solution. It was so simple in design, he should have conceived it in a nanosecond.

Reaching out to the floor, he grabbed a couple of shirts. Once recovered, he tied a knot into the end of one of the sleeves and then dropped his alarm clock down inside, so that it rested at the end. He subsequently joined the other sleeve to the first of the second shirt. Pulling himself semi-upright, he took hold of the heavy end and flung it towards the door, while hanging on to the loose end. It fell short, fortunately landing softly on top of some other clothes. His facial expression floundered, and he paused to regain strength before retrieving his lifeline. Once he'd fully recouped, he added another link to the chain and tried again. The alarm clock sped out towards the door, this time with sufficient slack, smashing against the wood just above the handle. The contact brought joy and despair simultaneously. His aim had been sufficiently accurate, but the force had caused the clock to disintegrate on impact. And as he listened to the pieces break apart, he knew in his heart that the damage was irretrievable to suit his efforts further. He collapsed, drained, onto the mattress. That was it. Without a suitable mass to drive through the air and offer some downward pressure to the handle, there was no way it was going to open. His chest resumed its steady self-consumption with greater ferocity. It was almost as if the disease knew what he was doing and expedited its grip accordingly. Pain began to register from within his intestines, buckling him in half. His hand released the loose end of his makeshift rope. The epicentre of suffering slowly edged its way back down towards his groin. His legs cramped uncontrollably. Stretching himself the full length of the bed, he soaked up the pain in a tearful grimace. Then, confused and exhausted, he passed out.

8

John had climbed out of his bedroom window at about five thirty, descending to the ground via a drainpipe. It was Sunday morning, and his parents were still asleep. He was heading towards the church for part one of his ritual. In a backpack he carried a fountain pen with a reusable ink cartridge and a piece of calf hide he had managed to get from the local butcher, having persuaded him that it was for a school project on how to make a drum. John didn't know if the calf could be considered a virgin as the ritual demanded. He had interpreted 'virgin' to mean 'purity'. A clean soul. To that end he was positive a calf would have one. What was there for it to sin over, anyway? Sin or no sin, though, it would have to suffice. Surely Shalek would display some tolerance to the criteria. Making up the remainder of the bag were some candles for protection and a jam jar of cat's blood, a substitute for child's blood.

Moving out of town, he left the main road, taking the shortcut through the woods. The darkness appeared more menacing this morning. Shadows merged to form conspicuous shapes that moved with the overcast sky. Last night the weatherman had predicted rain and thunderstorms, and from where John stood now, that seemed likely. The air sat heavy, making his clothes stick uncomfortably against his skin. A storm was the only way to break the mugginess.

The woods were silent. No birds sang. There was no patter of rodents' feet through the leaves. It was almost as if the forest was driven clear of life, with the sole exception of John's wandering figure. And yet he felt watched. Observed by something sinister.

Pushing deeper through the foliage, he arrived at the scarred tree and took a moment to whisper a short spell-like verse. The words fluttering softly from his mouth to begin with. Words of homage to the sisters who had shown him the way to salvation. Words pledging his devotion to their spirits and a promise to ensure their craft be returned to Shifton, more menacing and devilish than ever before. As the passage approached its close, his voice hit a crescendo. The wind rising to carry his promise deeper into the woods. Bowing his head, he turned on his heels and continued towards the church. It wasn't far, now, and paths began to open up in the undergrowth. His heart started to pound against his ribcage, his apprehension building for the task ahead. The air rushed around him, sweeping layers of leaves up from the earth, driving them into the air and swirling them about his head. Branches swayed with intent, seeming to form barricades across his path, but he pushed through.

The clouds moved swiftly in the sky, exposing snatches of the moon's brilliance to lighten the way. These same rays reflected off the whitewashed boards of the church, granting it an ethereal glow. The steeple and cross, displayed in its full glory, stretched up into the sky like a symbol of warning. He ignored it, striding onwards to the entrance, dragging his legs through the long grass. As he broke from out of the thick, he advanced at pace to the main door, opening and shutting it behind him to keep the blustering wind at bay.

The church was dim, moonlight only cascading intermittently through the glazed windows. The Saturday night candles of vigil had long since burned out, leaving reformed wax stalactites clinging to the underside of the candleholders. Moon shadows drifted effortlessly across the aisle, like angelic guardians of the sanctuary of God. Their faces and bodies flashing across his path with ever greater impact as he drew closer to the altar. Passing through the choir stalls, he noticed that the sacristy door on the right-hand side of the altar was slightly ajar, allowing a breeze to flutter the altar cloth. The air was cool but lacked the chill of a week previous, his exhaled breath barely visible. Bibles and hymn books sat ready at the end of each choir pew, waiting for their victims in morning mass. He picked one up, deciding to add the desecration of the holy book to his ritual.

Dropping his goods at the foot of the altar, he pulled out a couple of candles and lit them. He then carefully retrieved the cat's blood, placing it to one side, before kneeling down to face the crucifix. It was only then that he realised the high degree of thought he had put into what he would say later during the ritual of calling and how little he had prepared for this moment. He pondered.

"Dear Lord, this will be the final time that I will refer to you in that manner, for I no longer hold you affectionately in my heart." He paused. "You abandoned me in my time of need, allowed my suffering to take place in your sanctuary. At the foot of your table. I tried hard to understand why you forsook me. Why you stood watching over like a powerless child? And from this wondering I have drawn no positive conclusion or comfort. All I've discovered in myself is a distrust in your purpose. An abhorrence for your acts of neglect. As a result, I find myself unable to give testament to a false God, who is merciless in his actions, failing to display any compassion for his subjects." He paused again. He'd run out of words to say but felt he should say more. "I know you made your own son suffer on the cross, but that was to prove a point. That was to demonstrate faith. It was a route to begin your worship, to start your worldwide ministry, because only with such a strong display of faith through sacrifice would the feeble-minded even consider following." He swallowed. "Well, I already followed. I may never have wholeheartedly believed in your divine existence, but at the same time, I did believe that you were watching somewhere. But even if you are, I don't care anymore."

John picked up the container of cat's blood and removed the lid. Moving steadily, he tilted the container towards his mouth. He didn't falter once. As the plastic rim brushed against his bottom lip, he stretched his tongue out towards the advancing fluid. Its tip broke the surface tension, immediately sending a slug deep to the back of his throat. He savoured the flavour, allowing the juice to caress his every crevice and every tooth, and swallowed.

"On this day, I, John Garret, renounce God, and the One, Holy and Apostolic Church." Raising the container, he swallowed another batch. The candles flickered. "I give notice of my pledge to honour and obey a darker force. To follow those, you have banished from your chapel. To accept the power of those who were first to expose the true selfish nature of your existence. I pay homage to Shalek, wherever you are." He drank with greater passion, consuming three full mouthfuls. The wind blew through the sacristy, extinguishing one of the candles. John ignored it. "In this transference of faith, I will subscribe to the laws of the damned and will remain faithful to the pact I intend to cast." With these final words, he guzzled the remainder of the blood, cleaning the tub as best he could with his tongue and fingers. Another gust of wind blew, plummeting him into darkness. He grinned.

Throwing the empty container away, he turned to leave. Staggering out through the choir stalls, his backpack dragging limp on the floor, he stared at the position that would later be occupied by Gloria. She would be his first victim. She would be his proof of the pact. She would be his girlfriend for as long as he desired. The power of Shalek would seal his love in her heart. His grin widened dementedly.

Opening the church door, he discovered the sun breaking up the skyline, its rays casting a red hue above the forest. The time had reached seven fifteen, leaving him precious minutes before Father Hill would arrive to set up shop and even less time to get home and back into bed, before his parents would come to wake him. He had to be prepared by then to pull his sick card, faking a stomach illness. Nothing so serious that it would draw immediate medical attention, but just enough of a perceived discomfort that they would leave him to lie in bed while attending service. This single act would lead to typify the transference of his soul as the ultimate in descent from grace and godliness, by allowing his ceremony to take place simultaneously with his opponent's.

His walk broke into a run and before long, he was brushing through the woods, displacing everything in his path. He flew past the scarred tree before he realised it and joint the main road leading back into town by seven twenty-five. He slowed down at that point, the uneven territory having consumed all his energy.

As he rested, he started to think about Manton, Fletcher and Young, his three humbled enemies of old. All were still present and accounted for in the land of the living, Fletcher having begun his recovery after shedding just short of twenty kilos. John hadn't seen him personally, but by all accounts, he now resembled something close to a pale white totem pole. Even his muscles had been withered away. Returning to school on Friday, he had looked forlorn and fragile without his friends. However, despite this equalising of numbers and physical attributes, nobody stood up to challenge him or gain revenge for all the times he had worked them over. Maybe it was because they still feared the imminent return to glory of Manton. Or possibly, it just wasn't in their genetic make-up. Either way, Fletcher wandered the corridors and classrooms, suffering only the slow damaging indignity of whispers and giggles. In a way, though, that was probably a worse fate.

Manton and Young hadn't been seen for days and rumour had it that their bodies were passing through an equivalent metamorphosis. Manton, in particular, was shrinking in mass to a pitiful size. Surprisingly, nobody was suspicious about this small viral like outbreak. The doctors had concluded that it was some form of contact-driven contagion, thus explaining why it had been confined to the three boys. When this hypothesis had been questioned with respect to the parental contact, it had been postulated that the adult immune system was probably better suited to defend itself. When further questioning highlighted the possibility of an incubation period, the town council had stepped in, publishing an article in the local paper explaining that there was nothing to fear. That the disease had been contained and effectively treated, with each of the boys now making a slow but stable recovery. Of course, it was all bullshit, but only John knew that.

Eventually, John recovered, and he felt able to break into a run again, pushing himself on until he reached the end of his street. There he came to a halt, crouching down to rest a hand on the floor and regain his breath. Creeping back up to the house, he peaked over the front hedge for signs of life. There was nothing, so he proceeded, quickly ascending the drainpipe back to his room. He breathed a large sigh of relief, undressed and collapsed onto the bed, wrapping himself up in the duvet's warmth. Lying there, he already felt changed. Something inside him had been released. He felt contented. Dozing off, he was woken fifteen minutes later by his mother. The act began. He played them to perfection, and after brief deliberation, they left him to rest.

John lay there partially unconscious for a couple of hours, until he heard his parents depart with their usual religious punctuality. Outside the car engine fired up and the stereo gave an initial surge of sound before his dad managed to turn the dial down. Peering up over the top of his bed, he watched the car reverse out of the drive and pull out of sight. Breathing a small sigh of relief, he retrieved his clothes from underneath the bed and put them on. They were cool to the touch, having sat in the draught that swept around the floor of his bedroom. His spine shivered as the warmth drained from the surface of his body. It was now that he began to feel true trepidation about what lay before him. It wasn't that he no longer desired a pact with Shalek, but he dwelled on the uncertainty of his safety in 'calling' him. The text he had read was in truth vague with respect to covering one's own arse. It did provide the rites of ceremony and guidelines to adhere to, but now they just didn't seem substantial enough. But what was there to turn back for? He had renounced God and cast spells against his enemies. The only action remaining was to swear allegiance to an alternate master, and on that score, there was only one that he was aware of.

Picking up his backpack, he went downstairs, took his set of house keys from the dresser in the hall and unlocked the door. Outside the early breaks of blue in the sky had been consumed by swelling grey mountains of moisture. The wind had also subsided, returning the claggy stillness to the atmosphere with increasing discomfort. The clouds had gradually deepened in colour, displaying their stored potential energy with ever-expanding intensity. Soon they would break, streaming rain down and washing away the humidity. He turned, grabbed his coat from the stand and departed, locking the door behind him.

The street was relatively empty, the sole movements coming from neighbourhood pets, one of which was the now lacklustre cat from next door. Its movements were so slow and lethargic that it almost appeared to defy gravity by standing. Swaying from side to side, it spied John and endeavoured to cower away but only managed a steady stumble backwards, landing in a pile on its tail. John smirked and walked on.

As John progressed back out of town again, he watched the final few cars full of worshippers disappear into the distance. Like sheep steered by a good dog, they flocked from all directions, merging into a solitary procession. As each one passed, he endeavoured to remain out of sight, either hiding behind a wall or obscuring himself sufficiently behind a tree. There was only one instance where two cars passed in quick succession that he found it difficult to keep himself hidden from both of them.

The sky had now blackened considerably and when he re-entered the woods, he could have been forgiven for believing it to be night once more. His advance slowed, cautiousness seizing control. As before, the air was still and the undergrowth devoid of life. The forest had moulded itself into a perfect setting for such a black day. Despite John's steady advance, he came upon the marked tree with eerie speed, finding it somehow illuminated among the bleak surroundings. The etched bark displayed the same letters but with a new lustre, the wood chipped perfectly pale.

Just at that moment he heard the sound of the choir start to sing the first hymn. Despite the distance between them, he could almost decipher every word with perfect clarity. "The Lord God will see you through your troubles. The Lord will heal your wounds." The words became increasingly apt with each passing line. To John, it felt like a last-ditch attempt by his former deity to prevent him straying any further. It was far too late for that now, though. The church of God held no allure for him. It could offer no riches or power that he hadn't already acquired from more auspicious avenues. Malevolent avenues.

Dropping his backpack to the floor, he retrieved a handful of candles and spread them around in a wide circle, a little over seven feet in diameter. Within the circle he then carved the shape of a pentagram into the dirt, connecting each point of the star with an arc of three candles, spaced evenly around the circles intervening circumference. Next, he retrieved a bag of salt from his bag. Opening it up, he traced every groove, spilling the white granules into the etched pattern. Gradually the magic circle took form and he at last felt some reassurance of protection against his impending act. When it was completed, he stood back to admire his handiwork. It could have been a trick of the forest, but John was certain the emblem radiated pulses of light brighter than the crystalline reflections could possibly achieve. Maybe it was truly magical in more ways than by name. An animal of some kind rushed through the woods behind him and the spell of the moment was broken.

He dove back into his bag for the final time, withdrawing the pen, parchment, a tea towel and a knife. Drawing the knife along his forearm, he split the skin for two inches. Blood began to stream out and he wasted no time in drawing some of it up through his pen. He wasn't completely convinced that this was going to work, but he set to writing immediately. He got as far as "My Lord Shalek" before the liquid clogged up. Squeezing the cartridge, he tried to work the blood free from its chamber. Nothing happened. Finally, he resorted to using his wound as an inkwell, dipping his nib each time prior to drawing it across the dead calf's skin. Slowly, the pact took shape:

My Lord Shalek,

I have seen the power of your spirits and now harbour it inside my soul.

I have used your magic let loose in the world to fell my enemies.

I have renounced my love for God and my Christian faith,

and seek now that you will allow me to join with your minions here on earth.

While I respect your greatness and give myself willingly,

I do so under condition, for my honouring of you hangs on what you can offer me.

My desires are not great; all I seek is wealth and success,

and the granting of powers such that I may achieve this and other worldly benefits.

I seek to have your strength within me.

I want to be an extension of you in the world and for this I am willing to forfeit my soul.

Oblige my request, I dare to command thee.

John Garret

By the time he had finished, the flow of blood from his arm had begun to stem itself. But as a precaution, he wrapped the towel tight around it, placing sufficient pressure to prompt the skin to reseal. There should have been pain when he did this but there wasn't. His mind was now a tangled wreck of anxiety, shrouding all sensations. Pausing to take several long deep breaths, he stepped inside the circle, rolling the parchment up as he did so. Then, holding it out in front of him, he closed his eyes and began the invocation.

"Shalek, Master of the elements, controller of earthbound spirits, possessor of elemental life force, I beseech you to be favourable to me in my calling upon thy Great Minister which I make, desiring to pact with thee." He paused. "I pray thee also protect me in my undertaking and know that it is a request born from pure desire and want. Astaroth, Count, be propitious to me and cause that this night Shalek appear to me in human form and that he grants me, by means of a pact which I shall deliver, all the treasures of which I have need."

The winds started to swirl around him, lifting leaves from the floor and flinging dust into his eyes, forcing him to shut them.

"Shalek, I beseech thee once more, leave thy dwelling, in whatever part of the world you may be, to come speak with me; if not, I shall thereto compel thee by power of the mighty words of the Astaroth of Solomon, whereof he made use to force the rebellious spirits to accept his pact." He took a moment to catch his breath, his throat dry. "Appear then, instantly, or I shall continually torment thee with the mighty words of Astaroth."

Re-opening his eyes, he drew a torn page from 'Keeper of Fallen Angels' from his pocket and read directly from the text:

"Aglon, Tetragrammaton, Vaycheon, Stimulathon, Erohares, Retrasammathon, Clyoran, Icion, Esition, Existien, Eryona, Onera, Erasyn, Moyn, Meffias, Soter, Emmanuel, Sabaoth, Adonai. I call you."

The words represented Shalek's name, spoken in every tongue of his servants. It was the same incantation that Astaroth had been forced to use to achieve his desires. The air twisted higher above John's head, causing the branches to rustle deafeningly. He raised his voice and repeated himself.

"Aglon, Tetragrammaton, Vaycheon, Stimulathon, Erohares, Retrasammathon, Clyoran, Icion, Esition, Existien, Eryona, Onera, Erasyn, Moyn, Meffias, Soter, Emmanuel, Sabaoth, Adonai. I call you. I call you Shalek."

To his side, the scarred tree's bark began to fracture. John's fear swelled, but there was little time for doubt now, he had to proceed. He had to be strong. He watched the fracture grow, raising a hand to shield his eyes from the flying debris. The crack persisted towards the centre of the trunk, and he prepared for it to be felled. His knees weakened. The tree might come his way, and then what? He couldn't leave the circle, because that would expose him to his new lord's power. For a few moments his mouth froze in a trance, but then he continued:

"Aglon, Tetragrammaton, Vaycheon, Stimulathon, Erohares, Retrasammathon, Clyoran, Icion, Esition, Existien, Eryona, Onera, Erasyn, Moyn, Meffias, Soter, Emmanuel, Sabaoth, Adonai. I call you. I call you Shalek." He dug deep for courage. "Show yourself to me. I do not fear you. You are stronger than I, but I do not fear you."

The crack continued to forge deeper into the trunk. Instability began to set in, the wind catching the span of leaves high up, like a huge sail, swaying its mass from side to side. John closed his eyes and repeated once more the fixed passage in his mind:

"Aglon, Tetragrammaton, Vaycheon, Stimulathon, Erohares, Retrasammathon, Clyoran, Icion, Esition, Existien, Eryona, Onera, Erasyn, Moyn, Meffias, Soter, Emmanuel, Sabaoth, Adonai. I call you. I call you Shalek."

Still nothing.

"Show yourself. Don't endeavour to trick me into breaching my circle of defence, for I will not. What do I have to gain? You may not show yourself, but I know you are here. If I came outside this circle now, you would grab my soul for your own and I would be left with nothing. I know that and as such I am prepared to die here inside this circle now and hope that God will still be merciful and receive me to his side. For I am sure that it is not too late to repent."

John spoke straight from the top of his head, giving up the passage of summoning, knowing it to have already worked. "If that is the path you have chosen, what do you gain? Hey? What is your gain?" He screamed these last words with the full force of his lungs. "I'll tell you what. Nothing! You are stronger. You are more powerful. How do you add to your power through a single unseen sacrifice?" He waited for an answer, fully expecting Shalek to present himself at any moment. "Instead of a single demonstration of your strength, why not grant me my deal and extend your influence. Issue me with my sentence in the same breath if you wish but let me become thy servant first. Let me do thy bidding in ways that your powers cannot extend to. Give me your strength and let me be a medium, through whom you can channel your deceit."

In the distance, John could hear a barrier of sound approaching. It ploughed through the trees, the sound of their branches and leaves lashing closer and closer. It was a thundering disturbance compared to the tranquillity of ten minutes previous and the angelic choir voices that had precipitated down on those same branches. The ground rumbled beneath his feet, destabilising his footing, almost causing him to stumble into harm's way. But he regained his balance just in time, his foot scuffing the edge of the circle and knocking a candle over. When the swelling mass of air eventually arrived, he remained less steadfast, being pushed to the ground as if struck by a sledgehammer. His heart raced as he checked his feet remained inside the circle.

Just then the wind subsided, and he stood up. To the left of him, from where the wind had arrived, a bright mist was gradually advancing. There was no doubt in his mind as to what it masked. The time for summons had reached its close. Mouth dry, he waited nervously. As the white vapour encroached into the clearing, a silhouette appeared. An imposing figure, standing seven feet tall and equally as impressive in width. Its approach was slow and menacing, but its size diminished in equal proportion, reducing to a six-foot creature in no time. There were no supernatural features that John could see and as the mist revealed all, he discovered an ordinary-looking man. His eyes were fixed firmly on John, his speed of approach constant, but then, instantaneously, the figure closed the remaining ten metres in an instant, startling John backwards. Advancing right to the edge of the circle, the man towered above him, staring with piercing intent down at the child that stood before him. His hair was short cropped and black. Eyes looming large in deeply recessed sockets. His face was gaunt, the jaw and cheekbones pronounced in angular perfection. His lips and mouth were thin, smooth and tight, with emotionless attitude. His clothes were black, tailor fitted and designed to epitomise his subversive nature.

John returned his onlooker's stares. Unknowingly, his mouth dropped wide with wonder at the human form that had presented itself at his request. Shalek circled him, as if taking stock of his every aspect, contemplating what he should do with such a young and insignificant specimen. John chose to break the silence.

"Shalek?"

"You are an unintelligent creature, aren't you?"

"Sorry?"

"You invoke me, daring to challenge my strength, and then you see fit to insult with your first utterances." His words were slow and quiet but ever so penetrating. "Unintelligent, aren't you?"

"Sorry, I'm—"

"Stop talking." He raised a hand to interrupt and continued speaking, cold and calculating. "I see you've done your research." He pointed down to the parchment and the invocation rite. "I know what you desire and none of it is an issue. But what can you offer me in return?"

"I offer you my loyalty."

"Are you sure about that? Because I can stretch that a long way. Are you willing to follow blindly, without question?"

"Yes." John's nerves started to unsettle once more.

"Then I bind you with that promise. You will be my servant and in return I grant you my power. To do my bidding. As for your requests, I will honour them." He paused. "Hand me the parchment."

Shalek stretched out his hand, stopping before he crossed over into the air above magic circle. John's caution failed to be as precise, his hand leaving the circle's sanctuary. Shalek grasped it instantaneously. The coldness of his new lord's flesh stunned him, drawing the warmth from his own. John could feel the grip tighten, forcing him to part his fingers and release the parchment. He sneered and took the parchment from John's hand.

"I accept this as a contract between us. I will honour it for as long as you live, during which time you will do any acts I bid you do. And in death you will become mine always."

Holding the top right edge of the parchment, Shalek allowed it to unfurl. Once it was at full stretch, hanging perfectly straight, the words 'For this, I offer you my loyalty' scribed themselves below John's signature. It was only then that John started to realise his planned undertaking was nearing completion. His heart pumped so hard that he couldn't hear himself think anymore. He just stood, in fear of what he had accomplished, staring at the concentration of evil that was encapsulated by those penetrating eyes. The power of Shalek seeped up in his forearm like a chill. There was no going back now. The deal had been struck.

"I will retain this parchment as proof of our arrangement. And you, you will receive my gift." With that, he flipped John's arm over and released the towel wrapped around it. Then, with an elongated fingernail that appeared from nowhere, he split the skin once more. John's eyes watered as he watched Shalek's other hand stretch towards him. As it drew in, the palm mutilated itself, opening up a gash from which a dark red slime seeped. With intent, the wounds were pressed together.

"This signifies the closing of our agreement. My blood now courses through your veins, granting powers that you have only ever dreamed of. And with your blood in my body, you are bound to honour this day forever." He paused. "Do you understand this, John Garret?"

For the first time Shalek raised his voice, but it was the fact John had been named that unnerved him the most. He opened his mouth to speak but nothing came out. Shalek said nothing and waited. John tried again.

"I understand," he uttered feebly.

"The subtext of our contract is simple. You may use my powers as you wish, but they must never be exhibited or disclosed to any other living being. Do you understand this?"

"Yes."

"Then that concludes our business."

With that, he walked behind John again, this time accompanied by a gust of wind that snuffed the flames from each candle. He waited for his new master's re-emergence and when it failed to arrive, he turned to look and found nothing. His body began to relax, his nervous judder subsiding and his heart resuming a normal beat. A cold sweat erupted over his face; he was terrified by what he had seen. Even though he had planned the event and received all he had desired, comfort in success eluded him. In a strange way, he feared life more now than ever before. But he also felt different, in a good way, somehow cleansed of his ills, liberated from mundane life into some new blessed world, where every luxury and desire could be within his grasp. He closed his eyes and savoured the sensation.

9

"Hey, Freddy, wait up."

Freddy didn't recognise the voice immediately. He turned to see Ian shutting his locker, balancing a stack of books on one arm. He was wearing a blue pair of jeans, a white T-shirt that had the logo for a band called the *Propeller-Heads* on the front, and an over-washed faded purple denim shirt that hung loose, trailing out behind him as he advanced.

"What's happening?" Ian asked.

"Not a lot."

"Well, any more news? Any gossip? Anything happening out there?" he probed.

"Not that I know of."

"You heard about Manton and Young, following suit behind Fletcher? Man, it's so excellent how those three are the only ones to get sick. Teach them a lesson." Ian appeared jubilant.

"If it doesn't kill them?" Freddy responded.

"Didn't kill Fletcher, did it!" He grinned from ear to ear. "Just made him lose a huge amount of weight and muscle power. Christ, I could probably kick his ass now." He paused as if waiting for some comment, but Freddy remained silent. "Well, have you seen him?"

"Yes, I have."

"And?"

"Like you say, he's lost a lot of weight."

"So, doesn't that make you the least bit happy? I mean, he did partake in kicking your butt in the not-too-distant past."

"Yeah, but that doesn't mean I want him dead," Freddy responded harshly.

"I didn't say you did. All I was getting at was that it was due justice. They've caused a number of kids extreme pain. It's nice to see them get dished some. Especially since it leaves them in such a vulnerable position for the future." He rubbed his hands together gleefully.

"You've obviously not heard everything, then?" Freddy stopped just short of the main school doors. "Manton's father found him early Saturday morning, lying in his bed, out cold. Face gaunt and pale. Bed clothes soaked in sweat."

"Yeah, and? They're the same symptoms as Fletcher and Young."

"It took them two to three days to get into the same state and they didn't end up unconscious, waiting to be discovered by a steaming drunk."

"So? He's alright now, isn't he?"

"If you consider being in hospital, still unconscious, fed continuously through the nose but still losing weight as alright... Then yeah, he's just fine."

"Wow hang on there for a minute. I'm sorry. I hadn't heard it was that bad. But that doesn't mean it bothers me." He appeared annoyed. "So why's it eating at you?" He smirked at his pun.

"It's nothing."

"Bullshit. It ain't nothing if you gonna let off like that. So, stop wasting breath and tell me the detail." Ian sounded pissed off now. He obviously didn't appreciate getting a mouthful of self-righteousness, especially when he had no clue as to why he was getting it. A few seconds silence passed before Freddy began talking.

"Alright. First a question." He swallowed. "Have you noticed anything different about John? And I don't mean his weight or dress sense, but personality-wise."

"I don't know. He's gotten lucky with the girls since he kicked Manton's ass. Sometimes he's a little full of himself, but nothing I wouldn't be. Shit, who wouldn't get a bit pretentious after putting the school bully in hospital with a broken rib?"

"Maybe, but there's something else. It's like he's hiding something."

"You're just being paranoid because he's spending more time with his woman than you."

"Don't be a twat," he said dismissively. "I mean, don't you find him unduly interested in Manton and his cronies, and just a little bit too cheerful when he hears about their ill health?"

"I think you're reading into it too much, man. So, he gets a touch hyper about their misfortune, but there's nothing more to it than that. You can't tell me it doesn't warm your heart to know they're getting a touch of retribution for all the suffering they've caused in the past."

"Not in the same way as with John. When I see his joy, it's almost like he's congratulating himself."

"You're over-reacting. Just chill out, give it a couple of weeks and you'll see John come down from his high horse of grandeur and join the land of the living."

"I hope you're right." Freddy was still sceptical.

"Let's get off the subject. You going to the fair later? 'Cause we're meeting up at Chucks at about six."

"Who's we?"

"Me, Kevin, Nicola and 'spooky'." Ian put on a creepy voice and jabbed Freddy in the ribs. This time his friend laughed.

"I don't know why I even bothered asking your opinion. You're far too immature to understand anyway," he retaliated.

"Hey." Ian landed another punch.

"And you have absolutely no perception of right, wrong, normal or weird."

"Now you're pushing it." Ian rolled up his sleeves and pretended to be ready for a fight.

"Oh, don't hurt me, please!" Freddy exclaimed, cowering in mock fear.

"Only if you promise to stop taking the piss out of me."

"Alright, I'll do my best."

"Okay, then." Ian began to drop his guard.

"But you're such an easy target." With that he giggled and ran outside.

"Why you...." Ian chased after him.

Freddy was clearly the quicker runner, aided by his longer legs. Ian's pace started to wither as soon as they had left the school grounds and he shouted out his forfeit to Freddy, who then stopped and waited for him to catch up. Both of them were flush in the cheeks from the sudden burst of energy, but only Ian sounded breathless. As the two eventually joined company, Gloria appeared at the school gates and shouted for them to hang on. The two boys looked at each other in amazement. This was the first time they had been addressed by 'Princess Gloria', as she was partially affectionately and residually condescendingly known. It was an unofficial honour to be engaged by her in any form of activity and until John's recent rise to fame, the honour had been reserved for a select few 'jocks' and pom-pom bashers. She was wearing a tight-fitting red dress that hugged all the right curves. It displayed in full her unsupported bosom, through to her curvaceous hips. On her feet she wore a pair of strapless platform shoes with wooden soles, the uppers made of transparent plastic with a faint red dye smeared through it. Her hair wafted loose in the breeze and she was actually smiling at them.

"Hi, guys."

They were completely thrown by her informality. Ian failed to respond at all, except for a slight movement of his jaw, while Freddy casually raised his folder in acknowledgement.

"Hi, Gloria," Freddy said.

"Hi, Ian," she said.

He managed a grunt in response. She gave up and returned to address Freddy. "I was looking for John. You seen him anywhere?"

"Not today," Freddy answered.

"He was supposed to meet me after church yesterday but never showed."

"He was sick, that's why. I dropped around to his house at

lunchtime. His mum wouldn't let me in, said he needed his rest."

"You sure?" she asked.

Freddy didn't say anything, just looked at her simplistically.

"I'm not saying that didn't happen, it's just my little brother said he saw him on the outskirts of town, walking up the road towards the church as we drove past," she explained.

"Did you see him?" Freddy asked.

"No."

"Then you brother probably just saw another kid."

"Maybe." She started to sound uncertain.

"Look, we're meeting up at Chucks later. John's supposed to be there. If you haven't caught up with him by then, come along." Freddy suggested.

Ian's mouth opened, as if he was flabbergasted by the coolness with which Freddy was conversing with Gloria.

"What time?" she asked.

"Half five."

"Okay, I'll see you there." She turned to look at Ian for a moment. "Is he going to be there?"

"Yes," Freddy answered on Ian's behalf.

"Will he have regained vocal capacity by then?" She smiled and walked off before either of them could answer.

"You can talk now." Freddy chuckled.

"What just happened here?" Ian retained a bemused stare, waving his hands around in front of him.

"You made an ass out of yourself, but there's nothing new there. Now, come on." Before another word could be said, he started walking down the road. Ian quickly caught up. "You see, it's not just me who finds John's behaviour unusual. I mean, he's got a fine babe like that in tow and he stood her up without a word."

"Probably slipped his mind." Ian tried to hold a straight face.

"Give me a break. Bet you couldn't forget about her if she was your..."

Ian began laughing hysterically.

"You fucker."

"Wow, swear words. That's not one I hear every day. Not from Mr. Clean-Spoken," Ian said with a pretentious nasal tone.

"Well, I don't know what it is. Maybe the sight of Gloria's bazookas just brings out the animal in me."

"Bazookas. My, what colourful language!" He gave Freddy a nudge. "It was the thought of those supple creamy thighs that did it for me. The idea of them wrapped around my head just left me dumbfounded."

"You're going too far now."

"From that first moment after she shouted out, I couldn't think of anything else but her panties shifting to one side, exposing the full view of her—"

Freddy punched him hard. "Stop right there. That's no way to be talking about your friend's girl."

"Duh, okay." Ian said in mock submission.

"But just think. We'll get to see that steamy hot body again later." He grinned from ear to ear. "And that's enough to give me a major chubby." With that Freddy grabbed his groin and pulled a lecherous expression.

Ian cracked up.

Walking on for a while they discussed Gloria's attributes in greater detail, this time Freddy uncharacteristically displaying even less decorum. They even pondered over how much of her anatomy John had been privileged to see, and how much flesh he had caressed with his hands. In fact, if both of them hadn't been in full stride, they would have probably got erections there and then. Both guys felt major relief for this saving grace as they turned the corner to Freddy's home street to find Nicola standing there. Her eyes initially appeared distracted but fell down to gaze upon Freddy almost immediately.

She was wearing a red cotton dress with a yellow floral print. Her hair was tied back in a ponytail, the end of which had been lifted by the wind to sit on her left shoulder. A pair of spectacles bridged her nose, which was unusual, because she detested the way she looked in glasses. She had a point. They had large round circular lenses housed in three-millimetre-thick black plastic frames. So apart from looking like a second-hand seventies fashion accessory that added nothing to her street credibility, they also made her face look fat, when it was actually quite thin. In one hand she held what looked like the broken ends of a black candle, held delicately together by the wick. Small fragments of wax had crumbled off and stuck to Nicola's sweaty outstretched palm. As they drew closer, both of them could see the fragility in her eyes and the tears she was endeavouring to restrain.

"Now then, my precious, what's the deal?" Ian chirped up first, wanting to pull her out of the dumps, but she didn't respond.

"What is it, Nicola?" Freddy asked.

"John…" her voice quivered.

"What's he done?" Straight away Freddy was on the war path, his suspicions raised. Nicola failed to speak once more. Her mouth moved, but she was too emotional to forge the words. "Calm down, alright? Just take a moment to settle yourself and then try again."

Ian stayed quiet, amazed at the sudden paternal maturity his friend was displaying. Then, taking Freddy's lead, he straightened Nicola's hair and placed an arm over her shoulders. They stood like this for a couple of minutes and some tears spilled down her cheeks, but they were quickly dried up with a tissue Freddy produced from his pocket. Steadily, she composed herself.

"I was walking back home from school and I went up to John's house to see where he was. I hadn't seen him in school, and he wasn't in my math class." She sniffled. "I thought maybe he was sick or something. So, I went and knocked on the door and his mother answered. I asked if John was alright and she said why? I said I thought he was ill, and she said no. So, I asked if I could see him and she said he hadn't come back from school yet." Lifting her glasses, she dabbed her dress sleeve into her eye sockets.

"And?" Ian became impatient.

"I faded at that point. Didn't know what to say. I didn't want John to get into trouble, so I just said okay and goodbye."

"Is that it?" Ian retracted his sympathetic arm. "I thought you were going to tell us something devastating. Something scandalous. Salacious. Something I could spread around school."

"Shut up, you idiot." Freddy snapped. He knew there was more. "Ignore him. Carry on."

"Then I started to walk back down the drive and saw John cycling down the street. He was peddling so fast, head ducked down. As he cut across the street, he looked up and stared straight at me. For a moment he appeared uncertain, but then as he entered the driveway, he leapt off his bike and threw it down on the lawn. Then bashing past me, walked into the house."

"So, what have you done to offend him?" Ian asked.

"Nothing." She started to cry properly. Freddy placed his arm around her. The two boys stood listening to her sobs for a while.

"What's that, then?" He prodded at her hand. She raised it apathetically up, shrugging her shoulders. Freddy took it from her.

"It's a candle," Freddy said.

"Obviously. But why's she holding it?"

"I found it laying on the floor after he had gone inside," Nicola explained.

"You sure it wasn't there before?" Freddy asked.

She nodded.

"That's not a good sign!" Freddy remarked.

"What, so he's got a candle fetish?" Ian quipped.

"Doesn't it seem a little bit strange to you that a kid your age is spending his allowance on candles?"

"No. He could have been buying it for his mum."

"Finally, an intelligent comment, but it's unlikely he'd duck out of school to buy his mother a present. Particularly if he's deceiving her at the same time into believing that he's been to school."

"Fine, Columbo, what do you think?" Ian said, resentful of Freddy's belittling attitude in a girl's presence.

"He could be doing magic." Freddy was serious, but that didn't stop Ian from laughing out loud.

"Give me a break. You think he's doing card tricks?"

"No, you idiot. Witchcraft!" It was Freddy's turn to sound

offended now.

"Whatever gave you that thought?" Ian spoke dismissively.

"Black candles are a key element to practising any art of magic," he explained.

"Yeah, and so is having a cauldron of broth, but that doesn't mean my mother's practising hocus pocus every time she makes a soup."

"It does sound a little far-fetched." Nicola's weak voice broke the debate.

"Look, that's not it. You remember the other week I got the shit kicked out of me?" They nodded. "Well, John came to visit, and we ended up talking about these girl witches that used to live here, and I asked him to go to the library and do some reading up on it. Well, he did. After that, I've had about one rational conversation with him, when he told me what he had discovered."

"Come on. Cut with cloak and dagger bullshit," Ian said.

"You really haven't noticed any change?" Freddy questioned.

"Yes, I have, but like I said before, when you've got a babe like that, your priorities alter."

"But you aren't even beginning to get a little suspicious?" Freddy looked at Ian with incredulity. "What does it take to get you aroused about anything?"

"Well..." Ian was lost for words.

"That's three people who have told you, in the space of half an hour, that a close friend of ours is acting peculiar, and it washes over you like a case of the flu. You know, just lay back, take some rest and it'll all go away."

"What's got up your butt? You taking night classes in fucking parenting or something?" he retaliated. "It's not me who's gone whacko!"

"I know, but your reaction is so dismissive."

"Because if he's having problems, I don't see why it should be me who sorts it out."

"If being a friend isn't reason enough, I don't know what is." Freddy was stern, intent on bringing the needless discussion to a close. He briefly succeeded.

"Okay, let's see what he's like tonight when we meet up at Chucks," Ian said, ending the silence.

"What if he doesn't show?" Nicola put in.

"He told me yesterday he's coming, and I believe him. Besides, if he's a no show, then I'll accept your story." Ian took a breath and continued before the other two could interrupt. "But promise me – if he comes acting all normal, you'll drop the subject." They nodded. "Okay, I'll see you in an hour. I'm gonna get some grub." With that he raised a farewell hand and crossed the road.

"He has a point, you know," Nicola said quietly.

"Hey, I thought you were on my side?" Freddy's face softened. "And I know it sounds crazy, but so is the way John's acting."

"Yeah, but witchcraft?" She smirked.

"Why you…" He grabbed her around the waist and tickled her. She screamed and Ian turned briefly to see what was happening. "Come on, let's get you home." He placed his arm around her shoulders, and they walked on.

Nicola and Freddy arrived at an almost deserted Chucks ten minutes behind schedule, after Freddy had been roped into fudge brownies and a glass of coke with Nicola's mum, Karen. That experience had been a first for him, but apparently it wasn't unusual behaviour in the McKendrick household. Their casual chatter had extended to many subjects, leaving very few stones unturned in his speckled history. Everything from past girlfriends to future aspirations was covered. Hobbies, GPA, father's occupation and even his mother's age were gleaned from his mouth. Despite Mrs. McKendrick's courteous nature, relief had exploded through Freddy as they had departed.

Their late arrival at Chucks hadn't mattered though, because they were still first. Going to the bar Freddy bought two glasses of coke, while Nicola was despatched to find a free table with sufficient seats for all. Before he had chance to return to her, Ian and Kevin had appeared. When he reached the table, the three of them were laughing and giggling.

"What is it?"

"Nothing much," Ian answered.

"It must be something, or you wouldn't be having such a good time."

"Ian was just telling me about your—" Ian punched Kevin in the arm. "Hey, what you do that for?"

"You talk too much." Ian's face became stern.

"He was telling you about my what?"

"Now look what you've done." Ian gestured between his two male friends. "I was telling him that you think John's into witchcraft."

"Great! Are you going to tell John when he arrives as well?" Freddy's initial good humour dissipated.

"No, of course not." Ian shrugged off the attack.

"What about Kevin? Are you going to vouch for him too?"

"Hey, I won't say a thing." Kevin broke his giggles to speak.

"You'd better not!" Freddy threatened.

"Come on, Freddy, Ian was just having a bit of a laugh." Nicola became uncharacteristically vocal, attempting to diffuse the situation. "Neither of them will say anything." She stared at the two accused, seeking confirmation. They obliged her. "Now can we go back to being friends?" Their faces relaxed.

"Ok. But you've got to admit it sounds a little mental," Ian addressed Freddy directly.

Nicola and Kevin were dumbfounded by his tenacity and waited for the situation to erupt once more.

"Far-fetched, maybe. Implausible, no." Freddy grinned, and they all laughed.

"Thank God for that. I thought we were about to hit World War Three there," Kevin said, but before anybody could respond further on the subject, Gloria entered with John. The chatter ceased.

Gloria had altered her attire for the evening session and was now wearing jeans, a tight red low-cut sleeveless T-shirt, biker boots and a Shifton High varsity jacket, a relic of her former football player girlfriend days. The jacket used to be Matt Thompson's, but Gloria had never offered to return it after they'd split up and Matt had never asked.

John was dressed in his usual manner: T-shirt, jeans, trainers and denim jacket. But the expression he wore was altogether different – it was more commanding, a fixed glare of self-confidence that wasn't derived from his recent fighting glory days. They had already seen that picture. All of them noticed, but only Nicola and Freddy were unsettled by it. The four of them watched the couple traverse the floor to where they sat. Any of Gloria's earlier concerns had seemingly been dissolved over the past hour and a half. Her face flush with happiness as she clung to John's hand.

"Hi, guys," Gloria said chirpily.

"You found him without us, then?" Ian asked.

"Yup, he came around to pick me up." She turned to smile at John. He grinned back nonchalantly.

"So, where you been, bud?" Ian directed his attention at John.

"The usual."

"Why weren't you in school?" Freddy interjected pointedly.

"I was." His smile perpetuated.

"We never saw you. And you weren't in math class!" Freddy's tone verged towards accusation.

"That's because I didn't feel so hot. I went to the medical centre, the nurse gave me a couple of pills and told me to go home and get some rest."

"Then why were you out riding your bike later?" Ian butt in.

"I felt better late afternoon and decided to get some fresh air."

"Must have done you the world of good, by all accounts, because you nearly took Nicola's head off when you got home!" said Freddy.

"What is this, the Spanish inquisition?" John looked around at their puzzled faces, his own having lost its grin. "I needed a slash. That's why I dove past. I went back outside afterwards, and she'd gone." He pointed at Nicola.

The table went silent. Freddy had exhausted his questions.

And even though he didn't feel satisfied with the responses, there was little to be gained from pursuing the issue.

"Come on, are we going to the fair or what?" John said. He could tell that he had won the debate and allowed his smirk to return.

"Duh, of course we are," Ian said in a dunce's voice.

"Hey, try not to be such a fucking idiot," John snapped back.

"Umm." Ian pulled a funny face. "Tell me, do you kiss your baby sister with that mouth?"

"Give it a rest. Let's go." John didn't wait for a reply this time, turning around immediately to leave, pulling Gloria with him. Ian and Freddy glanced at each other, unimpressed by their friend's condescending attitude. Then waited with Kevin for Nicola to finish her drink before the four of them followed.

As they crossed the car park back to the main road, couples paired up. Kevin and Ian, the odd couple took the lead, followed by John with Gloria and then Freddy with Nicola, the two ever affectionate pairings. They remained in this formation until they reached the fairground entrance. Kevin and Ian waited at the gate for a good couple of minutes before the rest caught up. During this time both of them gazed at the attractions, the lights so bright that some blinded, as they spun chaotically, abusing their retinas. Reds, blues, greens, oranges. The field swelled with fluorescent activity that reached up magically into the night sky, competing with the stars. It was an uneven competition, though: the fair won. The big wheel stood proud in the centre of the feast as the adult of all rides. Even with the simplicity of its design, it was still the one to be revered the most. Braving the ordeal of clutching on to your stomach and being thrown randomly in multiple directions over the space of two minutes was nothing when compared to the challenge of defeating vertigo.

As the visual stimulation of mechanical madness wore off, Kevin and Ian's eyes began to wander around the remainder of the park. A land of tents presenting historical pastimes, where many a man had stood tests of expertise to win their woman trinkets of affection. These tents forming a canvass shanty town backdrop to the modern day illuminated mechanical wonders of fair life. A backdrop to a land where gypsies who needed to make enough money to support their families resided. The economic desperation behind these establishments was lost on the consumers though. Their purpose was pleasure. The providers circumstance was irrelevant. Ghost rides, houses of fun and carousels existed within this single storey pleasure land. Despite their low glitz nature, these were where the Kevin and Ian wanted to begin.

"So, where first?" asked John.

"Ian and I are going on the ghost train." Kevin turned to just check his buddy was in agreement.

"We'll come with you," Freddy said.

"Well, we'll come too," John confirmed. "Don't want to break the party up prematurely."

It was three dollars each to enter. From then on, the majority of the rides would be free, although some required supplements, like the dodgems. Freddy and Nicola were the last through the gates, Freddy paying for both of them. Nicola beamed from ear to ear as a consequence. Consumed by romantic thoughts, Nicola failed to register Freddy's ulterior motive for taking position at the back. He found John very uncomfortable to be around. His incessant grinning and new brash attitude were a lot to adjust to. And no matter what the others believed, it wasn't normal. There was something disingenuous about his friend's actions. And the control John seemed to have over Gloria exacerbated Freddy's anxiety.

They passed stall upon stall offering goods for skill and money. Kevin and Ian had stormed on ahead, but John and Gloria loitered towards a shooting gallery. Freddy followed, dragging Nicola behind him, but she didn't care. She was still overwhelmed by his chivalry in paying her entrance fee. By the time they had caught up with John, he had paid a dollar and was being issued with four pellets from a large, squat man with weathered hands.

"Now, kid, if you knock three cans over, the pretty girl here gets the choice of any bear on the top row. If you only get two down, she can choose from this equally well-crafted selection on the bottom shelf. If you get one down, and I hope you do better than that, she gets a five-cent chew." The guy leaned forward and semi-whispered in John's ear: "For your future happiness. Shoot well. Besides, I hate seeing unhappy girlfriends – just tears at my heart."

"Don't worry. I won't even need the fourth pellet," John said. He loaded up.

"What you talking about? You've never won anything on these stalls." Freddy had reached his side.

"How would you know?"

"Kevin said."

"Tonight's different. I'm feeling lucky." John turned around, the air rifle pointing up towards the sky.

"Hey, watch it there, kid!" An adult hand wrapped around the barrel and pulled it back towards the range. "You'll put a round through your friend's head. These are dangerous weapons, you know?"

"Yes, I know." John continued to stare at Freddy. Then, turning his concentration back to the stall owner, he sneered and raised the rifle toward the targets. Cracking his head to either side, he lowered his eye down behind the sights and fired. It missed.

"Bad luck, kiddo. Load up for the next one. And don't rush this time." The owner raised his mouth in a broad grin.

"The sights are out." John glared at the chubby man.

"I don't think so, son. I check them each day."

The stall keeper's response was nothing less than smug and that seemed to annoy John even more, but he said nothing. Reloading, he took aim again, this time setting his sights two inches to the left. Bang. He hit the can dead centre, sending it flying backwards into the blanket that hung at the back of the range. Without waiting for further rhetoric from the owner, he loaded and fired again. The second can was despatched to the floor. And then, before a stunned Freddy could raise his hands in applause, the final can was removed from its position. The stall owner's face had now plummeted through several levels of happiness to a grimace as he offered John a selection of stuffed teddy bears. John gestured for Gloria to make her own choice. She pointed at a big blue bear with red paws and nose.

"Would you like to chance your luck, kid? Win something for the little lady." The owner had recovered from his frustration and transferred his attention on to Freddy.

"Oh, I'm not very good at that sort of thing." He turned to Nicola, feeling uncomfortable under the pressure, but where he had hoped to find a scapegoat, he found a blushing young girl who was too embarrassed to comment.

"Don't be a chicken. If I can do it, anyone can," John sneered condescendingly.

"Alright, I'll give it a go."

"Good show, sport," John mocked.

"You won't mind settling for something smaller, I hope." Freddy turned and spoke quietly to Nicola. She smiled and shook her head, then stood on tiptoes to kiss him on the cheek.

"Oh, how sweet," John quipped.

Freddy spun round and glared defiantly. He had almost reached his limit for sarcastic remarks and if he hadn't feared John's potential capabilities so much, he would have smacked him on the nose by now. Freddy placed his money on the counter and raised the rifle.

"You got to load it, mate," John pointed out, but Freddy ignored him.

Loading up, he took aim and fired. The pellet clipped the side of the middle can, leaving it to rock on the spot. The four of them watched the can spin around on its axis, but it failed to topple. The owner spoke, but the words were lost on Freddy. He loaded another pellet and fired. This one struck the side sufficiently to throw the can off the ledge. John was saying something now, but Freddy didn't turn to make sense of it. With military style he targeted the next can and fired. This one smashed straight into the middle, breaking through the thinned aluminium and entering the can itself. It flew into the protective blanket. Freddy could feel the frustration in his friend's bones, even though he still refused to turn and look at him, because that would be like accepting defeat. Instead, he took it steadier, sharpening his aim and firing. Time seemed to slow down. He knew the pellet was on a direct collision course, he could feel it. He could see the small silver pellet streaking down the range, its line of travel taking it directly towards the far left-hand can. He was desperate to hear the noise of impact so that he could turn around and gloat, but it never came. Instead, the pellet appeared to pass straight through the can, leaving it completely undisturbed on the ledge.

"Bad luck, kid. I thought you'd got that one too." The owner sounded relieved.

"Yeah, real shame. Maybe you just lost your concentration at the end."

John's snide comment offended Freddy sufficiently this time and he turned around to retaliate. It was then that it struck him. What if the pellet had been on aim? What if John had caused it to miss? If he was truly into the craft, then it might have been a simple exercise for him. He already believed John had cast spells on Manton, Young and Fletcher; surely manipulating the course of a pellet was easy fodder in comparison?

"Which teddy would you like?" The owner tapped Freddy on the shoulder to get his attention.

"Lady's choice."

Freddy offered the task to Nicola without taking his eyes off John. She accepted the gesture, seemingly still floating in a dream world of delirious happiness. In his peripheral visons he saw her point at a small yellow bear with green paws and ears. The bear was about half the size of Gloria's, but it appeared to mean more to Nicola than any number of gifts would have meant to Gloria. Baring a rapturous smile, Nicola took hold of Freddy's hand once more, breaking his trance.

"Shall we catch up with the other two?" Gloria tugged at her boyfriend's arm.

"Yes, why not." John's smugness returned.

They walked on. Freddy watched every move John made, suspicious of everything. If he pointed, Freddy wanted to know what at? If he spoke to or touched anyone, he wanted to know what about and why? His paranoia grew with each second. He desperately needed to restrain it, because if he wasn't careful, John might get more suspicious about his interest and that was attention he didn't desire. Freddy kept turning the same thoughts over in his head. How could he reveal John's secrets for certain? He wasn't going to divulge them. Not willingly, anyway. And force wasn't an option, if Freddy's fears were founded. The thoughts circled in his head, with no visible way of finding direction. There was always the possibility that he could attempt a challenge in public that would force John to expose his nature, but that could only end one of two ways. Firstly, John could remain silent and not bite at the bait, instead saving his anger for that single moment he found himself alone with Freddy. At which point he would no doubt use his evil ability to wreak revenge. Funnily enough, that seemed the best outcome to Freddy, because the other option involved John's exposure to all who sat and watched, which could then only end with the same level of suffering extended to Freddy in the first instance, then subsequently to all spectators. He discarded the latter option as unacceptable. There were too many people he didn't want to see hurt.

They arrived at the ghost train to find Kevin and Ian nearly at the front of the cue. Kevin spied them and waved.

"What do you want to do, then?" John said.

"Wait for them, I suppose?" Freddy looked at Nicola to see what she wanted to do and she nodded in agreement.

"We can't do nothing! How about another shooting gallery?" John proposed.

"You can, if you like. We'll watch," Freddy replied.

"It's no fun without the friendly competition." He was clearly disappointed that another chance for exhibitionism had been withheld.

"How about getting our fortunes read?" Freddy suggested. He pointed to a four-by-four-metre tent that stood in the shadows between the ghost train and the house of fun. An awning was draped out in the front, suspended over two poles, one on either side, giving it a Bohemian air of mysticism. The tent fabric was striped white and red, with tassels stitched to the seams and edges, reinforcing the stereotype of prophetic power held within. A simple sign propped to one side declared: 'Gypsy fortunes told here'.

At the entrance, a young girl stood handing out leaflets to anybody who came close enough. She seemed a shy girl, remaining close to the comfort of the tent. She was about twelve years old, dressed in authentic gypsy costume, a style of dress with origins stretching back to the joining of early nineteenth-century Russian peasants with the nomadic people who wandered the lands of Eastern countries.

"Alright," John eventually replied, deciding that the situation could benefit him.

The four of them walked over. As soon as she realised their intent, the young girl prepared to usher them inside. It was at this point the two girls chickened out, cowering away from her widespread arms. Freddy began to question whether he should continue, now that the girls had opted out, but John caught his arm and dragged him in.

The inside of the tent was decorated with tall plants standing in large fake china pots, smaller plants, some mounted atop pedestals, and others scattered around on the floor. There was a round table placed centrally, with a crystal ball mounted inside an ornate gold stand that swirled like entangled branches around the base of the ball. Next to it, a small porcelain pot of smouldering coal stood below a small matching ornate tripod, which supported a tiny bowl of steaming liquid. Over the table was a bright multi-coloured cloth, finished at the edges with a row of tassels. Two chairs were pushed up to the table, one on either side, and two shaded lamps sat on top of a small side table, which, with the exception of the burning embers of incense sticks positioned around the room, provided the only light. At the back of the room a purple voile draped down to partition off a section to the rear. The sheen of the fabric distorted their view, allowing movement to be seen but not deciphered.

"What do you reckon to this, then?" John prodded Freddy in the belly with his elbow to catch his attention. "Cool décor, hey?"

"Yeah." Freddy was less concerned with the surroundings than he was about being alone with John.

The sound of something being dropped down on to a hard surface came from the back, then a cough. Both boys looked toward the partition. They could see the outline of a figure. Then a hand breached one side of the drape and pulled it back to reveal a woman in her mid-forties. Her face was weathered from years of travelling, with wrinkles contouring beneath her eyes and a redness in her cheeks that she had endeavoured to hide with make-up. A mole sat just below her left eye, a grotesque hair erupting from its core. Her eyes glowed green in the diffuse light. Her red and naturally curled hair rested around her chin, suffering from a recent amateur chop. A thin silk veil crowned her head, extending down to the sides and back but leaving the face completely exposed. She wore a dark brown dress with purple stripes imposed over it by a satin sarong. Her feet were bare, displaying the underlying frailty of her body. Veins strained blue. Her metacarpals were visible through the skin, pushing ever so gently at the underside.

"Good evening, boys." Her speech was slow and inquisitive. "What can we do for you this evening?

"We?" John questioned, his bravado knowing no bounds.

"Yes," she answered succinctly.

"Okay." John smirked, seeking a similar response from Freddy, but he offered none.

"Have a seat." She gestured towards John and the chair. "Are you staying here for this reading?" Freddy nodded. "Then have a seat also." The woman waited until he had settled himself and then began. "Before I can start, I require a couple of things. First, let me see your palm." She didn't wait for John to offer it but snatched at it from across the table.

"Hey, isn't it supposed to be my writing hand?" John was startled, sounding nervous for the first time that evening.

"No." She said abruptly but then relented. "Your writing hand is a symbol of your character, your capability. It doesn't represent what you will do with your life. That fortune is traced in your subservient hand."

She pulled him towards the table, rotating his left hand as she did so, revealing the pattern of his palm. She stared at it in puzzlement for a while. John accompanied her in this study, while Freddy chose to view her face. He wanted to see her reactions, because if she was genuine, then she would have no choice but to view the evil within him. Her expression remained void of emotion as she caressed John's skin. She followed each line with interest, pausing at each junction to determine where the real line extended. Three minutes passed and John started to get frustrated.

"So, when are you going to tell me my destiny?" His grin displayed more anxiety than ego now.

"In a moment. First I need a strand of hair." Before John could protest, she had already snatched at his scalp, plucking one out and placing it into the pot of steaming liquid.

"Hey, what do you think you are doing?" John objected. "What do you want next? Blood?"

"Yes."

"No way, lady!" John began to stand up.

"That'll be five dollars, please." She reached out a hand.

"I don't think so. You've done nothing."

"You said you wanted your fortune revealed to you and I have spent the last few minutes building up to that cause. Whether or not you wish to hear it is irrelevant. I have completed fifty percent of my contract and require fifty percent of the pay." The tent went silent for a moment, until Freddy disturbed it.

"You might as well finish it off." He was enjoying the look of discomfort on his friend's face. "You'd be giving your money away if not. And besides, I'm sure you're not chicken." He attacked the pride he knew welled within John's chest.

"Shall we continue, then?" The lady gestured for John to sit back down. He did, stretching his hand across the table at the same time.

The gypsy withdrew a two-inch long pin from the bosom of her dress and placed it into the burning coals of her makeshift fondue. Turning it back and forth she watched the metal end turn white, then, pulling it out, stuck it directly into the flesh of John's palm. He jumped in his seat but remained silent. A globule of blood slowly swelled from the rupture and the fortune teller rolled the tip of the needle in it, coating all sides before pulling away and mixing it into the pot of liquid.

That was when events began to get really strange. The liquid in the pot gradually began to change from clear to tinted green, through to a deep green. During this transformation the surface bubbled vigorously, steam rising and becoming thick as smoke, colouring the air all the way up to the canopy. Next the lady cloaked her face with both her hands, then, drawing them down across her features, she closed her eyes and placed her hands over the crystal ball. The globe itself now mystically filled with smoke. At first Freddy thought it was a trick of the light, projecting the liquid's effervescence through into the orb, but as he shifted his head the orb failed to display other images from around the room. The smoke inside began to swirl and open up. John's trepidation was now clearly evident from the panicked grin on his face and his twitching eyes.

"I am looking at your past. You had a loving upbringing in the arms of people who bore no relation to you." The striking accuracy of her first statement startled both of them. John more so. "They have raised you as their own and you have come to look on them with similar eyes. You were a happy child and have always had more ups than downs."

She moved closer to the table and peered deeper into the glass sphere, as it clouded over again. Her eyes strained to find an image. As she profiled the surface of the glass with her hands, the smoke displaced itself once more. Her face dropped. Concentration replaced by confusion. Words endeavoured to establish themselves on her lips.

"I see a struggle. You are fighting with someone and getting hurt, but in the end you win." She still looked perplexed. "I've never done a fortune like this before. I don't understand what I am seeing. While the shadows tell me you were triumphant, the overriding sentiment I receive is that you lost something more precious. Wait..."

She caressed the sphere again, her face plummeting from confusion into fear. Placing her hand down the front of her blouse, she retrieved a leather necklace with a golden talisman suspended from it. As she held it tight, her expression transformed from fearful into anger.

"You have embraced an evil spirit that will bring you nothing but harm. I can foretell no more. Your future no longer resides in the hands of fate but in those of someone else. Go!"

She stood up and pointed to the entrance. John's expression was caught between fear and hatred. Freddy knew she had hit close to the mark and felt triumphant that his previous suspicions had been confirmed, but once the happiness of being right had subsided, his dread resurfaced. He was safe for the moment, because John's attention was focussed on the fortune teller, but that would change soon, and he would remember all that had been said before. What would he do then? John's eyes were so glazed with hatred that Freddy knew he would have to strike vengeance at somebody to feel appeased of the accusations. In this instance, the most accessible people were the likely candidates, which left Freddy most immediate on the list. That being true, there was no way he could defeat John. If he could have, he would have tried already. The future didn't bode well.

15 years later...

10

Breathing deeply, he smelled the dank and stale basement air. Its years of neglect profiled in the decaying bricks and cobwebs. The natural lighting was poor. A single shallow window positioned high up on one of the walls peered out across the lawn, allowing little sunlight through. A chill seeped through the bricks and mortar from the surrounding earth, nipping at his skin. It had been so long since John had unlocked the door and descended the stairs for his weekly ritual. A thick veneer of settled dust laying testament to the two years' disrespect. His slippers dragged across the floor, leaving his passage clearly visible on the concrete.

Against the far wall stood a knee-high coffee table, simple in design and manufactured from pine. An array of candles were scattered across its top. Some sat in home-made candleholders, some in silver or pewter candleholders and candelabra, while the fatter ones stood on their own. All had been lit in the past, burning away a good proportion of their useful life and leaving the wax to drip down and fuse the candle or its holder to the table. There was no real sequence to their layout, except for four tall black unspent candles mounted in silver holders, one precisely positioned at each corner of the tabletop that served a distinct purpose.

Above the table, obscure symbolism covered a small area of the wall; lettering from a forgotten dialect developed by a sect long since dissolved for their blasphemous beliefs. The words were a sign of calling for 'the one who walks in darkness'. Historically this description had been commonly assumed to identify the Devil or the Prince of Darkness, when actually it referred to Shalek. The lettering was scribed in white paint and was now partially faded. He still knew its meaning, though, and that was all that mattered. To the left-hand side of the graffiti a small shelf supported books of demonology and Wicca, centrally amongst them pride of place was reserved for the three volumes of 'The Book of Fallen Angels'. All the books were well thumbed, the paper edges grimy from flicking fingers. Book markers separated pages at numerous locations and the bindings were worn through to the stitching and glue.

The torchlight flicked over the ground directly in front of the makeshift altar, revealing a magic circle painted in red on the floor. It was approximately two metres in diameter and contained a small square praying mat. At each of the five points of the pentagram stood a black candle, glued to the floor by wax left behind by its predecessor. At the head of the star, just underneath the table, a glass jar of rock salt waited to offer protection. Its purpose was to provide additional barriers between the mortal and immortal participants of any ritual.

Reminiscing wasn't his reason for being down here today. Nor was his intent to practise what seemed an art from his childhood, though it hadn't been that long ago. Turning around, he focussed the beam of light onto a pile of cardboard boxes stacked underneath the stairs. They were the only other objects he had allowed down here, containing forsaken artefacts from their wedding day. It was from these that Gloria had suddenly decided she wanted a vase. Apart from the annoying obscureness of her request, it was the fact she had asked at the most inopportune time, as he was about to leave for the office. He could have cast a spell on her if he'd wanted to, but he found it just as easy to pander to her whims as to eradicate them. Besides, he felt uncomfortable using the gift when he no longer worshipped its master.

Pulling out one of the boxes stacked at the top, he reached through the space it left and lifted out another box sat hidden to the rear. Opening the flaps, he revealed the desired present, undisturbed by time. A gift tag still remained taped to the side and his inquisitive nature couldn't help but look. 'From Kevin and Ian' was all it read. Not a particularly sentimental verse, but at least they had bought something. At the time of his marriage, they were barely still friends, his relationship with Gloria having distanced them. They spent some time together but nothing like the hysterics they had before his 'calling'. Everything had changed after that. His life had been spun around in any direction he chose and all he had to do was follow the flow. Information had come easy to him, swelling his mind. His school grades rocketed, and geeks asked for his help, which he naturally refused. With all this success came isolation from the masses and that was something he didn't enjoy but couldn't change. Kids feared him. Friends had trod cautiously around him in constant suspicion. Freddy had been the root of all speculation and John had tried in vain to curb his preaching, but no spellbinding had worked on him. After some investigation he unearthed the reason behind his friend's invulnerability, a talisman that had hung around his neck as a symbol of righteousness. John had spent two whole days in the library reading after his discovery, endeavouring to find a way of stripping the protection away, but there wasn't any. No magic would work, and evil could not physically touch it, without the attempt leaving scars. So, John had just suffered the isolation. What was friendship anyway, when you had the power to make a dream of your own destiny. True friends were just a lucky benefit in life. Besides, through his relationship with Gloria, he had inherited half a dozen bogus mates, who, while they offered no real conversation, sufficiently filled the physical void.

He and Gloria had become engaged at the graduation ceremony when they left Shifton High. Through modest supernatural input, they attended the same college. John had studied Law and Gloria American History. Not surprisingly, both had graduated. John was offered a position at his first interview with a legal outfit in New York. He had accepted, of course, on the proviso of a suitable five-figure salary, agreeing to start work in the fall after his wedding. Gloria hadn't been offered a job straight away, but once they had settled down on Staten Island, she had found a good teaching post at a local High School. It had been a long time since John had thought about any of this. His life had been too consumed by work and deceit to find time for reflection. Diluting the memories further, in his well-developed arrogance he had never paused to look back when there had been so much in the future to be conquered. Taking a stagnant breath, he picked up the tagged box and returned upstairs.

"Did you find it?" Gloria's voice came timidly from the kitchen.

"Yup." He shut the cellar door, locking it and placing the key in his pocket.

They lived in a pretty spacious five-bedroomed detached house on a quiet suburban street in Georgetown. It was a neighbourhood of sweeping curved roadways with well-spaced houses on either side. Theirs was one of the biggest properties on the estate and people often asked why they needed such a big house, seeing as children had never featured in their program. John would always claim that he was a moderate claustrophobic. However, the truth was more painful, in that they found it difficult to have children, John's poor fertility being the cause. Gloria had always wanted children but had kept it to herself. As a result, their torturous endeavours had only provided more disappointment. They had been trying in total for two years and were very close to visiting a fertilisation clinic when it happened. First her period stopped, then she tested positive and now she was well into her third trimester. It had been a strange time for John. Initially, he had been uncomfortable with the idea of children, the responsibility, the devotion, the ties. But then, as their persistence continued to be fruitless, his apathy towards offspring was superseded by the frustration of not being able to produce the goods. That had probably been the turning point for him. The cause of his desertion from heretical religion. The world had been promised to him. Yet with all that power, the act of procreation eluded him. Still, in the end it had arrived, which in itself was ironic, to John anyway, because the ability to give life was a foundation stone of Christianity. And that was a peace of mind he hadn't entertained for more than a decade.

For a while after conception, he had harboured doubts about his straying from the fold. Maybe God was a forgiving and caring person after all. Maybe he never really turned his back when John was younger but was waiting to display his power at a more poignant moment. However, those thoughts had quickly evaporated, being rapidly dispelled by the fact of his ever-perfect existence and success. But even through all that self-justification, he still remained faithless. Religion was a tired topic which could promise him little more than he already had and desired.

"I said did you find it?"

Gloria stuck her head around the kitchen door, her belly taking a peek also. Her eyes still sparkled like a child's, and through them he could still see that same popular little girl. However, the strong passion they had fired inside of him and had been the purpose of his existence for years, failed to rage so fervently now.

"Yes!" he snapped back. "Here. I'm off."

"What about breakfast?"

"I'll pick something up on the way to the office." He grabbed his briefcase and pecked her on the lips.

"But I made you pancakes."

"Well, I didn't ask for them, so throw them in the bin." He left her standing in the hall holding the vase.

Their marriage hadn't been smooth running for a while and that was one of the reasons she had wanted to have a child. She thought it would bring them closer together. There were times she believed her pregnancy had salvaged fragments of their former love, but they were sparse. She knew he would never leave, because she was the perfect display wife: pretty, intelligent and a good hostess. But she wanted more than a partnership based on financial stability. She re-entered the kitchen and did as John had instructed.

Outside it was a typical cold November morning. The moon was setting low on the horizon, while the sun rose in the east, its flaming crescent just starting to set the city alight. Their house stood proud at the crest of a hill, the street swooping down on one side, all the way to the coast, which was no more than a kilometre away. It was the only stretch of straight road longer than two hundred metres in the whole town. At its end, the choppy waters of the Hudson and East rivers merged to form the bay that stretched right across to Manhattan Island, crashing at the feet of Battery Park and the World Trade Centres. To the left of the towers, the red bricks of Ellis Island radiated in the morning sun, the steel water tank that stood atop the immigrants' processing hall winking across the bay.

John got into his car, a five series BMW, put on his San Diego Padres baseball cap and reversed out of the drive. He only had to travel the straight kilometre down to the dock, from where he would catch the ferry across to the city, but he was too lazy to walk it. His entire journey took him on average seventy minutes, comprising the two-minute drive and park at the dock, a thirty-minute ferry ride and a twenty-minute ride on the subway. The residual time was spent waiting and queuing for the various forms of public transport.

John enjoyed the journey, particularly when there was a strong swell on the sea, because then he would see the fear of his fellow passengers. He liked being spectator to their anguish, taking pleasure in their ever-paling features and stifled faces as they tried to retain their breakfast. It was amazing to John how so many seasick individuals could reside near New York. However, this morning the show was dull, a moderate yaw of the ferry being all that nature could stir. Kids ran around the deck playing cops and robbers, while mothers desperately attempted to keep them under control. Beyond the school traffic, there was the usual contingent of pinstripe-suit-clad Wall Street hustlers or would-be beggars, dependent on their aptitude for sin. These men and women scanned the financial pages looking for the traces of quick money. They would forgo big money stakes by gambling with other people's cash to test markets and follow-on smaller margin investments once their speculation bore fruit.

Next, the plain-suited individuals represented the cream of the crop indoctrinated into John's profession over the past three decades. In their laps they clung to briefcases, with a variety of papers then being perused on top. They all longed for that one high-profile case to land in their lap and grant them opportunity for advancement to partner. The rest of the vessel was packed with anarchistic cleaners grumbling about society's debt to them, vain shop assistants dolled to the eyeballs in make-up and drenched in perfume, and a myriad of other office workers – secretaries, accountants and errand boys – all oblivious to the ills of the world around them, content in their small sphere of activity. In fact, as John studied the faces, he decided, save for the children and some mothers. The boat was a perfect conglomerate of mortal sin.

Once off the other side he tracked toward the subway. Here a new breed of traveller joined the group. The bums, the drunks, the homeless, all searching to steal or scam unsuspecting tourists out of money. Their clothes were bedraggled, creased, holed and stained with a montage of food colourings, with odours to match their dirty faces. With these on board, the troop was complete. The train could take a direct route to hell now, with no stops required. John's type of crowd.

His stop was ten stations down the line at the junction of 5th Avenue and 32nd Street. It was an odd place for a legal office to be situated, in a predominantly consumer-orientated region of the city. But the building was amongst the oldest within the city limits, adding character and comfort to the working environment. It was only a five-storey building and John's firm were big enough to occupy the top three floors, ground level being taken up by shops and the second level for stock. The large stone brickwork, weathered by the elements, had a dark green hue to its facade. First-floor windows were formed in large semi-circles and provided a stunning feature for any passer-by. They would have also made a fantastic viewing facility as a reception area for offices, but the shops below refused to sell at anywhere near market value. The windows of Wilson, Schmect and Drummon weren't as salubrious, but they still offered superb views up and down 5th Avenue, as well as some of the city library sited across the street, the profile of its huge lion statues and grand entrance steps being in clear sight. The location of the library also provided convenient access for researching periodicals, the library holding the second largest set of legal archives within city limits. With this resource also came the peace, quiet and harmonious isolation required for submerging successfully into a deep train of undisturbed thought, which was all too frequently necessary to establish a suitably deceptive, for want of a better word, defence. This solitude was vital when working on cases where legal precedent failed to provide concrete retort for the facts of the prosecution. At those times, talent was required for twisting the relationship between all the items of evidence and legal statutes, with the sole intent of fabricating evidence in the minds of the jury. For this purpose, John was renowned within the state's profession. His remarkable success hadn't gone unnoticed at the firm, either. They had made him a partner back in September. A role he now relished.

The entrance to the office was a four-metre-wide corridor, situated between a bakery and a designer dress shop. The partners' names were engraved on gold plaques to the left of the front door, although they had yet to be altered to include Garret. Inside the corridor a security guard manned a reception desk, at which all entrants, including staff, were required to register. John tipped his head to the guard, signed the book and walked on. The corridor was lined in grey marble over the floors and walls, with grey plastic panelling substituting across the ten-foot-high ceiling for safety reasons. The access stretched for ten metres, deep into the heart of the building block, at the end of which two stainless steel elevator doors waited to consume all who entered. The lift always returned to the ground floor when it was inactive, so the doors opened simultaneously as John pressed the button. After a thirty-second ride to the second floor, the doors opened out into a relatively expansive reception area enclosed in diffused glass panelling, allowing light from the main office windows to shine through and reflect off the pastel colour scheme. The general layout meant that the four partners, the company treasurer and company secretary had external facing offices, which, once the door was closed, offered the required privacy for delicate client-to-lawyer meetings. Four of these offices were on the floor above, along with the company's own archive facility and periodicals library. Even though the two offices on the second floor held prime positions for view, they still left five large windows along the 32nd Street side to stream light through into the main open-plan space.

There was also a spare office that had always been kept empty. It sat to the back of the second floor facing on to 32nd Street, at the farthest point away from 5th Avenue. This had once been home to one of the founder members, who had gone through a nervous breakdown in the early sixties when he failed to prove an eighteen-year-old boy innocent of murder because he overlooked a vital piece of evidence. The boy had been sentenced to death and the execution carried out before he had realised what had happened. Apparently after that his health deteriorated rapidly. He worked non-stop, studying every case's evidence again and again. It had only been a matter of time before the mental crash arrived and when it had, no counselling could have retrieved the situation. At least that was the story that circulated the office whenever any new staff asked. Nobody knew the lawyer's name, because it had long since been expunged from the company title. And neither Wilson nor Drummon, the only two employees who were in the company at that time, would talk about it.

The firm employed twelve people beyond what you might call the key personnel, comprising five secretaries, two accountants, three researchers, one private investigator and a rookie lawyer who as yet hadn't been given an office and spent most of his time in either the company's or the city's library facilities. One of the secretaries out of the five was John's, Neve Locker. She was three years his junior and an exceptionally attractive lady. Her long dark brown hair generally hung loose and reached far down her back. It would be swept away from her face by a flexible comb, leaving her features fully exposed. Her face was thin but not such that it looked frail or gaunt. Her skin was youthfully pure and unblemished, with big deep hazel-coloured eyes that brimmed with hopeful naivety.

Her figure was a slender thirty-two B, converging into a twenty-six, blooming out into a thirty-four, and all of this was stretched over a five-foot-six-inch canvas. The proportioning of torso to legs was slightly askew, her thirty-six-inch legs taking a majority stake. Today she was dressed in a perfectly tailored purple suit with a tight knee-length skirt and waist-length cut jacket buttoned up to the joining curvature of her breasts, which were delicately connected by a silk camisole that was just visible.

John walked towards his office, ignoring everybody, as was his usual manner these days. Neve stood up to pass him a mug of coffee. He took it on the move, glancing his hand over her soft skin before latching on to the mug. She smiled anxiously. Entering his office, he shut the door behind him and placed his hat and coat on a stand behind the door. The room was spacious; being a corner cubical, it had windows on two sides, which added a vast amount of warmth to the environment. The windows had vertical pine-wood-slated blinds, which were drawn across but angled open. The carpet was an extension of the light turquoise pile that ran through the main office. He had been given the option to change it but found it oddly soothing. The walls were painted an almond cream, which reflected the invading sun's warmth. Two pine bookcases sat against the left-hand wall, while on the right-hand side a genuine Picasso was exhibited in pride of place, a small viewing light screwed to the wall above it. His desk and filing cabinets matched the bookcases and were cluttered with documents, a single clear spot residing squarely in the middle, in front of his chair. Two comfy visitor seats faced the desk, with two more placed against the walls just in case.

"Can I see you for a moment, sir?" It was Neve on the intercom.

He depressed the button and responded, "yeah, sure," then waited for her entrance. She opened the door looking less cheerful. The door shut behind her with a resounding *click*.

"So where were you last night?" She stood just inside the room, her hands fidgeting. "I waited for an hour and you never showed. Is it over?"

He tried to speak, but she interrupted.

"Have you had your fun and now it's over? Is that it?"

"No, that's not it. I got tied up, that's all. I do have work to do!"

"Oh, and the work prevents the use of your hands and mouth so much that you're unable to call?" She was clearly very distressed, crossing over the room to sit down in front of him. "Be honest with me. Do you love me?"

"Yes, of course I do." he lied.

"Well then, why don't you leave your wife to be with me?"

"It's not that easy."

"You've been saying that for the past year and a half." Tears began to breach her eyes. "I'm not getting any younger. I want to be with you, but if that's not going to happen..." Sniffle. "Then I don't want what we have anymore." She endeavoured to sound resolved but failed. John moved around towards her. Sitting on the edge of the desk, he took her hand in his and stroked it softly.

"You know I want to be with you. It's just Gloria's very vulnerable right now and as much as I want to tell her and get it out in the open, I don't want to kick her while she's down." He proliferated his lie.

She raised her spare hand up and placed it on his. "But where does that leave me?"

"Very much in my heart." She smiled and he rubbed his fingers over her cheeks, clearing the tears away. "I'm sorry I didn't call last night, but I just got so bogged down here that I lost track of time."

"Your dinner was ruined."

"I'm sorry."

"I love you so much." She stood up, creeping between his thighs. "I want to be close to you. Feel you." He leant forward to kiss her, but she pulled back, placing a hand over his mouth. "Did you know it's been a month since we last made love?"

"How can I forget. It was the first time I've ever had sex in my office. Brings a flush to my face every time I sit down to work."

He pinched her butt. "I visualise this cute sexy behind of yours, pressing its naked flesh down on to the wooden top. Skirt rolled up around your waist, knickers hanging from the end of one of your long stocking-clad legs." He moved his hand and unzipped the back of her skirt, then, sliding it inside, began to massage her bottom.

"Hey, get your hands off that." She pulled his hand out and closed the zip. "You want some of that, then you'd better call."

"What, I get nothing now?"

"You don't deserve it." She started to push herself away, but he grabbed her back, pressing his lips up to hers. For a moment she reciprocated his affection but then resumed her struggle to break free. He wouldn't let go.

"Stop it!" she said.

"Why should I?"

"Because anybody could walk in."

"So, let them. That would get it all out in the open."

"Well, that might work to ease your conscience, but I want to be treated with a little higher regard than a mistress, thank you." She pushed harder against his chest and broke free, then straightened her clothes.

"What about later?" John had a desire to be satisfied now.

"Maybe? We'll have to see how you behave today."

"What if I don't want to wait to find out?"

He wrestled her towards him once more. Her blouse fell out of her skirt, becoming visible from the bottom of her jacket. At that moment a knock came on the door and without even a moderate pause for acknowledgement, it opened, revealing Drummon and another man.

"Look, we'll finish discussing that later, if you could just finish that memo off for me," John flew off the cuff, giving Neve opportunity to exit the room before the new arrivals started to scrutinise and speculate over the situation. As Neve pushed through the door, Drummon gave her minimal clearance, doing his best to brush up against her midriff. The stranger was more of a gentleman, stepping clear to one side and conducting her past. Neve blushed and smiled at him.

Drummon entered in full, giving John a wry smile and a wink. John pretended to be confused by his colleague's gesture and Drummon quickly rearranged his expression. John's superior was fifty-five and had been with the firm since its inception thirty years ago, though he hadn't been a partner at that point. He had been taken on via a connection between his father and the mysterious insane founder member. His years within the profession were clearly evident across his chubby wrinkled cheeks and forehead, which although they established his age, also established his warmth of character. He was three stone overweight for a five-foot-ten man of his years, but he camouflaged it well underneath baggy shirts. The sexual flirtatiousness he had directed toward Neve, had been the stumbling block of four previous marriages, leaving him currently unmarried but with a partner.

The second man entered now, after giving a rather long stare towards the back of Neve. He was a man of similar age to John, possibly a year younger, which also granted him thicker hair. His eyes were piercing yet kind, softened further by his palatably cheerful smile, which exposed the fluoride whiteness of his immaculate teeth. These key features were established within a long, thin head, over-emphasised by a stature shorter than the national average. He walked over to John, stretching out his hand in front.

"This is Foster Logan." Drummon made the introduction. "And this is our most aspiring creation, John Garret." He then had the cheek to infer self-credit for John's capabilities.

"You didn't have to tell me that. You've been going on about a young protégée of yours all morning and this gentleman is the only one with an office who isn't knocking on retirement's door." He turned back towards Garret. "It's a pleasure to eventually meet you."

"Likewise." John was cautious in response, but he couldn't help himself from feeling an immediate affiliation towards Logan and his pleasant disposition.

"Foster here has just joined us from Smith, Hammond and

Sharp. Like yourself he represents the future potential of this law firm." Drummon took charge once more. "If you could set him up in the spare office and show him where everything is." The words drifted in the form of a command more than a request, but John didn't bite, intrigued by his new colleague. "I'll catch up with you two later." With that he departed.

"Smith, Hammond and Sharp, hey? Big firm. Why d'you leave?"

"Hard to make an impression when you swim with so many fish. Easier to do it in a fishbowl."

"I wouldn't let Drummon or any of the others hear you talk like that. They're a pretty proud bunch when it comes to the firm."

"They have every right to be. It's a good firm. On which note, may I congratulate you on your recent promotion. You must be one of the youngest partners in the history of the profession?"

"Nearly. Alexander Bartholomew Jones beat me. He was made a partner of Cedric and Collins in nineteen sixty-three, at the age of twenty-six. But hey, being second youngest isn't bad." He turned to pick up his coffee mug. "So, you had many big cases?"

"Just short of double figures. I did the background and pulled the cases together on all of them but only got to defend two."

"That must suck!" He took a sip. "Do you want a drink?"

"Yes, that'd be great." John depressed the intercom button.

"Neve, could you stick your head in for a minute?" She opened the door a couple of seconds later. "Neve, this is Foster Logan, our newest member of the team."

"Pleased to meet you." She spoke timidly.

"A pleasure to meet you." He took her hand and kissed it gently. She looked stunned and John felt a little put out.

"Yes, well, now that's over with, could you get the cleaner to unlock the office that time forgot and give it a once over." Neve registered understanding immediately, although Foster looked a little confused. "And my colleague here could do with a small refreshment. Coffee?"

"That's fine." He half turned to answer John, keeping a

wandering eye on Neve. She stared back.

"That's all, thank you, Neve." They both watched her leave.

"Very attractive girl. You two been seeing each other long?"

"Hell, no. She's just my secretary. Whatever gave you that idea?" John returned to his chair, forcing a smile. Foster followed, settling in one of the visitor's seats.

"I'm sorry, my fault. It's just when we came in it looked as though you two were..." He stopped himself from going any further. "I'll leave it there. I can feel the earth opening up to swallow me whole."

"She was upset about an argument with her boyfriend last night. I was consoling her."

"Dangerous game to play, that."

"What?" John said defensively, feeling uncomfortable with the continued inference.

"Becoming emotionally supportive to a colleague. Particularly one of the opposite sex. Takes a lot of restraint not to abuse that trust."

"I can handle it, thanks." He did his best to dismiss Logan's concerns.

"I'm just suggesting you take it steady there." John was about to speak, but Logan continued. "Look, I'm new to this office, but even I could see the way she looked at you. If you're not entwined already, it's definitely on her agenda." Neve knocked and entered, set the coffee down in front of Logan, then left.

"I take your forewarning, but I don't share your concerns." The moment's interruption had allowed John a chance to calm his anger. "So, how did you get the job, then? I knew nothing of any advertisements." He changed the subject, taking the offensive.

"It wasn't advertised. My father got introduced to Drummon through a business acquaintance, got to talking about the legal profession. I was mentioned as a young enthusiast like yourself. Drummon said they may be looking for someone and that I should come in for an interview."

"I would have expected them to show you around, then."

"They did."

"So why didn't I see you?"

"You have. It's today."

"They offered you a job on the day of your interview?" John was amazed and disgusted but tried to hide his emotion.

"Incredible, isn't it?" Logan's smile transformed into a grin now. One which lacked the same friendly charisma, exchanging it for something more sinister.

"Just a little." John was frustrated by the ease with which his new colleague had evidently walked into the business, but that wasn't his issue. He had discovered his success just as easily, probably more easily. He moved on. "So, you married?"

"No. Young, horny and ready for anything. What about yourself?"

"Married four years."

"Kids?"

"First on its way."

"Fantastic. You must be over the moon."

"A little. Probably as much terrified as I am happy," he lied in an attempt to lighten the conversation.

"You'll be fine." Silence ensued. Both men seemed comfortable with the break in chatter, neither diving to fill the void. Their talk had to progress some time, though, so John took the plunge.

"What's your history, then? Before your legal days."

"A bit of this and that. Usual childhood trauma, I then discovered religion. That was when I knew what my profession should be. You could say my Lord guided me on that score." Logan paused, as if waiting for comment, then moved on. "Surprised the hell out of the teachers."

"I hope you're more descriptive in court. You know you've got to say enough to allow the jury to make a decision."

"Don't worry about me on that score." He remained succinct.

"Well, I don't want to be rude, but that's all the hospitality I can accommodate for now. Work calls. If you ask Neve, she'll be more than happy to show you around the facilities." He didn't bother standing to show Logan out, just began looking over the case files that littered his desk.

"Well, thanks for your time. Let's go out for a drink sometime. Get to know each other a little more," Logan persisted.

"Yeah, just give us a call."

"Or you can call me. Here's my number." He scribbled on the back of an old business card and placed it down on top of the file John had settled on.

"Will do." Feeling a little embarrassed now by Logan's cool attitude, he picked the card up, studied it and placed it into his wallet. As his colleague approached the door, John called out. "What about tomorrow night after work? That at least gives me the opportunity to tell my wife not to bother with supper."

"That'd be great." He opened the office door. "As long as you are certain she's gonna be alright suffering her pregnancy alone for one night, cause I'd be looking for a bit of a boys' night on the town."

As Logan's words evolved, John could see where they were leading. His eyes dropped down to view Neve, who was within earshot. He hadn't told her about the pregnancy as yet, because he knew it would be the death of their relationship. Neve would know there was no chance of him leaving his wife while she was carrying their child. It was also a near certainty that he wouldn't leave afterwards either, not least because of the ensuing financial support. Neve's head dropped and he knew the game was over. He didn't respond to Logan before the door shut, being in a state of shock as to how he could possibly repair the damage so swiftly distributed. He had no idea where to begin, if indeed anywhere. Waiting in contemplation, he listened for those delicate steps to approach, the door to open and the flying rage to erupt. When she eventually arrived, his worst fears were far from accurate. She knocked and entered composed but struggling to fight back the tears. Saying nothing, she sat down. He pre-empted her.

"I'm sorry. I've been meaning to tell you."

"So why hadn't you?"

"I didn't know what to say. I don't want to lose you."

"How long have you known?" she asked.

"Eight months," he mumbled.

"And you couldn't bring yourself to tell me about it." Her anger started to reveal itself. "When were you going to let me know, when it was born? Or maybe on its fifth birthday?"

"I'm sorry." He got up.

"Stay away from me." She did the same and backed toward the door.

"I'm still leaving her."

"No, you're not, don't lie. You're always lying. It's just endless bullshit." Her voice reached a crescendo and he knew the main office would be able to hear them now.

"I'm not, I promise." He reached out to grab her.

"I said don't touch me. I can't stand the thought of your skin against mine."

"Come on, don't be like that."

"Don't be like what?" Her voice raised in disgust. "You treat me like crap and I just sit back and take it. I've been blind for so long, but thanks to a stranger, a true gentleman, I know the truth."

"Neve, please!" He was desperate, stretching out for her once more.

"Get off me!" She opened the door. "Just leave me alone." Everybody stared. The door slammed shut.

11

A couple of days passed before Neve began talking to John again and when she did, it was like they had never had a relationship beyond the professional. Speculation was obviously rife throughout the office. Rumours of lovers' tiffs, illicit children and abortions caused contemptible stares to fly at him from every angle. Neve fared well out of the entire experience. Females had automatically sided with her, while the men maintained a diplomatic vow of silence, leaving their vote open to female interpretation. John weathered the festering storm as best he could, but it was beginning to take its toll. He found it difficult to maintain a train of thought, which on one occasion had left him blushing with embarrassment after spewing his defence tactics for a murder case to a client in for drug pushing. The embarrassment came not so much during the misjudged incident itself but from the subsequent request made for a different lawyer. What made the situation worse, was that the case had been reassigned to Logan, who he was still trying to tolerate after his seemingly unintentional disclosure the other day. As a consequence of that event, John had cancelled their 'getting to know you' evening session but had agreed to reschedule it for tonight. This morning he had contemplated rescheduling once again, but with the current office atmosphere had decided he needed as many friends as he could muster. There was a knock on the door.

"Come in." He raised his voice moderately. It was Neve. She entered looking tired and frustrated.

"We need to talk. Is now a good time?"

John nodded and she closed the door behind her. Waiting patiently, he gave her time to settle and begin. She said nothing.

"What do you want to discuss?" He encouraged, attempting an affectionate tone.

"Us."

"I didn't realise there was an us anymore?"

"Well, that depends."

"On what?"

"On whether you actually care for me at all?" She raised her eyes to meet his.

"You know I do. But you also know my predicament. I'm about to become a father."

"Yes. And now that I have had time to think, I understand why you don't want to leave her at the moment." She paused to swallow. "What I need to know is if you would ever leave her at all, for me?"

"Neve, I love you. I would do anything for you." He began to move closer to her.

"No. Just stay there for now." She signalled for him to sit back down.

"I tried to figure out a way of telling you about Gloria. But in the same way that I can't bring myself to tell her it's over, I couldn't tell you about the baby, either."

"That's well and good. But I'm beyond that now."

"So where do we go from here?" John was finding it difficult to contain his enthusiasm. He never conceived that the opportunity to be with Neve would rise again.

"Well, you still haven't told me whether you would leave her to be with me?"

"Yes, I would." he lied.

She smiled, believing herself to be in control of the situation.

"So, show me how much I mean to you." Her smile turned wicked. "And come around after work."

John's face dropped.

"I can't. I'm going out with Logan."

"So, cancel!"

"I just confirmed it with him this morning. It's like a 'getting to know you' session."

"And that's more important than me?" Her temper was fraying fast.

"No, but he's told Drummon that we're going out and there'll be hell if I cancel."

She stood up, her chair toppling behind her.

"You know, I don't know why I bothered coming in here." She started to cry, but her face was still angered. "I open myself up to it every time." She moved towards the door. "If you don't mind, I'm taking the rest of the day off."

She didn't wait for an answer. She left, leaving the door wide open. He watched her grab her coat and walk straight across the office to the lifts. Gradually, silence possessed the office, eyes watching the spectacle in amazement. Time seemed to stop; taking an eternity for the elevator door to close behind her and end the performance. At that moment all eyes turned on him. To close the door immediately would have been a poor move, so he remained exposed, looking bewildered for about half a minute. Ironically, at that point he was saved by the individual who had caused him this strife in the first place.

"Looks like you're having a bad secretary day. What did you do? Wear the wrong aftershave?" Logan quipped as he walked in and pulled the door to. "Are you this much fun to watch in court?" he jibed.

"I just don't know what's going on this week."

"Looks to me like you could use a few drinks, a little table dancing, maybe even a little something extra for further relief." Logan tilted his head forward and smirked. "What do you say? Shall we blow this joint?"

John took a moment's contemplation before speaking. "Why not?" He picked up his jacket. "Lead on."

"Okay. You trust me?"

John nodded.

"You'll follow wherever I go?"

"Yes."

"Excellent!" Logan was acting almost like a teenager. As they entered the main office, it remained surprisingly active, nobody paying much attention to the two of them. "Your secretary's left her handbag." Logan pointed to a black Chanel bag sat at the foot of Neve's chair.

"Leave it. It'll still be there in the morning."

"Okay, if you say so. We may catch up with her outside, though, and she could be grateful."

"I think today she and I have past well beyond the stage of gratefulness."

They walked on.

Logan's first port of call was a baseball bar called The Babe two blocks away eastbound on 32nd Street. There they had a couple of beers and talked. Most of the conversation was orientated around John's past, but he allowed Logan to dominate the direction, finding it soothing to his tense state. Together they relived John's history from when he left Shifton High School through to when Logan entered his office with Drummon three days earlier. It was around eight o'clock that the topic of Neve Locker surfaced, by which time John was heavily lubricated.

"Okay, now what's the story between you and the cutest woman in the office?" Logan slurred his words.

"Hey, you keep your hands off her. She's mine." John asserted.

"That's not what it looked like to me earlier." Logan shook his head in uncertainty. "Looked to me like there's nothing left to preserve."

"No, she just needs some time to cool off."

"What about your wife?"

"Blissfully unaware!"

"Doesn't she ever get suspicious?"

"That's the best thing about a well-paying job. You can afford to buy two sets of identical clothing. One for one house and one for the other," he exaggerated. He had only been to Neve's flat four times and he certainly didn't have a wardrobe there, though he did keep a spare set of fresh clothes at the office, just in case his became tainted with lipstick or perfume.

"You crafty beggar." Logan sounded almost admiring of his new acquaintances position. "So, what's the deal for the future? You gonna leave your wife?"

"Hell no. I love Gloria."

"So, what the hell are you doing with a mistress?"

"Having fun." John smirked.

"Just remember what you give out, you get back double." Logan's face turned serious as he uttered the words softly.

"What you say?"

"I said what's fun?"

"That's impossible to discuss unless you've been with Neve."

"Is that an offer?"

"I'm only going to tell you one more time, leave her alone." He clenched his fists on the desk.

"Alright, just kidding." Logan took a swig from his bottle. "Okay, let's get out of here and go somewhere a little more up your street."

"Hey, what do you mean?" John grabbed Logan's arm, the booze making him increasingly physical.

"I mean a venue that is visually invasive." He refused to expand any further but beckoned John to follow. He did.

They walked back towards Broadway, zigzagging up and across alternate streets. Finally, they turned down a side alley off 42nd Street. It was the most obscure part of town to have a club of any kind, but there it was, sat smack across the end of the passage. A subtle neon sign, no bigger than a metre square announced 'Hell's Open' mounted up on the wall. A set of closed double doors beneath it were protected by two big black bouncers, one either side. The lighting was dim, the brickwork black and grimy. A small plaque bolted to one of the side buildings listed the alley as 'Dead End 54'. Two plastic dumpsters were pushed flush against the left-hand wall and John half expected to find a street bum lying behind them, clutching at a brown paper bag filled with bourbon. The alley floor had been recently hosed down and was free from rubbish, the traces of which were exposed in the small puddles of water had formed in the cracks and potholes. As they drew closer, John noticed that two security guys were twins, identical from their weight, stature, appearance and clean-shaven heads, down to their suits and shirts. In fact, the only distinguishable difference were their ties. One was black, the other was grey.

"Evening, sirs." The one on the left spoke, his voice deep and booming. "Nice to see you again, Mr Logan."

"You been here a lot, then?" John asked. Logan didn't answer, just grinned.

"Nice to see you too. Mr Thumper." The silent guard rumbled. "And you as well, Mr Basher."

"Friend of yours?" Thumper asked.

"Yeah, a new work colleague who has a little woman trouble."

"What, he can't get a woman?" Thumper smirked.

"No, he can get them. He's got two. Problem is, one's pregnant and the other talks too much." A smile almost cracked across Basher's face, but he quickly recomposed himself.

"Well, you brought him to the right place for uncomplicated women pleasures." Thumper grinned. "We got every colour and flavour you could ever possibly want. A regular candy store to the sufferers of social celibacy."

Thumper placed an ape-like hand centrally on John's back and ushered him through the door. As it slowly opened in front of him, he saw an onslaught of scantily clad females clinging and clutching at men in suits, who eagerly stuffed five-dollar bills into their knickers. The club wasn't massive, covering an area about fifteen metres square. There was no reception, save for a sultry-looking blonde in an evening gown, who suddenly latched on to John's hand, leading him away from Thumper. Slightly stunned, he followed his escort to a booth on the left-hand side of the room.

"Thanks, Eve." Logan winked and passed her a ten-dollar bill. She walked away and he watched her bum swing underneath the loosely tailored chiffon dress. "I tell you, that is the best piece of ass in the whole fucking world. You know I've offered her up to a hundred and fifty dollars before to get her clothes off for me, but she never accepts. I'm dying to explore her curves. But hey, I guess you can't have you cake and eat it."

"You come here often?" John enquired.

"About once a week. You know when you're without a woman, you need relief from somewhere, and all these girls are clean girls." He smirked again. "Of course, that could be because they cost so fucking much to have." Logan laughed. John didn't. He couldn't. He was too absorbed in the surrounding activity.

A stage sat to his left, which had a catwalk jutting out six metres centrally into the room, three fire-station poles spaced equidistant along its length. Around two of these, a couple of girls in their late teens were dancing in white nylon stockings and frilly underwear. Their bras only served to support the heaving bosoms, without covering them. Pert nipples poked out towards the lusting male onlookers. The front entrance was back to his right and across the far side a glitzy mirror-covered bar. Shimmering reflections of naked flesh shone from every angle. It was serviced by two large looking white males, who presumably doubled as security back-up. They weren't twins. Three waitresses worked the room, continuously streaming drinks in the direction of less than lucid men. All three of them were naturally attractive blondes with moderately sized breasts. The youngest looking of the three had spotted their arrival and started towards them. Her figure was a perfect pepper mill on legs. Wide at the top, long and thin in the middle and wide at its base. She wore a tight white cotton tank top that exposed her pierced belly button. Her legs were stocking clad, the snapper cords extending up underneath a pair of hot pants that left very little room for access. John tried to imagine how he could get his hand up anyway, his hormones in overdrive. In one hand she balanced a tray, while the other swung at her side, allowing her to walk fluidly, swinging her hips gently. John got hotter and hotter. The alcohol pumped through his veins. Logan laughed.

"Hey, don't pop your head just yet." He looked the girl up and down. "She's cute. But she also doesn't have a price. Believe me, I've tried. Hi, Monica."

"Now then, you, no funny stuff, alright?" She talked with a thick Brooklyn accent.

"Would I?" Logan raised his hands in playful surrender. Then, as he brought them back down, he reached out and grabbed her around the waist, pulling her down on to his lap. She squirmed. The two bruisers at the bar launched into defence, one of them mounting the bar. She signalled for them to stand down. "You see, it's times like these that I know you really do care for me and that you just enjoy playing hard to get," Logan said.

"Don't count on it. I just don't want to get blood on my clean clothes." She pulled herself free and stood up. "Now keep your hands off, cowboy, or I'll unleash the dogs on you. And you want to trust me when I say that's messy." She turned to John. "Why can't you be more like your friend here? Watching, politely imagining." Monica turned back to Logan. "It doesn't all have to be force and grubby hands to get what you want." She sat down on John's knee. "What would you like to drink, honey?"

"Now that's unfair!" Logan protested.

"No, this is unfair." Balancing the tray in her lap, she caressed John's cheeks and then, pulling his face close, kissed him on the mouth.

"You're right, that is unfair. What's he got that I haven't?"

"Innocence!"

"Ouch, that hurt."

John was amazed at how smoothly she handled Logan.

"So, what can I do for you, gorgeous?" she asked.

"Well, you can sit there for a little while longer." John rediscovered his tongue. "At least until I get a full-on chubby."

"I think I can accommodate you with that. Would it help if I rubbed my bum up and down against you like this?"

She eased her weight off him and wiggled her arse across his groin. John nodded, a bulge beginning to display itself. Logan sat watching in disbelief. When John's erection appeared to have reached maximum firmness, Monica dropped her hand down underneath her bum and caressed its outline.

"Now that is something to write home about! You sure it's not going to try and throw me off if I sit down?" She winked at him and dropped her weight back on to his lap. "Wow, the way that thing's pointing, it could almost be considered as invasion without permission." Her face turned serious. John's and Logan's expressions followed suit at the litigious inference. "Maybe you should consider getting a licence for it?" She started smiling again. The two guys relaxed.

"Come on, Monica. Tell me the truth. Why you never done that for me?"

"'Cause you beg too much. Now shut up, I'm tending to your colleague. That's what you brought him here for, isn't it?" She raised an eyebrow and he confirmed. "Now we've felt the goods, what can I offer you?" John's grin expanded, but she interrupted him, placing a finger across his lips before he could say a word. "And don't spoil the moment. I meant what can I offer you to drink? If you want anything else, that's a discussion for later."

"What would you recommend?" John played up to her.

"You can have a plain old beer, but I get the feeling you've already seen enough of those. You could have a spritzer or a cocktail, but that would make you look like a couple of bisexuals as soon as I left your lap. So, I'd recommend something long and strong, just like your other half." She wiggled her bum once more.

"Okay, we're in your hands. Bring us a couple of what you have in mind and a partner for my friend." John joked.

"I've told you once: don't push your luck."

With that she stood up and sauntered back to the bar. Both of them watched her every step, transfixed. Her firm calf muscles were taut as her weight was transmitted down through her high heels. As if she sensed they were tracking her moves, she put an extra emphasis into her swing and as she reached the bar, mounted the foot railing, lifting herself up so that she could stretch over and speak to one of the lads.

"So, what do you think so far?" Logan grinned across the booth.

"Not a bad choice of venue." John's words were playfully reserved.

"Yeah, it's not bad at all." Sitting back, he took a look around the room. "So, what time do you have to get home?"

"Not for a little while yet."

"Good, because I've got a small errand I need to run. Shouldn't take more than an hour."

"What, you just gonna leave me here?"

"I don't think you've got any worries about being taken care of." Logan flicked his eyes across the room and stood up. "I'll be one hour, that's it. Be back before you know it." John grumbled, but Logan ignored him and walked on. As he passed Monica returning with the drinks, he stopped to whisper something in her ear. She smiled and he departed.

"So, it's just you and me now, is it? Well, I'm sure we can enjoy ourselves. You know they have bedrooms upstairs?"

12

After leaving the club, Logan had taken a taxi back to the office. It was getting close to nine o'clock and at nine thirty, the guard would do a sweep of the offices, check the register and, subject to the coast being clear, lock up and go home. Logan caught him just as he was getting into the elevator.

"Hey, wait up!" He raised an assertive hand.

"Not working late are you, Sir?"

"No, just picking up something from my office. I can play catch-up overnight that way." Logan could see the guard had smelt alcohol on his breath.

"I see, Sir."

Logan didn't attempt further conversation. He waited for his floor and exited. The guard had gone straight on up to the next floor, attempting to ignore Logan's departure. But Logan churlishly pulled an aggressive facial gesture at the bowed crown of the guard's head and then flicked his teeth with his fingernail. The guard had looked up as he heard the click, just in time to see the doors close. Grinning triumphantly, he headed for Neve's desk. It was just as they had left it two hours earlier, her handbag still propped up against the side, partially open. Picking it up, he searched for some identification and found her driver's licence. From the scraps of conversations he had shared with her over the past week, he knew she lived on the island and had gotten the distinct impression that her apartment was near the Village somewhere. According to her licence she lived off west Marilyn, which was about a twenty-minute taxi drive away. He took note of the address on a pad and returned the licence and bag to its original location.

As he turned back towards the elevator, its doors opened and the chubby guard sauntered out; then suddenly lurched backwards, startled as he saw Logan approaching, despite only having left him minutes earlier. Failing to be discrete, the guard maintained his distance, appearing unnerved by Logan's smirk.

"Night. See you tomorrow." Logan winked.

The night guard didn't respond verbally, raising a slow hand of acknowledgement instead. Logan watched the guard stare at him all the way into the lift, maintaining eye contact until the doors prevented it. He found the man's intuitiveness unnerving. He had never encountered it before and now felt concern over whether it could damage his future plans.

Once outside he hailed a yellow cab, which he ended up fighting over with a business-woman. She was a young semi-attractive woman in her mid-thirties, well dressed in a knee-length skirt and jacket. With a briefcase in one hand, she strode with purpose towards the rear passenger door. As her hand had barged passed Logan's to latch around the handle, his chivalry had been discarded. He detested a woman who believed it her God given right to abuse her femininity. She, in turn, seemed completely taken back by Logan's stance, obviously unaccustomed to anybody questioning her actions. After a brief exchange of words, thirty percent of them expletives, she shied away. He watched her slowly back off grimacing, wounded in retreat, a humbled posture that she obviously felt uncomfortable wearing.

As the taxi pulled away, he gave the woman one final glare, which she attempted to ignore but couldn't. He felt good inside. The taxi slowly drove north up 5th, until 52nd street, where it turned left towards the Village. Logan watched the beggars, thieves, businessmen and lawyers that patrolled the streets. They all preyed on the innocent in some form. He sensed their aggression and hate. Revelled in their disdain for life.

The taxi pulled onto Marilyn, a predominantly residential street with seven step-fronted town houses on each side. It was easy to distinguish, by the cars parked outside, those houses were single-family dwellings and those that had been subdivided into flats. The building facades were late nineteenth century, with three storeys, constructed from large bricks. Entrance ways were positioned central to each dwelling, with rooms running off from either side. The neighbourhood's class sect was confused. Parked on the roadside, convertible Mercedes, BMWs and the odd Lincoln, suggested a higher paid, well-to-do occupant, while motorbikes, Fords, Chryslers and empty parking spaces offered evidence of a more menial living standard.

"That's fifteen bucks." The driver slid the glass partitioning back.

"You got to be kidding me?" Logan had expected the fare but never liked to give up his money that easily.

"You want it cheaper next time, take the subway or walk." The driver laid out his palm in readiness. Logan furnished him with the payment and got out. The cab drove off.

Waiting until the cab had moved out of sight, he retrieved a San Diego Padres baseball hat from his pocket and put it on. The pavements were fairly deserted, a solitary couple across the road offering the only company. He bobbed his head and moved on. Dustbins littered the sidewalk, the steam rising from manholes obscuring them from vision. An occasional tree, planted along the pavement edge, added to this domesticated picture.

Neve lived in 411c, which was about a hundred metres further up the street. As he drew closer a diminutive male figure exited, tightly wrapped in an overcoat and woolly cap. Logan avoided eye contact as the man turned in his direction, brushing past his elbow as he joined the pavement. Flicking his head around, Logan gave a pained glare. Adding insult to injury, no apology was forthcoming. Shaking his anger off, he mounted the steps, glancing back only once to see the man sit behind the wheel of a Porsche 911 with the number plate 'High 1'. Then, targeting the man's head, he lifted a finger, took aim and fired, blowing imaginary smoke from the tip afterwards. The car sped off, spinning its wheels to leave a trail of rubber and narrowly avoiding an oncoming removal van. Logan grinned and pressed Neve's buzzer.

"Who is it?" her clearly distraught voice responded.

"It's Foster, from the office."

"What do you want?" Her voice cheered up slightly.

"I saw you leaving depressed this afternoon. I tried to catch up with you to check you were okay, but by the time I'd got to the street, you were long gone." She remained silent. "You still there?"

"Yes." She sounded puzzled now.

"Well, I haven't been able to concentrate this afternoon, wondering if you were alright, so I got a cab over." He paused. Still, she said nothing. "I wouldn't sleep alright if I didn't know."

"How..."

He knew what she was about to ask and cut her short. "You left your handbag in the office. I apologise, but I sifted through it to find something with your address on it. Found your driver's licence. Cute picture." He could sense her smile. "Well, as long as you are okay, I'll get on." He let go of the buzzer to fake his departure.

"No, wait. Come up for a coffee." She released the door lock. "I'm on the second floor." Her last words were cut off as the fused glass door shut behind him.

Inside the decor was late sixties wallpaper, matched with tiled floor. The stairs were stained dark wood and led in a straight flight up to the first-floor landing. Every footstep elicited creaks of varying magnitudes, pitch and audibility. As his eye line met the floor of the next level, he discovered the poor decoration was perpetuated. A single apartment door was in front of him, a card displaying the letter 'B' fixed to the left-hand side of the frame. He paused briefly to listen, sensing that this was from where his ignorant street acquaintance had just emerged. Inside he could hear the scurrying of delicate footsteps. There was intention in their chaos, as if they were preparing to depart. Then, all of a sudden, the door opened, and a thin, interestingly plain woman appeared. Dressed in a short tight-fitting dress, stockings and high heels. Over the top she wore an ankle-length wool overcoat. 'Hooker" was Logan's first thought. And when she said hello, it did nothing but confirm his assessment. He didn't respond but ducked his head towards the floor once more and proceeded up the next flight of stairs that ran back toward the front of the house. He heard her mumble something, which he was certain contained the word 'fuck', but he still didn't respond. Upon reaching the second floor, he noticed the door to Neve's apartment was slightly ajar. He knocked.

"Come in. I'll be with you in a minute," a voice hollered out to him from behind a closed bedroom door. He did as was asked, entering a marble tiled hallway, approximately three metres square. Two doors led off in front of him, while another positioned to his right opened up to a corridor that ran the full depth of the building. In the bedroom he could hear hurried activity. Moving on through the right-hand door into the lounge, he found a relaxed environment. A tranquil peach colour covered the walls, complimented by a pine floor and wicker furniture with large padded cushions. A yew coffee table and Persian rug centred the room, with matching wood drinks cabinet and dresser pushed up on the left-hand side. An imitation fireplace had been created centrally between the two front-facing windows; the hearth filled with a vase of dried flowers. On the mantlepiece and dresser were a variety of family and personal photographs. Logan walked over to study them. Upon closer inspection, he noticed the reoccurrence of a single male posing with Neve, with greater than family familiarity. He was in his late twenties, attractive in a chiselled manner, had a friendly smile and a strong but thin physique. The intimacy they shared was personified in the final picture that he came across. He was carrying her on his back, both of them bare foot, standing on a beach in front of crisp blue surf. Trousers were rolled up to below their knees and thick jumpers indicated the coolness of the climate. They were both smiling, capturing the warmth and love of the moment.

"What you looking at?"

Neve entered the room behind him wearing a pair of blue jeans, a brown baggy jumper that extended long enough to warm her bum and a pair of slippers. Her face was freshly spruced, her exquisitely shaped lips displaying the dazzling moisture of fresh lipstick. A touch of mascara layered her eyelashes, but nothing more unnatural was present. In total her appearance was the perfect extension to the presentation of the woman he had met at the office; unassuming, with low self-esteem and seemingly unaware of her beauty. Her eyes sparkled like those of an excited child, full of hope, a gorgeous smile supporting their wishful expectations.

"Pictures. Who's this guy?" He pointed at the beach photo.

"Old boyfriend." Her face dropped slightly, displaying the anguish of reflection. Logan noticed and moved closer to her.

"What's wrong?"

"Nothing, really. I always get a little emotional when I think about him."

Logan could tell that the memories contained more than simple love spurned and waited for her to continue.

"He was very dear to me at one time, but he died."

"I'm sorry." He managed to sound genuine.

"No, don't be. You didn't know. The only reason it depresses me is because of the memories I have, sitting by his side in the hospital, talking to him. Caring for him. And we weren't even going out anymore at that point. We'd been split up about six months but that hadn't changed our friendship. Our relationship was always strange. Closer to a brother-sister feeling, really. There was still some passion, but it fizzled pretty quickly."

"How long were you together?"

"Eight years."

"Jesus."

"Hey, don't be blasphemous."

"Religious as well as devout friend. You're too good to be true." He found it easier to ignore her vulnerability in light of her religion.

"I'm not a groupie or anything. It's just you see death once or twice and it makes you hope that there's more to life than what we touch on the planet surface."

"Hell, that's deep." He smirked at the potential connotations of his words. "You must've freaked that kid's parents out when he brought you home."

"Never met his parents. They died when he was fourteen."

"I don't know. Can I stick my foot in my mouth anymore tonight?"

"Forget about it. Would you like a drink?" Neve asked.

"Love one, thanks. Lubricate my brain." He played dumb.

"What can I get you?"

"I'll have a beer."

"Sit down." She left for the kitchen.

"Nice place you've got here," he shouted out after her.

"Thanks."

He sat down and looked around, absorbing the other features and paintings mounted on the peach walls. She owned a selection of nouveau art, mostly prints of obscure painters, the meaning of which was solely in the eye of the beholder. Looking at their creations, their vision, was almost like taking a psychological test, like the Rorschach test, with the images conjured up reflecting the psychological profile of the individual. The manner in which they transformed in Logan's head would have to remain secret, but he grinned while entertaining their depraved construct.

"You know, it's really strange," Neve said as she came back in with the beers. "I've known you for only a few days. In fact, this is the first real conversation we've had, and I already feel closer to you than I ever have with John."

"Maybe he's just not a listener." Logan suggested.

"He's just not a great many things – like honest, caring, compassionate." She sat down in a chair near him and handed him his beer.

"I suppose nobody's perfect."

"I didn't expect perfect, but I did expect more than I got. But that's in the past now. Time to move on and seek new adventures."

"I'll drink to that." They chinked bottles. "So how long have you two been an item?"

"It's not really an item when one of you is married, but we were together for a little over a year." She emphasised the 'were'. "I don't think you could ever have classed it as an attachment. I've just been convenient for him. Played the role perfectly, of course. Let him use me and then break it off with no obligations." She started to cry.

"Hey, don't do that." He handed her a tissue. "He's not worth the tears. Besides, he'll get what's coming to him!"

Yet despite the words of comfort, there seemed to be something in his voice that had unsettled Neve. As if she knew there was something amiss, an underlying malicious intent.

He laid a hand over hers. "You've nothing to worry about, anyway. He's the one who needs to worry. He's the one who has to suffer the guilt of ignorance."

"I thought you and him were becoming friends?" she asked, looking confused.

"That doesn't mean I have to like everything he does. Besides, for now we're only colleagues. Casual acquaintances. Though I'm sure over the next few weeks he and I will get more familiar." His eyes wandered, as if in a daydream. "But for now, just imagine he doesn't exist, that he'll never bother you again." His hand clasped tighter around hers. She pulled it free. He stood up. "You know, when I saw you in the office the other day, I was jealous that you were his secretary and not mine. I mean, forgive me if this embarrasses you, but you are beautiful. There are guys out there who would give up their souls to be with someone like you—and look what you get—a guy without a soul."

She started to relax again. His words of compassion ringing true.

"You know what else I saw behind that attractive exterior?"

She shook her head.

"I saw pain, suffering, anguish. A woman tired of being placed in second position when she knew she beat the competition into the floor. I want to help you with that. I want to take the pain away. I want to give you something a thousand Johns could never give you." He said the words as if he was in a camp Broadway play, but she waited, captivated, on every syllable. "A purpose!" he finished. He checked his watch.

"Do you have to go somewhere?" She looked towards one of the front windows as if she had heard something. Rain began to patter against the glass.

"Well, I've got to get back and pick-up John from this club I left him in." He dropped the act, starting to talk very matter of fact.

"I thought you said you were just acquaintances?" she said, seeming startled.

"We are. For now. Look, this can't wait any longer."

He moved towards her, clutching at her upper arms and raising her out of the seat. Her face drained white. Then he kissed her. Initially her eyes opened wider as his tongue invaded her mouth, but as his internal caresses continued, she calmed down and reciprocated. Now that he knew he had captured her attention, he let go his hold and started to roam his hands over her well-disguised contours. He guided her baggy jumper up effortlessly over her smooth skin. Her eyes were fixed shut, settled in the passion of the moment. He picked her up, their kissing sustaining its momentum throughout, her trust so easily accomplished. As her feet left the floor, she raised her legs to wrap them around his waist. She was as light as a feather in his arms, quivering with anticipation. Walking around the sofa, he moved towards one of the windows that faced the side street, looking straight out across into the adjacent apartments.

"The bedroom's that way," she said, smirking.

"I know, but I promised to give you a purpose, and for that we need just a little bit more exposure."

Her smirk transformed into a grin and she resumed the kiss.

In a flat on the other side of the alley a young boy was taking excessive interest in what was happening. Logan pretended to have missed the pre-pubescent voyeur, playing up to the boy's interest by flashing him glimpses of Neve's bare back and bra strap, sliding the jumper up and down her spine. Then, with all his force, he pushed her away, fixing his hands firmly across her chest. Her eyes changed from contented, to shocked, to panicked. Her legs remained wrapped around Logan's waist, refusing to detach in spite of his rejection. Consequentially her upper body went flailing into the windowpane, shattering it from the centre out. Shards of glass broke free, showering down into the alley, but the edges remained fixed by resin into the wooden frame.

Neve looked terrified at Logan. He just glared back, his eyes manic. Her panic now turned to self-preservation as she released her legs, attempting to manoeuvre herself away from him. She failed as he yanked her back toward the window, holding on with a vice-like grip. Lifting her clear off the floor, he flung her once more at the broken glass. This time he retained his hold, pushing her torso straight through the fragmented pane and spewing another wave of glistening particles across the alley. Half her body was now outside of the apartment. Logan could see the face of the young boy paralysed by what he was witnessing, his eyes frozen wide, his jaw dropped low. Logan was still holding on to Neve and she was struggling to pull herself back inside. Blood streamed from every limb as she grasped at the jagged window frame. At this point Logan released his hold on her arms, dropping his hands to her thighs. Then, in one final decisive movement, he launched the remainder of her body out into the air.

Unprepared for this, she only just managed to retain the feeble grasp she had on the frame as her legs passed underneath her chest. Her head re-entered the room momentarily but then gravity took charge. As she started her descent, her neck caught the windowpane, a shard of glass jabbing like a knife deep into her throat. Blood spewed out like a fountain, spattering the frame. Logan jumped back out of the way to avoid it. This momentary resistance to nature's number one force caused Neve's scrambling body to spin back towards the wall. Then as it accelerated downwards, her head was released, and she vanished out of sight. Logan tugged his baseball cap peak back down to obscure his face and then stuck his head quickly out the window to check where she had landed. Three storeys down her body lay still on the tarmac, surrounded by a pool of rapidly dispersing blood. Then, casting a half glance across to the boy, he left.

13

"So, where were you last night?"

"I told you I was out." John's tone was defensive.

"You told me you were going out with a new work colleague. A couple of beers and you'd be home. So where did one o'clock in the morning come from?"

"It wasn't one." His brain throbbed as he spoke. It was taking every ounce of his strength to remain calm.

"Sorry, you're right. I'm being generous. It was one fifteen!" She dropped a saucepan into the empty sink.

"We got talking. I lost track of the time." He tried to pacify her. "And stop shouting please. It's not good for the baby."

"Yeah? Well, neither's worrying until the earlier hours of the morning where its father is. You could have called."

"We couldn't find a phone."

She ignored him. "It would have only taken a minute at the most. I was sat by the phone anyway. Waiting for the police to call and tell me they'd just dragged your body out of the East River."

"Come on, stop overdramatising."

"I'm not, I was worried."

"Well, you shouldn't have been. I was fine." The interrogation was beginning to wear thin.

"What, so I'm not allowed to worry about my husband anymore? I should just let him do what he wants?"

John began to think that he should never have given up spell-casting. "I'm going to work now." His temper was fraying.

"Typical. So, when am I going to see you next? Maybe you'll be going out again tonight or are you just going to tell me tomorrow?" she said with vicious sarcasm.

"If I go out, I'll call." With that he closed the door firmly behind him.

As she walked to the front window, to watch him get into his car, a pain in her belly started to grow. It was a sensation she had never felt before. Nerves flared agonisingly. She cradled her belly with one arm but continued to look out the window. The sky had failed to seal itself during the night-time hours, the rain disfiguring her husband's appearance behind the windscreen. The abdominal disturbance returned, jabbing sensations hitting randomly at her insides. It was stronger than any kicking the baby had done before. She lowered her other arm down in comfort. For the first time during her pregnancy, she no longer felt in control.

Outside John sat for a couple of seconds in the driving seat, staring back at Gloria. He could partially see her jerky movements but decided that she was faking it in an attempt to get him back inside. He turned the ignition key.

His work journey was as normal, the same nameless faces wandering around the boat and on to the subway. The only variation to this routine was in his head, which was filled with thoughts of the night before. Pictures of Monica giving it some on top of him. Impaling herself in continuous wet ecstasy, her tits bouncing in the palms of his hands, head and hair flung back as if she was so familiar with the road she travelled. Their encounter had lasted a full three hours, during which they'd done everything. Some of which had been new to John, but she had offered, and he had tried. Whenever their acts had allowed face-to-face contact, her smile had shown pleasure, supported by her delicate wispy voice repeating "Oh, God, I can feel that" every time she enveloped him. The whole event had made John ponder why he had ever resorted to magic for love. He should have stuck solely with using it for money. At least then he would have been able to pay for last night's kind of adventure again and again. John stirred from his daydream to find a couple staring at him from across the train carriage. They seemed disturbed by his vacant stare and for once John felt slightly embarrassed. He looked away.

As the train pulled into his station, he was relieved to get out and feel the breeze of fresh air rushing down the stairs and along the tunnel. His head was in poor shape, having consumed too much alcohol with Monica. As he climbed the steps, the fume-drenched air filled his lungs, soothing his body's tension, created by the suffocating confines of the subway. Up on the street, the city was its usual hive of activity, sidewalks spilling over on to the roads as pedestrians rushed to their places of work. Fortunately, John's time amidst this hustle and bustle was limited. As he pushed the office door open, the guard offered greetings, but John ignored them. His mind was focussed solely on getting to the sanctuary of his office. The lift, though confined, offered some comfort. As it opened up at the second floor, the receptionist stood to catch his attention, but he passed by her, moving rapidly with fixed intent. The only thing that caught his attention as he twisted between desks was Neve's absence.

Once through his office door, he closed it behind him and sat at his desk. In the top left-hand draw he always kept some Hedex. Breaking them free, he popped a couple of tablets, chasing them down with the dregs of stale coffee that sat in his mug from the day before. He winced, nearly vomiting the pills straight back up. Slouching in his seat, nestling his stomach, he waited for the discomfort to subside.

"Neve." He pressed his intercom button. There was no answer. "Neve."

"Yes, Mr Garret," a female voice answered.

"Neve?"

"No, Sir, it's Jane. Neve hasn't arrived yet this morning."

"Oh. Well, could you get me a fresh coffee?"

"Okay, Sir."

John stood up. Pulling the blinds open, he looked down the street. The masses still scurried to make work on time instead of resigning themselves to a late arrival. Letting the blinds slip closed once more, he moved to a mahogany corner cabinet that housed a wash basin, concealed by a hinged lid. Plugging the hole, he filed the basin sink with cold water and dunked his head. Water filled his ears, further numbing his chemically suppressed headache. He heard the door open and retracted his head from the sink.

"Just leave that on the desk please, Jane." He turned to find that three people had entered his office, one of whom was Jane. He dried his face and hair.

"Sir, these are detectives from...." She broke into tears.

John stared at her as if she was insane. The younger of the two detectives, a woman, comforted her. The other walked towards him, an introductory hand stretched out in front. This man was aged around fifty-three, a desk belly straining his lower shirt buttons. His attire was ordinary low-income work clothing, which bore the trademarks of a few years' use. His shoes were also a signpost for his occupation and class. With greying hair and tight piercing brown eyes, he presented himself as an uncaring nemesis to the higher echelons of city society. Namely lawyers.

"Mr Garret?" John accepted his hand, shaking it three times before letting go.

"Yes, that's me."

"Neve Locker is your secretary?" The detective questioned.

"Yes." He was puzzled. "What's this about, officer?"

"You may want to sit down, Sir."

"No, I'm fine just standing for the moment."

"Miss Locker was found dead late last night."

John fell into the closest seat. He couldn't believe it. Despite his lack of true affection for Neve, lust in itself was still a hard thing to accept losing.

"How?"

"It appears someone threw her out of her apartment window. We have an eyewitness, but they are a little too shaken to talk at the moment."

"I just can't believe it." He stood up again and went to

comfort Jane, but she pushed herself away and ran outside, leaving him standing spare. The female detective followed her.

"Is now a good time to ask you some questions?"

"Yes, I suppose it's going to be as good as any."

"Okay. Do you mind if I sit down?" The detective posed the question but didn't wait for a response, so John didn't answer. "You've known Miss Locker for how long?"

"Two, maybe three years."

"Did she seem happy in her work?"

"Yes."

"To your knowledge, was she in any financial trouble?"

"Don't think so."

"Did she have any enemies at all?"

"No."

"Boyfriend?"

"No, not that I know of."

"Did you have a close relationship with her?"

"As close as any boss, I suppose." He replied cautiously.

"Did you ever see each other socially?"

"Occasionally. Sometimes she needed to talk." John offered a half truth.

"Does she have any family?" The detective continued to fire questions at him.

"I don't know about her parents, but she sometimes mentioned a sister up in D.C."

"Right, well, thanks for your time."

"No problem, officer." John stood up to show him out.

"Oh, just for clarification – where were you last night, between eight and ten o'clock?"

"I was having drinks with a colleague," John answered instinctively, momentarily forgetting the imperfection of his alibi.

"And your colleague's name is?"

"Foster Logan. He has that office right across there." John pointed to the far side of the floor.

"Thanks. Right, well, if you think of anything else that may be of use, give me a call." He handed John a calling card. "We'll be around for a little while longer. Need to ask your friend a few questions and some of Miss Locker's other co-workers. I assure you, though, that we'll minimise the disruption."

"With the news you've brought, I doubt anybody could do that today."

The detective managed to muster a sympathetic smile.

As John opened his office door, he could see the female detective already canvassing Neve's work mates and his nerves immediately began to feel slightly on edge. He shook the detective's hand once more and closed the door. Looking down at the card he read 'Detective Chris Harrington'. Now at least the face of trouble had the courtesy of a name.

Outside John's office Harrington had joined his partner, a twenty-nine-year-old woman called Reilly Fox. She was an out-of-character blonde, with a degree in philosophy. Despite her hair colour, her physique was unremarkable; she wasn't curvaceous, but neither was she fat. The perceived outline from her baggy clothing suggested a weak skeletal frame, available to be pushed around. In truth, though, she worked out regularly and had a very toned muscular body. Unfortunately, the same exercise had choked her female development, leaving her flat-chested and narrow hipped. Her face was plain, and she made no attempts to hide it. The seriousness with which she attacked her work penetrated the air through sharp eyes and furrowed brow. This characteristic was her only real failing, because it gave the impression of continuous scrutiny, automatically raising barriers. In truth, it was her own defence mechanism for low physical self-esteem and a moderate paranoia over how others perused her figure. She was wearing a dark green suit, recently dry cleaned, offering sharp contrast to Harrington's lived-in look. The skirt was knee length, and fifteen denier tights hid her pale complexion.

"Morning." Harrington addressed the man Fox was interviewing, subsequently turning his back on him. "You got a second?" He didn't wait for her to reply, leading her towards the reception so they could talk away from inquisitive ears. "I'm gonna go back to the station, see if our boy's ready to talk yet. I'll come back and pick you up later."

"How much later? I'll be done here soon."

"I don't think you will." He played the condescending mentor. "Let's look at what you've got." She handed him her notepad.

"No. You need to delve deeper than that. Find out about her love life, who she was sleeping with, office lovers, that type of thing. I don't want to know about her personality, I got that information from looking around her apartment. What we need is personal details."

Reilly's insecurity displayed itself through a blush. She was new to homicide and to New York, having transferred from Houston after the failure of her high school marriage. In the southern states she worked in vice, which required a much more simplistic style of investigation. She hadn't specifically asked for this transfer, just took the first option that presented itself. This was it. And she had grabbed at it, both feet forward.

"Okay, I'll dig. I'll give you a call when I'm done."

"Fine. And make sure you interview a guy called Foster Logan. Garret in there says they were out together last night," Harrington spoke as he entered the elevator, taking his eyes off his partner.

By the time he had turned around, the doors had closed. He knew that the thought of working alone would unnerve Reilly, but he could think of no other way of opening her up, making her city wise and homicide tough. Just like a man he thought. And just like a man, he pushed her with typical bull-fistedness. Harrington was positive she would respond to his approach, because below that vulnerable exterior was a strong woman. A woman who wanted to protect herself.

Once outside, he headed for his car, which was parked up on the kerb. He shielded himself from the rain that had resumed falling. The car was a beige nineteen eighty-eight Cadillac, complete with peeling paint and rusting panels. The motor underneath the hood was a different class altogether, being a police-customised V six-cylinder engine, which was on special trial in the city. The idea was to provide the exterior impression of a car on its last legs, while providing power and speed suitable to the trade. The looks made the car undesirable to thieves and the engine made it close to unescapable by the same individuals. The interior was imitation leather that squeaked as Harrington slid across from the passenger seat to the driver's side. He turned the key in the ignition and the engine purred into life.

Pulling into the steady flow of nose-to-tail traffic, he listened to the police radio band. The conversation was generally pretty quiet, mostly mundane domestic issues at this time of day, the thieves and drug pushers still sleeping off the previous night's activities. The precinct was only ten blocks away, but it took fifteen minutes to drive. An underground car park provided both parking spaces and a maintenance area. Which while at first glance appeared normal, was notorious. The notoriety being attributable to its subterranean location, the subway having been driven in close proximity, the planners having failed to take cognisance of the parking area. The result was a car park that vibrated regularly from the air blasts, as trains accelerated the ventilation through the tunnels. He remembered the first time Reilly had felt it, he had thought she was going to have a heart attack, believing it to be an earthquake.

The station itself was late nineteenth century. The car park had been retrofitted in the nineteen twenties through modification to its basement. The building spanned a seventy-by-seventy metre square area and had five floors in total, including the basement. The masonry was fairly standard in the style and structure common to the older buildings in the city centre, although its facade had been renovated recently, making it stand out more. Homicide was on the third floor and Harrington took the elevator up. Despite the face lift that had occurred outside, the inside had retained a lived-in look. The last time any kind of decorating works had taken place Lyndon Johnson was still President, and that refurbishment had been from necessity, after the Mob had bombed the floor in an attempt to kill a state witness. They had succeeded. The informant in question had disintegrated into more parts than were worth counting. The device had been planted underneath the chair he was sitting in while being questioned. He had only sat down a couple of seconds before – boom! The event had been so well planned that no more than ten minutes after detonation, the Mob's lawyer was on the doorstep demanding his client's release. Harrington remembered the day because it had been his first in the department. Fresh from the academy, he had arrived really believing he could make a difference. Then, the next thing he had known, was someone else's beliefs were splattered all over his face. He learned in the most horrifying way that righteousness has many enemies. The event had scarred him mentally and he had become intent on policing the law aggressively. At times through the seventies little had separated him from the men he sought to reap justice on, save for a badge and the public's faith. Moving into the eighties, his vengefulness had calmed, and he had taken on wisdom, and with it a more precise method of law enforcement. Instead of driving to bring criminals to justice no matter what, he transcended from the cannibalistic approach to a predatory one, lying in wait, accruing evidence so that when the strike came, it hurt. The eighties had been very good for him; he had held the highest arrest rate for the majority of the decade. His cases were watertight and many fancy defence lawyers failed to work their expected magic. Crime lords and gangs were unhappy. This same record had also led to him receiving the largest number of death threats. They hadn't disturbed him initially, but then a car bomb had been discovered rigged to the axle of his Ford Mustang and for the first time, he had felt unprotected by his badge. That had been the last day he had driven to work. The device had been primed to explode on axle movement, which, given that he had driven all the way from Newark in the morning, meant it had been installed from inside the station. The encounter had reminded him of his first day in sixty-nine, but this time he had cowered away from it. Truth be told, he was afraid. That had been in eighty-nine, and since then he had been assigned partners. This pairing up hadn't been a sign of his captain's distrust, more an acceptance that he required support to continue his work. Harrington had showed a lack of tolerance for the majority of these partners; others showed a lack of tolerance for him. Since eighty-nine and now, he had been through the equivalent of one per year. Reilly Fox was the latest, and in a strange way he liked her. She had a way that made him feel comfortable, an insecurity that he could pander to, making him feel stronger. More in control.

Harrington's floor was built around a central corridor that ran the width of the building. The walls were painted stony grey and the floor was black sheet plastic. Glass-paned office doors sprung off to one side, the occupants' names brushed in gold paint on the frosted glass. On the left, transparent glass partitions separated the specialties of the force. Homicide and narcotics were the only two to occupy this floor, which made the layout easy.

Harrington's desk sat alone in a corner surrounded by its own partitioning. Weaving through the office, he said his good mornings. A couple of his colleagues handed him transcripts from other cases he was working on, but he gave them only cursory glances. After passing by the coffee machine, he entered his workspace. Filing trays were piled up and a small desk calendar still displayed August. He picked up the phone and dialled the desk sergeant.

"Bill, it's me." He spoke with familiarity. "Has that kid from last night come in yet?"

A voice answered briefly from the other end of the line.

"Did you say room three?" Harrington asked.

Confirmation came.

"Thanks, Bill. You still on for poker Saturday night?"

As the response came, Harrington let loose a small laugh. "Okay, I'll see you there. Then we'll see how smug you are." He hung up.

Slowly taking a gulp of his coffee, he thought about Neve Locker. She had apparently been an unassuming, attractive lady, with a good job, no debts and no enemies. There was as yet no report from the coroner, but as that thought passed his mind, he checked his desktop to make sure, though he knew there wasn't going to be much it could tell him. The body had been laid out in the rain for a good fifteen minutes without protection. Any evidence accrued would almost certainly be limited. There was also the high potential for contamination. The only hope he had was that they would find fingerprints, hairs or something inside her apartment. The murderer had obviously been known to her, because there was no forced entry, either at the front door or to her apartment. This fact alone made it easier to narrow down the suspects, as long as an accurate picture of her private life could be established. He took another swig of coffee.

One of the new recruits entered his cubical and handed him an envelope. It was the coroner's preliminary report. After a brief exchange of words, he didn't even have to open it to know that he had been right. No traces of DNA on the victim had been found. Her death had been caused by a glass shard that had jabbed through her neck. According to the coroner, she would have been dead before she hit the ground. He still had to have the deposits under her fingernails analysed, but he suggested holding no hope for skin or blood traces. Her nails had been bitten short, and they had laid sodden in a puddle for a long time before getting bagged, reducing the probability of recovering anything viable tenfold.

Taking one final swig from his mug, he got up and made his way to the interview rooms situated on the ground floor. He had to pass through the lobby on the way. Bill gave him a wink as he wove through a crowd of out of city schoolgirls who had managed to lose their teacher on a field trip. The entrance to the back passageway was security swipe card activated, as was the access to all other floors. Harrington's card was getting old, though, the magnetic strip scratched excessively, requiring him to slide it through a couple of times before it was acknowledged.

Passing through, he opened the third door on the left. Inside sat a young boy, next to what was presumably his father. The young kid was about thirteen years of age and was clearly nervous. His hair was a mousey brown colour, thick and combed in a parting. Glasses enhanced his eyes, and a retainer straightened his teeth. To add to his childhood afflictions, he also suffered from severe acne, which had already scarred his youthful skin. Harrington couldn't assess his stature because he was seated, save to say he was boy height.

"Morning." He stretched out a hand. "I'm Detective Harrington."

"Hi. I'm Cliff." The father spoke. "And this is Billy."

"Pleased to meet you, Billy." He offered his hand to the boy, who reluctantly took hold. "Thanks for coming in."

"Not a problem, detective," the father replied.

"Right, well, I don't want to keep you any longer than necessary, so let's crack straight on." He opened up a notepad. "Now, you were watching out your window last night when the woman fell. Yes?" The kid nodded. "I understand this is difficult for you, Billy, but so that I don't misinterpret anything, you're gonna have to speak. So, was that a yes?"

"Yes."

"Right. Now, starting at the beginning, I want you to take me through what you saw. Okay?"

"Well, the guy turned up and she went to get him a drink." The boy's voice was shaky.

"What time was that?"

"Nine o'clock."

"Are you sure?"

"Yes."

"How long had you been watching through Miss Locker's window before the man arrived?" Billy didn't answer. "Was it five minutes, ten minutes? Longer?" He nodded. "You have to say it, Billy."

"Longer."

"Did you look through her window a lot?"

"What's that got to do with it?" the father interrupted.

"It establishes the importance of Billy as a witness. If he looked through her window regularly, then it's easier to believe he saw what he did, than if he happened to be looking at the moment it happened." Cliff rested back in his chair. "So, Billy, did you look through her window regularly?"

"Yes."

"So how long had you been watching when the guy arrived?"

"About an hour." The boy still sounded uncomfortable.

"Alright. Tell me what she was doing." Harrington tried to settle him.

"I don't know everything. I usually watch as soon as she gets home, but yesterday she was back before I'd finished supper."

"Okay, so what was she wearing?"

"A pair of pyjamas to start with. She was watching television, drinking a hot mug of something. I watched her go towards the intercom and then after a minute or so, she started to run around, picking things up and straightening cushions."

"Then what?" He made notes as Billy talked.

"She got changed. Put a jumper and jeans on." The kid evidently didn't enjoy the recollection, looking towards his father for support.

"Carry on, son."

"Then that guy appeared. She looked happy to see him. He looked around a bit and then they sat and talked."

"Describe the man."

"He was youngish."

"Thirty?"

"He looked as young as Tom Cruise in *Days of Thunder*."

"Okay." It wasn't the description Harrington was hoping for, but it was a start. "What colour hair did he have?"

"I don't know."

"He had hair?"

"I think so, but he was wearing a baseball cap."

"Any particular team?"

"The San Diego Padres."

"Are you positive about that?" he said slowly.

"Yes, because I remember thinking that they were beaten by New York in the World Series the other year. I thought that was funny."

"Good. So, what happened next?"

"After the talking, they got close. Started kissing and stuff."

"I take it you began to pay even more attention at this point?"

Billy smiled nervously.

"He started to touch her body and that was when he threw her at the window." His smile withered.

"Did you get a good look at him then?"

"Not really. He saw me so I moved back into the room."

"How come he saw you and you didn't get a good look at him?"

"I was scared." The boy started to cry.

"Hey, don't worry about that." He stretched out a reassuring hand. "What you've given me so far is great. He patted Billy on the shoulder. "You alright to continue?"

The kid nodded.

"Okay, so what happened then?"

"He looked down to check where she had fallen and then left."

"Now, that wasn't so bad, was it?" He continued to speak in a soothing tone. "I've only got a couple more questions." He paused. "Right, did you have your glasses on or off?"

"On." He sniffled an answer.

"Good." He took note. "Did the man have a coat on?"

"Yes, a black overcoat."

"Right. Well, that's it for now. I just need to have a quick private word with your father and then you two can go home." Harrington stood up and signalled for Cliff to follow. Taking him out into the corridor he shut the door behind him. "There are a couple of things. Firstly, I may need Billy to come in and look at a line-up. Are you okay with that?"

"Yes, sure."

"Thanks. Secondly, if Billy is right about the man seeing him, then he could be in danger. So as a precaution I'm going to post an unmarked squad car outside your house, just in case. Don't answer your door to anybody, and I'd take Billy out of school for at least a week. Tell them he's sick."

Cliff was speechless.

"Look, I'm not trying to panic you and I know this may sound like desperate measures, but it isn't. It's just standard procedure," he lied. "It's always better to be safe than sorry. Now, you need to remain upbeat about everything, don't give the game away. I've seen too many freaked out parents to wish that paranoia on anyone. So, you just take Billy home and tell your wife there's nothing to worry about. I'll be in touch. Thanks for coming in. This officer will show you out." Harrington grabbed the sleeve of a passing uniform. Then, opening the door, ushered Billy to come out.

As he watched them leave, he took a couple of moments to consider the kid's testimony. Everything led to the conclusion that she knew the victim and that she found him appealing enough to make an effort to clean up. Getting in the lift, he went down to the car park, got in his car and drove himself back to see how Reilly was doing. When he entered the second-floor reception area of Wilson Schmect and Drummond she was just finishing with the lady sat adjacent to Neve Locker's desk. She turned to look at him as the elevator doors clunked shut and he signalled her to come across.

"Okay, well, I've spoken to the kid and let's just say he doesn't make this an open and shut one. He saw the guy, but only a partial. So, a solid identification may be difficult." He took a breath. "On the positive side, he was watching the whole time. His description confirms the fact that she knew him. It even goes to suggest that she liked him."

"All this is beginning to tie together." Reilly remarked.

"What do you mean?"

"I've spoken to everybody now and the one reoccurring theme is a relationship between Locker and Garret."

"You spoken to Garret about it?"

"No, he's been upstairs in a meeting since you left."

"What about his colleague? The one he claims to have been with."

"He's a no show. They've tried him at home but got no answer."

Harrington stayed silent.

"What do you want to do? Do you want to go?" Reilly asked.

"No, I think we'll stay and question Garret a little bit more. He's not been honest with us about his relationship. Who knows what else there may be?"

"Shall I go and fetch him?"

"No, let's have a quick look in his office first. Never know what we might find."

As they walked back across the floor, all eyes were focussed on them. When the two detectives entered Garret's office, there was a mixture of relief, confusion and 'shouldn't we say something' written across their faces. Harrington shut the door behind them, wanting to keep their snooping private. Fortuitously, the action also reaped the most benefits, because it immediately exposed the coat stand, atop which sat a Padres baseball cap. His heart nearly soared out of his mouth.

"I think you can stop looking now. We've got enough to bring him in on suspicion." He pointed at the cap. Reilly looked confused. "Our eyewitness says the perpetrator wore a San Diego Padres baseball cap," he explained.

"Do you want to bring him in now?"

"I think we might. No point in wasting time. You get him and I'll see you down at the car."

Fox walked away, but Harrington stayed for a while longer. He took the baseball cap down from the coat stand and placed it in a plastic evidence bag. Next he moved over to the desk and began tugging at drawers. The first couple opened without much of a problem, exposing pens, paper, stapler, envelopes, the usual office equipment and stationery. However, the bottom latch was solid. He studied the lock for a moment and then quickly rummaged through the open drawers to see if he could find a key. Nothing. He stared at it for a minute, contemplating whether he could release the latch without leaving a trace. The last thing he wanted to do was blow the case through an illegal search, but at the same time he didn't want to really leave any rock unturned before he left. The necessity for discrete enquiries to protect the company name was paramount in legal firms such as this one. A nervous partner wouldn't think twice about clearing away any incriminating evidence. He needed to see what was hidden within that drawer and he needed to do it before they interviewed Garret. A brainwave struck. His secretary would have probably kept a key, so that she could access any of his files for the partners in his absence. Following this instinct, he found two sets of keys in her desk and bringing both back to the drawer he searched for a match. Three keys offered potential, so he tried each in turn. Predictably, the last one did the job. As he pulled the drawer open, Harrington discovered an assortment of files, with a telephone book and diary sat atop them. He immediately reached for the telephone book, flicking through to the 'L' section, tracing his finger down to find the victim's name. It was there. Next, he opened the diary. This was a more time-consuming task. Studying each entry, he prayed for anything that could associate Garret to his secretary on a personal level. As he read journal entries from the past few weeks, he found no clear reference to Neve Locker. In general, the entries were written in a personalised abbreviated text, words were stemmed short and initials replaced names. For the most part, irrespective of names, Harrington could get the gist of each appointment. There was an exception, presented in a series of single-letter entries scattered across the preceding months. Some appointments were at lunchtime, others were late afternoon and early evening. The lone letter that represented these engagements was an 'L'. The phone rang, breaking his concentration.

He picked up the receiver. "Hello."

"Mr Garret the..." an assertive feminine voice began, then trailed off.

"No, this is Detective Harrington."

"Oh. Where's Mr Garret?" The female on the other end of the line sounded startled.

"He's on his way to the station. Can I help at all?"

"Yes." She regained composure. "Could you let him know that his wife has been admitted into Kennedy's Infirmary?"

"With what?"

"Premature labour. He's to get down there as soon as possible."

"Okay, I'll pass the message on."

With that, the woman hung up.

14

"Okay, shall we take it from the top one more time, then?" Harrington was starting to display signs of frustration. Garret's story was clinically precise and identical with each repetition.

"No, I won't! I think I've given enough of my time to you without actually being charged. I'm going to see my wife."

John appeared equally distressed by the course of their conversation. The only person who had remained close to tranquil was Fox, and that was easy for her to do, because she was just following her partner. However, her coolness was beginning to fray. Garret had given his statement five times now. With the other evidence in mind, they would usually be able to arrest with conviction or discharge him from their enquiries. Bearing all these factors in mind, Harrington could see Fox starting to look confused by her partner's escalating frustration. Over their days of working together, he knew she had witnessed a couple of instances where his response to an action could only be considered excessive. He also knew she had smelt alcohol from his direction a couple of times, on both occasions early in the morning, which he believed she had generously dismissed as leftover vapours from the night before.

"I will hold you on suspicion of murder if I have to." Harrington's words were forceful. "But I would just as soon eliminate you from our enquiries in a pleasant way."

"Well, I believe my testimony has already done that. Go to the club. Talk to Monica. Talk to Foster Logan, he'll verify everything."

"We'll do both of those. Though unfortunately for now, Mr

Logan is nowhere to be found and your office doesn't appear to have any personal details on him at all. And then, ironically, we can't check at the club either, because you have failed to tell us exactly where it is."

"What you talking about? It's off 42nd Street, on Dead End 54."

"No, it isn't, because there is no such thing as 'Dead End 54'. Neither have we found a place called 'Hell's Open' anywhere along '42nd Street'!"

John looked confused.

"Hey, you were drunk! You probably don't remember the night that clearly. The club could have been anywhere." Harrington toyed with him.

"No, it was there. I remember it clearly."

"Are you so certain of that? No creeping doubts?"

"None at all." Garret immediately regained composure.

"Then you wouldn't mind taking a polygraph."

Fox was startled by her colleague's request, given they hadn't charged Garret yet.

"Not at all." John accepted the challenge.

"Right, then. Fox, could you get that set up? Thanks." He didn't wait for her to answer. "We'll put you against the machine and then take a little excursion to find this mystical club." The door shut behind her as she left.

"What about your diary?" Harrington probed.

"What about it?"

This was the first time that Harrington had brought it up, due to the less than perfect procedure he had followed to obtain it.

"There are some frequent entries in it making reference to Miss Locker. Yet you say, sorry, claim, to have had only a working relationship with her."

"There aren't any such entries." John raised his voice.

"You sure?" Harrington played it more casual.

"How did you read my diary?" John's forcefulness remained.

"It was on your desk. Your employers had given us permission to look around. So, we did." He smiled sheepishly.

"That book was locked up in my side drawers."

"You must be mistaken. The diary was sat on your desk and your side drawers were unlocked."

"This is getting more like a set-up by the minute."

"You think that, then straighten us out. Tell the truth."

Garret glared across the table at Harrington but said nothing.

"Let me make things a little bit clearer for you. We have several testimonies that suggest activity beyond typing and shorthand between you and your secretary. We have a single testimony from a person who Neve had only recently confided in about your relationship and how you were talking of leaving your wife. We have an eyewitness to the murder who saw a man in a baseball cap. A 'Padres' baseball cap."

Despite his innocence, John could feel his face begin to show signs of despair.

"I have a telephone book – your telephone book – that has Miss Locker's home telephone number in it."

"That's not incriminating. I'm her boss, I need to ask her to come in at odd hours and I need to check where she is if she doesn't show."

"That's true, but on the back end of all the other testimony it looks more like evidence of a more intimate association. Don't you think?" John remained silent once more. "Then we have this diary showing your engagements with Miss Locker."

"What engagements?"

"The references to 'L'. Some during the day but the majority early evening."

"'L' stands for Library. It's across the street from our offices. You may have noticed it. I put that in so that Neve knew where I was if anybody needed me." He had previously planned his response to this query if anybody had asked the question.

"I suppose that explains those that have historical reference, but what about those in the future?"

"Don't tell me you don't make plans for getting your work

done?" For the first time John came over smug.

"Not two weeks in advance, no," Harrington retaliated, catching him by surprise. "What? Cat got your tongue?"

"Like I have said, can we get on with this? I want to go and see my wife."

"All in good time. I wouldn't want to be accused of not giving you fair opportunity to state your case."

John understood Harrington was attempting to exploit his clear anxiety to see his wife for everything he could. As pressurised police interviews went, Johns' desire to leave had gifted Harrington the perfect natural circumstance to probe for flaws in his story. If there was a confession to be had, this was the environment to secure it and John knew that. Though, for all Harrington's requests, it hadn't started to play on John's mind as much as it could. At that moment Fox re-entered the room.

"All set up. If you'd like to come this way." She gestured towards the door.

They moved next door into an identically decorated room with a polygraph machine laid out neatly on the table. John was quite comfortable with the situation related to his testimony of the events of two nights ago, but after the final direction his conversation with Harrington had taken, he was concerned about exposing other facts.

Fox and Harrington followed him into the room, bringing the complement to four, a female police technician already being at hand to administer the test. Silently she guided John into a chair, unbuttoned the top of his shirt and attached the sensor pads. He could already feel his pulse starting to race. Deceiving humans only required theatrical flair. But to lie to the machine meant the extension of this facade through his entire biological make-up.

"Okay, just relax," the technician said. "I need to ask you a couple of baseline questions and then we'll move on." She picked up a pencil and set the machine running. John could hear the needle as it delicately scored the paper. "Okay, now you must give 'yes' or 'no' answers only. Is your name John Garret?"

"Yes."

"Are you an attorney?" Her voice drifted out, placid and monotone. John tried to find humour in it to soothe his nerves but failed.

"Yes."

"Are you married?"

"Yes."

"Are you twenty-seven years old?"

"Yes."

"Are you a homosexual?"

"No, I'm not."

"Yes or no answers only, Sir!" She raised her voice for the first time.

"No."

Fox had now moved round to sit in front of Garret, taking a chair in the corner. Harrington, however, remained behind John out of his peripheral vision, but John knew he was there. He turned his head slightly to locate him.

"Please remain facing forward," the technician instructed. Silence fell for a moment. John could tell from the look on Fox's face that an exchange of some kind was taking place behind him.

"Okay." Harrington's gruff voice erupted. "Did you know Neve Locker outside of work?"

"Yes."

Fox appeared surprised at his answer.

"Were you having an affair with her?"

"No." He could feel sweat seeping out along his arms, clinging to the underside of his shirt.

"Do you know where she lives?"

"Yes."

"Have you ever been to her apartment?" Harrington's style was more direct than the female technician's, his questions attacking in continuous barrage.

"No."

He lied, not knowing why. He just did it instinctively. He knew the moment the words had left his mouth that the sensible thing to do would have been to say yes. His heart fluttered. Staring at Fox, he watched her eyes twitching backwards and forwards between himself and Harrington. Within that blue glaze he could see his worst fears evolving. He could tell that with each incorrect answer, he incriminated himself further.

"On the fifteenth of this month. Two days ago." Harrington clarified the date further. "Did you see Neve Locker?"

"Yes."

"Did you see her after she departed the office?"

"No."

"Did you go to her apartment that night?"

"No." He felt a little more comfortable with this line of questioning because his answers would be honest. He had nothing to hide.

"Were you out with Foster Logan on the fifteenth?"

"Yes." Tension drifted out of his body.

"Did you go to a bar called 'The Babe'?"

"Yes."

"Did you then go to a club called 'Hell's Open'?"

"Yes."

"Was the club on 42nd Street?"

"Yes."

"Did you spend time with a woman named Monica?"

"Yes." John could tell that the answers now weren't producing the indicators Harrington wanted to see.

"Did you sleep with her?"

Fox's expression showed as much surprise to the question as John felt. His pulse raced momentarily.

"I want to see my wife." He evaded a response.

"I've told you that you can, but only when we're done here. Now answer the question. Did you sleep with the woman called Monica?" Harrington spoke aggressively.

"Why can't I see her now and finish this later?"

"Because that isn't how we operate. Now, for the last time,

answer the question. Did you sleep with a woman named Monica?"

"No." His temples throbbed from the pressure.

"Does the letter 'L' in your diary refer to Neve Locker?"

Again, Fox appeared surprised by the question.

"No." He was beginning to feel exceptionally vulnerable. He'd never been under scrutiny like this before. His master's power had seen to that.

"Does it refer to you meeting her outside of work?"

"No." He started to fidget with his hands, picking at the seams of his trousers.

"Have you ever had sex with Neve Locker?"

"No." He began pulling at a loose thread. Fox noticed.

At that moment the door opened, and a heavy-footed person entered. There was a brief exchange of whispers before Harrington said thanks and the newcomer departed. John's anxiety grew.

"Did you murder Neve Locker?"

"No. I didn't."

"Yes or no answers only."

"No." He raised his voice.

"Have we got enough there?" Harrington was addressing the technician now. She obviously nodded. "Right, then, let's move on." He grabbed Garret around his bicep, directing him back out of the room.

"Do I get to see my wife now?" John was becoming increasingly frustrated by Harrington's stalling tactics.

"No."

"Why not now?" His voice was stressed.

"Because I am arresting you on suspicion of murder. You have the right to remain silent. Anything you say will and can be used against you in a court of law. You have the right to an attorney, and if you cannot afford one, they will be provided for you. Do you understand your rights?"

John was dumbfounded. He was innocent.

"You're making a big mistake. I didn't kill her."

"I think it only fair to tell you that we have matched a hair from Miss Locker's apartment to one from your San Diego Padres baseball cap."

"But I didn't do it! I was with Foster Logan! Find him, he'll tell you!"

"We are trying to locate him now, but I don't see how his story can help you, given that we can't find the club you allegedly spent the night at. And quite frankly, I think you are just seeking to confuse the situation."

"No, I'm not. Why don't you let me take you to the club?"

Harrington looked less than enthusiastic about the idea, but Fox shrugged her shoulders at him, as if to say, "it's not such a bad idea". He thought about it for a moment.

"Alright. I want him processed first." Harrington was talking to Fox, but before she could respond, Garret spoke.

"What's the point in doing the paperwork, if I end up driving you direct to the club and introduce you immediately to Monica? You'd only have to release me again."

Fox did her shoulder shrugging thing again.

"Okay. Handcuff him." He indicated for Fox to do it.

Taking the lead, Harrington directed them downstairs to the car. The three of them walked in silence, each mulling over their own thoughts. Fox's was the most simplistic. She was solely preoccupied with her partner's attitude of blanket guilt towards Garret. She couldn't refute some of the evidence and would be the first to confess it tended to flag him up as the principal suspect. However, to her, he just didn't seem that kind of guy. In her eyes, he had acted with sincerity when first talked about his secretary's death.

Harrington, on the other hand, believed solidly that he had caught his man. He required no more proof to achieve that, unless this club thing panned out.

Finally, Garret was sandwiched in the middle of this. His thoughts were filled with emotion. Terror of going to prison. Fear for the unknown about his wife's hospital admittance. Creeping uncertainty over the club's location and whether he was going to be able to lead them there directly, if at all. Logan's face flashed in his mind as the only person who could release him from this nightmare. Every time his features appeared, though, they gradually transformed into a forlorn picture of Gloria in a hospital bed.

"So how do you explain your hair appearing in her apartment?" Harrington started out of nowhere, as he placed a hand atop Garret's head to duck it down into the car.

"Well, she worked for me, didn't she? I'm sure it's not beyond the realms of possibility that she could have picked up hairs on her clothing, which subsequently got deposited back there. If you checked, you'd probably find some of your hairs at Fox's apartment. Doesn't mean your partnership has extended to another level, does it?" His words were precise, striking for the first time with a legal philosophy, but his voice showed his true colours, wavering in the emotion of isolation from Gloria.

"That hypothesis may account for one or two hours, but we found quite a few."

"Well, who's to say how often she cleaned?"

The car fell silent until they emerged back into the city mayhem above.

"Where now?" Fox questioned Garret, sensing that Harrington had retreated.

"Head to 42nd Street like I told you. East side of the Broadway end."

Progress was a challenge, traffic stacking up like a slowly parading rack of toast, the steam having been replaced by the products of combustion. Businessmen and families sat inside their vehicles of stature, slaves to a mechanical age that damaged the earth's delicate ecosystem with each explosive thrust of the piston head. Despite each occupant knowing this harrowing fact, of gradual self-extinction, they sat nonchalant, sucking up the vapours into their lungs. As the police car lurched forward, he gazed upon the front seat occupants, seeing mothers. They made him think of Gloria. Despite the way he acted, he cared for her. That was one reason he had ceased to use his craft. He wanted the love to be real, but he was so easily led astray. And when Neve had started working for him, he had found it impossible to avoid flirting with her. The words just fell naturally from his lips. Nothing crude or crass. Subtle innuendoes that could be construed as harmless, if casually observed, but if sentiment was mutual, would be deciphered to reveal their true intent. A piece of him enjoyed the flirting. It was something he had never done with Gloria, because she had been captured by darker means. In that way, his provocative speech was a way of escaping to the childhood he had never had. He needed to see how Neve would react, like an experiment of the mind, to establish whether he was appealing without the magic. Inevitably, once he had been drawn into the experiment, it had become very difficult to stop. It became a test of how far he could push and get away with it. As he gradually achieved more without detection, the experimental side of the act ceased, and the relationship's perpetuation became founded solely on his egocentrism. He enjoyed seeing himself fucking one woman, then going home to another. The ultimate challenge for him was to have both in the same day. That was a challenge to end all challenges, because a woman at the best of times was the embodiment of twisted rationale. Fluctuating hormones acted as a catalyst, causing simple misunderstandings to erupt into screaming matches. Now, for any male to handle and control one of these so-called natural partners was enough, but to control and indeed harmonise two of them, so that they both felt horny within twenty-four hours of each other, needed a miracle, not a mortal. Yet all of this spent disrespect had now transformed into solid guilt. With the death of Neve and the hospitalisation of Gloria, he had suddenly discovered that he felt sickened by his behaviour. In some ways, where he sat now would be a fitting end to his adultery. But he didn't want it to be. He wanted to make things right, to be honest and true to the wife he had acquired all those years earlier.

"Okay, where are we going from here?" They had arrived in the general area that John had indicated.

"Look for a clothes shop called Kenton's. It's next to the alley that you want."

Driving steadily up the kerbside, they eventually came across the shop and as John had described, an alley jutted off behind it. Fox pulled up square to its entrance, so that they could all get a good look down. John stared in disbelief at the emptiness before them. There was no plaque on the wall registering the alley as 'Dead End 54' and there was no neon light shimmering at the end displaying 'Hell's Open'. Yet he knew this was the place, despite the rubbish skips and bums.

"You want to tell us the truth now?" Harrington said.

"I have been." His voice was soft from shock.

"Sorry, what'd you say?"

"I'd like to look down there, if you don't mind?" John requested.

"There's nothing there. What do you hope to achieve?" Harrington sounded annoyed.

"An explanation."

"Give up the act. You've been caught out."

"No." John raised his voice. "I was here. There was a club down there. That was one night ago and now it's gone. I want to know where."

Harrington said nothing and Fox waited for his decision.

"It's not going to hurt to let him look," she prompted her partner.

Harrington thought some more and then indicated for Fox to proceed. Switching the engine off, she got out and opened the back door to allow John out. Her partner steadily followed. On entering the alley, John studied the walls, discovering screw holes where he remembered the plaque sitting. Raising his cuffed hands up he felt across them. Fox watched him inquisitively.

"There was something there." He flicked his head towards the holes. Fox said nothing.

Walking deeper into the alley, he spied other markings to the walls, that, although they weren't evidence in themselves, offered additional reassurance for John that it was here he had visited the night before last. Harrington had stalled at the entrance to the alley, disinterested in what John was doing. Fox continued to follow Garret down to the end, where a loosely chained door prevented further advance. John looked above the door and, as with the alley name, empty screw holes were clearly visible. But unlike two nights ago, the door was graffitied and dirty.

"Come on, that's it." Fox reached out to pull him back, but he evaded her grasp, and before she could try again, he was tugging at the security chains. He didn't pull particularly hard, but they fell away to the ground. Fox managed to catch his arm. He turned towards her.

"Aren't you even the least bit curious?" he asked.

Fox thought for a moment, then let go.

Garret didn't wait for her to change her mind or for Harrington to voice his opinion. He pulled the left-hand door back and entered. The air smelt stale, dust falling from the ceiling. Blocking his passage were a couple of chairs laid on the floor with broken legs. As he pushed one aside, a trail was traced across the floorboards. The room was dark. Spying the light switch he flicked it down, but the power was cut. Momentarily he stood still, surveying the club as he had never expected to find it. As his eyes gradually adjusted, more became visible, until finally he could focus on the torn and moth-ridden curtains that draped down across the back of the stage. Everything was still set out as it had been that night, except now it appeared gilded with five years of neglect.

"So, is this your alibi?" Fox was standing by his side.

"It wasn't like this. This club was open. There were women dancing and stripping."

"Maybe you've confused it with somewhere else?" She entertained his conviction.

"No, it was here."

"Well, it ain't here now." Harrington had come to see what they were doing. "Let's go."

15

"Where the hell have you been? I've been stuck in here two fucking days." John stared through the glass at Logan.

"I've been around." Logan's answer was cool.

"What do you mean you've been around? Haven't you been back to the office? Didn't anybody tell you where I was?" His colleague said nothing. "Well, have you told them the truth yet? Are they going to release me?"

Logan pulled out a cigarette and lit up. "No."

"Why not?"

"They don't believe your story, you know?" He tilted his eyes menacingly. "For a moment I didn't even think they were going to ask me anything, but then this enthusiastic young woman – Fox is her name. Well, she insisted that I give some sort of account of the night of the fifteenth, just to make sure there were no holes in the case. Least that's what she said. To be honest, I think maybe she's fallen for you. Felt sorry for your perfect portrayal of a man suffering an injustice. Alternatively, you could have just put a spell on her."

John was stunned by the comment.

"What do you mean?"

"Don't play dumb with me. I know you better than you know yourself."

"Who are you?" John raised his voice, suddenly feeling threatened by Logan's presence.

"Do you read the papers much, John?" Logan pulled a newspaper from his coat pocket.

John didn't reply.

"I do. Fascinating, really, looking at pictures and reading stories about events that have happened. Wouldn't it be great if there was a way of knowing what events were going to happen? A method by which we could mould our future and change others' destinies. That would be incredible, don't you think?" He paused to look at John's paling face. "I guess that kind of philosophy would get frowned on a lot. Pretty certain the Church wouldn't condone it."

"Who are you?" John repeated.

"Take this, for instance. This man here. Drove his car straight into the side of the bay bridge. While the car was balancing on the edge he managed to climb out. Then, just as he was about to get off, it lost its fight against gravity and started to plunge toward the water. See this photograph was taken just before the car dropped."

Logan put the paper up to the glass so that John could see it clearly. The car was a Porsche with a personalised number plate, 'High 1'. In the picture, the car had just begun to tilt forward, and the man was standing on the trunk, poised to step back on to the solid foundations of the bridge.

"You know what happened next?"

John shook his head and Logan pulled the paper away before he could read it.

"The guy jumped and managed to grab a bent piece of the side barrier. Everybody started to cheer, thinking that he was okay. Then the car smashed into a fuel tanker that was passing below. It exploded, enveloping the man in a mushroom of flames. Nobody saw what happened after that, but investigators found his skeletal remains inside the boat, his skull having been spiked through by a railing. I don't know. What do you think actually killed him? The flames or his brain being kebabbed?"

"I don't know." John responded cautiously.

"I'm sure it was the skewer effect. Don't think the flames would have had chance to work their magic before he landed. Must have all been very painful." He paused for a moment. "I've seen this guy before, you know. You know where he lives? Bet you can't guess?" Logan paused as if waiting for an answer but didn't really expect one. "He lived right next to your lover." He raised the paper up to the glass again, indicating with his finger where John should focus his attention. "Sometimes, as you know, fate just needs a little hand." He smirked.

"Who are you?" John sounded exasperated.

"You know, I hadn't thought about it before, but there are so many similarities between this guy and you. Principally, the fact that fate had them in the wrong place at the wrong time." His expression took a turn for the worst. "What is fate, anyway? Is it truly a random phenomenon that causes specific significant events to happen in people's lives? Whether the event be good or bad, fate gets the blame or credit based on the impact it has on the lives of those involved. Or is fate more sinister than that? More planned and contrived?" Logan folded the paper and placed it back in his pocket. "Are you familiar with the concept of good and evil? Hell, what am I asking, of course you are. Well, what if good fate was an act of God or one of his disciples, or his angels and bad fate was the intervention of the Devil and his demons? That would make sense, wouldn't it? That would then make your current situation attributable to demons. Now, why would they have a grudge against you? Any ideas?"

"What are you?" Garret rephrased his previous question.

"You're catching on now, kiddo. Slow out of the gate but leaping in front now." Logan drew closer to the glass. "Do you want to know why fate has sought you out? Do you want to know why demons have sought you out?"

John nodded, feeling increasingly uncomfortable in Logan's presence.

"You've disowned your faith." The words lashed viciously at the glass and John collapsed back in his seat.

"Which one are you?"

"I'm Foster Logan, attorney at law," he quipped.

"That's not what I asked. What's you real name?"

"I am Semjaza, the eighth protector, the eighth watcher." Fear gripped John's face as he recalled the name he had read so long ago. "A former angel of God's empire now descended to work with the darker natural forces of the earth. My former task was to prevent the use of enchantments by the unworthy. Now my jurisdiction is further reaching and far more uplifting. I am autonomous in my assignments. My sole goal is to perpetuate the dissemination of chaos through the force of Shalek and his disciples."

"Guard!" John shouted in a panic. He wanted out. Wanted to get away.

"Go now and you will certainly die. With the lack of any evidence from me, you'll go down in about five minutes flat. Lethal injection leading to massive systems failure. Bowels responding uncontrollably, heart beating irregularly, muscles spasming as they scream for oxygen, your brain slowly turning to mush, and all the while you are fully conscious." Logan smiled. "It's no skin off my nose. You can die now, or you can simply undertake what you pledged to do fifteen years ago."

The guard appeared. "What do you want?" he asked, seeming annoyed by John's disturbance.

"It's your choice." Logan offered him a final escape option.

John thought for a couple of seconds, sweat bursting through his pores. To stay could mean anything, but he had no desire for death. And he was curious.

"Nothing. Sorry, thought I needed the toilet."

The guard cursed out loud and left.

"Smart choice."

"What do you want?" John was timid in his enquiry.

"Only what you promised all those years ago."

"And what is that?"

"Your servantship and your loyalty of course."

"What? I pledge that to you, and you get me out of here?"

"Almost." Logan smirked. "It's just not quite that simple."

"What else do I have to do?" John hated the way Logan

was looking now, his face tilted forward, eyes firmly fixed on his. Piercing his skull.

"You have to give us what you vowed to deliver all those years ago. You have to make sacrifice to Shalek. You have to destroy those who persecuted you into calling Shalek."

"You want me to kill Manton?" he exclaimed.

"I wouldn't shout about it if I were you. You never know who's listening."

"You want me to kill Manton?" John repeated more quietly this time, seeking clarification of the ransom to which he would be submitting.

"And the others. Young. Fletcher." Logan seemed to be basking in the moment. Relishing the control and power he held over John.

"No way." John's response was swift.

"If you don't, you'll die for certain." He pointed at the entrance door. "Once I walk out of there, I'm gone. No testimony, no second chance. Are you sure you want that? Your wife in hospital, your baby in jeopardy!"

"What do you mean?

"Oh, I'm sorry. Haven't they told you? Gloria. She's lapsed into a coma. Doctors aren't sure whether the baby will survive." He watched as the colour drained from John's cheeks. "I can help with that as well, you know. Make sure you have a healthy little baby who can live through to be a grandfather."

"What assurance do I get that you will save my child?"

"The same assurance that I have from you that you will be true to your word if I get you out of here!"

John sat confused.

"I don't want to put the pressure on, but I can just as easily bring an end to both their lives now if you retract from your pact."

The room fell silent for a while. Then John answered, "I'll do it."

"Good."

"I'll conjure up a spell and be rid of them as soon as I get out."

"That's not quite what we had in mind." Logan's tone was dismissive.

"What was in mind?"

"You see, you've been away from the religion for a while now, so this, to you, will be like a re-initiation. For that, no magic is allowed. This offering must be made by hand."

John knew there wasn't an alternative. "Okay." He smiled with trepidation. "When do I get out of here?"

"Unfortunately, paperwork is slow at the best of times and that's something us supernatural beings can't get involved in. I would have thought you'll be out by the end of the day. Then you can see your wife."

"Well, make it quick." John got up the courage for demands.

"It'll happen as quickly as it can, but you make certain the visit to your wife is brief. Like everything in life, there is a deadline. Yours is a week. A week to make amends with your master." Logan stood up to go, then drew back toward the glass. "A word of advice." He waited for John to pay attention. "After this, don't lose sight of your true faith again. You won't get a second chance. Shalek's not that forgiving."

With that Logan knocked on the door, signalling for the guard to open it. He didn't turn around again, because he knew what he would see. He'd seen it before. A man reduced to a feeble wreck, terrified of what he'd done. Scared to move forward and scared to stand still. These were the situations Logan lived for. The scenario where his subject met with disagreement, no matter which way he turned. He thrived on the exhilaration granted him by the power that shifted through his body at the moment of submission. His fellow watchers persisted in visions of becoming Shalek and how great it would be to control humans as he did. To be able to impose such fear. They missed the point. Shalek had power to intimidate, but he rarely used it. When he was summoned by a caller, they were inevitably protected by a pentagram inside the magic circle, rendering him powerless. Then, from there on, he had to use his watchers and disciples to police the race he sought to perpetuate. In this capacity, the likes of Semjaza, Logan, were the means for tangible contact. They were the real fear givers. The punishment deliverers.

Logan had promised to return to Harrington's office once he was done talking to Garret, though not to give a statement; he'd already done that before. Harrington had refused to give Logan access to Garret until they had an account of the evening. In that way, Logan had played his cards skilfully, pushing Garret successfully towards where he wanted him, without even a pair of twos to his name. If his former colleague had thought twice about it and hadn't been so wrapped up in the events, he would have figured out enough to question that. He hadn't, though, and so Logan's job had been easier, but no less pleasurable. His return to Harrington's office was solely to stamp a confessional name to the text, confirming it as a true story of the evening's proceedings. It obviously wasn't. If it had been, then he would have had to explain the whole devils, demons, servant relationship and how he had called on those forces of evil to open up a derelict old building for one night to deceive Garret. Instead, he had redirected their attention on a club that did exist, one block away, with parallel coordinates, at which Monica did work and would swear to her liaison. It all seemed like a lot of work for such meagre gains, but what price could be placed on a soul.

"So, was he happy?" Fox asked Logan. Harrington remained silent, clearly frustrated to have lost his prime suspect.

"Yes, he can't wait to get out and see his wife. In a similar vein, I can't wait to get off."

"Well, if you could just sign here it will be all over." Fox pointed to a document on the desk.

"For now, anyway," Harrington quipped, but Logan ignored him and signed.

"Thanks for your help. The officer will escort you out." Fox stretched out her hand and shook Logan's. He said nothing further and left.

As he walked down the outside steps to the pavement, he felt a sense of pride in his accomplishment. Emotions weren't something he had been presented with all those years ago when God had first assigned him down on earth, but it was something that Shalek had bound him with. Naturally, the only emotions that Shalek had imparted on him were those that could be twisted toward evil. Logan loved his life. He loved the powers he held, the magic he could perform, but most of all he just took pleasure in reeling his victims in through their own deficiencies rather than through spells. It was important to him for them to suffer their mistake. It was for this reason that he rarely employed his supernatural powers. Like now, he could transmigrate his body to anywhere he cared to imagine, but he didn't. He could run amok, binding people with crushes even though they were married, driving them to adultery and the consequential misery. He could cause men to thieve, maim and murder. But he would gain no enjoyment from such acts. Instead, he preferred the more hands-on approach. He enjoyed walking amongst them at night, appealing to their true evil tendencies. He would taunt women and men alike with offerings of extreme pleasure, gaining their devotion. In the web he spun, nothing counted greater than loyalty and the strongest of these came from the willing. He would usually sexually enlist at least one human a night and once bedded they couldn't resist doing his bidding.

As time had passed and the world had grown around him, he had craved more of a challenge and that was when his purpose had blossomed. He used his enlisted servants to manipulate others towards darker mortal means. Like pawns, he used his troops to incite men and women into committing sin. For a period of time his contribution to Shalek's flock had been minimal in comparison to his counterparts, but what he offered was a quality subscriber, not just an understanding based solely on fear. Logan's legion had grown and was still growing. Each time it reached a critical mass, he would perform the ritual of the demon and promote his most trusted subjects. In this ranking they were like his commanders and he was their general. His fingers could spread wider and stronger in this way. His congregation were empowered to do his will. It was because of this style that he believed Shalek left him to his own devices, trusting in his loyalty. Occasionally, like with Garret, he would be called upon to pursue a failing pledger and in those instances he thrived.

Walking the streets back to his apartment on 5th Avenue, he brushed shoulders with the world. His smile held attraction for women, prompting them to make heavier contact in search of conversation, while for the darker element of the city it gave a warning, flashing glimpses of the insanity that dwelled behind.

He was dressed smartly today in a black suit with an open-collared electric blue shirt. His shoes were the finest Italian, and his overcoat was black, long and made from pure cashmere. To all intents and purposes, he looked every bit the lawyer he had professed to be, even down to that winning smile that mesmerised and intrigued. Walking into an establishment called Faye Rays, he perched himself on one of the bar stools. It was a large bar with only the highest of city life for clientele. They were all businesspeople here, with the exception of the few secretaries who dressed above their status to snare a wealthy husband. All too frequently it was these that Logan prayed on. Apart from his natural sexual allure, he had the ability to offer them what they wanted. He could lay the husband of their dreams out on a platter for them, if only they would relinquish their soul. Tonight, though, he fancied something with richer blood. He wanted to score a new partner, someone who could open the doors to new congregations. Someone who could give the cause supplemental finance to perpetuate. He needed a disciple to help coordinate his ventures, because he had servants in the thousands. It was a rare day that he walked the city and didn't pass a minion of some level, which was good. But there were just too many for effective control with his current regime. He needed a right-hand woman.

Sitting there casually drinking whisky, he felt the constant gazes of the husband seekers seeping into his back. Over the course of a couple of hours, three had attempted to buy him a drink and two had unsubtly bumped into him, hoping to stimulate conversation. He rejected all of these, pleasantly, of course. He never wanted to deter future potential. And as the minutes ticked by, he started to resign himself to pursuing one of the former offerings, but then it happened. A woman who had been sat commandingly at the other end of the bar, conversing with a swarm of males who verbally jousted for her attention, looked over to him and smiled. The game began. Over the next ten minutes several glances were cast between them, like silent negotiation. Finally, Logan bought her a drink and that was when she parted company with the group that evidently bored her, making diplomatic verse of departure before collecting up her briefcase and walking with professional esteem to the stool adjacent to him.

"Thanks for the drink, Mr...?" she spoke with a demanding, yet polite attitude.

"Logan, Foster Logan." He offered his hand in greeting. She took it, shaking it firmly.

"Jane Trubile." She introduced herself and sat down. There was no 'Do you mind if I join you?' or 'Is this seat taken?'. Her character was strong enough to acknowledge the obvious. Logan liked that. She held potential.

"So, what do you do, Mr Logan?"

"Call me Foster." She nodded in acceptance, indicating politely for him to continue. "I'm kind of in the legal profession."

"Thought as much. You have that evil eye of the profession."

"What do you mean?" Logan was amused by her perception.

"Please don't take this the wrong way, but you have the demeanour of a man who's continually dispersing eighty percent truth."

"I have to confess that after eight years in the city, that's the most interesting approach I have ever heard." He tried to catch her of guard and suppress her confidence in the process.

"I'm sorry." It had worked. She blushed slightly. "I said I didn't mean to offend. It's just I work with lawyer's fifty percent of the time and you get used to their mannerisms and anaesthetised to their honesty." She smirked to indicate the sarcasm. "Still, it was wrong of me to stereotype and immediately class you in the same category."

"Apology accepted." There was a momentary silence as she searched for a follow-up sentence. Logan watched her briefly suffer before bailing her out. "I guess it's my turn now to ask about your livelihood, but I won't. Instead, I will endeavour to demonstrate equal intuition." He laid a compliment, wanting to remain on the knife's edge between comfortableness and embarrassment. "By your style and the attraction, you hold for your male colleagues, I would have to say that you are either their boss or that you are the best lover in town." He grinned and took a sip of his drink waiting to see the reaction.

"Well, I can confirm that in that situation I am certainly the former." She paused with a wry smile. "That doesn't mean I'm not the latter as well. It's just that none of them will ever discover that. Very few men have, or will ever have, a stake in that camp." She rose to the bait, exactly how he had wanted her to.

"Okay, we know status, but we don't yet know the profession." He placed a hand to his face in portrayal of careful musing. "Taking into consideration you're understanding the characteristics of members of the legal profession, you must work within a company that requires excessive legal contact. In that respect, I would suggest you are a member of a financial institution. Your specific tasks being mergers and acquisitions." He grinned triumphantly.

"Ever thought about going into fortune-telling?" She was impressed. "If I was to grade with a percentage, that would have to be in the mid to low nineties. Which I must say, is very impressive for ten minutes' worth of eye contact and five minutes of conversation."

He shrugged his shoulders.

"Do you want a job?" she joked.

"What can I say? It's a talent. I'm sensitive to personalities."

He gave a wry smile.

"You must be fantastic at cards."

They laughed.

"So where did I get the ten percent wrong?"

"My underwear colour," she flirted.

"No, seriously." His tone turned sarcastically serious. "We'll get on to assessing your knickers later," Logan flirted back.

"Is that a promise or a threat?"

"Neither. But all being well, something that you will never forget."

"My, aren't we a sharp one? I like that." She didn't wait for him to make any further sexual innuendos – she had clearly decided they had travelled as far as they should at that moment. "I run my own enterprise that buys and sells a variety of things. We are part financial institution, doing some stock trading, but really that was just the foundation block of the company. I traded until I had enough funds to offer high risk development capital myself. You know, lend good investments the money for company purchases, management buyouts, technology developments. That kind of thing." She paused, looking at him quizzically. "You still interested?"

"Yes. Just feeling a little insignificant," he joked.

"It was during one of those ventures that I met Matt. He's the guy with the grey suit and green tie," she whispered, pointing over her shoulder. "He was one of the guys seeking to do a management buyout. He's an engineer but with a strong sense of business about him. Well, he had these grand ideas about taking this firm over and developing its systems, structures and strategy. His concepts blew me away the first time he explained them. I agreed almost immediately to funding him. Not blindly, mind you. I had his house listed as collateral and the interest rate started at ten percent for every month in the first twelve rising by two percent each twelve-month cycle after that."

"He must have been mad." Logan played up to her story.

"No. Just knew his limitations, which weren't many. He turned the company around within a year, from a break-even wreck to a twenty percent profit, forty percent higher revenue firm." She took a sip of her drink. "That's when I changed my mind about my future ventures and became more than a one-man show. And that was when the other guys turned up." She inclined her head back to the men she had left. "Got into buying companies for ourselves, developing them and then selling them back or stripping them to component parts and selling them separately. Make a lot more money doing it this way and it's so much more satisfying."

"Is tonight a little celebration, then?"

"Your intuition strikes home again." She grinned. "We've just finished our biggest strategic development programme, as we call it. Quadrupled our money on a twelve-million-dollar capital outlay over a fifteen-month period. And we've just completed the deal to sell the final section of that business."

"So, is tomorrow a day of rest for you?"

"Day of rest?" she smirked. "I'm a good boss. I've given them the week off."

"Well, all I was wondering was if you would like to spend tomorrow with me?" He played his hand cool.

"Why do we need to get back together tomorrow? Why not just continue on through tonight?" Her over confidence was starting to make it all too easy for him.

"That would be just perfect."

"That's later, though. First, buy me another drink and tell me more about yourself."

"Okay!" Logan caught the bar tender's attention and pointed at their glasses. She watched attentively, studying his form.

"So, about you?" She reached out and touched him on the sleeve.

"Well, my job is evil and misery," he said frankly.

Jane laughed.

"No, seriously, I perpetuate the darker side of life."

"What are you, a defence lawyer?"

"In a manner of speaking. I am the prosecutor, the public defender, the judge and the jury all rolled into one tidy package. In my profession I save a fortune in legal bills. There's never a hung jury and there's never a mistrial."

"Are you a God?" She laughed.

"No, but you're getting warmer." His eyes remained serious, but he allowed her a small smile just to retain the mood.

"You're a devil," she joked again, seeming confused by where he was going. The fresh drinks arrived, and Logan paid.

"Let me put it this way. I work for an institution that is to people's souls what you are to their pockets."

She looked increasingly confused.

"Okay, try it this way. Both our institutions provide a service, and for that service we expect a return. Yours provides money; my company provides whatever's missing. And within that I ensure that payment is just and timely."

"You're a debt collector," she persisted with her humour.

"Bang on." He knew she was growing weary of his evasive riddles.

"You don't work for the Mob, do you?"

"No, but they are one of my best customers." He paused. "Does that bother you?"

"Not particularly. I've lent them money before – legitimately, mind you. They've always been good credit."

It was Logan's turned to laugh this time. She was perfect. Everything he needed. And he just knew she was going to be the fuck of his decade and that was quite a statement, considering the numbers of contestants that had gone before her. She also deliriously outclassed all her predecessors in personality and that made her even more alluring. To dupe and penetrate a sophisticate was a much greater conquest and so much more invigorating for him.

They talked for a little longer, while consuming two more rounds of drinks. During that time, Logan had listened to her life's history and tactfully remained silent about his. She didn't seem to be particularly bothered about his background anyway and that one attribute enhanced his sexual anticipation further, because initially she would set herself out as the one offering the goods to him. She imagined herself as the one in control. But once she had felt him inside her, all that would change. She would want him deeper and deeper. Her appetite would be impossible to stifle. And afterwards, her allegiance would be so much more potent, having made that mental journey from superiority to inferiority. In the future she would want to be near him for nothing but to feel the sweet sensation of vulnerability. He smiled at the thought.

"Don't just think it. Let's go do it!" Jane grinned and brushed her foot up the side of his leg.

"Okay." He stood up and took her hand. "I would say your place or mine, but in mine there's something I want to show you."

"Lead on." As they turned around, she noticed her colleagues had departed without telling her and she pulled a puzzled face at the fact, but she got over it quickly. "So, where's your place?"

"On 5th Avenue, up by the park."

"Very nice. You must be a good debt collector?"

"Well, let's just say I have a few ventures on the side."

"The more you talk, the more I think I'd better hang on to you." She put her spare arm through his, testing the water. He clenched it tight to his side.

They walked in silence until reaching Logan's apartment building. It was a ten-storey block, with one of the lowest profiles and fewest occupants along the west side of the park. Externally the building was fashioned in the sixties, while internally it had been gutted during the late eighties and renovated to a higher modern standard. During the same process, they had changed the desired occupant profile by knocking sets of four small flats together to establish larger grand pads. Logan's den of iniquity was on the tenth floor and was one of the biggest in the building.

As they entered, Jane's mouth dropped as she slowly rotated to view the layout. The front door opened immediately into an open-plan greeting area come lounge. Laid down on the floor were grey slate slabs, with ornate medieval rugs strewn across them randomly. Designed like tapestries, each one told a tale. Jane scanned them steadily, her interest stimulated, but also slightly perturbed by the evil suffering that they portrayed. She dismissed the feeling quickly with an each-to-their-own philosophy. Two similar, larger tapestries hung from metal railings with pointed finials on the left- and right-hand walls. Blackened windows dressed the east-facing wall, draped with deep red velvet curtains. In everything she viewed she could see age. The European dark ages to be precise. The room was history, and with the windows blackened so, only the entrance door stood firm to tell you which century you were in. Two openings led off this central chamber, their doors having been removed and replaced by curtains of identical deep design and fabric to those across the windows. As with the tapestries they ran on twisted iron rods with spear-like ends.

"Don't you like the twentieth century?" She looked towards him, slightly bemused.

He grinned. "I love it. So much financial potential. So much natural evil. But there is nothing more peaceful than the past. A time when nature and God liaised to run the world. A time when the darker emotions were the minority. They were taboo."

"So, you like this stuff, then?"

He didn't answer but indicated for her to follow him through into the next room. She did as he bid, dropping her briefcase on top of one of the benches. As she brushed the curtain back out of the way, she found herself in a kitchen dining area. There were no mod-cons, just an open hearth on the far wall, with a heating plate sat across one side for pots and spits for cooking meats fixed across the other. A long wooden table sat in the middle of the room, eight high-backed chairs positioned around it. Each chair was fashioned with a triangular section at the top of the back rest, above head height, a single name carved into each. She moved to read one of them.

"So, who's this Arakiel bloke?"

"Not your concern yet. Follow me," he commanded. She followed.

Passing through another drape they entered the bedroom. There was no bed, though, just a large flat mattress covered with silk sheets and around twenty cushions of different sizes and colours. The room was candlelit. Clumps of candles sat together in tactical positions where lamps would have normally been placed. The walls were stripped back to bare blocks the size of shoe boxes, presenting the illusion that they were inside a castle. Jane couldn't believe they were real and stretched out to touch the surface, expecting to feel the twentieth-century texture of plastic. Instead, her palm was greeted by the chill of cold sandstone. In the far-left corner, an iron spiral staircase led to a bolted wooden hatch in the ceiling. The bolt was padlocked shut and for the first time Jane felt uncomfortable about her surroundings. Logan took hold of her hand and pulled her closer to him. His touch settled her, but she still stared quizzically at the rest of the room. On the bare walls there were various weapons of war, spanning from medieval swords and axes to samurai swords and nunchakus. They were positioned in four arrangements, each signifying a period of history or religion and backed by a banner displaying a coat of arms.

"Now, this is where I've been wanting to get you for the past two hours." Logan pulled her close, grabbing her other hand as she spun in. "You feel nervous. Don't! There's nothing to fear but what you conjure in your own mind."

She started to open her mouth to speak, but Logan covered the void with a kiss before the words could be delivered. Inside her guts had been knotted, but his touch untwined them. Her anxiety drifted away. Kissing was the second most sensual experience. Naked skin on skin, untethered by exposure to the outside world and heightened in sensitivity. They kissed long and hard, Logan wrapping his arms around her back in a strong embrace. Slowly sliding one hand up her spine, he fixed it firmly to the back of her skull, interlacing his fingers with her hair. Then, pulling her away, he dropped lower to kiss her neck.

Frozen to the spot, Logan could tell she was terrified and unable to do anything, except languish in the tender impulses his caresses were bringing. As his tongue drifted lower towards her bosom, he started to release her shirt buttons one at a time. As he revealed her lace bra, he felt her hands land on his head, plunging him in between her breasts. He allowed her direction, using his tongue and teeth to unclip the front snapper. Then, tugging the cups to either side, he released the fullness of her white flesh, allowing her breasts to land warm and smooth against his cheeks. She squeezed her elbows tight, nuzzling him in the cradle of her chest. Kissing and licking at her now swollen nipples, he removed her suit jacket. Flinging it to the floor, he pulled her shirt free of her skirt and glided his hands up her naked spine. She started to moan. Reaching the top of her back, he clustered the shirt fabric in his hands and pulled it down, exposing her bony frame. As the shirt fell from her, Logan stood upright again, lapping kisses over her shoulders and neck as he did so, eventually resting back on her mouth. Jane now started to take greater participation, balancing out the clothes situation by rapidly removing his shirt. Logan could feel her fingertips sliding over his hairless skin, she felt the strength of his pectoral muscles as they flexed. Pulling her chest towards his, Logan finished stripping her torso bare by flicking the shoulder straps of her bra loose, leaving their skin to saturate in contact. As it did, she flinched momentarily, her hairs standing proud from the chill of his body.

Suddenly Logan pushed her down on to the bed. Catching her off guard, her arms flailing around, she landed softly amongst the cushions, her expression one of uncertainty. He quickly rectified her understanding, dropping headfirst down into the well of her thighs. Immersing his face between them, he pushed them apart, forcing the hem of her skirt higher. She knew what he wanted and assisted, wriggling her body to allow her skirt to ride up and her legs to be spread wider. The hem's gradual elevation revealed her stockings tops and Logan paused for a few moments, lapping at the naked skin up towards her crotch. Then, with a careful slip of his left hand, he caressed the nylon sheath from her ankle up to her thigh, completing the movement with a delicate flick of the suspender clip, releasing the front and back in sequence. Her moans turned to groans, emerging ruffled from her gaping mouth.

He repeated the motion with her other leg, all the while retaining tongue to skin contact in the cusp of her slender thighs. When both stockings had been released, he pulled them off, discarding them behind him.

By now her desire for penetration was out of control. She wreathed on the bed, thrusting her knicker-clad vagina down on his head. The cotton of her pants was already lustfully damp, and Logan could feel it on his cheek as he turned to address each thigh in turn. It had been a while since he had managed to instil so much pleasure into such a virtuous woman. Lifting himself back up, he ripped at her knickers, exposing her private sanctuary. Then, removing his own trousers and pants, he moved straight back up, priming himself to invade her.

"Wait!" She spoke softly, but her hands stopped him less delicately. "I'm a safety woman." She pointed down at his dick. "Condom?"

"I've got one on." Startled, she looked back down. Logan allowed her to see what she wanted to see.

"How did you do that?"

"It's a talent."

"Well, carry on, then." She fell back down to the bed and the illusion disappeared.

Her skirt was the only item of clothing left on her body now and he rolled it up, ensuring that her legs held maximum flexibility, before pushing in. Immediately her back arched away from the silk sheets and she exuded a loud gasp. At first, he only partially entered, moving in and out in a slow, steady rhythm. Then gradually penetrated deeper and deeper with each thrust. Eventually he had entered as far as he could. Her hands tugged at the sheets, pulling them free of the mattress, drenching them in her sweet sweat. Eyes fixed shut, Logan watched her bite at her lip as she had orgasm after orgasm, each time clamping him tighter inside. After the fourth he withdrew altogether.

"What?" She looked panicked that he was dissatisfied.

"Are you game for an experiment?" He smirked.

"That depends?"

"There's no depending. You have to trust me on this one."

"Okay." She sounded uncertain, but he knew right now she would do anything to feel him inside her again.

"Come here."

He stood up and walked towards the spiral staircase. Climbing it, he unlocked the padlock and slid the bolt back. Then, with a swift movement, he flipped the hatch up, exposing another room. Jane stared up, scared of what he was doing but still overwhelmed with a desperate desire for him to penetrate her once more. She was loving the vulnerability she felt while in his embrace, helpless to his sexual assault. The dull light above silhouetted Logan's face, altering his appearance and increasing the sinister sneer of his grin. He beckoned her up with his finger. She followed. The iron steps felt cold under her feet and she clutched the railing, steadying her ascent. As her head entered the new room, she saw more candles scattered on the ground in clusters, but also individual ones sat in wall fittings and four-foot-tall candelabras. The walls retained the same medieval theme, but on one wall, a large two metre by two metre slabs of limestone was inset, a pentagram carved on it. At each of the five points sat squat black candles on small block ledges, the wax of their predecessors forming fingers that stretched out toward the floor. Around the star a larger circle had been inscribed with what appeared to be the same names as on the dining room chairs etched equidistant around its external circumference. Marked around the inside was a passage written in an ancient tongue that held identical structure to the mottos listed below the personalised dining chairs.

"Come over here," Logan commanded. She capitulated, but as she walked toward him, her attention drifted to the floor and a similar tribute to that carved on the wall. The only difference here was that within the outer circle, four shackles rested open in preparation for something.

"You don't expect me to let you lock me up in those, do you?" Her sanity was returning, the deep-seated lust drying up within her as the cold air nipped at her skin.

"I asked you to trust me and you agreed. I assure you, nothing but pleasure awaits."

He stood aside and took hold of her hand, then kneeling, he tugged her down. She relinquished control, feeling somehow appeased by his touch. Ripping her skirt from around her waist. Logan fixed her spreadeagled to the floor. The rough surface of the slab made her twitch, her muscles tense in discomfort. Logan walked around her once, speaking under his breath. She couldn't understand him, but her mind told her that he was chanting in the same foreign language etched beneath her. Slowly she felt a tingling sensation as if a hand was gliding over her body, caressing her calf muscles. Steadily the sensation rose towards her waist and she felt her sexual anticipation return. Logan was still circling her, chanting and moving his arms about in silent prayer. Slowly the tingling started in other locations, building up until it felt as if a multitude of hands were shifting across her flesh, concurrently tenderising her breasts and inner thighs. She closed her eyes, twisting in the ecstasy. The sensations slowly moved inside her vagina, the flesh parting as before. She kept her eyes firmly fixed shut, afraid to witness what was actually happening around her. She knew the presence wasn't physical. She knew something else was taking advantage of her, but she endured the invasion with lustful terror. With the entity taking an ever-deeper presence, she felt her vagina twitching in readiness for something special. As the orgasm brewed to breaking point, it suddenly happened. She felt cold naked flesh lying against hers and with a single thrust, it broke through deep into her womb, deeper than before. She screamed in pleasure. There was no delicate nature to what was happening to her now. They weren't making tender love anymore. The event had turned into a consensual fuck. She wanted him thrusting into her and he pumped her like a whore, without a care to her pain. He rammed harder and harder. She was in pain but loving it. With him on top she wanted to feel dirty. She thrived on the new lack of respect he displayed, as well as the contempt she held for herself. As he drove forcefully into her, it was as if his penis was taking a different form. Stabbing inside her.

Cutting through her fragile skin. Despite the pain, she savoured a continuous orgasm, her flesh clenching at his manhood. Even her inner thighs were bruised raw, the nerve endings screaming as his legs chaffed at the surface. The pleasure of pain was almost excruciating, and she wanted to burst free of her shackles, but concurrently, she also loved the way they dug into her flesh as she writhed in agony underneath him.

She began to feel a warmth welling in her womb. His thrust was getting heavier, reaching a crescendo. Suddenly a flush of liquid spilled into her. She could feel it filling every crevice. But he didn't stop, he persisted, spilling more alien liquid into her with each thrust. She screamed in pain.

The pleasure had gone now. She wanted him out of her, but he continued. For the first time she opened her eyes and saw the hatred on his face. The powerful disdain. She screamed again, trying to wriggle away, but he just followed her. As she moved, she felt the floor wet beneath her bum and looked down to discover that she laid in a pool of blood and blackened semen. She screamed again, suddenly realising the blood was hers. Her terror became uncontrollable, her mouth opening in high-pitched protest but exuding nothing. He stopped. Pulling back and standing up, he displayed the splatter of their combined fluid over his body. She could still feel the fluid seeping out from her, filling the pentagram with colour.

"What have you done?" she managed to say.

"I am making you one of mine." With that he dipped his finger in the liquid and painted a symbol on her abdomen. "Now taste this and feel truly alive for the first time."

He glazed his finger once more in the liquid and pushed it between her lips. She didn't resist. The pain drifted away, and her shackles fell loose. Her confusion had dispersed. The taste of their liquid had given her an instantaneous understanding. She knew now what he was and what she was to him.

"Now go downstairs and wait. I need to talk to our master." Logan instructed.

16

As the sheriff entered the press room, he immediately flinched at the sound of dripping. A slow steady drip that was impacting on something metallic. The vintage printing machine stretched out down the full thirty-metre length of the shop floor. Pages of the *Shifton Chronicle* were interlaced around rollers, prepared to pass delicately through the printing process at a surprisingly rapid pace. He stopped for a moment and cocked his head to see what today's front page was going to read. 'Horse Boy Born to Bum' was the title that glared back at him, with a hazy picture of the suggested hybrid baby cradled in his mother's arms. He shook his head and walked on, continuing in the direction of the dripping sound.

The sheriff was a tall man with a slim athletic build. He wore the office uniform of beige shirt with brown lapels and double pockets, in which bulged a pair of sunglasses, a pen and notepad. His trousers were chocolate brown, matching the colour of his holster, which housed a six-shooter standard issue. On his feet he wore ankle boots and, on his head, a brown baseball cap that had 'Sheriff' embroidered in gold lettering across the front. He walked proud, though without the air of superiority that was common to many law enforcement officers in these parts. He was the oddball of the crop in that respect; always courteous, never presumptuous and always generous. This latter attribute had been with him since childhood and developed further in adulthood thanks to his wife Nicola's unquestioning generosity. There was no doubt that she was the driving force in that arena, a quality that benefitted her work at the library organising reading classes for the dyslexic and under-developed.

Up ahead he could see his deputy and the coroner standing over the remains of a body that had come into full contact with a printing press. They both looked up momentarily towards him on hearing the click of his heels on the concrete floor and then looked back down at the corpse. Kevin Shane was Freddy's deputy, and they had a very close relationship, having grown up together since he had arrived in Shifton at the age of thirteen. They had been through some good times since then and Freddy had asked Kevin to stand as his deputy five years ago, when he had lost his job at the mill. Initially, Freddy had some doubts about his decision, but these had been quickly appeased and he now quite happily confessed that it was the best decision he had ever made. Kevin had taken to law enforcement like a nymphomaniac becoming a prostitute. He loved it, had a passion for it and even sometimes got depressed that there wasn't enough crime going on. This would be his first death though. Not that Freddy was an old hat at investigating fatalities. He had only investigated two and they both transpired to be the most extreme resolutions to domestic discontentment. Still, it had given him a basic understanding of how he wanted to proceed, and he had no worries that Kevin would be enthusiastically involved.

Freddy was standing directly above his deputy now and could see the complete mess he had been viewing. The body, which was beyond immediate identification, had been dropped headfirst in between the two main feed rollers. The skull had been fragmented, creating a speckled montage across the reams of paper that had been flying through. The torso had also been damaged under compression but had been more suited to withstanding the pressures of the press, quickly causing the machine to trip out on overload before the legs had been pulled in.

"Who we got here?" Freddy tapped Kevin on the shoulder.

"Andy Fletcher." He handed back a bagged wallet, pointing at the driver's licence.

"How did it happen?"

"The best we can tell is that he fell down off that viewing platform." He flicked his head towards the meshed walkway that provided access across the press.

"Surely that would have caused more damage than this? It's a seven-metre drop, for Christ's sake."

"Not necessarily. It's a tight fit between these two rollers and it's only the bottom one that actually drives, the others guide. So, there was no real additional force to drag him through."

"What was he doing up there to start with?"

Kevin had stood up now and turned to face his boss. "Well, according to Sally, that's the worker who found him, he often walked the lines to check the print was running smoothly. Apparently, he took considerable pride in his paper."

"Really?" Freddy pointed to the front page.

"Well, maybe not so much pride in the content, but he liked his rubbish to be well presented."

"What was this Sally lady doing here?"

"She comes in to help on early morning runs. Sometimes they don't meet the deadlines and have to come in early doors to print off. Today was just one of those weeks."

"Is she the only one who comes to help?"

"Yes. At least she was this morning."

"Have we ruled out foul play?" Freddy asked.

"Don't see the need to consider it?" Kevin paused a moment to give the sheriff chance to answer. Nothing came. "Do you?"

"I have to confess; it is puzzling me how a man who walked that gantry on a frequent basis could manage to lose his balance sufficiently to allow him to topple over a four-foot-high railing and plummet straight down into this machine."

"Accidents happen. Human error and all that."

"Did this Sally hear a scream?"

"No. She was out back at the time fetching a new roll of paper. The forklift is a bit noisy."

"Odd, don't you think?" Freddy questioned. Looking up

puzzled.

"What? The fact she never heard anything?"

The sheriff ignored him. "I don't know. It's just that if it were me, I'd be standing there, leaning over to get a better view. For arguments sake, let's say I'm standing high on that first railing, because something's caught my eye and I'm afraid the print's not coming off how it should. I'm hanging on to that top railing to give me as much support as possible." He acted out his story on the spot. "Then I lose my balance enough to topple forwards over the top. If it was me, I'd still be holding on to the bar, trying to stay alive. So, my body would rotate, meaning that if I fell, my feet would hit the floor first."

"Maybe he rotated in mid-air?"

"He was falling, not diving." He took a breath. "No, whichever end went first, I figure that was the one most likely to hit the rollers first." Freddy took a look at the body and then back up at the gantry. "Have we dusted for prints yet?"

"No. Didn't see the need to. I'd put it down to an industrial accident, accidental death, that sort of thing."

"That sort of thing? You may well be right, but there's enough here to cause doubt and that means we do a thorough job. So, let's get the kit out and get on with our job."

"But there must be hundreds of prints."

"Yes, and one of them might be a killers. So, come on. Go get the gear while I talk with the coroner."

Kevin departed disgruntled, almost like a petulant child. He had been playing big man until Freddy had turned up, showing off to Louise, the coroner. In a way, Freddy had been showing off as well; she was, after all, an exceptionally attractive woman and the only eligible lady of their age group in town. Obviously, that was excluding those with too free and easy a disposition. She was aged around twenty-eight but compared to her peer group she had a wiser head. Her hair was styled into a layered bob, giving a ruffled appearance. Sections of hair had been tinted red, which ordinarily may have appeared tacky, but on her it didn't. She wore silver, thin-framed, elliptical glasses, emphasising her deepest blue eyes. Her skin was smooth and fair, making her look, at times, ever so delicate. She had arrived in Shifton a year ago, after spending time in the Big Apple completing her training. This was her first solo posting and as such, Freddy had been party to her maturing phase, witnessing the 'I may be young, but I'm qualified' syndrome.

"Hi, Louise, what we got?"

"Okay, finally the chief says hello." She smirked.

"Hey, you know I'm not one of those touchy-feely city folks. We're just plain old speakers out here. Talk when you need to talk."

"What a shame. And there was me thinking that one day we would build a relationship." Her smirk transformed into a smile. "You've dashed my hopes again Sheriff."

"Don't toy with me, Lou, you know I'm a happily married man. But if I wasn't, you'd be first on my list," he joked.

"Don't, you'll make me blush."

"Come on, stop your teasing and tell me what you know." His voice hollowed regimentally, and she knew it was time to be serious.

"Alright." She paused to think. "I can't see any signs that death was caused by anything other than massive head trauma from falling between these two rollers. There are some bruises to his wrists and ankles that were generated prior to death, although I can't say for sure that they were a result of any foul play."

"Will you be able to give me a better indication later?"

"I'll obviously try." She took a breath. "There's a scrape to his left knee, which looks as though he stumbled and gashed it on some of the mesh flooring up there. It dug in pretty deep. Ripped straight through his trousers. It's the closest indicator that I have toward a sign of a struggle."

"Any traces of skin under the fingernails?"

"There's some residue." She picked up the bagged hand and indicated a collection of matter trapped under his left index finger. "But it's gonna take analysis to determine what it is and where it's from."

"You gonna send that over to Charston?"

"Yeah, I'll do it first thing tomorrow."

"Can you tell whether he was conscious at the time?"

"Give me a break. Humpty Dumpty looked better than this!" Louise jibed.

"Just asking. No need to lose it. It's not very professional, you know!" he said in mock condescension.

"You know what I like about working with you? It's the fact that it's difficult for you to preach superiority when you're younger than me." She smirked.

"How d'you know that?"

"Kevin told me."

"So, you've been asking about me, hey?" he teased, grinning from ear to ear.

"I thought you were married?"

"It depends what you're offering as to whether that's relevant."

She bobbed her head quizzically. "So, there's room in your heart for more than one woman?"

"I didn't say in my heart." He indicated with his hands that she would have to look at a lower part of his anatomy to find dual parking spaces.

"I think we'd better end the conversation right there and return back to work." Smiling, she took a breath. "As you were about to ask, I shall have the report on your desk by close of shop tomorrow. Is that okay?"

"Louise, your service is always okay. Anytime you want to expand your remit, you just let me know." He teased.

"Hey, I thought we'd agreed to leave that subject?"

"You must know that men think about women at least once every minute. So, you can't blame me for bringing it up now I know how you feel."

"Alright, then." She moved in close to call his bluff and whispered in his ear, "Stop by the morgue on your way home later. Say about six o'clock. I'll show you how much I can expand my remit and your knowledge." She casually brushed her hand across his thigh.

"I think, like you say, we'd better leave that expansion alone." He stepped back. "We wouldn't want it to get in the way of our work."

She started laughing. "Thought you might say something like that."

"You cow." He realised her insincerity and let out a small chuckle. "You better not have any outstanding parking tickets."

"Me? I'm a model citizen."

"Oh, I don't know about that. So far I've got you on soliciting a police officer."

"Yeah, and I could have you for sexual harassment," she retorted.

"Okay. Let's call it quits."

She nodded.

"You'll have that report on my desk back end of tomorrow."

She nodded again.

"Okay. I'll speak to you later." With that he left.

Flirtatious behaviour aside, Freddy had seen all he needed to see. The next bit, the hardest bit, was contemplation. With the few facts at hand, he had to determine firstly if there was crime to pursue and, if so, who did it, why they did it and finally uncover evidence to prove the case. Nothing he had seen so far directly suggested foul play. Yet his instinct saw too much implausibility in the accident.

The sun was still rising as he left the *Shifton Chronicle* building. Kevin was in his squad car, relaying details back to the station. By the look on his face, Freddy could tell he was also having a grumble. As soon as Kevin spotted Freddy, he finished his conversation and began rummaging across the back seat.

The *Chronicle* building was in the centre of town opposite the library. The space had previously been occupied by two second-hand clothing stores and before that, in Freddy's youth, a record store and soda fountain. Both of the previous ventures had hit financial difficulty. The last owner shut down at exactly the same time as Fletcher was lobbying the council for a grant so that he could start up a local paper. They had been sceptical at the time, because it had been tried before and had failed. Nobody had taken an interest in local stories. However, over several weeks he managed to convince them that he could print a paper everybody in the community would want to read and they had believed him. Freddy had been annoyed at the time, still remembering the little runt who had bullied and taunted kids at school. He didn't believe he could have changed. And when it came to business, he saw Fletcher as having all the panache of a bent used-car salesman. Unfortunately, Freddy's appraisal of Fletcher had never been called for. The town had watched with great interest as the site had been cleared. Speculation had been rife over what was to replace the demolished buildings. When the news broke that it was a newspaper office, intrigue stimulated huge debate and eagerness. When the first issue had been printed and racked on shop shelves for purchase, it had sold out in under four hours. To be fair to Fletcher, Freddy had actually bought a copy and read it cover to cover. It had been quite interesting and informative, even insightful in places, though credit for the latter went to the one real journalist on the paper's staff, who was at the start of his career, looking for experience before searching for work with the big boys. He didn't have to wait long, being offered a position at the *Washington Times* within three months. After that, the quality of articles had gone south, along with the readership. Every now and then, a big enough local event would take place and Fletcher would write about it in his own inimitable style. People would buy the paper to find out the scandal and it limped on. Freddy had no idea what would happen to it now that its founder, editor and owner had died.

"Okay, whereabouts do you want prints taking?" Kevin had got organised and was awaiting instructions.

"Just go over everything within a ten-metre radius of the body." He didn't even look at his deputy as he spoke, something catching his eye across the street. Kevin moved off. "Hey, and don't forget to take prints from all the employees!" Freddy shouted after him, his attention still focussed elsewhere.

Eyes wide he stared across the street, watching a figure move along the far sidewalk. It had mannerisms he felt familiar with but failed to place. The feet plodded forward in physiological drudgery, shoulders sagging in tune to fit the visible mood. A long coat draped down, shrouding his body, covering all but his jean bottoms. The man's hand fidgeted with his coat pocket in a manner that suggested agitation, despite his depressed demeanour. His head lolled to the left, which again sparked déjà vu. He continued to glare at the back of the guy's head as he walked away, desperately searching his memory for an answer to the familiarity. Nothing came. He crossed the street, having no intention of addressing the man but keen to continue his study. Eventually the figure turned out of sight and Freddy entered Charlie's convenience store.

"Did you see that guy?" he asked Nina, who was standing behind the cash register.

"Yeah, Sheriff," she said in her quaint thick southern accent.

"You recognise him?"

"No. Never seen him before in my life. Why?"

"Oh, nothing, just appeared familiar. You know?"

"No, can't say that I do." Her answer surprised Freddy, breaking him out of his trance, but before he could say anything she grinned. He didn't pursue it.

"You got a copy of last week's *Chronicle*?"

"Now with that I can help you." She dropped below the counter. "Been waiting for them to drop this week's off and collect the unsold copies, but if you'd care to reduce my sale or returns, you are quite welcome." She reappeared. "That'll be fifty cents." She handed him the paper and he scanned the front page. "You know you should really keep up to date with local events. If you stick around, I'll sell you one of this week's as well."

"I don't think they'll be coming."

"Why's that?" She smiled, thinking he was joking.

"Well, you see the commotion across the road? My car parked up on the kerb?"

"Yes."

"Inside the editor is lying dead in the middle of this week's edition."

"You shittin' me?"

"Nope."

He walked back across the street. Louise was just packing up her car. "You done?"

"I am now." She slammed the car boot down. "Pleased to see one of us has the time to read a newspaper."

"I wish that were true. But I'm only just managing to stay a week behind the community." He showed her the date and tipped her a wink.

"You can't be reading it for its community insight, so there must be something else!"

"So, you're not just a pretty face." He jested.

She scowled.

"Motive!" he announced.

"So, you're just playing dumb, then, when you're actually quite intelligent," Louise quipped back.

Freddy started to stammer a response but couldn't think of anything suitable. "Just make damn sure you've got that report on my desk at the end of the day."

"Oh, so the deadline's come forward now!"

"Well, if you think you've got time to chatter…"

"Don't you worry about that. It'll be there." She got into her car and he watched her drive off before climbing up into his Land Cruiser and driving back to the station.

17

"Is it true?" Freddy looked up to see the local Father standing on the other side of the counter. "Fletcher's been found dead?"

"It appears to be Fletcher. We're still awaiting confirmation." He addressed the slim figure of a man clothed in jeans and white-collared black shirt, who had now gone quite pale and was whispering a prayer to God. Freddy stood still and waited for him to finish, though he had no real respect for the religion, not since Manton had been ordained. That was the ultimate irony. A boy who had been in and out of squad cars regularly for the early part of his teenage years was now the local priest in that same town. It wasn't that Freddy held a grudge, but it was difficult to believe in the compassion of a man who had previously caused you to be bedridden for a week. Every time he looked into Manton's eyes, he could still see the viciousness of that day, but that was a long time ago now and Father Manton entered the police station sparingly and voluntarily.

The complete transformation of Manton's character had been much talked about over the years, but the majority of the town had accepted with his reformed presentation. The metamorphosis had all started not long after that fateful day in the locker room, where Freddy had pitched in to rescue his friend. It was about two weeks later that Manton had taken ill, really ill. He had lost slabs of weight in hours. It had been a wonder that his body had been able to endure the rapid shedding. In total he dropped three stone in weight. The doctors had been flummoxed by the undetectable contagion that ate away his fatty cells and muscles. Events had climaxed one night when his father had gone down to the local bar on one of his infamous drinking binges. Manton's condition had deteriorated, and he had attempted to get to a phone but had failed, passing out instead. He was found later that night by his glazy-eyed dad, who nearly had a coronary when he saw his frail son's white body lying lifeless. According to the paramedics, it had woken him up better than a bathtub full of coffee. They'd got Manton into the hospital and on a drip, but the weight still evaporated from underneath his skin. His skeleton became clearly visible, skin stretching tight around it. His father stayed sober by his son's side, holding his hand, talking and praying. He vowed to be a better person, to take care of his son. To bring him up the right way. Manton's condition reached the bottom when he entered into a coma and they had to force feed him. But then, one morning, it all ended. Manton's dad had peeled his head away from his son's hospital bed to see a pair of open eyes staring back at him. They had become close friends after that and Manton had drifted away a little from his former mates, choosing to spend his spare time with his father. Neither of them had drunk a drop of alcohol since then, each keeping the other on the straight and narrow through times of temptation, though they were few and far between. Both men had been strengthened by the experience, and despite the fact that it looked all too staged, they discovered God in the process. It was impossible to go to a Sunday mass without seeing the two of them sat up near the front. Manton's dad subsequently found better employment and they moved out of the trailer park into a house on the Riverside Drive. It was then that Manton had decided he wanted to join the priesthood.

He had left Shifton when he was eighteen to study for his ministry and was finally ordained and given a parish in Louisiana. That had been a real eye-opener for him, seeing first-hand a way of life that few acknowledged existed within the United States, a simpler way of life without necessity for monetary status. He had thrived on the charitable work he could do, the support he could give, but then his father had contracted cancer and he had requested a posting closer to home. The Church had been kind and given him the position of Father at Shifton. That had been four years ago. His father had passed away three years ago. When he had returned, it had always been with the intention to move on again, but now his father was dead, the memories of this town were all that remained of his family.

"If I may ask, Sheriff, why are you awaiting confirmation? Do you need somebody to identify him? I'd gladly oblige!"

"No, Father, it's not that." He paused for thought, trying to determine the correct words. "It's the way in which he died. It has left him a little disfigured."

"Oh, dear." He dropped his head and spoke a further verse of prayer.

"If it's any consolation, I doubt he suffered much. Death would have been pretty instantaneous."

"The Lord takes care of his flock, so I am sure you're right."

"You might actually be able to help us. We're trying to find details of a next of kin, somebody we should contact about his death?" Freddy asked.

"Fletcher had nobody. His parents died around about the same time as my father and he has no brothers or sisters."

"Anybody who may want to hold a funeral for him?"

"No, but if you're wanting to know what you should do with the body, leave that to me. I'll arrange a burial spot for him in the cemetery."

"Thank you, Father." Freddy felt frustrated by being benevolent towards his former enemy, but he had no choice but to be courteous.

"I'll speak with you again later."

"Okay, Father."

Raising his hand in departure, Freddy turned away, exiting the reception area via a key-coded side door. The station was plain looking, single storey with a basement cell facility. All windows were barred, even the office ones, just in case anybody decided it would be a convenient escape route. Inside the main entrance, a shatterproof glass partition stretched from floor to ceiling behind the reception desk. The door that Freddy had just passed through was the only access to the rear offices. The walls were painted a pale grey matt emulsion and the floor was plastic sheeting with a tile pattern. A panelled false ceiling hid the electrical conduits and ventilation system, with recessed sections holding strip lights that were obscured by a panel of diffused semi-transparent plastic. Four desks were neatly laid out, three of which provided space for his deputies to work, the fourth being occupied by Doris, who answered the daytime phone lines, did some typing and generally helped around. Nobody worked nights in this capacity. As for law enforcement, Freddy and his deputies took it in turns to work the night shift for a week.

"Morning, Doris."

"Sheriff." To an outsider her answer would sound cautious, if not cold in its short nature. Truth was that it was neither; she had just always been economical with her words.

"The coroner's report come in yet?"

"On your desk."

"Can I get a coffee, please?"

Doris didn't acknowledge his request, but Freddy heard her chair screech along the floor behind him.

"Doris, has Kevin turned in yet?"

"Squatting on the dunny." Her directness made him smirk.

Leaving his office door open he walked towards his desk. Freddy's office was the only section of the entire station that had any style. He had a bookcase covering the whole left-hand wall filled with volumes of legal transcripts and texts on psychological profiling, through from the Freudian to the psychotic. There were historical references of famous serial killers like Bundy and Manson. Local history had almost a column to itself, only being intruded on by Shakespeare. The other walls were painted a blue grey colour, mounted with a collection of library photographs of the town since the first settlements back in the mid-nineteenth century. Breaking up these black and white stills of time were Freddy's re-election certificates, of which he was very proud, along with a couple of photographs of him with Ian, Kevin and his wife, Nicola. The furniture was sparse and modern, with complete disregard for any creature comforts. His desk was positioned so that his back faced the window, leaving him silhouetted to visitors. The window glass was fused so that nobody could see in through curiosity and nobody could see out to get distracted.

Sitting down, Freddy ripped open the sealed brown envelope containing the examiner's report. It was concise, to say the least, but that was Louise's style. In many respects it was good, because it didn't take an eternity to run through and drag out the fundamentals. It also restricted the subjectivity that could creep into any investigation, by leaving the facts to speak for themselves. The flaw with this approach was that sometimes the conjecture was the spark that led to the arrest. Without it, inspiration could be harder to source. Flicking through the pages he found little more than she had already divulged, with the exception of some bruising around the wrists and to the upper back, which she confirmed showed potential signs of a struggle. She had tried to take prints from the bruises, but nothing came of it, leading her to believe they were either innocent bruises from something else or the culprit, if there was one, had been wearing gloves.

"You wanted me?" Kevin had appeared in the doorway.

"Yes. I can't see any forensic information on my desk." Freddy played mildly with sarcasm, not wanting to offend his old friend.

"That's because I've still got it."

"So that's the problem." He grinned at Kevin, hoping that he would subtly receive the message and fetch it. After a couple of seconds delay and an embarrassed flush, he did. Freddy waited, poised for his return.

"Here it is." He brought it in and handed it over. Doris nearly passed him on route with Freddy's coffee, disappearing again before either of them had further opportunity to speak.

"Five sets of prints. Was that it?" Freddy was amazed.

"Yeah. Surprised me as well." He waited for his boss to read on and then provided commentary. "Only two sets were found in the area we believe Fletcher to have fallen from. Both of those have already checked out as the deceased's and Sally Barnett's. We're printing all other employees' today, see if we can eliminate some of the others. Hopefully we'll have fewer questions by mid-afternoon."

"You'll not find any unidentifiable now. Coroner's report indicates that if indeed there was a murderer, he was wearing gloves." He let Kevin's document drop to the desk and pondered.

"What do you want to do next?"

"Pull all the employees in one at a time and interview them. Get a better feel for Fletcher, see if he had any enemies, if he was a good boss." He took a breath. "Post signs along the main street as well, asking anybody who was in that area in the early hours of yesterday, say between four o'clock and eight o'clock, to call and tell us if they saw anything, no matter how insignificant it may appear to them. And take Charlie to interview all the shop owners along that front, see what they saw as they were opening up."

Kevin nodded an okay and turned to leave.

"And while you're interviewing everybody, ask them if they've seen any strangers in town. Anyone that has stood out from the general tourist trade. Particularly single males."

"What you going to do, Freddy?"

"Go over to Fletcher's house." He stood up. "Have a look around and see if there's anything strange there. If you find something important, call me on my radio."

Kevin walked over to Doris and got Charlie on the radio. Freddy could hear them arranging to meet up on the main street as he left the building. Outside the sun was still failing to break up the cloud cover and the horizon threatened harsher weather to come.

Fletcher lived out on the west side of town, on Maple Drive, which was sandwiched between Pine View and Crescent Drive. It was one of the oldest areas of the town, with houses dating back forty years. If there was a lower class in Shifton, this is where they lived. Accommodation was cheap and simple. In fact, some houses were only good for keeping the water off their owners' heads. All the houses were wooden construction, with tiled roofs. The colours of paintwork varied from plain whitewash through to decorative yellow and blue. Few had been overhauled in the past five years and Fletcher's was no exception. It stood second from the end, white paintwork peeling and crumbling away from unprotected wooden planks. The house was on stilts about four foot off the ground, the space between the house and ground obscured by wooden lattice panels that provided the illusion of a continuous structure. The roof was in a poor state of repair, dislodged tiles littering the garden and hedges.

Opening the front door, he discovered the inside was similar in standard to the outside. Carpets were badly worn, wallpaper peeled away, and door frames were chipped and scuffed black from years of stray feet bashing at them. The visual decay was accompanied by a peculiar odour that wafted around the house, only made tolerable by a faint herbal musky smell. Through the archway, the dining room and lounge area spread out immediately to his right. To the right-hand side of this, a small table stood with the phone and a pile of unopened mail on top. At the far end of the hall, a door led through to the kitchen, which then provided access to the staircase. He entered the lounge. A television stood in one corner, with two chairs facing it. Lying on the floor adjacent to the furthest chair was a diner tray still carrying the remains of Fletcher's last supper. The walls were bare, faded plain blue wallpaper simplistically covering the plaster. Taking a couple of slow glances across the room, he departed for the kitchen. Room after room did nothing but solidify the perception that Fletcher was to all intents a loner and not a particularly hygienic one. The kitchen held a dirty stack of cutlery and crockery from the previous week. Upstairs in the bathroom, he discovered a tub with a water mark of scum that almost formed a sufficient ledge to provide leverage for the occupant to stand up and get out. He also found a toilet whose white porcelain was ashamedly patterned in an unnatural manner for any self-respecting human being. Areas of carpet around the house had worn through to the base weave. Floor tiles in the kitchen were absent and light bulbs only occupied the essential fittings, leaving the remainder to dangle free. The smell he had detected earlier had become increasingly pungent as he had moved upstairs. And as he drifted through Fletcher's home sampling his life, he became less inclined to field any thoughts of abnormal death, accepting his deputy's opinion. But then he entered the bedroom. Inside was a single bed which had been pushed across the wooden floor to the centre of the room. Around it twelve discrete piles of some granular material had been spaced equidistant in the form of a circle, with a single black candle mounted in each, slowly burning away. Freddy wetted his fingertip and dipped it into one of the piles, speckling the end with some of the granules. Then, tasting it with his tongue, he identified it as salt. Through this act he had also identified the source of the odour, the candles being scented and speckled with herb leaves.

Painted on the right-hand wall was a symbol that he didn't recognise. He took out his notepad and sketched it. When he'd finished, he moved back to the bed and studied what laid on top of it. The sheets had been stripped away, exposing the mattress, which had the same hieroglyphic graffitied on to it. Resting on the mattress, central to the marking, lay a decapitated action figure with its clothing stripped off. In the centre of its chest, a burn hole had been filled with what appeared to Freddy like a resin of some nature.

His nerves started to fray. He had two options to believe. The first was to accept that this was Fletcher's own doing and that he secretly worshipped something other than God, although this theory did nothing for the memory of a guy who, hygiene aside, had tried to make something of himself. However, Freddy favoured that imagery, because the alternative was that a killer had set this up as some bizarre ritual before or after they had actually done the deed. Judging by the detail in the presentation, Freddy could only believe that it had been after, because there was no way this had been done in a rush. It was too tidy for that. Too precise.

Suddenly his attention was drawn behind him, to a creak coming from outside the door. His pulse began to race, and he swiftly drew his handgun, taking aim at the doorway. Creak! He took a step back, knocking one of the candles over in the process. He thought about announcing his presence but wasn't entirely sure whether that would be best. For the first time in his life as sheriff, he felt vulnerable. He hadn't realised until now how spooked he had become when he had seen this altar. He wasn't prepared to deal with it. Creak! He firmed his stance, taking hold of the gun in both hands. Sucking in slow breaths, he attempted to steady his aim. What if the killer was in the house? What if this really was some sick altar for devil worshipping and the killer was still in the house? A sweat broke from his brow. His nerves nipped at his brain. Another floorboard creaked, this one closer. He readied himself, stifling his breath, not wanting to miss a sound. He could hear breathing. A loud and steady panting. He homed the gun in tightly on the lip of the door, wanting to be able to release power immediately at whatever was advancing. Suddenly there was movement at the base of his vision. He lowered his gun sharply, depressing the trigger as he followed through. Just before it was too late, he realised he was taking aim at a large Dalmatian and relaxed his weapon. His heart continued to race, his face flushing in self-embarrassment. Walking over he patted the dog on the head and for reassurance casually stuck his head out into the corridor to ensure that it was clear. Even with the confirmation of his solitude, Freddy's discomfort still failed to ease completely. He couldn't help but feel that there was a relevance to what he had discovered, which troubled him severely, and it wasn't going to be quelled while he stood in full sight of it. Having one last look, he grabbed the dog by its collar and left, closing the bedroom door behind him. He led the dog outside before releasing it, making sure potential evidence would not be disturbed further.

After shutting the front door, he gulped in fresh air, feeling it purge the sickness that had taken hold of him. A couple across the street watched from their bedroom window and Freddy began to feel self-conscious. He got into his jeep. Picking up his radio handset he called into the station.

"Where you been, Sheriff?" It was Doris. "Kevin's been trying to get you for half an hour."

"Sorry. Left my radio in the car. What's he want?"

"Got another body." Doris declared.

"Who?" The shock snapped him back to his senses.

"A guy called..." He could hear her checking her pad. "Young."

"Where?"

"Over at the guy's house on Washington Drive."

"Call Kevin and tell him I'm on my way," he said with urgency. "And can you get somebody out to keep an eye on Fletcher's house? I'm going to need some prints taking."

"Everybody's out, Sheriff!"

"Then get down here yourself, Doris." With that he clipped the handset back to the dashboard and drove on.

18

John pulled into the motel forecourt, keeping his head low as he passed the reception. While he did his damnedest to remain inconspicuous, his endeavours did nothing but stir greater interest. The old guy inside the reception, Mr Dillon, was a stereotype elder, nosy and pushy. For example, John had used the term 'recreational' to explain the nature of his stay, but that hadn't been clear enough for Dillon. He strove to discover where the recreation was, who it was with and how it would all be paid for. The old git epitomised the very essence of society that John had sought to avoid by staying at a lowly run-down motel. Even as he passed the reception window, he could see Dillon sticking his mottled nose up in the air and straining up on his toes to see who was driving past.

The motel was called the *Blazing Stump*, though there were no signs of its namesake anywhere. It was typical low-budget, single-storey fabrication, with wooden boards and tiled roof and a small canopy extending all the way around the square court, providing shelter from the sun or rain. There were only sixteen rooms and fortunately fourteen of them were unoccupied. A small swimming pool sat empty to one side, an idea gone bad. Leaves covered the blue-chip tiled base and rusted sun loungers sat around its perimeter, laced together with some construction tape to deter stray pedestrians and keep them safe from falling into the six-foot void.

Parking his car up, John got out and headed towards his room, number eight. Swapping keys, he primed himself to unlock it, but as metal was about to slide into metal, he heard a shuffle of feet to his left. Turning sharply, he saw a figure cloaked in the shadows.

"You're back late. Where you been?" John recognised the voice as Logan's.

"Driving around."

"Trying to release that guilt you've freed within yourself. I wouldn't bother. You'll never get rid of it. It sticks like shit, my friend." He moved forward and raised a hand to John's shoulder. John stepped away. "That's no way to embrace a kinsman."

"I didn't realise that was what we are. I thought we had more of a blackmailer and victim relationship."

"Oh, not at all. I am your friend, and I am here to help you. Show you the error of your ways. That's all."

"Then why don't I feel like I'm being saved?" John was unimpressed with Logan's talk and was fuelled by the anger he felt over his recent murderous deeds.

"That's because you are forgetting why you're doing this." Logan took a breath and moved closer still, lowering his voice. "You have misconceived what is going on here. There is nothing I am forcing you to undertake. This is something you promised a long time ago. And a debt can never be forgotten. Particularly not one with a price this high."

"Well, I'm starting to wonder if the debt is worth it?"

"I wouldn't do that, if I were you. Honesty is important in any relationship; so, too, is trust. You were entrusted with a gift and you have used that gift. Now you are only making good on your own word. So, if you have an axe to grind, I suggest you point it at yourself and sink the blade deep. I am not your enemy. That monster is within you." John despised Logan's every word, because of their truths. "Besides, if you need more motivation, just think of your present and future family."

"You told me they would be safe if I came here," John said, sounding panicked.

"I know, and I'm true to my word. They will remain in perfect health as long as you play your part. But only if you play your part!"

"They'd better be alright!"

"Or what?" Logan challenged him, stepping forward once more. John held his ground. "Just finish your sacrifice and they'll be fine." He smiled, as if to break the tension. "I've enlisted the help of a couple of nurses. They're keeping an eye on her for me now. Making sure she's properly looked after. Caring for her every need." He took a deep breath. "So, your mind can rest easy and get on with the job." Logan pushed at the unlocked motel room door and it fell open. "Shall we go in? It's cold out here." He led on, John followed.

The room was basic. The walls were painted in a cream paint and damp bubbling had forced peeling around the skirting board. Dirt marks sat as evidence of former occupants and poor cleaners. A bulb without its shade hung from a central rosette in the ceiling. The bed, disguised by a cloth quilt, had seen better days; the springs sounding off as Logan sat down. A black and white fifteen-inch television set was mounted off the wall on a swing arm, allowing viewing from any part of the room. Below it, a chest of drawers offered the chance to unpack belongings, but nobody had remained sufficient nights to warrant that, at least not after they'd viewed the bathroom, which had a white porcelain suite that was slowly turning grey. Dirt clung to the grout holding the tiled floor together and the sink drain hole was clogged by a cluster of entangled hairs. A transparent shower curtain hung ready for action, stuck together by mould that grew between its curves. The only reason John had stayed after having seen it was through his desire for anonymity and seclusion from the masses.

"So it's two down and one to go!"

John looked in surprise at Logan for a moment, but then realised what he was referring to.

"I have to say that I admire your work so far. It's definitely been inventive. Printing Fletcher's brains all over the *Chronicle*." He gave a chuckle. "And what you did with Young – that was a dream killing, if ever I saw one. I'd liked to see the coroner pronounce the cause of death on that."

"What do you want?" John didn't appreciate the praise.

"Nothing, really. Just thought I'd check on you, make certain you weren't faltering."

"Well, now you've seen me, you can go." John's voice was elevated, revealing his frustration at Logan's small talk.

"Hey, that's no way to treat a friend."

"I thought I had clarified that I'm not talking to a friend."

"I guess we will have to work on that, then." Logan sniffed, as if he was upset. The charade was brief. "Well, if I'm not a friend, have you bumped into any of your older friends?"

"No."

"Shame. They're all still here, you know." He smirked. "You're the only one who escaped. But then I suppose you have your own unique prison." Logan studied the room. "And even that ended up in your return to this quaint little town."

John pulled himself a beer out of the fridge and sat down. He had no desire to engage in conversation with Logan but realised that he wasn't going to disappear. He was sure Logan had come to accomplish something. Even if it was just to feed his sick pleasure of watching minions crumble away from humanity, falling hopelessly into a world where wrong is right and individual will be secondary to that of a greater being.

"Yup, they're all here. Nicola married Freddy; did you know that?" He attempted to coax John into conversation. John remained silent. "They got married the year after you and Gloria. Of course, they were truly in love, not hiding behind a spell. Yeah, it was a great wedding. Nicola looked gorgeous. She had this beautiful white dress, with stockings, suspenders and garter belt underneath. Oh, I don't know, there's just something about a bride that makes you want to fuck her, don't you think?" John could tell Logan was pretending to look distracted, while in reality he knew John's frustration was mounting. "A feeling smack in the middle of your loins that makes you want to just lift that skirt up, yank those virtuous nickers off and hump that peace of ass. Hey, and my, what a fuck machine she's turned into. Okay, she's only been with the one guy, but she makes prostitutes look like amateurs. She's so in love with

Freddy now that she greases his pole every fucking night. I'd give anything for that kind of action."

"Would you fuck off?" John interrupted.

"So, you are listening. Thought for a moment you'd gone to sleep." He ignored John's comment, casting his eyes around the room. "You know, it's a nice place you've got here. Perfect little inconspicuous hideaway." He walked over to the bathroom. "Not too roomy but pleasantly cheap decor, with moderate comfort. Bathroom's a bit grim, though."

"Did you just come all this way for sarcasm?"

Logan sniffed. "Don't you just hate it when you go into a bathroom after someone has just had a DIY colonic and released all that age-old smelly crap from their deepest recesses? And there you are! Sniffing it and stifling your breath simultaneously, thinking solely of the particles of shit layering your nasal passage."

"I give up!" John laid back on the bed.

Logan ignored John's despair. "Anyway, I'm digressing. Where was I? Yes, Nicola! Well, I suppose if you're gonna fuck someone in a small town, it might as well be the sheriff. Now did you know that? Your mate Freddy is the sheriff of this backwater dumpster. He's ogling over your last masterpiece at this very moment."

John showed a glimmer of interest.

"Do you want to know who's with him? Hmmm." Logan continued to coerce him into speaking, but John wouldn't. He knew Logan would tell him no matter what. "Kevin. Your humorous playmate of youth, though he has misplaced a great deal of that funny streak. Turned into quite a weak-minded fellow, actually, considering all the mouthing off he did when you were young. Yeah, that boy knew how to stir things up."

Logan got himself a beer from the fridge. Twisting the screw cap open, he sat down beside John. "Ian's here too, though for an intelligent guy, he's not doing particularly well. He's only one step better than that piece of scum you rolled this morning."

"Are you going anywhere?" John's patience was thinning.

"Not particularly. I just decided it was time to get to know my client better." He took a swig from the bottle. "So come on, then. Don't keep me in suspense."

John's expression transformed to one of confusion.

"How you gonna do Manton?"

No response.

"You have found him, haven't you?"

Nothing.

"You know what he does? Where he works?"

"No, I don't."

"Oh, then this is the best bit. La *pièce de résistance*. You are gonna like this so much it'll make your dick hard." Logan's grin extended from ear to ear. "He's the fucking priest." John's face dropped. "Ordained ten years ago and a self-righteous forgiving bastard now."

John tried to speak but couldn't. He already loathed himself for what he had done that day. He regretted his childhood pledge.

Logan was clearly picking up on John's distress, grinning with pleasure. "Hey, don't be sad. You've still got me."

"You enjoy this, don't you?"

"You bet."

"Enjoy making me suffer?"

"More than anything." Logan enthused.

"You fucker." John thrashed out with his right fist, letting go of the beer bottle on route. He could see Logan waiting, watching his fist close in. Then John felt the hairs on Logan's cheek make contact with his clenched hand and he waited for impact, but there was nothing. Instead, John's fist continued to follow through, still expecting to find stability in Logan's face. Through its absence he tumbled down on to the floor, bouncing off the edge of the mattress.

"Now that was clumsy, and I wouldn't try it again." He smirked. "Is it really all that bad? You don't have to complete your task, you know. I could take your life this instant if I wanted. Save me a lot of hassle, that's for sure."

John could hear the voice behind him and rolled over to see Logan standing by the bathroom door, hands clasped behind his back, face angered. His stance was threatening and powerful and for the first time John feared him. He feared his lack of options, the lack of escape routes. He was terrified by the fact that for once he wasn't in control. He didn't have the power to change his predicament. He was subservient to a greater being and that was a sensation he hadn't encountered since his childhood and the days of Manton.

"Now, are you gonna try that shit again or have you got the message?"

"We're clear." He clambered back to his feet. "I'm a quick learner."

"I know you are."

With that short exchange John retook his seat. Both men eyed each other, suspicious of the other's intent and actions. Despite his attempt to appear relaxed, John knew his newfound unpredictability had caught Logan off-guard.

"How did you get into this?" John retrieved his beer bottle from the floor.

"Well, you can only do God's dirty work for so long before you want something more out of it. Shalek offered the something more." He took a sharp, wistful breath. "Look at it this way: God is omnipotent, but he does nothing with that power. Shalek is omnipotent and uses the power to his advantage. Who do you think leads the more exciting life?"

"Excitement doesn't mean it's right!"

"I think it's a little too late for you to be playing that card. You chose the same life. Difference is that you just don't like the price."

"You're right. I don't." John confessed.

"That's too bad. But don't think you can ever revoke your pledge. You can do that with God, but it doesn't wash with Shalek. He may not be able to reach you, but I can. My servants can." The room fell silent, each man taking a swig of beer. "You realise this is one of the greatest inventions of all time?" He raised his bottle to draw attention to it. "Do you know how much more crime there is while people are under the influence of this shit? It's fucking brilliant. In fact, if it weren't for guys like you, with your natural dark instinct, the drunks would be our only source of recruits."

"What do you mean naturally dark? I'm nothing like you! I hate doing this!"

"Whether you hate it or not is irrelevant. You subscribed to it and you're doing it!"

"You're wrong."

"Really." Logan's smirk returned. "Didn't see your high moral standards when you were on the up and up. When you got married. When you got that cool fucking job and the flash beamer. You stayed pretty fucking quiet through all of that."

John could offer no defence.

"Yeah, that's it. You just think about it a little bit more and then you'll see how similar we really are."

"Are you ever going to leave tonight?" John changed subject.

"I'll leave now. There's no bloody pleasure in talking to you further." Logan stood up and dropped his beer on the sideboard. "Just remember one thing." He flicked his wrist out, grabbing John by the throat before he could put up any resistance. "You can turn away from God without consequence, but never think you can do that from me." He increased the pressure around John's larynx, ceasing the flow of air. "Don't forget that!"

With that he let go and departed. John rubbed at his swelling neck, caressing the inflamed skin. He hated Logan on so many levels, but he had no choice except to obey. He couldn't defeat him, and he couldn't hide. The only way out was to do his bidding.

19

Freddy was at a loss. Two deaths had taken place within the space of twenty-four hours and neither had revealed any traces of the perpetrator. Except for any evidence that might have been recovered from Fletcher's house, but that little sacrificial arrangement hadn't seen the day out. Someone must have been waiting for Freddy to leave, because by the time Doris had arrived, it had been swept clean and restored to its former bachelor squalor. He'd recounted what he had seen to Doris and Kevin, but they had both listened sceptically. On a thread of hope, he had gone to Young's place thinking he might uncover a similar shrine, but there was nothing. Just a corpse, for which he was still awaiting the autopsy report.

The facts he did know were as follows. One: the motive was probably not theft. There were no secondary owners at either of the guys' homes to further verify this, but all electrical appliances, pictures and silverware had remained untouched. At Young's they had even found a three-hundred-dollar bundle of ten-dollar bills in his bedside drawer left undisturbed. So, the criminal had to have been the worst burglar in history if he had missed that. Plus, Fletcher was killed at work. Second on his list of facts was that it was probably a single male. He based this deduction on the physical aspects of committing each crime. If a single female had committed them, then she would certainly stand out in a crowd. And in line with that logic, if a group had been involved, then they would probably have been clumsier. Probability and logic also suggested that they would have been noticed by somebody. So that left him with a single, male criminal who had a connection to both men.

Freddy sat back in his chair and thought further, staring at the fused glass pane fitted in his door, reading the letters of his name and title backwards over and over. There had to be something he was missing. Kevin and Charlie had drawn a blank, and Kieran, his other deputy, was off sick. It was Kieran who was usually Freddy's first sounding board. He was a good bit sharper than the other two and Freddy guessed that in a couple of years' time he would be running for sheriff himself. Freddy didn't mind that. He respected Kieran. And if he was to lose an election to somebody, then he would prefer it to be him. Allowing his gaze to fall back to his desktop, he studied Fletcher's examiner's report further. It was irrelevant how many times he went over it. There was nothing in it that could assist him. He was just killing time before the next one showed up. His mind wandered back to the day before and the stranger he had seen walking down the other side of the street from the *Chronicle*. A walk so familiar to him, but he couldn't place it. Possibly someone from his childhood. It was the way the man's head had lolled to the left side and the steady bounce in his step, even though he otherwise looked deflated. Maybe if he hadn't been shrouded so well inside the long coat, Freddy would have remembered more. As it was, he was left tormented by a trace memory. He had even run through the guy's mannerisms with Nicola, but she couldn't place it. Shaking his head clear, he stood up to go check where the report was, his impatience growing beyond control.

Opening his office door, he could see Kevin standing in the reception, talking seriously to a stranger. His conversation partner was stern looking, in his late twenties, with hair combed back tight to his scalp. Black clothing covered him from head to foot. His eyes were deep, dark and penetrating, even from Freddy's ten-metre viewpoint. On his left-hand Freddy could see an ornate ring, sculpted in what appeared to be platinum or silver. The two men were in heated discussion, Kevin displaying his aggression, hands waving like birds in front of the stranger's face. The panelling between the reception and the office area absorbed the sound, but the silent show painted enough of a picture. He began to walk towards them. As soon as he had taken his first stride, the stranger flicked his eyes towards him. Immediately Freddy could see the change to his temperament. The man appeared to notify Kevin of Freddy's approach. His deputy took a quick glance over his shoulder and before Freddy made it through the security door, the two had made their final exchange of words and parted company.

"Who was that?" Freddy pointed at the back of the man as he crossed the street, his long black raincoat protecting him from the pouring rain.

"Visitor in town?" Kevin walked away, passing by his boss and entering the main office.

"D'you two know each other?" Freddy pursued.

"No!" Kevin sounded nervous about the accusation. "Why?"

"You just looked familiar. What did he want?"

"Directions."

"Looked pretty steamed up to be only asking for directions."

"Well, he had heard about the recent deaths, too. Was a bit concerned."

"D'you put him straight?" Freddy quizzed further, uncertain of the sincerity in his deputy's voice.

"Yeah, I did."

"Okay." Freddy left it at that. "You got my coroner's report?" Kevin said nothing, passing him the brown envelope he had been holding. Freddy took it. "So, what's it says?"

"Nothing that you're gonna believe."

"Why?"

"Let's begin with the cause of death." He paused for effect. "Young drowned!"

"He what?" Freddy didn't believe it. He ripped into the envelope to view the confirmation.

"Yup, drowned. It would appear that he was locked up in that steam room for so long that all that vapour had accumulated in his lungs and he drowned."

"Bullshit. Is that even possible?"

Doris looked up.

"Why didn't he cough it up?" Freddy challenged.

"Because he was unconscious. Passed out from the heat. It was a good forty-five degrees in there."

Freddy read the text as he walked back to his office. Kevin followed, closing the door behind them, so that Doris wouldn't hear anything further.

"Did you find any prints?"

"No. Nothing outside, and inside the persistent condensation kept all the surfaces pretty clean. Nothing on the broom handle used to secure the door shut either."

"It's definitely murder?" Freddy questioned.

"That's for sure. Just the weirdest fucking method that I've ever heard of."

"You found nobody who saw anything?"

"Nope. The area's pretty quiet and there are few vantage points that give a view around the back to Young's pool house." He took a breath. "Besides, the coroner reckons he'd been in there for at least seven hours. So that would put the killer there at around six in the morning. Few people up at that time."

"Did you find anything peculiar in the house?"

"You know we didn't! You were there."

"Yeah, but after I had gone?" Freddy clarified.

"Nothing. No disturbance, nothing visibly missing. Although we are waiting to check that with his girlfriend when she finishes blowing off the rest of the men in the town."

"What d'you mean?"

"Girlfriend's Karen Stiffler. From what I hear he's been ridden more times than the paper boy's bike." Kevin didn't refrain from painting a poor image.

"You speak with familiarity, Kevin. Something you should be telling me?"

"No. She'd probably ask me for money if I asked for favours."

"Where's she now?" Freddy asked.

"Nobody knows. Got everyone on the lookout for her and Charlie's staying up at Young's house in case she returns there."

"Alright." He paused for moment. "You didn't find any ceremonial type arrangements or symbolism?"

"No." Kevin gave a shallow laugh. "You're not going to go on about that shit over at Fletcher's again, are you? We found nothing. You probably passed out from that foul smell and dreamed it."

"No, it was there!"

"Yeah, well, we both know it ain't there now! So maybe you should just leave it at that?" Kevin was getting dangerously close to patronising.

"I'll leave it where I want to leave it and you had better watch your lip." Freddy pointed. "There was a ceremonial offering made up at Fletcher's house and I'm going to find out why."

"Okay. Best of luck with finding the evidence."

Freddy was shocked by his deputy's disrespect. It was completely out of character with his usual subservient nature.

"Did you climb out of the stupid side of the bed this morning?"

"No." Kevin acted confused.

"Then quit while you're ahead." He paused to give his friend opportunity to demonstrate that the words had sunk in. "Good. Have you recovered any evidence from Fletcher's house at all?"

"No. Completely clean. Forensically speaking, of course."

Freddy relaxed again, smiling at his friend's joke. "Have you and Charlie found any witnesses to that morning's events on the main street?"

"Yeah, a couple. We got the old man, Mr Vicars from the 7-Eleven across the street. Says he saw a stranger around about six when he was just setting up. The other's a woman who was walking her dog, passed somebody suspicious up on Johnson's Street about five minutes later. We think it's the same guy, description fits, times fit. Not many other people to get him mixed up with at that hour."

"Description?"

"Sorry?" Kevin made like he didn't understand.

"Of the man!"

"Late twenties, approximately five ten, one hundred and eighty pounds, dark hair, no distinguishing features. He was wearing jeans and a long coat, that's about all either of them could remember."

"Either of them happy about participating in an identification parade?"

"Yup. No problems in either camp." Kevin waited for his boss to say something. "So, what next?"

"I don't have a clue." Freddy's enthusiasm was dampened. He'd done everything he should and now was at a loss. "What about your visitor friend this morning? He fits the description."

"Yeah, but he's only just driven into town."

"That's what he told you."

"Yeah, but—"

"You said he was even asking about the deaths," Freddy interrupted his deputy, who was now coming over a little more than defensive. "Well, that's pretty typical of serial killers. They return to the scene of the crime or at least remain close to it." Kevin looked distressed. "What, don't you watch the *X-Files*?" Freddy's joke did nothing to alleviate the tension in his friend's expression. "I'll grant you that walking into the cop shop is a bit gutsy, but these guys are all a couple tins short of a six pack."

"No, I'm sure it wasn't him." Kevin's nervous tone persisted.

"Don't be so trusting. Let's go find him, ask him a few polite questions." Freddy stood up and put on his hat. "Come on." He patted Kevin on the shoulder as he passed.

Walking outside, Freddy fumbled with his keys, hastily trying to open the land cruiser and get out of the rain. His fingers moved too quickly, though, and they fell to the floor. As he bent down to pick them up, water spilled off his collar down the back of his neck. Reflexes twitched his shoulders. As he straightened himself again, he caught a glimpse of a long-coated man through the car window. The guy was about to turn off the main street on to Johnson's Street, about two hundred metres away. Freddy pointed and Kevin turned to look, his face displaying heightened dread when he turned back, which puzzled Freddy. The key clicked home in the door, and they climbed in. Unlike the vehicle door, he slid the key into the ignition easily and they were reversing back out onto the street before Kevin had time to put his seatbelt on.

Driving like a man possessed, Freddy manoeuvred up the main street, dodging jay walkers, instinctively slowing enough to give them a quick visual warning. A car reversing out of a parking space did so with complete disregard for anything else in its vicinity and Freddy had just enough time to swerve to the other side of the road. Turning on to Johnson's Street, they found the figure had only made moderate progress. Before Kevin had time to acknowledge what was happening, Freddy had screeched to a halt behind the man and was jumping out of the car, his left arm raised, hand assertively stretched out in a stop symbol.

"Excuse me, Sir!" He was ignored. "Excuse me!" He got close enough to stretch out and clip the man's shoulder, exposing a bewildered face as the stranger turned to see who was reaching out for him. "John?"

"Freddy." While there was every surprise in Freddy's voice, there was none in Garret's.

"Jesus. What the hell are you doing here?" He forgot all about his work.

"Passing through," John answered hesitantly.

"What, on holiday?"

"John?" Kevin caught up.

"Hi, Kevin. How you doing?"

"Great. Christ, what you doing here?"

Freddy gave his deputy a sharp glare for interrupting.

"So, sheriff and deputy! Where's Ian? Does he complete the complement as the cell master?" John joked.

"No, Ian mercifully went a different path. Still lives in town, though. We meet up once in a while. What about you, though? Where you been? Last I heard you were getting married to Gloria?" Freddy enquired.

"Well, that happened. You were invited remember?" John

said. Freddy checked him up and down with official curiosity. "Something up?" His voice splintered across his larynx, coming out frayed with nerves.

"Nothing. Just haven't seen you in such a long time, thought I'd study for all the changes." He smiled. "So how is the prom queen, then?"

"Pregnant, actually."

"Brilliant. Congratulations! Is it your first?" Freddy maintained enthusiasm.

"Yes."

"No problems, I hope?" Kevin pitched in, catching John off guard. There was something peculiar about Kevin's tone, a sense of knowing.

"No, it's all going normally." John's words were cautious.

"That's good." Kevin asserted oddly and Freddy caught a strange intonation in his deputy's words.

"Where are you living?" Freddy asked.

"Up New York way. I'm a lawyer in the city."

"You must really miss this place, living there," Freddy joked, trying to lighten what was an awkward conversation. It didn't work particularly well; it just laid the foundation for a momentary suffocation by silence.

"So, you two married? Kids? What?"

"Kevin here isn't quite ready for commitment yet. He's far too content working himself around the females of the town. Which as long as he steers clear of the married ones is fine."

"Yeah, I'm a law enforcer by day and a law breaker by night," Kevin chuckled.

"We just have to keep a close eye on which laws you're breaking, don't we?" Freddy made the comment as if with reference to fact but offered no elaboration. Kevin fell silent once more.

"What about you?" asked his former best friend.

"I married Nicola."

"Well, there's a bombshell I wasn't expecting." John's voice was sullen with stilted surprise. "How long?"

"It's been about three years now." He took a breath. "No kids, before you ask. Not yet anyway."

"It's good to hear that you're all okay and happy."

"Yeah, we're that alright. Just never managed to break out of this town. Only you managed that trick." Freddy's eyes were focussed on the ground as he made his final comment, but he knew it had startled Garret.

"I guess some of us have all the luck." John's cautiousness returned, followed by the uncomfortable silence.

"Sad, isn't it, when nearly ten years apart, we can't stretch a conversation beyond five minutes," Freddy quipped, trying to soften the mood. "Tell you what. Why don't you and me go and get a coffee? It'll be more relaxing than standing in the street and we might actually get to know a little more than the base fundamentals about each other."

"No, I can't. Things to do."

"Surely they can wait half an hour while you catch up with a school time friend." Freddy knew John wanted out, but he wasn't going to let him off that easily. "What is it, work? We'll call them and tell them you'll be a few minutes late."

"No, it's not work," John replied.

"Well, if it's not work, then it can definitely wait. I won't take no for an answer."

Freddy's insistence left John no choice but to agree, though his entire body expressed his discomfort. As Freddy led his old friend back towards the main street, Kevin started to follow.

"Hey, you're still on duty. Take the car back to the station and look over those autopsy files again." Freddy watched John's expression eagerly as he spoke to his colleague. "See if you can put that grey matter to effective use for once. Then scout around to see if you can find that stranger of yours. I want to talk to him." He just finished shouting out his instructions as the cruiser door closed. "I have to guide him by the hand a touch. He's not what you would call a blood hound, unless it's female." Freddy grinned. "Shall we go?" He offered the question rhetorically as he ushered his friend on. "So, how long you been in town?" He began the interview.

"A couple of days." They turned back on to the main street.

"Where are you staying?"

"About fifteen miles away in a motel." They entered Evette's Coffee Emporium.

"Yeah? What's it called?"

"The Blazing Stump."

"Yeah, I know that one. Bit shabby for a lawyer, isn't it? Particularly a defence lawyer. It is your kind who makes all the money?"

"Who said I was a defence lawyer?"

"Nobody. I just guessed. What d'you want?" Freddy offered.

"Mug of coffee." John delved for his wallet, but Freddy restrained him.

"I'll get these. Have a seat and I'll be with you in a moment."

Freddy could see his friend had the jitters; he just didn't know what about. He was confused as to why John was visiting, and he found it more than coincidental that he wore the same clothing as the stranger identified from Kevin and Charlie's enquiries. He paid for the drinks, held brief small talk with Evette and joined John.

"So, why didn't you get in touch when you got back?"

"Didn't know any of you were still here." John replied.

"Wouldn't have taken much to find out. It's not like we're hiding out of the limelight."

"Didn't think that way," he responded hastily. "Besides, I haven't had much spare time."

"You're finding the time now?" Freddy pushed further, intent on keeping his old friend on the defensive. John shrugged his shoulders and took a sip from his mug. "Why isn't Gloria with you?"

"Couldn't make it. Didn't want to travel with the baby. Too much stress."

"That's fair enough. Still, would have been nice to see her as well." The two of them fell silent, both sipping steadily from their steaming mugs. John's eyes danced nervously, trying to avoid Freddy's, which were firmly fixed on him.

"You always amazed us you know. Suddenly achieving so much after such a poor start." Freddy took a complimentary turn, searching for an avenue to relax his friend and get him to drop his guard. "Going to college! You were never really the academic type."

"A late starter."

"Suppose so." Sip. "I always attributed it partly to Gloria. She was always smart. I figure that she must have been giving you some additional tuition."

"Well, maybe a little."

"You know, we kinda lost touch when you and her began going steady." Sip. "Before then, you, me, Kevin, Ian and Nicola were inseparable."

"You have to pay attention to your girlfriend if you want to keep her." John smiled nervously.

"Yeah, but it got so we never saw you at all outside of class. Nicola took it hard, you know? She had always fancied you."

John looked startled by the comment, but he half smiled. "She doesn't anymore, obviously."

"No, you ignored her one too many times for that. You did that to all of us." Freddy accused.

"I'm sorry."

"No, don't be. Guess we all have to let go of our childhood sometime. It's just more difficult when the memories are so much fun. Anyway, I haven't seen you in ten years. So, I'm not going to bust your balls now. We had a heap of good times before then."

"Yeah, we did." John was starting to ease up.

"Hey, remember that time you kicked the shit out of Manton?" They laughed together. "I ended up in bed and you became a folk-lore hero."

"That's right."

"Always thought that was unfair, seeing as it was me who saved your ass to begin with."

"I'm sorry again." This time he smiled properly.

"Nah, forget it. What else are mates for but to get beaten to a pulp so that their friends can become the most popular guy in school?" He sighed. "They were funny times. Remember how you looked up those books in the library for me?"

John feigned confusion.

"Come on, you must remember, the stuff about witchcraft. The ceremonial stump out in the woods."

"Yeah. We did some stupid things, didn't we?"

"That was about the same time that you and Gloria hooked up, wasn't it?" Freddy pulled back the reins of interrogation, sensing John's comprehension of where he was being led.

"Yes, it was." John kept his response concise.

"Christ, has it been that long?" Freddy paused. "That was the year Manton, and his crew took ill as well, wasn't it?" He managed to utter the words as if they were being realised for the first time.

"I can't remember."

"Come on. How could you forget? You were all joyous about it at the time." Freddy contested.

"No, I don't remember."

"I recall you came running into school the day after you'd heard about Manton, quizzing us, asking if it was true."

"Sure, you're not confusing me with Kevin? He was the wise-cracking one, you know."

"No, it was definitely you. I remember it distinctly." Freddy's tone verged on accusatorial. John shrugged it off. "Well, they went down badly sick, that's for sure. Doctors never found out the reason." He sipped. "Appears as if it's all happening again for them now." For the first moment since their reunion, Freddy spoke without thinking. Unfortunately, they happened to be the truest words he had uttered.

"Look, I've really got to be going." John announced.

"No, you can't. We've only just sat down."

"Got to. Work's work."

"You said it wasn't work."

"A favour for an acquaintance doesn't always seem so bad."

"I'm sorry, but I can't just let you leave like that."

John's face contorted as if in silent panic.

"You'll have to come to dinner. Nicola would love to see you," Freddy continued.

John breathed out. "I can't, I'm leaving straight after this next appointment."

"Can't you stay another night?"

"No, I've really got to get back to Gloria. Don't like leaving her on her own." He stood up and extended a farewell hand.

"Okay. Well, it was good to see you again, though a little brief. Next time you come, get in contact and bring Gloria. We'll have a proper reunion."

"Sure. See you." John turned to leave.

"Hey, wait!" Freddy walked after him. "Here, take my card. It's got my office and home numbers on it. Give us a call."

"Sure." He placed the card in his shirt breast pocket and started to turn away. Freddy snatched at his arm, startling him. Freddy's face was silently stern.

"How come we use to be such good friends and now we run from each other?"

"We're grown up, Freddy. A lot has changed about both of us. We're nothing like the kids who were friends." There was a peculiar tone of resignation in John's voice.

"Hell, that's cold."

"Maybe. But true."

"We don't change that drastically. Me and Kevin still tolerate each other!"

"Maybe for friendship he's worth tolerating." He gave an exasperated grin. "You just have to trust me when I say, I'm not worth getting involved with anymore."

"Shouldn't I be the judge of that?"

"No!" With that, John shook Freddy off and departed.

Freddy watched him go, his mind mixed with instinct and guilt. He had no explanation for why he had been so tough on Garret. There was nothing to say it was him and though he had inadvertently made a connection between him, Fletcher and Young, he hadn't as yet acknowledged it. He shook his head, feeling an embarrassed glow come over him as he realised his behaviour had predominantly been based on childhood resentment and suspicion. His speculation over Garret's method of success had long since been pushed to the darkest recesses of his mind. Age had brought with it maturity and a lack of imagination to believe the implausible. To judge the guy based on his coat and the fact he happened to be in his hometown was thin. It was more likely that a stranger had entered the community and had decided the population required culling. Kevin's early visitor had to be top of the list for that. Finishing his coffee, he regained composure and walked back down the street to the station. Inside Doris was just departing for her mid-morning break and Kevin was reading a newspaper.

"So that's your idea of working over the evidence, is it?" Freddy questioned Kevin.

"I studied it. Couldn't think of anything."

"Tell me something I don't know." Doris gave a small laugh. He entered his office and Kevin followed.

"How's John these days, then? Still up to mischief?"

"He's fine. Nervous about being around town, I think. Not surprising; he's been away for long enough."

"Is he our man, then?"

"What makes you say that?"

"Well, that was why you picked him up to start with, before you realised who he was."

"Yeah, and that's as far as it went." He lied.

"You didn't find it the least bit unusual that he matched our stranger's description."

"No. In fact, I find it a great deal more plausible that your stranger friend is our culprit than a guy we've both known for half our lives."

"You really believe that?" Kevin pushed him.

"Yes, I do!"

"So, what happened to all those accusations when we were kids? The 'there's something strange about John now' and the 'have you noticed how weird John has been acting lately'?"

"That was just boyish stupidity."

"Freddy, you were eighteen before you stopped going on about it."

"Well, I've changed my mind." He picked up the pathology report and began flicking through the sheets.

"No, you haven't. You're just ignoring the memories."

"So, what's the deal, then? You're positive it's him." Freddy challenged.

"Well, shall we look at the incriminating evidence?" Kevin sat down to face his boss. "He's in town. Then there's the aforementioned articles of clothing." Freddy opened his mouth to speak, but Kevin raised his voice and continued. "Which we have already covered, but I felt the need to re-highlight. And finally, he must have held a lot of grudges against those two. All the times they kicked the crap out of him. Not to mention that final onslaught Fletcher and Young, along with our resident holy man, claimed to have carried out." Freddy looked puzzled. "You must remember. They said they'd beaten him up and left him whimpering in a ball on the floor. But then the next day our mate arrived at school as if nothing had happened. Denied the entire experience. I mean, even I found that strange. But what do you reckon, group hypnosis? Pubescent adolescent macho bullshit dreams?"

Freddy was startled by his deputy's uncharacteristic turn of words. "Okay, I remember," he conceded. "You know I do. But the man's clean and we've no proof."

"Not so clean as you may have thought!" Kevin proposed.

Amazement glazed Freddy's eyes as his deputy passed him a piece of paper.

"I didn't sit around doing nothing while you were socialising. Did a bit of checking up and it would appear that our old mate has been recently questioned on a murder charge. His secretary's."

"But they let him go?" Freddy asked.

"Only while they follow up other leads." He clarified.

"Still doesn't mean he did it."

"No. But it's a bit much of a fucking coincidence, don't you think?"

"Do you know how the girl died?" Freddy questioned.

"Thrown from her apartment window. Leaves it consistent with our MO."

"What MO?"

"Exactly." Kevin smiled smugly, and for the first time Freddy felt a little inferior to his colleague.

"So, what next?" Freddy prompted.

"Well, it's up to you, but I'd keep an eye on him. See what he does? Because if this is all just a big old vendetta or therapy for a tortured mind, it ain't over."

Freddy's face contoured with panic.

"There's still the big fish to fry!" Kevin added.

"Okay, I'll accept your argument, but that doesn't mean I want to rule out the other guy you were talking to or anybody else fitting the description, for that matter," Freddy asserted, regaining his composure. "While I keep a track on John, I expect you to find your guy."

"Whatever you say, boss." Kevin grinned.

"Get moving, then!" Freddy hollered.

20

Freddy decided to stop off at the library before setting out for stakeout land. There were a couple reasons behind this decision. Firstly, Nicola was working there today, and he wanted to tell her that he would be out all night. And secondly, he thought it would pay to pick up some literary material of the alternative kind. Catch up on some background reading, just in case his old paranoia became reality.

The library hadn't altered in the slightest over the past fifteen years. It still possessed the power to daunt all who entered. The domed skylight extended high up into the sky like an inverted chasm. The help desk, worse for wear after years of under investment, still resided centrally underneath the shaft of light that shimmered off airborne dust particles. Nicola stood in the middle of this luminescent column and as Freddy walked in, she spied him immediately. Her face was puzzled but pleased.

"You'll never guess who I've just seen," Freddy said.

"Oh, I don't know? Father Manton?"

"No. But interesting that you should bring him up." He paused in thought.

"Well, who, then?" She quizzed.

"John!"

"Fredrickson?"

"No. Garret!"

"Really?" Surprise took over. "Where is he? Did you invite him for dinner?"

"Still burn a flame for him, even after all this time?" he joked.

"No, don't be silly. You know I only want you. But that doesn't mean I can't be hospitable."

"Okay!"

"So, did you invite him?" She asked again.

"Said he didn't have the time. He was acting strange, though," Freddy said cagily.

"You're not going to start that again!"

Her familiarity and recollection tripped him quickly. "What?"

"Don't play coy with me. That ritualistic crap you spewed on about when we were young."

"You can't say there was nothing weird going on."

"Nothing but teenage peer pressure." She riffled through some index cards laid on the counter.

"You're wrong." He proclaimed.

"Yeah. And you went on about it so much that even Kevin started to come down here to look things up for you."

"I never sent Kevin to look up anything." He was shocked by the accusation.

"That's even worse, then!" She chuckled hysterically.

"When was this?"

"You're not going to start on him now, are you?" She cautioned her husband.

"Just tell me when, Nicola." He asked assertively.

She sighed. "About four, maybe five years ago." Freddy mused over the answer. "Oh, for Christ's sake, give up and come back to the real world."

"You mean to tell me you don't find it the least bit coincidental? Fletcher and Young dead and then I tell you John's back in town?"

"Coincidence? Yes! Linked? No!"

"Not even after that illness happening simultaneously with John's transition?"

"Big words, hon."

"That's not answering the question."

"What's really got you thinking like this again? It can't be John's return, because we got you over that suspicion." She waited patiently for a response. It was slow to arrive.

"Kevin thinks there's a link, too."

"Oh, fucking marvellous. Now we've got superstitious crackpots for sheriff and deputy! What's Charlie do in his spare time, voodoo? And does Doris run a secret coven?"

"Now you're being stupid."

"I'm the one being stupid!" She raised her voice, then quietened down, embarrassed. "At least I have reason for talking fiction. Working in the library and all!"

"Talk about character changes." Freddy uttered flippantly.

"Yeah, well I spent two years loving a guy who had more interest in his best friend's behaviour before he began showing any interest in me!" She paused to dignify her tone. "I'm sorry if I don't roll over quietly in anticipation for the return of those days."

Freddy was stunned into silence. This was the first time Nicola had ever truly expressed her emotions.

"Hey, Freddy," said a voice behind him.

Nicola made a sign for quiet, seeing immediately who it was. She knew Louise, though the reverse wasn't true. She had been pointed out to her several times in town by neighbourly housewives poking their mischievous noses in where they didn't belong.

"Doris told me I could find you here," Louise spoke softly. "We need to talk."

"I'll see you later," Freddy said to his wife.

"Yeah, run off with your little floosy," she spoke under her breath, but she knew both of them had heard.

Louise flinched as if she was about to turn and retaliate, but Freddy prevented her.

"Please don't!"

"Why not?"

"That's my wife."

"Right." She took a moment to process the fact. "Friendly, isn't she?"

"Just a bad time. What did you want?"

"Found a print on Fletcher around his wrist. Showed up under ultraviolet." She informed him.

"Got a match?"

"Give me time. I'm trying to get it run through the system now."

"Good." His voice sounded strained with frustration.

"What's up?" Louise asked.

"Nothing."

"Yes, there is."

"I can't really talk about it."

"Woman troubles?" she persisted, but he said nothing. "Told you the other day I can help with that."

"Now's not the time for flirting." He smirked briefly, but his voice remained sullen. "Nicola's not the problem anyway." He stopped talking, mulling things over, trying to find structure of some kind. She waited expectantly. The expected confessional spurt didn't arrive, though. Instead, he started to climb the staircase to the first floor. Louise followed.

"So, you gonna tell me what it is?" she spurred him on.

"Alright. You're impartial to all of this. So, I'll bounce something off you and if you tell me I'm crazy, then fair enough."

"Fire away." She grinned.

"When I was fourteen, I had this friend and we got in some scuffles with Fletcher and Young, and believe it or not, Father Manton." He started to walk around, studying the index cards at the end of each aisle.

"You beat up a priest?" She seemed appalled at the idea.

"Trust me, he wasn't so pious back then." He took a breath. "Well, one day, Manton and our two recently deceased decided on revenge of the grimmest sort. Least that's what they professed." He entered one of the aisles of books, his eyes now beginning to stream over the spines of each volume in turn, tracing the index numbers toward his goal.

"What'd they do?"

"That's not important." He tried to regain his train of thought. "Problem was my friend told a different story. One in which nothing drastic happened." He stopped for a second. "After that event, our priest and corpse pals went down with something serious. It was like they had contracted 'the consumption', or something. They wasted away down to nothing, until they were banging on death's door. Doctors didn't have a clue. But then, just before hitting the critical list, life rejuvenated within them and hey presto, they're back in school. Only now they're a little humbler." Staring in sudden discovery, he pulled the stepladder along and ascended.

"I'm sure this is going somewhere, but if there is a link, can I have it soon? 'Cause so far I'm just hearing stereotypical teenage angst." She paused, scrunching her face up slightly. "Of a decade and a half ago."

He returned back down with a book in hand.

"Okay. Well, during this hive of retaliatory activity, my friend was reading up on some really weird shit." He pointed at the book he had retrieved. "This, to be precise. He began acting very peculiar."

"Stop right there. You're not going to try and palm off witchcraft on me, are you? You know, Kevin told me about your freak attack over at Fletcher's. Talking about sacrificial settings and all that jazz. 'Cause if that's what's coming, then you are nuts." She sounded unnerved.

"Just bear with me for a little while longer. You know me. You know I'm a pretty rational guy." He paused for some reassurance and she nodded for him to continue. "Okay, now the book talks of a demi-God called Shalek. He is the keeper of the titular 'Fallen Angels'."

"And they are?" she interrupted him as they sat down at a reading table at the end of the aisle.

"I was getting to that. They were angels despatched to earth by God to maintain the good-to-evil equilibrium. Trouble was that Shalek converted them. Now they work for him."

"You really believe in all this, right? Does your wife know?"

Her tone was strongly tainted with sarcasm.

"Why do you think we were arguing?"

"I think I'm beginning to like her." Louise joked.

"You said you'd listen with an open mind!" His eyebrow was raised as a reminder.

"Didn't say I'd check it in at the gate," Louise quipped, then gestured for him to carry on.

"Reading through here, it talks of a magical place in Shifton. Out in the forest." He tapped the book's cover. "Been used for years to worship differing forms of the occult." Louise's head was tilted patronisingly to one side, but he ignored it. "I know my friend went up there. And I know he read this book. And I know his three enemies simultaneously got horribly sick." He went silent, waiting for her comment. It was a few seconds in coming.

"And that's all you got?"

"Save to say after that time nothing bad ever happened to him. And now he's back in town and bodies are appearing all around."

"Well, at least that point is a hard fact. Otherwise, this is not the kind of talk I like to hear from my sheriff."

"Now you're sounding like my wife." He opened the book and started to flick through the pages. He had evidently hoped for more from her.

"So maybe she's a smart woman." She rested a hand on his forearm. "Just got a viper of a tongue." She laughed.

"Just take a look and read some," he pleaded.

"I don't need to." She sighed and retracted her hand. "Forget the superstition for a moment." Her voice turned serious. "You have a guy in town known to be pissed at the deceased, albeit a long time ago, but at least it holds potential for a revenge motive. Though I must say at this juncture, he potentially holds the record for suppressed vendetta instincts. But at least it's a more rational scenario than his being a witch."

"I never said he was a witch. Besides, he's a man." She looked confused. "He'd be a warlock." Freddy smiled to ensure she realised it was a joke.

"Anyway." She glared at him. "I'm digressing into irrelevant comments like you. All I'm trying to say is, from historical association and commensurate re-emergence alone, you've got enough to question him."

"I've kinda already done that," he said timidly.

"And his reason for being here is?"

"Business of sorts."

"And you don't believe him." She sat back in her seat. "Okay, so now all you've got is superstition and a severe case of obsessive-compulsive tendency."

"Kevin suspects him as well."

"So, what did he suggest as a motive? Or does he subscribe to your tripped-out theories too?" Her condescension returned.

"That's irrelevant."

"Okay. So, what does he think you should do?" She questioned.

"Follow him."

"Well, at least it's low profile. Balanced. Maybe he should be sheriff."

Freddy stared sternly at her.

"Just kidding. He tries it on too much anyway." She cringed. Silence fell.

"So, you gonna tail him?" she asked.

"Yes."

"So, what you still doing here?"

"Stakeouts are a lonely business. Thought I'd take some background reading." He tapped the book with his hand.

"Alright, just promise me you won't tell anyone else what you told me. I'd hate to see you locked up in an asylum," she said in an attempt to relax the atmosphere between them. It worked.

"Just you go and get that fingerprint ID."

"I'm on it." She stood up to leave, then turned for one final comment. "Be careful."

Freddy smiled.

He closed the book and returned to pull another from the

shelf. Then, with both tucked under his arm, he walked back downstairs toward his hostile wife.

"So, did she have a whole load of sweet nothings for you?" Her sarcasm hadn't subdued.

"Give it a rest, will you." He cut her short. "I'll be gone all night."

"Oh, that's convenient."

"I said give it a rest. I'm on a stakeout."

"Alone?"

"Yes." He glared, annoyed at her persistence. "I'll call you when it's over." He didn't wait for another speculative remark, just walked away.

21

After his oddball discussion with Kevin earlier, Freddy had left the office feeling positive of mind and determined to track Garret's every step. That was now six hours ago, and his emotions were running far less pure. He had homed in on the Blazing Stump, sure that his suspect would return there after his appointment, if indeed he had one. But the gradual numbing sensation that had conquered his butt had also started to infiltrate his enthusiasm. There was a limit on how long he could spend staring at the same empty motel room. There was an even lower limit to the number of overly inquisitive passers-by that he could tolerate. Up until now he had remained incognito, having changed his clothing to avert excessive attention, but was increasingly considering disclosing his purpose to the office manager, to facilitate an impromptu search of Garret's room.

The night sky had closed in unnoticed, bringing with it a clouded weather front and rain that had steadily built up from a drizzle into a thick downpour. Along the street, halogen lamps began to flare, just in time to illuminate a Ford rental pulling up on the other side of the road against a barren patch of wasteland a hundred yards in front of the motel entrance. Rain sizzled off the metallic silver bonnet, despatching steam upwards into the night air as if the car was breathing. Lights switched off, it sat there for a moment, its occupant hidden by the darkness within. Freddy slid down in his seat, feeling suddenly naked to scrutiny.

The driver's door opened, and an internal light automatically switched on above the rear-view mirror, revealing Garret's confused features. He moved slowly, as if each action was being internally questioned. He still wore his raincoat, but his exposed hair soon soaked up sufficient water to leave it lying limp across his scalp. Locking his car, he walked towards the motel and through the archway into the courtyard. He raised a hand as he passed the manager's office and Freddy could hear him holler a greeting of some kind. He sat upright again, watching every last movement until the bedroom door closed behind Garret and the window was filled with dancing blue rays of light from the television screen. Freddy stared mesmerised at the projected rays, almost missing a coated figure appearing five minutes later from the adjacent rough ground. It was only as the internal car light flicked on again that Freddy fully regained his focus. Turning, he caught Garret's face briefly, just before the car door closed. Freddy reclined back in his seat and watched as the car drove off without its lights on. Once it had passed, he sat up again and turned the key in the ignition. There was a brief whir, then silence. He tried again, only to receive the same response. Four more times he attempted to fire the engine, but each time it failed. He smacked his hand against the steering wheel and checked his rear-view mirror to see where Garret had got to, but he was already out of sight. Climbing out and slamming the car door behind him, Freddy raced across the road to the motel.

"I need to borrow your car," he shouted at the manager, while revealing the sheriff's badge clipped to his shirt pocket.

"I don't know you," the old man responded from his sofa chair. "Why the hell should I lend you my car?"

"I'm the sheriff of Shifton and—"

"We're not in Shifton now, son!" He smirked.

"Look, while you're wasting my time, a murder suspect is getting away."

"A murder suspect, hey? And you don't have back-up. Give me a break." He started to laugh.

"Do you want to be arrested for obstruction of justice?"

"Not really. Particularly if you'd have to walk me back to the station." He showed further appreciation for his own humour. "But we're not in Shifton, so I guess I'm good."

Freddy was moving around behind the desk to take hold of the guy when he spotted the keys dangling from a hook underneath the counter.

"Fuck it." Freddy snatched them.

"Hey, give those back right now, sonny boy." The old timer started to reach for a baseball bat hidden by the side of his chair. "Lest you want your head caved in."

"Sit down and shut up!" Freddy spun around, unclipping his revolver from his holster. "And tell me where your car's parked." The man turned a bright shade of purple and pointed to the back door. "Thank you, sir. I'll return it later."

With that he bolted out back to find a white rusted four-door Lincoln reversed back into a garage. Giving the door two quick tugs in succession, he climbed behind the wheel and started the engine. She struck up perfectly first time, the engine ticking over much more quietly than his cruiser. Sliding the stick shift into first, he pulled away and out onto the main road. There was no chance of catching up with Garret, but that wasn't necessary. After his discussion with Kevin, he knew there was only one place he would be going to and that was back to Shifton.

John had covered a lot of ground in the short time Freddy had been delayed. Ignoring state speed limits, he was driven by a burning desire to conclude events, to get it over with and return to something that resembled a normal life. However, this passion for closure still failed to alleviate the asphyxiating fear strangling his lungs and throat. Neither of his previous outings had caused him such stress, but this one seemed somehow different. Killing Fletcher and Young had felt more like a service to Shifton. There was nothing good in what they had become. They had added no real value to the community, at least none that couldn't be replaced by somebody else. Manton, though, had become a focal point of communal praise. And he was a priest. This latter pill was the hardest to swallow, because no matter how much John tried to convince himself that his teenage religious severance was just, it didn't ease the burden of guilt he faced. To desecrate books and denounce God was personal, a self-sought sealing of his own fate and his alone, carried out under the hazy influence of hate. But now, to betray God and Christianity through the slaying of one of his disciples. That required him to have firm belief that it was right. That it was just. And that it was the only way his baby could be saved. With all these questions, John harboured doubts, but no alternative cried out to him. Even God remained silent again, and in his absence, he signed away his minion's life.

As he drove along Main Street, lights from the oncoming traffic flashed in his eyes. The town arcades were brimming with juvenile life and McDonald's was equally packed. As he passed Chucks, the average age for nightlife shifted from the barely teens to the near twenties. That place hadn't changed much. Still the same layout, the same external canopied seating area, the same lighting. Only now the clientele had risen a few grades.

Once past his old haunt, the town settled into suburbanite doldrums. The land of self-absorption. Here people wanted to break from society, to move out of the spotlight suffered at work and in town, where continuous scrutiny was an aspect of daily routine. In their homes they thrived on the perception of seclusion and the ignorance of others. Neighbourhoods had changed vastly since John's youth. Back then, socialising was paramount. "The door's always open" philosophy was embraced by all but strangers, and even they never sat outside the loop for more than a week. It felt different tonight, not least because there were no children to be seen playing on the streets. They were all in town, at the arcade, or inside, watching television or playing computer games. Parental control and childhood imagination had suffered major losses, all but vanishing over the past generation. This time of fond reflection and comparison managed to distract John for a few moments. But as he turned up the heavily forested road to the church, his mind refocussed on the carnage that awaited.

It was Saturday night, and he knew that Manton would be

at the church preparing himself for the morning service. For quick reassurance, he had called Manton's home number before leaving the hotel, just to check he wasn't around. The phone had rung out uninterrupted. His mind as yet hadn't really focussed on how he was going to deal with the impending confrontation. Young and Fletcher had been easy in comparison. Neither had really seen him coming or been in any position to put up a struggle. He had sacrificed their souls as required through ritual, setting up the ceremonial altar to Shalek and burning the black candles in his honour. It had been easy. Their houses were empty, their wits slow, and they represented only a questionable loss to society. This would be different. He would have to face Manton to begin with. There couldn't be any cowering in the dark waiting for an opportunity to reveal itself. His approach must be forward, direct and most importantly, understood.

He cornered the final bend, bringing the church into sight, the windows flickering with orange candlelight. A single car was parked out in front. He pulled up slowly, his eyes wandering across the rough land where so much pleasure had been captured in his youth. He imagined Kevin, Ian and Nicola playing football, calling him across to join in. How they had laughed and joked in the summer sun, clueless as to what the future would bring.

As he parked up outside the church, Manton crept back into his subconscious and John snapped back to the present. The church loomed darker and more mysterious than he had remembered, like a symbolic edifice that housed wonders. Its once white wooden structure had been weathered over the past decade and a half, telling the financial story of the parish and the strength of the congregation. Wooden gargoyles had been added to the porch roof, leering down on all who entered. They were only there to instil some sense of safety in the penitent, a peace of mind from worldly ills! Protectors! He passed by them, lowering his eyes, feeling the dread they emitted in his muscles. As he pushed the main door open, he slung a small rucksack taken from the back seat of his car over his shoulder, leaving both hands free for whatever lay in wait.

The door swung silently open, revealing an empty nave in front of him like a nightmare. Every minute detail remained unaltered and he could feel the mental pain of his penultimate visit. The burning candle wax drawing every drop of moisture from his skin. The pain in his ankle as it prevented his escape and added to his torture. The sadistic drive of Manton as he took pleasure first in ordering Young and Fletcher into action and then as he took charge himself. His memories were so vivid, they almost managed to stimulate the same level of hatred he felt when he had returned on the Sunday when he had denounced God. The abuse he had strewn in disrespect at the altar. The shredded and scattered bible pages and hymn books. His passion to embrace a religion that cared for its flock. If Manton had been within his grasp then, it would have all been over in a flash. His rage was high, sweat seeping from his brow. Glancing from side to side, he sought his childhood nemesis, but he was nowhere to be seen. Then the remainder of his life shuttered through his mind. His wedding, job, degree, car, house, wife – they were all lies. None of it was his. He had achieved nothing, save for that single precious entity that lay inside his wife's womb. A tiny human being made by him and Gloria. It was the only thing of worth he had created in his life and even then, he had to do it in partnership with another. That baby represented all that was good about his life.

"Can I help you?" A familiar voice resonated along the aisle. John was caught by surprise and failed to respond. "Hello. Can I help you?" The voice repeated.

Looking up he saw a slight man dressed completely in black, save for a white collar of the faith, walking toward him. His hair had receded, his skin was mottled and pitted, the tell-tale signs of teenage acne long since departed. With a confused smile on his face, he continued to approach. In one hand he held a rag and in the other, a bar of soap. His sleeves were rolled up his forearms and it appeared as if he had just been scrubbing the floor. As he drew nearer his face reflected greater concern at John's extended mute response, and instead of moving up close, he came to rest five metres away. At this distance John was sure he would be able to see traces of the man he had come to slay, but he didn't. If it was possible that a person could completely alter their appearance, then Manton had achieved it.

"Hello. I said, can I help you?" he repeated himself. John stared down at Manton's hands, searching for any indicator. "Oh, don't mind these, I was just cleaning the steps over there." Manton misunderstood the glance.

"Father Manton?" He sought confirmation.

"Yes."

"You used to live in this town, right?" John was still a little uncertain.

"Yes."

"You look nothing like you used to." John uttered quietly.

"Sorry? What did you say?"

"Nothing."

John stepped forward, reaching out his hand in greeting. Manton's head was muddled, but he didn't want to be rude, particularly considering the familiarity with which the stranger addressed him. So, he reciprocated. As their hands clasped tight around each other, John swung his other hand around, landing a punch square to the side of Manton's temple. Manton's eyes twitched momentarily before his limp body dropped to the floor. It all happened in slow motion, the body falling vertically to begin with, before spilling to the side as his legs buckled. With this sideways motion his body picked up momentum, all of which seemed to get absorbed by his head as it smacked the tiled floor. The collision of skull and stone rippled around the church and made John wince. Standing over the motionless body, he doubted his courage once more. But the doubt disappeared as soon as his thoughts converged back on his wife and child.

Grabbing hold of Manton's right arm, he dragged him up the aisle toward the altar. A thin trail of blood left traces of the journey and added a colourful air of artistry to the event. With the others there had been no in-between phase, just life and death. Death had been explosively messy with one and sadistic with the other. And he had retained sufficient emotional detachment from both his victims, executing his retribution when opportunity had struck. There had been no mental engagement. In their declining seconds, they would have been none the wiser as to who was attacking them or why it was happening. Manton would be different. Not because that was what John wanted, but because Shalek desired it. He knew the gesture had to be symbolic and he knew the victim must understand why his life was ending.

Reaching the altar step, he pulled some climbing rope from his bag and began to tie Manton's hands together with one end of the cord, lashing the loose end around the altar pedestal. With two other pieces he completed his one-man re-enactment by fixing each leg tight to the first pew on either side. Manton moaned, starting to regain consciousness.

"What...?" He couldn't get any more out, seemingly confused. John ignored him. "What's going on?"

"Payback time." John announced with playful delight.

"Why? Who are you?"

"You hurt me. You mean you don't remember?"

Manton shook his head.

"Well, let me try and jog that memory of yours." He paused for effect while he desperately sought to rediscover his vicious streak. "Does your broken rib still cause you pain?" For a second Manton still failed to register, but then the realisation slowly dawned. He stared at his attacker, as if searching for physical confirmation.

"Garret?"

"That's me."

"Why?"

"Well, that's the uncanny thing. I don't want to be doing this. But then I don't make the rules."

"That doesn't answer my question." Manton replied.

"Look, just shut up and let me get on, will you? The information's going to be useless to you in a couple of minutes anyway."

"Maybe, but at least I'll have understanding." Manton's voice was relatively calm, subdued by shock.

"You priests always talk a lot, don't you?" John crouched momentarily, rucksack in his hands, pondering whether to bother divulging his reasons. "Remember after our big fight all those years ago, you chased me here one night and tortured me?"

Manton remained silent, as if languishing with the memories of his former self.

"Well, not surprisingly, I wanted revenge, so I pledged myself to Shalek."

Manton appeared confused.

"So, you know your scripture, but not your folklore. They should train you guys better. Shalek is the earthbound God, created by your master to offer substance to his faith. He is the ruler of the land and the master of the fallen angels. He is my master, and he gave me the power to enact revenge on you. Remember the illness that gripped you and your friends? That was my work, but his power. The only thing is, that I misinterpreted my side of the deal. I had to kill you; not just make you suffer. And that's why I'm here now. I have to finish what I started."

"But why does it have to be that way?"

"Because he demands it!"

"That's not a reason."

"It's reason enough for me."

"No, you're just afraid," Manton said, his voice soft and calm.

"Stop trying to fucking psychoanalyse me. The truth is you've only got yourself to blame. You created me." John was becoming slightly agitated, feeling compelled to justify himself.

"No, you did that to yourself."

"Maybe, but you were certainly the inspiration."

"I have done a great many things that I regret in my life and one of them is the persecution of others. I can't take those memories away, no matter how much I wish for it. But God has taught me the lesson I sorely needed to learn. He has humbled me and demonstrated the error of my ways."

"None of that changes anything." John dismissed his confession.

"Maybe not for you, but it does demonstrate that it is never too late to change."

"That probably works with your lord and master, because he's so absent from life. My master takes a somewhat more active participation. Makes sure that I never stray from the straight and narrow of his work."

"No matter how hopeless you feel it is, the Lord can protect you!"

"What? Like he protected me all those years ago against you? Fat fucking chance. While God may rule in people's hearts and minds, Shalek and his minions are raping the surface of the world for self-gain."

"It won't help them in the longer term. In the afterlife." Manton challenged.

"They don't care about an unproven state of being or reaping the rewards that are supposed to be waiting for them there. They care about the here and now," John said as he laid candles in a circle around Manton's body and lit them.

"What about hope and faith? Don't they matter?" Manton probed.

"Hope and faith are tired. They may have worked over nearly two millennia, but don't forget, their foundation stone was a man who performed miracles. Even back then God knew that he had to provide something tangible to instil his faith. Well, the cycle is now almost complete. Humans are tired of the dusty images. They need something new. Something they can touch." Taking a piece of chalk from his bag, he marked a pentagram on the floor, closing the tips with arcs to form a magic circle.

"If that's what you believe, then there is no hope."

"What I believe is that if I was starving in the middle of the street, on my dying legs, and a person walked up to me and offered me an apple from his hand, or the promise of ten, if I could just walk a hundred metres down the street and around the corner, I'd rip the apple from his hand so fast that he might lose a finger."

"Then do what you must." Manton started to pray. "Our Father, who art in heaven, hallowed be Thy name."

"I wouldn't bother with that. He won't save you. Just like he never saved me from you." With that John drew a hunting knife from his rucksack.

Manton ignored his comments and continued reciting the Lord's prayer.

"Shut up, will you! It's time to bring an end to this."

Manton took no notice.

Garret tried to shake the noise from his mind. Taking a slow breath to steady his nerves, he began the ceremony. "Shalek, Master of the elements, controller of earthbound spirits, possessor of elemental life force, I beseech you to be favourable to me in my calling upon thy Great Minister which I make. I offer thee this soul in penitence for my poor faith. I promise to abide by your doing from this moment through the rest of my life. Please forgive my neglect and know that my pact was honest."

"And forgive our trespasses, as we forgive those who trespass against us. And lead us not into temptation." Manton's words increased in volume.

Garret compensated: "Aglon, Tetragrammaton, Vaycheon, Stimulathon, Erohares, Retrasammathon, Clyoran, Icion, Esition, Existien, Eryona, Onera, Erasyn, Moyn, Meffias, Soter, Emmanuel, Sabaoth, Adonai. I call you to witness and accept this offering."

"Our Father, who art in heaven," Manton started again, raising his prayer to a shout.

"Shalek, accept this offering of body and blood as a symbol of my devotion to thee." With that, John raised the knife into the air, tilting its blade towards Manton's chest. "Aglon, Tetragrammaton, Vaycheon, Stimulathon, Erohares, Retrasammathon, Clyoran, Icion, Esition, Existien, Eryona, Onera, Erasyn, Moyn, Meffias, Soter, Emmanuel, Sabaoth, Adonai. I call you to witness and accept this offering. Take this man from the earth."

With that, his outstretched arms began to arc downwards toward Manton's torso. From nowhere a shot blistered the air.

The strength was suddenly smashed from John's right hand, destabilising him. Pain screamed through his head as his left hand sought to comfort the wound that had appeared. His knife flailed effortlessly forward, falling uselessly on the stone slabs beneath the altar. Blood seeped through John's fingers, initially warming, then numbing his arm. As his body lunged to the left, his ankle caught one of Manton's shackles, sending him spilling uncomfortably onto the altar steps. Without a free limb to protect himself, his left shoulder slammed onto the edge of the top step, his body following through, colliding with the remaining ones. Rolling down, he came to a stop facing upwards, next to the front choir pew, obscured from his attacker's vision.

As he lay still, paralysed by shock, his arm pulsating, his mind began to fade. He heard footsteps approaching, but for a moment found himself on the verge of fainting. Everything seemed dreamlike around him. But then the sharp agony returned clarity to his thoughts. The unknown party still hadn't stepped into John's line of sight, so he wriggled himself away from the central aisle and crawled around the front outside edge of the pew. He took short silent breaths, so as not to reveal his progress, but he knew that it was all just playing for time. The trail of blood alone would betray his position. But every second was crucial, if he was to recover the situation.

Moving onto his knees, he sped up his pace, listening cautiously to the strange footsteps advancing towards Manton. For a moment they slowed down, as if their owner was readying themselves to take aim. But as they continued advancing, he heard them trip with uncertainty. John had reached the back of the church now, managing to clear the next line of sight. He could hear the stranger running to see where he had got to, then the flurry of footsteps was broken by a short exchange of words between Manton and the unwelcome visitor.

John knew he couldn't outrun his hunter and would have to turn and fight at some point. So, shuffling on the spot, he readied himself, listening to the hard steps draw closer and closer. His only hope was that the element of surprise would allow him to dislodge his aggressor's weapon from his hand, leaving them on an almost even keel. His leg muscles tensed in readiness, his heart pounding at his ribs. The front of a foot appeared cautiously into view. John knew it was a split-second move, else he would certainly be seen. Then just as he initiated his pre-emptive strike, the door opened behind him, but it was too late for him to do anything about it. All he managed to acknowledge was that his aggressor was Freddy and that he was felled with ease. Next thing he knew was yet more pain as they slammed into a wooden pillar. Freddy took the brunt of the impact, his gun spilling away and his head cracking on the edge of the upright. John made no contact with the wood at all, but the action had inflamed his wound beyond all comprehension. The two of them separated like a shattered rock, falling either side of the pillar. Freddy's body fell lifeless and unconscious. John, on the other hand, fell at an obscure angle yet again, landing conscious in a heap against the wall. Rolling over, he turned to face the newcomer.

"Well, look here. What a predicament!"

As John's vision settled, he could see Kevin standing in front of him, gun poised at the ready.

"What the fuck has been going on?" Kevin demanded.

"I don't know. Freddy just started to attack me."

"Yeah? Then what is Manton doing all tied up over there?" Kevin flicked his gun toward the altar.

"I don't know. He had him down there when I came in." John wriggled around, resting his back up against the wall.

"And what were you doing up here?" Kevin stepped to one side so he could get a clearer view of his boss, who was still lying motionless.

"I just came to pray."

"Why here?"

"Just wondered what it was like th—"

"Oh, cut the crap, will you?" Kevin cut him short. "You haven't got any interest in how this place has changed."

"What do you mean?" John was unnerved by the tone in

Kevin's voice.

"Pick up the gun!" He pointed John toward Freddy's weapon.

"Why?"

"Just pick it up!" His voice sharpened.

"So you can shoot me?" John managed to raise a defiant tone.

"No." He took a breath. "So that you can complete your job." He lowered his weapon.

"What?" John's confusion soared.

"Get on with your sacrifice. Then we can get out of here." John pulled himself up the wall bemused. He still didn't fully understand what was going on. "And you can dispense with the religious crap, just shoot him. Shalek won't give a shit."

The truth sunk home. Kevin was on the books. He was a minion, a disciple, a follower. John started to rest easier, but he was still confused by the deputy's intervention. Surely it would expose him. John's mind was muddled. No matter how he now tried piecing the bits of the jigsaw together, they didn't equate to a simple resolution. Nevertheless, he did as instructed and retrieved the gun. It was only as he started trudging back down the aisle that he realised Manton had been screaming out for help the whole time. As John re-entered his vision, he went silent and reverted back to prayer. It was really only then that the penny dropped. There was no way out of this situation for all of them. At least two of them weren't going to make it. He spun around to see what Kevin was doing and found him hovering over Freddy's body.

"What about him?" John spoke loud and clear to ensure he got Kevin's attention.

"I don't know. You just get on with that and then we'll worry about Freddy boy." He dismissed the enquiry with an air of confidence.

"But he knows who you are now."

"No. He didn't see me come in. Just caught sight of the door opening."

John accepted the answer, though something still troubled him. The expression on Freddy's face had been a blend of relief and surprise. John was certain Freddy had acknowledged somebody. Someone he knew.

"How can you be so sure?" John asked.

"Just sort him out, then we'll worry about the big sheriff man here." He ignored John's question.

"Why are you here?" John altered his approach.

"What do you mean?"

"Well, why did you turn up at that precise moment? What's your remit?"

Kevin said nothing.

"I wouldn't have thought that you would jeopardise exposure just for the sake of me. Did Shalek send you to watch me? Or did Logan?" His recent saviour started to look agitated. "Or is there something more than that?"

"Just kill him, will you!" Kevin spoke with a vicious sneer.

"No. I want you to explain your involvement first."

Kevin started to shake his head. "Why can't you just do as you're told?" He raised his gun and took aim at John. "Why am I here? It's simple, really! You can't be trusted. You've failed in your duty once and you've been making a right fucking abortion of it this time. I've had to trudge around after you, clearing up your stupid fucking messes. I mean, are you trying to give the game away?" He paused for a second. "No, don't answer that."

"That still doesn't explain why you're here now."

"That's because I know you're not going to like it. I think you'd better drop the gun now." He indicated down towards John's side and waited for him to let go.

John did as instructed, feeling his heart sink as the metal clashed with the stone floor once again.

"You see, John, I'm pretty much like you." He started to move toward the aisle. "I wanted something more out of my life. Unlike you, though, I decided to work hard at it for a while. See if I could make it on my own. Didn't happen, though. Then, one day, I was driving around with Freddy here, and he told me this cockamamie tale about witches and burned tree stumps, and then about you and what he thought you'd done. Well, I got intrigued. Started reading up, just as you must have. Tried summoning Shalek, but he wouldn't come. So I lost faith. Then, three weeks ago, this guy turns up, says he can give me what I've been wanting and all I have to do is watch over you and then kill you. Things have even turned out better than I had planned. I never dreamed Freddy would be here. Now I can get rid of him, too."

"But why me?" John hadn't quite grasped the significance of the facts.

"You're my way in. My sacrifice. Just the same as Manton there is yours."

"It's not worth it, you know."

"Give me a fucking break. Don't even think about getting all sanctimonious on my ass, when the reason we're in this predicament is because Freddy there caught you about to stick a knife in Father Rehab."

"That doesn't mean it's right. I just don't have a choice. Gloria and my baby are in hospital. Logan will kill them if I don't do this."

"My heart bleeds." He sneered. "Took you fifteen years of the good life to come to that conclusion. Now I want my fifteen."

"It's not worth it!"

"Let me be the judge of that. Now turn around, kick that gun to one side and go pick up that knife. Slowly, mind you. You're gonna finish your job, then I'll finish mine." John did as instructed. "Now get down and gut him or whatever it is you want to do."

Standing still, John looked at Manton praying beneath him. His eyes were shut tight, words flowing from his lips in a ceaseless drone. John glanced back at Kevin, but all he could see was the barrel of a gun sighted on him. His former friend's posture was fixed solid, his hands clasped tightly around the pistol grip, his breathing steady. There was no more discussion to be had with Kevin. His body broadcast his resolve. John took a final look at the priest lying on the floor and dropped the knife.

"I can't do it!" John exclaimed.

"Makes no difference to me. I'm going to kill you either way!"

"You'd better get on with it, then, because I will not kill him." He pointed at Manton.

"Fair enough."

With these final words, John heard a shot ring out. He braced for the impact, his eyes cowering shut, but nothing came. For a split second he thought Kevin had missed and waited for a second bullet to be despatched. Silence. Fearing next that it was some cruel trick, he squinted out of one eye, expecting to see the gun still poised and Kevin winking mischievously before pulling the trigger again. Instead of this image, he saw Kevin lying on the floor, blood seeping through his uniform, his eyes glazed, his legs twitching. Nobody else was in view. He dove for the discarded gun and cocked it. Then, slowly, he peered above the front pew. Still nobody. Standing up, he begun a steady progression to the rear of the church, casting a glance down every row as he passed. All the while his weapon remained loosely directed at Kevin. As he reached the deputy's body, he crouched fumbling with one hand for signs of life but found none. All the while his gun hand remained alert in search of the shooter. Standing back up, John kicked Kevin's gun away from his body, then focussed his attentions on the remaining blind spots. The air was silent, disclosing no clue as to where he should look. Absent of caution, he stepped forward, right into Freddy's gun sights.

"Drop it!" Freddy's voice wavered.

"Only if you lower yours away from my head." He took a short breath to ascertain the reaction.

"It wasn't a request, John."

"Okay." He let go of the gun.

Freddy started to clamber to his feet, the gun falling away from its target in the process. But John didn't move.

"What now?" John asked.

"Well, first you can untie Manton down there." Freddy swooned with the sudden rush of blood. He clutched at his head, as if he would remain conscious if he did.

"What about Kevin?"

"Don't think we need to worry about him anymore. I got him smack in the middle of his chest. Now get moving!"

John made his towards the alter for a third time and started to smirk to himself. He couldn't get over the complete irony of the entire evening. He had started out with the intention to sacrifice a man who had been the root of his evil, to finish being pursued by the boy who believed something was amiss fifteen years ago, while discovering that yet another friend had uncovered the source of power and had pledged to do its bidding against him. Then he had found righteousness amidst the carnage, refusing to murder his former adversary, by default determining a course of action that would surely result in the death of his kin. The events had elapsed so comically compared to the plan; he couldn't help but laugh. He no longer cared about anything. And for the first time, he actually felt at peace with himself. It was a strange sensation.

"What's up with you?" Freddy asked.

"Oh, nothing, really. Just finding humour in the unpredictability of life," he responded cryptically.

John arrived at Manton and knelt down immediately. Taking the knife back into his hand, he cut the ropes.

"What now?" John shrugged his shoulders quizzically and dropped the knife. Then, before Freddy could answer, a gust of wind blew down the length of the chapel, extinguishing all the candles, leaving them stranded in the laminated shimmer of moonlight cascading down through the windows. The sudden gloom left their vision blurred, their pupils rapidly dilating to adapt.

"Who's there?" Freddy called out.

John knelt down and felt around for Kevin's gun, eventually clipping it with his fingers.

"Your worst fucking nightmare!" A voice echoed around them. Freddy looked confused, but John knew the tone immediately. There was only one person left it could be and the words used were fitting for his epitaph.

"This is the sheriff speaking. Who are you?"

"I don't give a shit who you are. You're mine now!"

Something moved to their left. Freddy and John turned simultaneously and fired a couple of rounds. One bullet shattered a pane of glass, the others impacted on the wall.

"Missed me. But I got one of you!"

Both Freddy and John turned instantaneously to see where Manton was, but he had disappeared. Then, from the back of the church, they heard a muffled groan and a squelching noise. Something landed on the floor ahead of them. They raised their guns and fired again.

"Hey, guys. I don't want to sound like I'm a nutter or anything, but you're wasting your ammo. What you gonna kill me with when it runs out?" The speaker finished with a snigger. "You look so alone and confused up there. Would you like your priest back?"

With that, Manton's limp body came sliding up the aisle of the church. It seemed to move effortlessly, coming to rest at their feet. Blood seeped from several puncture wounds across his torso. His neck had been broken, the larynx torn out. His belly was ripped open, his guts expanding from out of their confines.

"Who the fuck is this guy?" Freddy said, sounding panicked.

"Wow, there's a million-dollar question. You gonna tell him, or shall I?" A voice came from the darkness.

"His name's Logan," John said hesitantly.

"So, what the fuck does he want?" Freddy demanded.

"Your lives," Logan answered in a sinister whisper that arrived so close to their shoulders, they felt his hot breath tickling the backs of their necks. Spinning, they shot randomly again, wasting three more bullets. "You're nearly out now. Have you thought about what you can use next for defence? And try to be inventive – don't jump straight on to the praying and begging lark. It's just no fun."

"Garret, what the hell does he want?"

"He told you." John was coping slightly better than Freddy, because he knew the enemy.

"Yeah, but why does he want us dead?"

"Think of him as a debt collector. I made a deal and now he wants the payback."

"Succinctly and eloquently put my friend." It was Logan again, this time his voice more distant. "Problem for you is your method of payment is already expired at your feet. Now you have to pay in person."

"So, is this the reason I shouldn't get involved with you as a friend again? Or is there something else?" Freddy asked John.

"No, this is it," John replied.

"Good. I don't think I could handle anymore."

"I know you couldn't." Logan's words drifted around them.

John and Freddy twitched from side to side, checking all angles of approach.

"Tell me one thing, John, before this goes any further. Did you kill Fletcher and Young?" Freddy asked.

"Yes."

Freddy didn't have a chance to respond to his friend's confession because just then a gust of wind passed swiftly in front of them. They saw nothing, but Freddy felt a hand thrust at his chest, launching him over the altar and into the wall. John vanished momentarily from sight on the other side of the stone table. The square smack of wood across the span of his back emptied his lungs. And as he landed on the floor, he gasped for air as his body tried to recover. The winding was compounded by a fearful urgency that further stifled his intake. Panic set in and he could feel his face exploding with heat.

"Here, let me help." A face appeared at the side of him, its eyes black, its mouth dripping in blood. "Don't want you to die just yet. No pleasure in that!"

With that he placed a hand across Freddy's chest. Immediately his body relaxed, sucking in oxygen like gold dust. For a second he couldn't move, gripped by fear and restrained by a single powerful hand. But then Logan just grinned, raised his eyebrows and disappeared. Freddy jumped to his feet, moving sharply back around toward John.

"Do you.... see..... him?" Freddy was still slightly breathless.

"No. You just went flying and that was it."

"He was just there." Freddy's voice was manic.

"Are you alright?" John asked.

"No, I'm not fucking alright."

"Ha ha ha ha." They could hear Logan laughing from the back of the church.

"Come on. Let's get out of here." John grabbed Freddy's arm and started to pull him towards the exit. "I'll be damned if I'm going to stand around and wait to be executed."

"Damned is exactly what you are, Johnny boy." Logan appeared instantaneously in front of them, blocking their path. "And you ain't going nowhere. This is such an appropriate setting to conclude these events. Wouldn't want to lose that production value." Reaching out, he grabbed Garret by the neck and raised him up off the ground. Freddy cowered back in terror, tripping over Manton's body as he did so and landing in a pool of blood. As his wet palms touched the slickened surface, they gave way underneath him, his backside following through to an identical reception. The blood quickly drenched his trousers, driving him to get up.

"Ha ha ha ha. You know John, your friend here is quite the comic. Maybe I'll keep him alive for a while."

John tried to speak, but Logan tightened his grasp.

"What's that? You'll have to speak up, Freddy boy can't hear you!" Logan sneered and then dug his nails deeper into John's throat, breaking the skin and drawing blood. "Hey, check that out. Isn't that just marvellous? I've wanted to do that since the first moment I met you."

Freddy's head was a mess. He didn't have a clue what to do. There was no way he could take Logan on directly; he didn't have the strength. He couldn't shoot because he was shaking so much. And if he did, he could say with some certainty that if he hit Logan, it would have to pass through John first. Twitching forward as if to launch into action, he clipped Manton's body once more, lowering his eyes instinctively and viewing the carnage. John's face was now turning shades of purple, his hands tearing at his captor's skin in such a fashion that would have any mortal howling in pain. Logan was positively thriving on it, savouring every gash. For a brief second of insane ecstasy, he closed his eyes and relaxed his hold. It was only then that Freddy understood John's wish, as he managed to release the stranglehold enough to break the words out.

"Kill m—"

Logan's senses returned. "No, no that won't do," he protested playfully, shaking John's head in his hands. But it was too late. Freddy had begun the initiative, lunging towards the pair of them. He had three bullets left and he knew what he had to do. Ducking his shoulder down, he endeavoured to evade Logan's grasp, knowing full well that if he caught hold, it would all be over. John's eyes were so vacant now that death couldn't be far away from him already. Anything Freddy did would only provide minuscule relief from his final suffering. As Freddy closed in, his shoulder dug underneath his friend's armpit, using John's body as a blockade against Logan. Planting the muzzle hard into his friend's belly, he prepared himself to fire.

John managed to smile and say a final reminder: "Gloria."

The shot ripped straight through John. The zero-distance impact meant that the bullet retained much of its force, breaching his back and entering Logan. For the first time since Freddy had set eyes on him, Logan looked startled, as if in true surprise, but then the expression turned to pleasure once more. Freddy fired again, and then again, keeping the gun muzzle buried in the same spot. The way Logan's face reacted indicated that these had also hit home, the third one appearing to cause discomfort. Ever since Freddy had first made contact, he had been pushing Logan backwards, his initial momentum carrying them. But then as the third bullet found its course through Logan's intestines, Freddy felt his power give and the drive turned into a steady stumble, until all three of them crashed down on to the floor. John's limp body fell between them and Freddy used that barricade to his immediate advantage, clambering back to his feet and retreating away. Logan's recoil was less spontaneous. Blood oozed from beneath his jacket and he clutched at his stomach in devastating acceptance.

Outside they could hear police sirens approaching. Freddy only had to survive minutes before back-up would arrive. Taking a glance down to his left, he looked at the lifeless mass that was John and then back up at Logan.

"Does that piss you off?" Logan tormented Freddy, but his expression still displayed pain.

"Yes, a bit." Freddy's reply was spiked with bitterness.

"Good, because you're gonna need that hate to give you the strength to fight further." He removed his clasped hands from his stomach, exposing the wound. The blood flow had stemmed. Licking his fingers, he exaggerated the savouring of flavour. "You know, it doesn't matter how many times I taste my own blood, I always prefer to spill someone else's."

Logan dove toward Freddy, catching him in the ribs and despatching him down the aisle like a discarded coke can, his body moving effortlessly until Manton's corpse got in the way. For the second time Freddy found himself winded, but he moved, nonetheless. If he didn't retreat, Logan would only catch him sooner. There was no doubt that his attacker's movements were more lethargic than before, his force notably suppressed by the wounds Freddy had inflicted. However, that didn't mean much in terms of bringing them to an even status. Logan was still far superior, but his overconfidence spilled with each passing comment and any weakness was one that could be exploited. The blockade across Freddy's lungs slowly receded and he sucked in great quantities of air. Searching side to side for a weapon of some kind, he spied the crucifix used to lead the procession into the morning service. Lifting it out of its stand, he removed the cross from the end of the pole, revealing a shiny gold conical end.

"Give up, man. You'll not achieve anything with that." Logan taunted.

Freddy took no notice, raising it in defence. Logan tried to swot the end to one side in defiance, but Freddy retracted it out of his reach. That angered Logan.

"Come here, you little fuckwit." Logan lunged clumsily

forward, expecting to find support when he embraced his target. Freddy wasn't going to play ball, though, kneeling backwards just far enough to ensure Logan was completely off balance, before jamming the base of the mast in-between two floor slabs, angling it on a perpendicular vector to Logan's descending torso. By the time Logan realised what was happening, it was too late. His hands moved swiftly to grab the end of the pole, but they couldn't prevent the clumsy movement of his body being skewered. Freddy watched in trepidation as Logan's body slid down the pole, the pointed end protruding out of his back. Blood poured out, spilling on to the stone slabs in an endless torrent, rapidly forming a pool that reached out to Freddy's knees.

Freddy stayed fast in his position, watching for the last signs of life to vanish from Logan's face. The hunter had become the hunted and that sudden realisation was the most satisfying fact. His predator's face twitched with disbelief. Words wanted to form in his mouth, but he had neither the air nor the neural power to pull them together. Reaching out desperately, he tried to grab Freddy in one last effort to take him also but failed to achieve more than a passing glance. Eventually, the spasmodic jerking subsided. Freddy got to his feet, and stumbling up the aisle, calmly left the slaughter behind him. As he exited into the night, a police car and ambulances arrived, lighting the church like a disco.

Charlie jumped out of his car like a professional. "What's happened?"

"What you doing here?" Freddy asked, puzzled.

"Couple of kids heard gunshots while making out in the woods. What's happened?"

"I'll tell you later. There are four dead bodies in there. So be prepared." With that he walked up to the ambulance.

His head swirled as he endeavoured for the first time to make sense of the preceding events, knowing full well that he would have to explain it in some detail. Especially because it involved the shooting of an officer by an officer, let alone the death of the local priest. He wasn't sure that he could convince anybody of the story he would recount. There were far too many twists, turns and curveballs. The whole thing was just a complete mess.

"Hey, Freddy." Charlie had reappeared from the church. "How many bodies did you say there were?"

"Four."

"Not anymore there aren't!"

"What do you mean?"

"Well, I've got Manton, Kevin and what would appear to be an older version of John Garret, our former school friend. And that's it!"

"You can't have. What about the big guy staked at the front?"

"There's nobody staked at the front." Charlie looked perplexed.

"No way!" He began to head back toward the church.

"I'm sorry, Freddy, can't let you do that." Charlie grabbed his arm.

"Why not?"

"Can't run the risk of contaminating or tampering with the crime scene."

"I'll take that chance." He tried to pull away.

"No, you won't."

"Look, I'm in charge here." Freddy lost his patience.

"No, you're not. You're a suspect and I should be detaining you for questioning."

"The hell you should." He tried to break free, but Charlie gripped tighter.

"Please don't make this any harder." Charlie went to reach for his handcuffs. After a moment's thought, Freddy relaxed. "Good. Now get yourself seen to, then go sit in my squad car. We'll go back to the station when I've got things sorted here." He started to walk away but then stopped and turned. "And you'd better call Nicola. This could take all night."

22

Freddy sat outside the church for almost three hours before Charlie got Doris to drive him back to the station. She wouldn't normally have gotten anywhere near a crime scene, but the department was now irreconcilably undermanned at the moment, despite the appearance of the county sheriff. State troopers had been called in and were expected within the next half-hour. They would have usually arrived much sooner, but a chemical tanker had overturned near Clayton Falls, taking out a school bus, a truck load of beer and several cars.

Louise had arrived at the church a couple of hours prior to Freddy's departure to begin her preliminary examinations. She was also helping to capture evidence, taking fingerprints, blood samples, gun powder impregnation tests and a host of other forensic assessments. With her working on the scene, Freddy stood a chance of being cleared sooner rather than later. At least that was what he hoped. Though hope wasn't sufficient to calm him. He was finding it impossible to relax with the uncertainties of his future. Doris had stupidly attempted to quell his anxiety by plying him with cup after cup of coffee, but the caffeine just exacerbated the problem. To make things worse, she had also called his wife, and the prospect of having to explain all this to her increased his nervousness.

It was six thirty in the morning now and the sun was just starting to torch the horizon. Freddy imagined the air to be crisp and clear outside, but he couldn't see clearly through the frosted pane of his office window. Doris had locked him in there because she didn't feel right about putting him behind bars. To his surprise, Charlie hadn't objected when he had returned. He'd given him the low-down on what he could and couldn't do in there, but at least he could await his fate in dignified comfort.

"What's going on?" Nicola asked as she entered the room.

"Don't start freaking on me. It's not that bad."

"Stop trying to pacify me, then, and tell me what's not that bad." Her response was quick and more accusing than sympathetic.

"I got involved in a shoot-out, that's all."

"So why are you under guard?" She pointed at Charlie.

"Procedure."

"Don't wrap me in cotton wool. I'm not dumb."

Freddy let the silence hang before answering. "I did some of the shooting. So, Charlie has to view me as a suspect until my story checks out."

"And how long's that going to take?"

"Not long."

At that moment Louise opened the door, dressed roughly in jeans and T-shirt, bed hair straggling in disarray toward all corners of the room.

"I thought you were just going to follow him?" She addressed Freddy with an air of concern.

"Great, the floosy!" Nicola was evidently unimpressed by her arrival and consequential captivation of her husband.

"Hey. What is your repressed trauma?" Louise snapped from her exhaustion, retorting overly assertively.

"Stop it, you two," Freddy snapped, putting an end to the squabbling before it could degenerate further. "You don't even know each other, for Christ's sake!"

"Well, what's she doing here?" Nicola demanded to know.

"Her job." He spoke firmly. "Louise, this is my wife, Nicola. Nicola, this is Louise. Now both of you start acting like adults."

He shook his head and sighed, stifling the strain of dealing with the situation. There had been some fairly incessant questioning at the church by the county sheriff before he had been despatched back to the station. And on top of that, he was still trying to piece the sequence of events together himself, in an endeavour to add logic to the slaughter. The last thing he needed on top of everything was a cat fight.

Freddy regained composure. "Okay, now what you got?"

"Well, it didn't take long to figure out you shot Kevin."

"Kevin's dead?" Nicola stumbled back into a chair.

"Yes," Freddy answered her.

"Why?" Nicola questioned.

"Later!" His response was short and firm. He wanted to use the small amount of thinking time he had to full effect.

Louise continued upon Freddy's indication. "It would also appear to be your gun that killed your friend Garret. So, you're easily pinned for those two. But you confessed to them anyway, so let's move on to the more ambiguous parts of your deposition. Namely Father Manton's demise and this alleged third party."

"Alleged?" He objected to her phrasing.

"For now, let me focus on physical evidence." She paused to structure her thoughts. "Okay, you're covered in blood, although simple test work has already shown this to be Garret's, which, incidentally, reaffirms you as Garret's killer. But I would suggest that if you had also been the instrument of our Father's demise, you would resemble an Andy Warhol painting." Nicola sighed in disbelief at her phraseology. Louise stopped and raised her hand. "I don't need to tell you that all this is in confidence. Out there, we never had this conversation." He nodded. "And your wife?"

"Yes," he answered for Nicola. "But just keep the explanation simple and brief."

"Fine. The splatter pattern that would have been discharged and the blood found toward the rear of the church rule you out of that one."

"That should rule out Garret as well!"

"Normally, yes, but he was found lying in the pool of blood at the back and so could have been the culprit."

"But he didn't do it!" Freddy stressed the point.

"Don't bite my head off. I'm just telling you what I can prove."

"Have you got anything on my mystery man?" He sounded desperate.

"Well, where you claim to have left him staked, I found a blood residue mixed with a black gelatinous plasma. It's really strange stuff. I also found splatter marks of the same substance across the back wall."

"So that proves my fifth man!" His enthusiasm returned.

"Not entirely."

"Why?" He was starting to disbelieve what he was hearing.

"Before I divulge any more, I would firstly like to stress that I believe in science and not the occult. And I will only put my name to what I can tangibly prove and preferentially explain."

"What did you find?" Freddy's enthusiasm was irrepressible. Even Nicola was beginning to show a less admonishing interest in Louise's comments.

"The traces of blood didn't come from anybody in the room."

"Different blood type?" Nicola interjected.

"As it happens, yes." Louise seemed slightly taken back by Nicola's sudden interest. "But more importantly, the blood was dead."

"Well, it's bound to be," Nicola retorted.

Freddy sat quietly, waiting for the rest.

"Not like this," Louise said. She took a breath. "These samples hadn't just died. They had been dead a long time. The cell structure is substantially degraded and coagulated. There is no way that they could have come from a fresh wound in this half of the century."

"Are either of us having déjà vu yet, ladies?"

"I'm not finished yet." Louise placed her hands to her head, as if in disbelief of what she was about to disclose. "The plasma, on the other hand, is alive and continuously multiplying at a cellular level. It's like nothing I've ever seen before."

"That's great, you've got my fifth man." Freddy made the improbable leap of faith with ease.

"No way," Louise disagreed.

"Why?" Freddy raised his voice.

"I'm not putting my name to this secretion being able to support life."

"Why not?"

"'Cause I have absolutely no proof. This stuff could have been brought to the scene for some other reason. Garret could have been planning to use it in his ritual. Traces were found on his clothes."

"So, you believe about Garret being into the occult?"

"Not entirely."

"Why not?"

"All I mean by 'ritual' is that evidence shows Father Manton had been tied up, spreadeagle style on the floor near the altar. As if Garret intended the murder to hold additional significance."

"Why won't you believe me?" Freddy was starting to lose hope. Every fact of the event that didn't involve him was slowly being eroded to expose him as the sole linkage.

"I'm not saying that."

"Sounds like it to me." Freddy looked across at his wife, who sat silently. He could see in her eyes that she was struggling to know what to believe.

"All I'm saying is it would be remiss of me to make a leap of faith to there being a fifth man in the absence of any acknowledged scientific fact." Louise fought to get herself back on the side of friendship.

"What about corroborating absence of fact in my favour?" he challenged Louise. She appeared puzzled. "Like if Garret had brought it to the church, then where's the container? And what happens when state forensics corroborate with me that the splatter pattern across the back wall is consistent with a gun shot?"

"If all that comes true, then I would be happy for you. Meanwhile, all I can conclude is the presence of an extraordinary and peculiar substance that could offer credence to your claim of there being a fifth man."

"Are you going to write it like that?" Frustration frayed Freddy's voice.

"Yes."

"The judge will need a fucking dictionary to translate." He turned away.

"Don't get bitter with me. I'm just doing my job." She emphasised the final word. "Besides, you must appreciate that it's difficult to swallow the existence of a guy who was shot multiple times in the chest, was subsequently staked through his breast plate and then managed to just up and walk off without a trace." She waited for him to respond but he didn't. "You must admit it sounds a little far-fetched?"

Freddy ignored her and the room fell into silence. He was struggling to find any means of convincing even his wife that he was innocent. And if he couldn't do that, how would he convince a jury?

"What about the fingerprint on Fletcher?" he started again.

"Out of my hands. Charlie's got the report on that." Silence briefly consumed the room again. "Look, I'm sorry I can't help more."

"No, I'm sorry for shouting. It's not your fault."

Freddy stumbled around to sit at his desk. He began flicking through the files that still lay there, opening up both Young and Fletcher's wallets side by side. The door opened.

"Hey, I told you not to touch anything." It was Charlie. "You're a fucking suspect, Freddy! I could get my ass in a sling for not reading you your rights already."

Freddy stood up. "Give me a break, Charlie, you know I didn't murder anybody other than in self-defence."

"No, I don't know that. Much as I would dearly love to believe it."

"Fine. So how much longer until either you arrest me or let me go?" Freddy sounded exhausted.

"As long as it takes."

"That's not good enough." The words lashed out. "I told you Gloria could be in danger."

Nicola's eyes opened wide at her husband's statement, seemingly confused as to how Gloria fit into the equation. At the mention of this other woman Louise looked puzzled, almost jealous. Nicola noticed it.

"I might be your deputy, but I'm not stupid, Freddy. I've called New York and spoken to a Detective Harrington."

"Who's he?" Freddy interrupted.

"He's the guy who was investigating John. He's gonna put a couple of guards on her."

"Fat lot of use that'll be when they haven't got a clue what he looks like."

"That isn't completely true, because this Logan fellow was Garret's alibi when his secretary died."

"Jesus, how could I have been so stupid?" Freddy proclaimed to nobody in particular, his mind evidently whirling toward some connection. "That's the missing piece!"

"What?" Louise asked.

"It's so simple." Freddy thought some more, then turned to explain. "Logan frames Garret so that he had to do what he was told. Then because Garret thinks twice, Logan kills him."

"Sounds great, but we still don't have a motive."

"Yes, you do!" Freddy had it all figured out.

"No, we don't. This piece of shit supernatural deposition of yours does not substantiate motive." He held up his right hand, which clutched at the form. "And I would strongly advise you to reconsider this before the state boys get finished at the church."

"I can't change the truth." Freddy sat calmly back in his chair.

"Then at least give me some hard evidence in your favour. Something more than the scraps Louise has cobbled together." He turned to look at her. "No offense intended, Lou."

"None taken."

"Because to play Devil's advocate for one more second," Charlie continued, "if this is what you want to present as your defence, plus that little scenario you just concocted, then the prosecutor will have no trouble making it look as though the grudge against Fletcher, Young and Manton was yours. That you planned it all to frame Garret, who you despised for getting out of this shithole of a town."

"But that doesn't explain why Garret was here?" Freddy challenged.

"No. But you saw him here one day and seized the opportunity to instigate revenge." He paused. "The rest of us just played into your hands, listening to your stories of ceremonial set-ups that just disappeared, and strangers being spotted around town."

"That's good, but it's not true." Freddy dismissed him.

"Don't be dumb now. You've been around long enough to realise that truth in a court room is solely what you can prove, and failing that, what sounds the most reasonable. So, between your tale and the one I just cobbled together, which sounds the most believable?"

"The only evidence I have left to give you is this Logan guy in person. But you ain't gonna get that while I'm sat here." Silence returned as Charlie postulated.

"Ladies, I think you need to step outside for a moment." Charlie's voice was soft but formal.

"Why?" Nicola questioned.

"It's alright." Louise reached out to take her by the arm. "I don't think this bit is something we need to hear."

"Freddy?" She looked toward her husband, but he ushered her away with his hand and a reassuring smile.

Charlie waited until he heard the door latch click behind them before continuing. "If I do this, Freddy, it's on my terms, okay? 'Cause if you fuck up or don't come back, this town will need a whole new department."

"I promise I'll be back."

"Alright, the official line is this. I have sufficient evidence here to detain you on suspicion of murder and not in self-defence. However," he emphasised this last word, "in my opinion, some evidence tends to your version of events and the subsequent presence of a fifth man." He took a breath. "Your description of a man named Logan ties in with that of the NYPD and his last known address was in New York. So, on that basis and the suggested danger to another civilian, I am releasing you under your own cognisance. You are to travel to New York and report immediately to this Detective Harrington at the 7th Precinct. You will then be under his custody."

"Thanks, Charlie." He extended a hand.

"Just catch the guy."

As their hands detached, Freddy moved toward the door. Opening it, he turned. "See, I knew you believed." With that he departed, before anything further could be said. The women watched in disbelief.

"What you doing, Charlie?" Louise asked.

"Giving him a chance."

23

The early morning dew had long since evaporated in the glare of the sun as he departed Shifton. The air felt claggy. A thin film of sweat sticking his clothes to his body. The discomfort elevating his tension. His mind played through differing scenarios of the future. How would he introduce himself to this Harrington? What would follow? Finding Logan? The sequence of capture? The potential heroics? Death? The uncertainties left him clueless over how to proceed. He blinked, trying to divorce himself from the continuous role play.

It was three in the afternoon as he pulled into the Queens-Midtown tunnel. The hypnotic amber flashes of the roof lighting flared up his windscreen, providing timely distraction. He drove on autopilot, taking little notice of activity ahead. His progression steadied as he left the interconnection thoroughfare to join 54th Street. Taxis dodged, horns beeped, pedestrians chanced their lives. He had checked a map prior to entering the tunnel and had a fair understanding of where he needed to go. He reached the precinct a little before four o'clock, flashing his badge to the entry guard and parking up in the underground garage.

As he climbed the stairs, uniformed officers looked at him quizzically, but nobody challenged his presence. At the front desk he obtained directions for homicide and continued his ascent. As Freddy reached the appropriate floor he enquired after Harrington once more and was directed across the main office, towards a man on the far side. Initially, he was dismayed to see the age of his pending supervisor. It wasn't going to assist him at all in spinning a less than coherent story. His pulse started to race.

"Detective Harrington?"

"Yes." The old guy studied him quickly up and down. "Who are you?"

"Sheriff Wayne." He extended a hand. Harrington turned away from it.

"So, you are the infamous sheriff."

"I'm sorry?" Freddy was taken back.

"Oh, it's nothing. Just you've become quite a phenomenon around here in the past four hours."

"How so?" He composed himself.

"Well, when a deputy sheriff calls and asks a favour of you that entails taking his boss into custody, while assisting him in finding a murderer; ears tend to prick up and tongues wag." He shuffled some papers on his desk. "From what I hear of your little back-water retreat massacre..." the words oozed sarcasm "...I'd have locked you up straight away." He paused to look directly at his guest for the first time. "Guess you must do things differently," Harrington finished with a smirk.

"I've worked with Charlie a long time." Sitting down, Freddy fell instinctively into his defence. "He knows I'm honest."

"Then you're a phenomenon twice over." He returned his attention to the reports on his desk. "Still, I have one unsolved murder. You killed my previous and, I should say, only suspect. So, if you've got a theory, I'm all ears. Before you start, though, I think I should get my partner in."

He lifted the phone handset and dialled a four-digit number. It seemed to ring for ages before someone answered. Freddy began to feel nervous about elaborating on his story. He had thought it over meticulously in the car, deriving a tale that held to the general theme he required but excluded the more contentious connection of occult inclinations. The phone was answered.

"Reilly, it's Harrington. Could you come down here for a moment? Our sheriff has arrived." He didn't appear to wait for a response, almost dropping the receiver while he was still talking. "She's on her way." They stared at each other for a moment.

"Charlie said you'd got Gloria Garret under protection?"

"Yup, we do. And it had better be for a good reason, cause my captain hates wasting manpower." Freddy sensed the pointedness and distrust in Harrington's words. His discomfort grew. "And here she is, the delectable Detective Reilly."

Reilly ignored the comment and extended a hand of greeting. "Hi. Detective Fox Reilly." She in-formalised her introduction by giving her first name.

"Sheriff Freddy Wayne." He clasped her hand tight, finding a reassurance from her introduction and from the extension of Harrington's dismissive attitude to others apart from himself.

"Pleased to meet you." She sat back against a side cabinet and smiled.

"Alright, let's not get too friendly." Harrington seemed aggravated by her composed entrance. "Remember, you're still a suspect." He took a sip from his coffee cup, grimacing at the tart taste before swallowing. "So, give us what you've got!"

"Right. Where to begin."

"Just skip the 'it was Wednesday morning and raining outside' country folk routine," Harrington said.

"Your previous suspect," Freddy started straight in, "came out to Shifton direct from leaving your cells. After a couple of days, he had left us with two murders."

"How do you know it was him?" Harrington questioned.

"He told me before he died."

"You mean before you shot him." Freddy nodded. "Convenient." Harrington quipped.

"It might help me a touch if you just stuck to the innocent until proven guilty routine for now, thanks!" Freddy objected.

Reilly sniggered at the sheriff's jibe towards her partner.

"He was supposed to carry out a third, but I stopped him. At which point, this Logan guy entered the scene." Freddy omitted the fact that Kevin had arrived first.

"And he was there, why?" Harrington's scepticism continued.

"To ensure John did as he should. And if he didn't, kill him."

"You saved him a job, then." Harrington smirked at his own humour.

"You still haven't made any connections for us," Reilly cut in, adding a serious tone.

"Okay. John told me that Logan had killed the secretary to frame him. Make him vulnerable," Freddy lied.

"So why didn't he tell us this?" Harrington now began to show some sincere interest in the interrogation. He clearly didn't want to be bested by his young female colleague.

"Because Logan was having his wife watched and had threatened to kill her if John didn't do as he was told."

"So why did Logan want these three guys dead?" Reilly asked.

"That, I don't know," he lied again. "I guess they owed him."

"Nice story but pretty thin," Harrington said.

"I don't know," Reilly began. "It goes some way to explaining why Logan just disappeared for two days. And why Garret's story fell through without him."

"And it could also be a story fabricated by an inexperienced cowboy sheriff who screwed up," Harrington said, staring straight at Freddy.

"If that were true, how would I know what Logan looked like? Hey?" Freddy was beginning to resent Harrington's cynicism. "And how on earth would I have thought to check Garret's rap sheet?"

"So far your first point is the only thing extending this conversation."

"Come on, it's worth following up," Reilly intervened, trying to ease the building tension. Silence fell across the corner of the room.

Harrington was the first to break it. "I'm still confused as to why Logan would go after Garret's wife, now that all the parties you claim were indebted are dead?"

"John told me." His answer was quick, simple and a part truth.

"Yeah, but how does Logan benefit?"

"I don't know. That's just how he operates." Freddy kept it simple.

"How do you figure that, with your limited exposure?" Harrington changed tack. "This guy a friend of yours? Did you plan it together?"

"Don't be bloody stupid."

"So, I'll ask again: where's the benefit in killing the wife?" Harrington leaned forward.

"Give him some slack," Reilly chipped in.

"I'll cut him some slack once he starts to tell the truth, instead of this bullshit." Harrington seemed certain that Freddy was hiding something.

"I am telling the truth," Freddy asserted, but the words just bounced of Harrington's ever-expanding bravado.

"You've given me nothing to make me believe that. You might be just setting up your partner so that you walk."

Freddy fell silent.

"You must understand my scepticism. 'Cause I know even the Mob wouldn't be that persistent or ruthless. They have respect for disassociated families. So, what makes this guy that ruthless?"

"I don't know."

"Bullshit. Friend or no friend, you wouldn't just come down here on the word of a killer if you didn't have any other proof."

"I've just got a gut feeling that he wasn't lying."

"Crap." Harrington still refused to accept any of it.

"Logan's been pretty persistent so far. He came up to Shifton!" Freddy pointed out, matching Harrington's aggression.

"So, you say."

"Hey, if you don't believe me, send me home." Freddy turned passive again. He was tired of fighting an argument when they should be acting decisively.

"Don't tempt me."

A disgruntled and uncomfortable silence fell around them once again. Reilly searched her mind for some positive comment to progress the situation but failed. Harrington just sat wide-eyed in frustrated anger, staring at Freddy. The words the sheriff had spoken had begun to hold some foundation, stirring his inquisitive nature. But he was too proud to back down now, afraid of losing face in front of what he perceived to be his student.

"Alright." Freddy decided on one final angle. "If you really believe that I'm making all this up, just to divert suspicion from me, why don't we give Logan and some of those other people who gave Garret an alibi a call? See if they want to change their stories? If they even still exist?"

Harrington didn't look particularly pleased at the suggestion.

"We already tried his apartment, or at least, what he told us was his address." Reilly shrugged her shoulders as she spoke. "A Mr Chan actually lives there, and he's never heard of our man."

"And you say I'm holding back." He smiled in disbelief. "Doesn't that feature as peculiar to you?"

Harrington ignored Freddy, trying to save face, speaking straight to Reilly, his voice reserved. "Give the others a call." He passed Reilly the file sat on his desk and she departed. "So how long had you known Garret?" He started on Freddy again, though with dignified restraint this time.

"Since he was thirteen."

"And you never met this Logan?" The detective's voice remained suppressed.

"No. John and I hadn't been in touch for over ten years."

"What, did he do something to piss you off?"

"No. He just left town." Despite Harrington's softer approach, the questions still riled Freddy. "Moved here."

"Did you know any of the other victims?"

"Yes." He paused, feeling the same exposure to questioning that he felt subjected to before he left Shifton. "I was at school with them."

"Shit." His expression and tone were so matter of fact. "Do you see how this just looks worse for you by the minute? What, did they piss you off as well?" The accusations returned.

"I don't see how any of this has relevance to you." Freddy decided to take the offensive. "They're not your crimes to solve."

"Just trying to figure out the probability that we'll be chasing a ghost, set up by you, to get you off the hook."

"Christ. And you say my story's convenient. Sounds to me like you've lost a suspect, so you're going to make a whole new one up." He paused. "I mean, that's not thin. It's fucking wafer." Freddy stood up. "Doesn't it rouse even the smallest amount of intrigue in your brain? The fact Logan disappeared for three days and then falsified his address? How d'you get that fucking job anyway? Did you fuck the captain?"

"Watch it," Harrington warned.

"No. I'm not going to sit here and take this shit from an old washed out, redundant detective that they give a young naive kid to so that he still feels as if he has a purpose."

"I said watch your mouth." Harrington stood up now.

"I bet you've got a bottle of whisky stashed away back there!" He reached out across the desk as if looking to clarify. Harrington grabbed hold of his hand, twisting it around with greater strength than Freddy had anticipated.

"Am I interrupting?" Reilly returned, her face displaying equal surprise and ridicule at both of them in turn.

"No." Harrington let go. "What you got?"

"Nothing. Four of the witnesses' home phone numbers are payphones. And that club? Well, they've never hired a Monica Levine before! Never hired a Monica period!" She waited for her colleagues' comments. "So, what do you want to do?"

Harrington remained in quiet contemplation.

"It's worth ago?" She tried to stimulate an answer. "I'll be the first to admit it's stretching intuition a bit far in places, but it's better than anything else we've got for Neve Locker's death. And with these bogus numbers and everything." Still no answer. "You know what they say: eliminate the plausible and you've got the possible." She was clutching at straws now to incite a reaction. "Besides, he'd have to be an idiot to drive straight here to us if he was guilty."

"Okay." Harrington ended her speech. "But he remains cuffed."

"You're kidding me?" Freddy took a step back, raising his hands in protest.

"No, I'm not. You're under my custody and I have no intention of losing a potential murderer from under my nose so late in my career."

Freddy looked at Reilly in disbelief, expecting to find support, but she returned his stare blankly.

"Fine." He had no choice but to concede.

"Do the honours, Reilly. I'll get the car." With that, he removed his jacket from the back of his chair and departed.

"Is he always this distrusting?" Freddy attempted to break the ice in Harrington's absence.

"Just doing his job. You'd want him to be that diligent if it was your relative lying dead."

Freddy was taken back by the speed and wording of her response, as much as by the fact that she remained loyal to her partner, who quite clearly showed her less respect.

"I suppose you're right. But that doesn't excuse his lack of faith in your ability." Now it was Reilly's turn to be stunned, though she half smiled at the fact that he had been astute enough to notice.

24

"Looks like a no show." After they'd waited twenty-four hours, Harrington's smugness started to reveal itself as he paced the room.

"Give it time, he'll come."

Freddy was desperately trying to sound convincing, when in truth his self-belief was actually starting to falter. Ten hours earlier he had convinced them to stay on, instead of taking shifts with another team. His insistence had since quelled inside to a nervous hope. Reilly and Harrington had taken shifts sleeping through last night, but Freddy couldn't, he was too scared. The two sensations seemed like a mega contradiction. One half of him was fearful that Logan wouldn't show, the other fearful he would. His mind was fatigued, and his eyes blazed as if a match flared in front of them. He knew he had to get some sleep soon, but night was closing in again and that was when he feared the most. He had prayed so hard for Logan to turn up during the day, but he knew in his heart if Logan did come, he would not offer them that advantage or that comfort.

"As far as I'm concerned, you've got tonight and that's it. After that, you're going back to Smallville, or whatever it's called."

"Shifton," Freddy made a point of telling him, then turned toward Reilly who was sat beside him. "Is he always like this?" She laughed and he smiled. "You don't appear native. Where you from?"

"Down south."

"Oh, yeah. Been there, nice place." He made fun of her lack of description and she smiled. "So, what brought you here?" He scratched at his handcuffs.

"A bad marriage," she said curtly. Freddy could clearly see the recollection depressed her.

"Sorry for asking," he apologised.

"Forget it. What about you? Why sheriff?"

"They weren't taking any more on at the hardware store." She laughed again and Freddy turned to view her partner's reaction, only to see him sneering with resentment at their sudden friendliness. He turned back and carried on. "Trust me, it was an accident, not design. Fate held my future in its hands." Reilly looked confused. Freddy went on to explain, "You see, I was all set to go to college on a sports scholarship—basketball—when I ripped a ligament in my right knee during the final quarter of the last game of my high school career."

"Jesus!" Reilly frowned in sympathy.

"Needless to say, said scholarship was retracted and I was left futureless."

"So why law enforcement?"

"Wife put me up to it. Town voted me in. That was five years ago." He shook his head in mock despair. "Think I'm stuck in it for life now."

"It mightn't be the job that you're stuck in for life," Harrington interrupted, but they both ignored him.

"You must enjoy it?" Reilly pursued her questioning with fresh interest.

"Pays the bills." He ran his hands over the metal cuffs once again, laughing nervously.

"Yeah, for piss easy work," Harrington scoffed.

"You know, I don't know how you tolerate his upbeat attitude."

Reilly laughed again.

"So why was law enforcement the job for you?" Freddy asked.

"Unfortunately, nothing quite so melodramatic. Just the

family trade."

"You enjoy it, though?"

"Pays the bills." She replied.

They both grinned at each other.

A quietness descended. Freddy looked around the visitor's room they were sat in and then at Harrington, who was studying some activity through the corridor window. Freddy watched the old guys' eyes quiver in thought, his eyelids twitching as he stared the length of the corridor with intense interest.

"Say, Harrington, any chance of these cuffs coming off?"

"Same as for you becoming president." He didn't bother turning to look at Freddy. "I'm just going to check on something."

"What?" Freddy asked quickly, his heart starting to flutter with panic. But Harrington ignored him. "Don't suppose you've got keys for these?" he said to Reilly, his voice taking on a distressed resonance.

"Yes, but he'd go ballistic." She paused. Freddy slumped forward in his seat. "Give him time, he'll come around."

"I may not have much time available." He buried his head in his hands.

"Why are you so nervous?" she asked.

"You forget, I've come across this guy before and was lucky to survive." He sat upright. "And that time I was free-handed and armed."

"Come on, he's just a man." She reached out to touch his hand, but then clearly thought better of it and retracted it before making contact. "Stick near me and you'll be alright. I'm a good shot."

"I wish it was that simple."

Freddy started to find strength somewhere within, gradually resolving his fears and determining his mind to face up to the future. Standing up, he wandered across to the window to see what Harrington was doing, viewing him in stern conversation with Gloria's guard.

"I'm going to see what's going on," Freddy announced.

"No, don't." Reilly's words weren't delivered as an instruction but as a request. "You'll only annoy him more. Just sit down and try to relax." She stood up, grabbing his arm to hold him away from the door. He let her win, knowing she was right. Then Harrington reappeared.

"What was it?" Freddy's anticipation was fierce.

"Nothing." He shut the door slowly behind him, clearly enjoying the superiority he held over Freddy. "Just her sister come to visit."

Freddy's face dropped. "She doesn't have one."

With that he launched for the door, ripping his arm out of Reilly's clutch. His first few strides down the corridor were difficult as he struggled to come to terms with the lack of balance enforced by his shackles. As he gathered pace, a woman in casual clothing entered the corridor from Gloria's room.

"Stop her!" Freddy screamed at the guard sat by the door, who raised his head toward the unfamiliar voice. The woman wasn't as slow, pushing the guard to the floor before sprinting away. Freddy let her go, turning into Gloria's room instead, knowing instinctively that Harrington would barge on past in pursuit, wanting to rectify his mistake quickly. Coming to a standstill in the doorway, he was immediately comforted by the electrical pulse of Gloria's heart transmitted by the array of monitors. The light was dim, and nothing appeared to have been disturbed. He made amateur checks to ensure all the relevant drips and sensors were still connected. It was only after that he noticed a bowl positioned centrally at the foot of the bed, a black candle burning in the middle.

Moving closer, he knelt down. The pot was filled with a dark liquid. He poked the side of the bowl, the liquid's surface barely rippled. Puzzled, he extended a finger and dunked it in. The substance felt dense around his skin. Drawing back, he held his finger up to the light cascading through from the corridor. Staring at it, his heart sank as he realised what it was. Blood.

"She alright?" Reilly startled him.

"Did you get her?" His nervous tone had grown.

"No," she replied.

Freddy's face dropped.

"She vanished."

"Where's Harrington?" he asked, suddenly concerned by the absence of the disgruntled detective.

"Back-tracking with Krueger. The guard who was outside." Her answer calmed him moderately. "What's that?" She pointed to the clay bowl.

"A symbol of the future." He walked out into the corridor.

Reilly knelt down to study it, then followed him out. "Is that blood?"

"Yup."

"What kinda sick fortune is that?" Freddy could hear concern in her voice.

"I think the worst kind," he answered, frowning.

"Harrington was right, you're holding back," she said.

He turned away from her, but she grabbed his arm and pulled him back.

"Tell me!" she cried.

He yanked his arms free and rattled his cuffs in front of her.

"You know I can't." She declined his proposition.

"Then forget it."

Freddy looked past her, down the corridor. It was empty, the dim light shining off the linoleum floor and cream walls. A phone began ringing behind him and he turned. It was sat on the reception desk ten metres back; in the direction of the visitor's room, they had spent the previous twenty-four hours cooped up in. The duty nurse appeared and lifted the receiver.

"Hello." There was silence as the voice on the other end spoke. "Yes." She looked up towards both of them. "Uhhh." She acknowledged something. "Uhhh." She did it again. "Okay. Excuse me, Sir." She moved the handset away from her mouth, resting it on the counter, and said directly to Freddy, "This is for you." She vanished from sight.

Freddy was bewildered, trepidation freezing his legs to the

spot.

"Anybody know you're here?" Reilly asked, seeming equally perturbed.

Freddy shook his head and started to walk towards the desk.

He raised the handset to his ear. "Hello." The word was fearfully delivered.

"Now what are you doing here, Sheriff Freddy?"

He recognised the voice instantaneously.

"This isn't your debt. You should have quit while you were ahead. Then I may have overlooked that stake incident."

Freddy couldn't speak, the words were blocked by a swelling lump in his throat. "But seeing as you're here, I'm incited to rip out your fucking heart." A threat would have usually snapped Freddy into verbal action, but all this did was made him feel weaker still. "You gonna speak, dumb fuck? Why you here?"

"To protect Gloria." His words fumbled over his lower lip.

"To protect the wife of a low life who deserted your friendship years ago!" The words echoed loud in Freddy's ear. "That's fucking rich. Guess Harrington was right when he said you were a phenomenon." He started to laugh and somehow that made him sound human, granting Freddy release from his fear.

"That's not the way I see it."

The laughing stopped. "Then you're blind." Logan asserted.

"Maybe it's you who is living in blinkers, 'cause the last memory I have of John, he was giving up his life to save mine." Freddy's inhibitions dropped altogether. "Allowing me to kill a piece of shit like you!" He kept his voice low and pointed.

"Interesting memory, because I'm still alive."

"Night's still young."

"Yes, it is, isn't it?" The phone line went dead, but the words continued in his other ear. "And you don't have the slightest idea of what you're dealing with."

Freddy dropped the handset and stumbled away from the reception. His bravado of a few seconds previous drained away.

"Who was it?" Reilly's words startled Freddy and he flinched away. "Who was it?"

"Him." He looked up and down the corridor in rapid succession. "He's here."

"What did he say?"

He turned to look straight at Reilly. "I'm fucked!" He began studying the length of the corridor again. "Don't suppose you'd consider taking these off now?" She shook her head. "Didn't think so."

He moved back toward Gloria's room. Midway there, he stopped and cocking his head to one side, strained his ears to capture the slightest sound.

"What is it?"

Reilly was behind him. He raised a hand to silence her and listened on. He didn't have to strain his ears for much longer, there was a sound starting to resonate through the walls. An electrical humming sound, like high voltage cables. The floor started to vibrate under their feet. Reilly instinctively looked down to see what was happening. Freddy remained alert, waiting for what was to follow. It arrived with a gradual pulsing of the lights, as if the power was being sucked away. Rapidly the pulsing grew into a flicker, throwing shadows flailing across the corridor. Then, suddenly, every bulb blazed brilliant white, momentarily blinding both Freddy and Reilly. One by one they then started to blow, beginning at the far end of the corridor. A wall of sparks cascaded shimmering light and glass over the floor. They shielded their eyes as the explosions travelled above their heads. Eventually, the last light blew, and as the sparks hit the cold floor, they were plunged into darkness.

An eternity ticked by before the emergency power kicked in, filling the corridor with a red hue. Freddy shook his head clear of glass before spinning from side to side, trying to check all angles at once. Nothing. Focussing back on Reilly, he noticed she had drawn her gun.

"You'd better watch where you point that," Freddy said nervously.

The corridor fell deathly silent.

"What's that?"

Freddy caught movement in his peripheral vision. A figure flying across the corridor to their left. Reilly spun around, raising her weapon and taking aim in the direction of his stare.

"What?" She couldn't see anything.

"Something moved."

"Nothing there now!" She was obviously trying to sound calm, but her voice wavered.

"Fuck!" Freddy was getting more agitated.

Listening in silence once more, they waited. Reilly stood poised to shoot. Suddenly, Freddy felt a chill across the back of his neck. He turned to see nothing. It came again, like the breath of the dead this time, an intoxicating stench, stifling his breathing. He twisted around once more to find emptiness and Reilly. She stared at him strangely. Running his hand over his skin, he tried to generate some warmth, simultaneously taking a step to one side to avoid the smell. But the coolness settled deeper and the stench followed.

"You shouldn't have come, Freddy boy." This time the breath arrived carrying an all too familiar sound. Spinning around in panic, he saw the corridor was still empty. "You can't win. I won't let you!" The words wrapped around him like a serpent. "Shalek won't let you. His debts are always paid."

Freddy spun around, sensing Logan over his shoulder.

"What is it?" Reilly's voice was concerned, but Freddy didn't hear her. "Sheriff!" she shouted.

"Nice girl. She your new partner?"

Freddy spun again, losing his balance and knocking into a trolley stacked with medicines. A bottle of pills fell to the floor, smashing and scattering its contents. "Can you trust her, though? Can you trust anybody now?" Turning continuously, he caught a glimpse of Logan's eyes, but they disappeared as quickly as they appeared. "Remember Shifton! Remember Kevin! My helpers are everywhere!" His final word was screamed into Freddy's ear just as a violent thrust smacked into his chest, sending him hurtling to the floor.

"Hey, you alright?" Reilly moved towards him, offering her hand in assistance, but Freddy cowered back, his face screwed up in uncertainty, raising a hand to warn her to keep a distance. "What is it?"

"You didn't hear him?" His voice was suddenly filled with distrust.

"Hear who?"

Reilly started to feel unsettled by Freddy's rambling and found herself reciprocating his aversion to touch, though it wasn't paranoia fuelling her uncertainty, more a strong sense for self-preservation. She even allowed her gun sights to fall partially in Freddy's ever-changing direction, just in case he turned nasty.

"God, I am so fucked." Freddy declared. Reilly watched him twist on the spot, not knowing which way to turn. "Can you take these off now?" He advanced nervously, but she retreated a commensurate amount.

"I don't think s—"

Before she completed the sentence, a noise came from the reception area. Both of them turned to view the source. Reilly raised her gun away from Freddy and toward the disturbance. They discovered the nurse from earlier walking towards them, her face pale and eerily vacant. On viewing the woman Reilly allowed her aim to swing back on to Freddy, who was already stepping back from the advancing woman. Reilly matched his retreat once more.

"Miss, are you alright?" Reilly addressed the woman. There was no answer. "Why doesn't anybody answer me around here?" Reilly muttered underneath her breath, but Freddy did answer her: "Because she's not feeling herself at the moment."

"What are you talking about?" Reilly thought he was just playing for time, positioning himself to attack her.

"Look at her right hand!" Freddy forcefully whispered the words.

Reilly flicked a cautious glance in his direction, afraid the opportunity was going to be taken by Freddy to jump her. The attack never came, but she saw what Freddy feared. A scalpel. Stepping back further, her gun now shifted between Freddy's retreating form and the advancing nurse.

"Miss, do you want to drop the knife!" Reilly dispelled with her previous calm nature toward the nurse, speaking authoritatively.

"It's no good, she can't hear you."

"Miss, put the knife down!" She raised her voice higher.

"Just shoot her, will you!"

"Look, you shut up and stop moving." It was only after Reilly spoke, that Freddy noticed the gun was targeting him as much as the nurse.

"What you doing?" He was really panicked now, sandwiched between two armed women.

"Protecting myself."

"From what?" His eyes flicked toward the nurse.

"You."

"Look, I'm on your side. Now shoot the nurse!" he started to shout.

"No. Lady, put the knife down, please." The words fell on deaf ears again.

"She's not going to do it, so shoot her." He started to move back again.

"I said shut up and don't fucking move!" Reilly demanded.

"So you gonna let her kill me?"

"Miss. Put the knife on the floor or I will be forced to shoot!"

The nurse's eyes failed to acknowledge anything Reilly said. She remained transfixed on Freddy. The gap had narrowed now to less than five metres and she started to raise the blade threateningly. It glistened red as if already coated with blood.

"Fucking shoot her!"

Freddy was screaming now, and Reilly half glanced towards him, opening her mouth to respond. But before she could, the nurse lunged with her arm stretched out in front. Freddy ducked out of the way and managed to grab hold of the woman's wrists in the process. The momentum of the attack left both of them off balance and they spilled backwards into Reilly, knocking the gun from her hands. The nurse bounced at an angle off the wall and followed Freddy down to the floor. There the struggle continued and for a second Reilly was frozen in disbelief.

"Get her off me!" he shouted at Reilly, snapping her out of her trance. Moving forward she tried to pull the nurse away, but all she achieved was a slash down her forearm as the nurse flicked the scalpel around in an arc behind her. Flinching in pain, she retrieved her gun and took aim on the woman's back.

"Shoot her!" Freddy bellowed.

"I can't get a clear shot." Reilly responded.

"Just shoot her in the leg."

Reilly did as ask. The nurse recoiled away, clutching at her bleeding left calf muscle, but she didn't scream. And as Freddy retreated behind the safety of Reilly, the nurse stood up and advanced again, limping towards them, her face as determined as ever. Reilly shot her again, this time in the shoulder, knocking her to the floor. The scalpel flailed out of her arm, skating away down the corridor behind her. This second shot rendered the nurse unconscious, blood oozing from her wounds. Freddy saw the guilt surface on Reilly's face as she stared down at the relatively young woman.

"First time you shot someone?" he asked.

She nodded.

"Try not to let it bother you. It was going to be her or me. You didn't really have a choice." He reached out to touch her reassuringly, his trust in her restored. She shook him off.

"Would you mind telling me what the fuck that was all about?" She demanded.

"You wouldn't believe me!" He knelt down to check the nurse's pulse.

"Oh, I think you'll find me pretty receptive at the moment." She looked nervously up and down the corridor. "Besides, if you still want my help, it's gonna be better given if I know what we're up against. Particularly now that normal civilians appear to have joined the fun."

"Yeah, well, next time just trust me and shoot."

Before Reilly could reply, a door opened behind them and a body lurched out into the corridor. Spinning round, she raised her weapon, pulling the trigger without even sighting the target. Freddy had seen who it was, though, and moved to knock her second aim high, the bullet taking out an exit sign.

"Don't waste all of those at once." He lowered her guard. "Particularly on one of your own."

It was only after Freddy had said his last words that Reilly noticed an NYPD badge pinned to a uniformed chest on the figure ahead of them. As they moved closer, she could see that it was Krueger. He was wounded, blood oozing from a gash in his trousers. Reilly started to hasten towards him, but Freddy grabbed her arm to restrain her, indicating behind them towards the nurse. She immediately understood what he was driving at, partially raising her gun in readiness.

"Krueger, is that you?" She raised her voice to make certain he heard. There was only a groan in return. "Krueger?" she asked again.

"Yes." The words strained through gritted teeth. Reilly relaxed as soon as she heard him speak, diving forward to check his injuries.

"Jesus, Krueger, what happened?" She examined a five-inch gash that ripped the length of his left calf muscle. "Where's Harrington?" She suddenly thought of her partner.

"I don't know. We were walking back, checking rooms..." He winced in pain. "Something dove at me, gashing my leg and flinging me to one side. Then I saw them drag Harrington off down the stairwell."

"Where to?" Freddy asked, while Reilly grabbed an operating gown, wrapping it tightly around Krueger's leg.

"It could only have been the basement." The officer replied.

"You said 'them'. How many were there?" he quizzed.

"Only the one." He grimaced in agony. "A man."

"How about dealing with these cuffs now?" Freddy addressed

Reilly.

"How about telling me the truth?" She matched his persistence.

"Do the cuffs first and we have a deal."

She contemplated the offer for a second, then retrieved the keys from her trouser pocket. Freddy raised his clasped hands and waited for her to insert one into the lock. As the shackles came loose, he was suddenly filled with a new confidence. Immediately he stood up and opened the stairwell door.

"Come on. I'll tell you en route." He waited for a response.

Reilly didn't give him one, turning to speak to Krueger. "You alright here?"

Krueger nodded.

"Make your way down to Mrs Garret's room and call for help. Okay?"

He nodded again.

She stood up to follow Freddy but then turned back momentarily. "Oh and get a doctor for that nurse down there." With that she joined Freddy in the stairwell. "So, you were saying?" she urged him.

"Okay. Firstly, we're not dealing with a human!"

"Tell me something I hadn't deduced."

Freddy was taken aback by her reformed composure in the face of the supernatural.

"Alright. Logan is a fallen angel, currently manifested in a long since dead male Caucasian body. The one that you've met." He paused, checking the next flight of stairs below them. They were clear. "He's the servant of Shalek, an earthbound demi-God, who my friend Garret made a pact with. Then, to put it simply, Garret failed on the repayments and Logan was despatched to sort him out. You diggin' this?"

"Uh-huh," she confirmed. "So does this Logan have any special powers – magic, shit like that?"

"The works, I think? That bit upstairs is the first I've really seen of them, though. He appears to favour the more hands-on approach." They arrived at the final flight of stairs. A large metal reinforced door sat at the bottom.

"One other question," she said softly.

"Fire away." He mimicked her whisper.

"Is this Shalek guy likely to show up?"

He paused for thought. That was something he hadn't considered. "I really hope not!"

On reaching the basement level, they discovered a pool of blood stagnating on the ground, a trail leading off underneath the exit. Pushing the door open slowly, Freddy peered out cautiously. A single passageway stretched ahead of them that was evidently the spine road to accessing all areas of the basement. Freddy could see three distinct offshoots in front of him and looking behind, a further four were evident. There was only one door visible off this central roadway and it was marked up as closet.

Moving out into the corridor, the trail of blood appeared black now and he could see it clearly against the tiled floor. Tracing its passage, he advanced steadily, poised to recoil back from any frontal assault. The stream of blood turned a corner and Freddy did likewise, only to discover Harrington's lifeless body; his viscera ripped out and splattered over the width of the corridor. Before Freddy could turn to warn Reilly, she had breached the line of sight. To his surprise, she said nothing. He could see pain welling in her eyes, but fear was still rooted as her primary emotion. Calmly, she knelt down by her partner's side, unclipped his gun from its holster and passed it to Freddy.

"You may need this." She moved on.

Continuing slowly, they checked the rooms to either side. One covered the corridor, while the other undertook recognisance inside. Through no deliberate intention, they took turns in the latter duty. In all honesty it was only a cursory glance being applied, the poor lighting providing camouflage for even the most obvious of features. The persistent emptiness and increased level of fear eroded their determination. They had heard and seen nothing except Harrington's dead body since arriving in the basement.

But then it came. A noise from the end of the corridor. The sound of utensils crashing to the floor. Without seeking confirmation, they moved simultaneously towards the source. The sound had drawn them to the morgue. Strips of plastic sheeting hung from the double door frame, acting as the only barrier between them and inside. Pulling several sheets to one side, Freddy stuck his head in and surveyed the layout. Across the back wall, fifteen columns of doors hid space for the systematic processing of the deceased. Three white marble operating tables with stainless steel inlays for the bodies were available for autopsies and two slave trolleys sat poised to deliver bodies around the room.

"My, my, my, what do we have here? Well, if it isn't Tweedledum and Tweedledee. What are we up for now, kids, a little necrophilia?" Logan's voice wafted towards them from all directions.

"No, just your heart and head," Reilly answered, displaying her disdain for Logan.

"Fighting talk, that's what I like." He paused. "You know, I used to relish tormenting the likes of your friend Garret, Freddy boy. But you know what? I've had so much more fun with you in the past couple of days." They could hear him smack his lips together in distasteful delight. "Not sure you should have brought the girl into it, though!"

"I can handle myself," Reilly snapped again as she spread out to the left of the room. Freddy taking off to the right.

"Yes, I know you can."

"Sure, you do!" she replied.

"Oh, believe me, I do. We've met before!" His voice lowered to a sinister level.

"Yes, but I don't think you really had time to sit and judge my character." His smart talk annoyed her further.

"I don't need much time." He chuckled softly. "But I'm not thinking about the station. I mean back in your old town."

Reilly was puzzled.

"You really don't remember, do you? Ha ha ha. God, you

humans are so stupid at times. I was the guy who picked your husband up when he left you. Incidentally, I was also the man who set him up with that slut bimbo he deserted you for." His voice sounded closer to her and she spun around, thinking he'd be there. But there was nothing. "You obviously weren't tight enough for him."

"Just ignore him, Reilly, he's trying to rile you, get you to waste your clip." Freddy offered support.

"Don't be so soft, Freddy my man. I told you before, bullets can't kill me." Logan's voice was relaxed and smug.

"They sure slow you down, though," Freddy retorted.

"You got lucky in the church." His pitch dropped an octave and Freddy knew he had touched on a sore point. "Please don't count on that lasting!"

An unsettling silence fell across the empty room. They still couldn't see the enemy and to lose the sound of his voice stirred a higher sense of fear.

"Anyway..." Logan's voice lightened. "Back to my young friend here. You know I like screwing frigid intellectuals. So how about it?"

"In your dreams," was the best rejection Reilly could muster off the cuff.

"Now, that's a very dangerous thing to say. Because I have a habit of making dreams come true."

"Can you see him yet?" Reilly ignored Logan's jeers, shouting across the room to Freddy.

"No."

"I tell you, it's like cat and mouse with you two," Logan continued. "Give up, kids, you'll not find me. I'm too quick. Just ask Harrington. Oops, I forgot. He's dead."

Unlike his previous taunts, this one hurt Reilly. As soon as Harrington's name had been mentioned, her mind visualised him sprawled on the floor, guts trailing away from his body. She could see the terror and suffering in his dead eyes. The emotions of his dying seconds mapped through the contours of his wrinkled face.

"Hello, kitten." Logan's voice whispered in Reilly's ear, his breath stifling her lungs. She tried to turn around, but he clasped her throat, lifting her off the floor and strangling her voice. As she was elevated higher and higher, she could see Logan's face hidden in the maze of piping riddled across the ceiling. And at the same time, Freddy disappeared from sight, too caught up in his own inspections to notice.

"Uhhh." She managed to make a sound. Her heart was thumping at over a hundred, giving her greater strength.

"Reilly!" Freddy heard her muffled announcement. "Reilly, you got him?" He started to move back in her direction, straining his eyes. "Reilly!"

"She'll not be talking for a moment, Freddy boy. She's trying to catch her breath. Ha ha ha."

"Where is she?" Freddy demanded.

"Oh, just hanging around."

Logan's voice had taken a darker menacing tone. Freddy knew the time for playing was over. This was where the ending began. And it did. Reilly's feet suddenly dropped into sight from the ceiling, quickly followed by her torso. Just as her head came into view, she jolted to a halt a foot off the floor. It was only then that Freddy saw the linen noose clasping her neck. She was still alive, holding on tight to the cloth underneath her chin. Breaking into a sprint, he cleared the space between them in seconds. The redness of the lighting emphasised the panic in her features as she tugged at the noose. Instinctively, Freddy grabbed her legs, lifting them higher to relieve the immediate pressure.

"Quick, Freddy boy. If you lose her as well as Harrington, you'll be back to zero alibi. And two more dead bodies."

He couldn't see Reilly beyond her waist now, but he heard her wincing breaths as she failed to find any slack in the cloth. His eyes flicked randomly around the room, searching for anything. His gaze fell on a lone instrument tray sat to the side of the central operating area. The problem was he had to let go of Reilly to fetch it. There was no choice. Letting her down gently, he felt her legs begin to kick violently as soon as he released them. He could have explained his actions and alleviated her terror, but calm rationale was the last thing on his mind. Speed was the essence for survival. In fact, he knew it was the only chance. Logan wouldn't wait forever to initiate his next assault. The pleasure he received from the moment would be rapidly lost. Decisively snatching a scalpel, Freddy raced back, retaking hold of Reilly's twitching legs. His initial intent had been to pass the scalpel to her, but she had no strength left. So, he had to reach up himself, holding her around the waist with one arm, while he sawed at the linen with the other. It cut free easily, releasing her full load on to his shoulder. Dropping the knife, he cradled his other arm around her back and laid her down gently to the floor.

"You okay?"

"Yes."

The reply was faint, and he could see her throat was starting to swell. He saw the temporary relief in her eyes, appearing for a moment to forget about their predicament. But it came streaming back, as those same eyes started to widen in panic. She tried to shuffle away, initially confusing Freddy, until he realised who she must be seeing. He stood up slowly, bracing himself for the attack.

"Right. Well, I think that's sufficient foreplay," Logan whispered in Freddy's ear. "Shall we dance?"

With this final tease Freddy was launched backwards through the air, landing squarely on one of the trolleys, which careered off towards the far wall. It hit with such a force that Freddy was flung forward before the trolley toppled down on top of him. Reilly watched in terror, her legs slipping in vain against the polished floor as she tried to retreat.

"No, don't you go anywhere. We're not finished yet."

Logan glared at her, paralysing her legs, before turning to follow Freddy. Reilly's distraction had given Freddy enough time to draw his gun and fire a flurry of bullets at Logan's chest. He buckled back in his step and it looked as though they had an effect. But as soon as the momentum of the final round had been dissipated across Logan's mass, his approach resumed, his eyes blazing in anger.

"You know they really irritate my skin!" he screamed in disgust at Freddy.

"What do you care? It's not yours anyway!" Freddy managed to quip, though he felt less than brave.

"My, aren't we quick-witted." Logan brushed the felled trolley to one side and reached down, grabbing Freddy by the scruff of his neck. Then, lifting his face to within an inch of his own, he continued. "It's mine while I possess it, you little fucker. So have a modicum of respect. Okay! I've had this body for fifty years. I'm kinda attached to it."

"Well, you'd better start getting used to the idea of leaving it." Freddy fired again at point blank range straight into Logan's belly. He winced in pain but soon recovered.

"I think that's you all spent now. So, what next?" He paused in mock contemplation. "I know! How about this?"

Pinching his hand even tighter around Freddy's throat, he flicked his wrist, flipping Freddy horizontally on to the nearest examination table. Freddy landed hard, his back smacking squarely against the steel insert, winding him. He started to struggle, clutching at Logan's hands, but achieved nothing.

"Okay. How can I make this as lingeringly painful as possible?" Logan mused playfully, then picked up a scalpel. "I believe I'll start with a few fingers. Beginning with your trigger finger." He grinned.

Freddy had no time to process this prospect before his hand was twisted around and the blade ripped through, severing his index finger.

"Ahhhh." The scream was faint, suppressed by shock.

"I wouldn't bother screaming about it. Nobody's gonna save you. And trust me, it won't ease the pain." He drew close to Freddy's face again, exhaling under his nose and forcing his cold dank breath down into his captive's lungs. Then, pulling back, he raised Freddy's hand so that he could view the damage. "Hey, look at that spurt!" Logan smiled in false wonderment. "Christ, your heart must be racing. I'd better dress that wound, though, before you lose too much blood." He pretended to look around for dressings. "Shit, we're in the morgue. Not much call for bandages down here. I'll have to improvise. Don't worry, though, I've seen this done in a cowboy movie."

Freddy was struggling to see Logan clearly, tears glazing his eyes. He had lost all thoughts of coming out of this alive. He couldn't even get his mind to think coherently about what Logan was going to do next. It was irrelevant. His pain was so bad now and it wouldn't get any better. He still struggled, but it was only a desultory effort. His body was too gripped by fear to breathe sufficient oxygen to give him strength. He was brought back to reality as he felt a cool liquid being poured over his amputated stub. Initially, the coolness provided relief, but then something in the liquid start to burn at his unprotected flesh.

"Here, you'd better bite on this."

Logan shoved a plastic spatula between Freddy's teeth, confusing him even more. But then he saw the lighter and knew what was coming. He braced himself as the flame took hold of his hand. He tried to move, but Logan held him fast with one hand, while the other raised Freddy's arm like a torch in front of his eyes. Sweat broke out from every pore on his body and he gasped for air before launching a newly inspired attack on Logan. It was short-lived. Logan swatted him back down and continued to waft Freddy's arm from side to side, thriving on the moment right until the flames burned themselves out.

"Okay! What next?" He placed the scalpel across his lips in thought. "What do you think? That wound look a little too neat for you?" He poked Freddy's singed hand in front of his face. "Yeah, it does. I'll use my hands and teeth now. That should really be excruciating." His expression became more gripped with insanity by the second as he threw the scalpel over his shoulder. "You know, I've always wanted to see whether I could remove a man's pectoral muscle from under his skin as easily as they insert those silicone implants in women. So, what's say we give that a go?" Freddy began his struggle for freedom once more. "Oh, dear, you caught your breath again?" He clasped his fingers tighter and Freddy felt his neck shrink. He lay motionless. "That's better! Good! Okay, where was I?"

Logan ripped Freddy's shirt apart, exposing his hairless chest. Then, he elongated a single finger, his nail seeming to grow instantaneously, the end sharpening itself. Logan watched with pride and then when the length was to his satisfaction, he pointed it towards Freddy and jabbed it straight into his chest.

He screamed, but it faded quickly. His brain was beginning to dysfunction, starved of life's sustenance.

"Hmmm." Logan sniggered. "I missed my mark. Sorry." Retracting his nail, he immediately reinserted it an inch to the left. "That's better."

He sounded happier with his positioning now. That was when the real pain began. Logan sawed the nail back and forth, slicing around the base of Freddy's left pec. Lashing out, Freddy caught Logan across the face with his own nails. Logan glared in anger. Then, withdrawing his finger, thrust the palm of his hand into Freddy's right shoulder. With a loud crack, Freddy heard his shoulder pop out of its socket. His arm dropped useless to his side. He didn't have time to scream over this, because the serration of his chest resumed immediately, overbearing all other trauma.

"God, that's beautiful!" Logan exclaimed as if no interlude had taken place. His eyes sparkled with enthusiasm as he watched the blood seep out and drench Freddy's shirt.

"Now for the big one." He chuckled. "This is truly going to hurt!"

Delicately, he wiggled his nail between the skin and muscle, skating over a plethora of nerve endings as he did so. Freddy reeled in agony. He had nothing left to give in defence, his body was consumed with pain. He started to black out.

"Fucking hell!" The scream came from Logan, taking Freddy by surprise as he felt the nail withdraw. Still dazed, he opened his eyes in time to see Logan's distraught face vanish below the table line. "You fucking bitch."

Freddy started to lift himself up off the table with his functional arm, to find Logan lashing out at Reilly's flailing legs as she pushed herself away from his reach. Blood saturated the floor, and for a moment Freddy thought it was Reilly's. But then he noticed traces of black plasma. Following them back, he discovered that the back of Logan's knees had been slashed open, the tendons cut in half.

"Come here!" Logan shouted. "I'm gonna rip your fucking tits off!"

Freddy stumbled to his feet, searching through dazed eyes for a weapon of any kind. His body was so weak with shock that he staggered from side to side, bouncing between examination tables to remain standing. Behind him, Reilly was gasping for breath.

"Got you now, you stupid bitch."

Freddy didn't bother turning to view the situation. That would have been futile. With one arm dislocated, he couldn't launch an attack without a weapon. He moved towards a cabinet pushed up against the left-hand wall, ripping drawers out on to the floor. Papers, surgical gowns and face masks scattered themselves around. Reilly's groans were getting increasingly fraught.

"Okay. I've tried muscular extraction, now let's do the mammary gland, shall we?" Freddy heard Reilly's shirt rip open. "Nice tits, babe! A little slender for my liking, but they'll still look good mounted on a plaque."

"Ah..!"

The scream was muffled, but Freddy knew Logan's nail had breached her skin. He tugged at the drawer handles in quicker succession, his senses returning. He struck gold: a mass of metal instruments spewed over the floor. Immediately, Freddy grabbed the biggest implement he could find, clutching at the handle of a seven-inch cleaver. Hastening back to the fray, he found Logan's raised arm readying itself to plunge a handful of nails into Reilly. Running forward, he swung the cleaver into action, detaching Logan's hand at the wrist.

"You bastard!" He fell away from Reilly, rolling to face Freddy.

"I'll eat your fucking eyes out of their sockets for that."

"Unlikely!"

Freddy's determination was reinforced as the cleaver swung a decapitating arc toward Logan's neck. The head didn't sever completely but lolled back, pulling the rest of Logan's body down with it. He stood waiting for Logan's resurrection, readying the blade. He knew it wouldn't be completely over until he committed one last act. And until then, he wasn't certain how far Logan's powers stretched.

"Are you okay?" he called to Reilly.

"Uh-huh." She gasped with relief. "What now?"

"Now I have to cut his heart out." Freddy's expression was staunch.

"No way!" She regained some life, stumbling to her feet and pulling out her handcuffs.

Freddy stood back. "If I don't, he'll come back."

"And how am I supposed to explain that?" She moved to cuff him.

"Please!" he pleaded. "You don't understand. His body may be easily corrupted, but his spirit is harder to dispose of."

She stopped to think. The two of them stood motionless, staring into each other's eyes, trying to see each other's thoughts. A minute passed and then, without explanation, Reilly turned and left the room. He could see her waiting outside beyond the transparent plastic sheeting of the doorway, her back turned towards him. He didn't wait for her to change her mind. Kneeling down in a pool of blood beside Logan's body, he raised the cleaver above his shoulder and struck it centrally between Logan's ribs, cracking the breast plate in half. Then, using the blade as a cantilever, he yanked one half of the ribcage up, exposing the still beating heart. Freddy recoiled in disgust, but then, gathering his resolve, he reached forward and ripped it free. Plasma oozed from the ventricles, enveloping Freddy's hand, biting at his skin like frostbite. Standing, he moved back to the mess he had created earlier, finding a white bag amongst the surgical coveralls. Placing the heart inside, he departed.

Looking up and down the corridor, he saw what he was looking for.

"Where you going?" Reilly shouted after him.

He ignored her, opening a large metal door about ten metres down the passageway. He disappeared from sight. It was a few minutes before he reappeared, looking more relaxed.

"What d'you do?"

"I had to burn something in the incinerator." He half smiled.

25

Staggering slowly, they re-emerged onto the hospital floor where it had all begun. Their back-up had met them halfway up the stairwell. After taking directions, they had moved on swiftly to check and contain the area to keep out stray civilians. Behind the police, a paramedics team had fussed for a few seconds, wrapping them in blankets and attempting to lead them somewhere more open, where their other wounds could be tended. Both Reilly and Freddy flinched at their attentiveness, eventually pulling away and continuing passed. Bemused at being shrugged off, the medical team had carried on downstairs in search of other injured. They would be disappointed. Back on the second floor, Freddy and Reilly instinctively checked both directions, noticing that shards of glass still littered the empty corridor. Although the main power was back on in the rest of the hospital, because of the blown strip lights, this floor was still lit by the red glow of the emergency system.

"Krueger?" Reilly called out timidly. After passing so many people in the stairwell, she had imagined this place to be a hive of activity. "Krueger!" She raised her voice. No response.

"Reilly." Freddy tugged at her sleeve. "I think you should take a look at this."

She was about to ask why, but as she turned back toward Freddy, all became apparent. Freddy was paralysed, staring with an expression of terror down the corridor. His eyes appeared to glow almost white, reflecting the brilliant light radiating from Gloria's room. Reilly's reaction was more fearless than Freddy's, almost as if she refused to accept what she was seeing. Moving forward, she clasped her new-found partner's arm, trailing him behind her. Drawing her weapon, she clicked the safety catch off. Broken glass crackled under their shoes, breaking the stillness of the air. That was what unsettled them both – the lack of noise. No phones. No talking. Nothing. Closing in, they strained their eyes to pierce the light and view inside, but it was too bright.

"You ready?" Reilly asked without turning.

"Y-yes." Freddy gave his stilted confirmation.

Without hesitation, they lunged through the door. Reilly led the charge, her revolver raised high, her index finger primed to depress the trigger. In the future, both of them would be incapable of explaining what happened next, because it was almost magical. The brilliance of the light reduced to nothing more than sixty-watt magnitude. The air suddenly started to reverberate with activity once more, initialised by a baby's cry. Inside they discovered nothing untoward, though they were confused as to why Krueger hadn't answered them. He was sat just inside the room keeping guard and must have heard them. Moving their gaze forward, Reilly and Freddy stared in amazement at the rest of the room's occupants. Two nurses worked in swift activity at the base of the bed. Between them they cleaned and cradled a new-born baby, while also tending to the mother, who now, remarkably, was conscious.

"Freddy?" Gloria recognised him immediately.

"Gloria."

"Why are you here?" She was confused. "Where's John?"

Before Freddy could answer, their reunion was interrupted.

"You two outside, now!" Reilly's captain had arrived and looked furious.

"It's alright." Reilly rested a hand on Freddy's shoulder. "Leave this to me."

"Freddy." Gloria tried to catch his attention again, as Reilly followed her commanding officer out of the room.

"So, what the hell happened here?" The captain's voice was raised. "I've got one dead detective, one injured officer and destruction of property littering three floors."

"We were protecting Mrs Garret as agreed, Sir, when the suspect, Logan, arrived," she explained, simplifying her story.

"And Logan did all of this?"

"Pretty much."

"And I suppose he's the one to blame for Harrington?"

"Yes, Sir."

"Then where the fuck is he?" His voice was strained and pointed.

"Downstairs in the morgue."

"I don't think so."

Reilly's eyes widened.

"All I've got down there is a putrid body and a coroner going apeshit, wanting the real body back."

"There's one body and it's on the floor inside the morgue." She was adamant.

"The only body in the morgue is flesh-eaten back to the bone and maggot riddled. It hasn't supported life in a long time."

With her boss's last words, she realised what had happened. The body had rapidly decomposed to its natural state, as if it had been dead fifty years. But how could she explain that? She had needed to be terrified out of her wits and taken to within an inch of death to believe it herself.

"Well." He was waiting.

"I don't have an answer for you, Sir."

"Trust me, you'd better find one, else you'll be back on a train to wherever it is you came from! I want that report on my desk by the end of tomorrow." He stormed away.

She turned and re-entered the hospital room to find Freddy squeezing Gloria tightly as her tears fell on his shoulder. Gloria's sobs were silent, but her grief was evident. To their side a nurse cradled the baby.

"It's a girl." The nurse said, anticipating Reilly's first question. Reilly smiled and extended a finger towards the baby's tiny hands. It was only then that she noticed the silk white hair and the blanket pale white colouring of her eyes. "She's albino."

Freddy turned around in shock. "Let me see." He moved quickly towards them, pulling the towel away from the baby's head.

"What's the problem?" Reilly was disturbed by his actions.

"I don't think it's over." He turned towards her, stony-faced.

"Why?" Reilly's face lost its colour.

"What's not over?" Gloria asked, having heard his comment, but Freddy ignored her. Taking Reilly by the arm, he led her into the corridor.

"In some of the historical text I've read, fallen angels can possess the newly born, without being invoked, if they lay claim to a debt of that blood line." He paused. "When that happens, the child is born albino."